To Peter Cameron
A father with too big a heart,
Even if it did tick with a hiccup.

Who taught me to see dragons in the clouds,
And that there's always a chilli hidden somewhere …
Probably in your next bite.

Copyright © 2021 JP Cameron

All rights reserved

ISBN: 9798746474919

Imprint: Independently published

Books in the Series:

Dog Days

Puppy Love

The Furry and the Furious

Barking Mad

Let Sleeping ~~Dogs~~ Gods Lie

Old Dog, New Tricks

Dogs of War

Let Sleeping ~~Dogs~~ Gods Lie

The Lycan Files: Book 5

JP Cameron

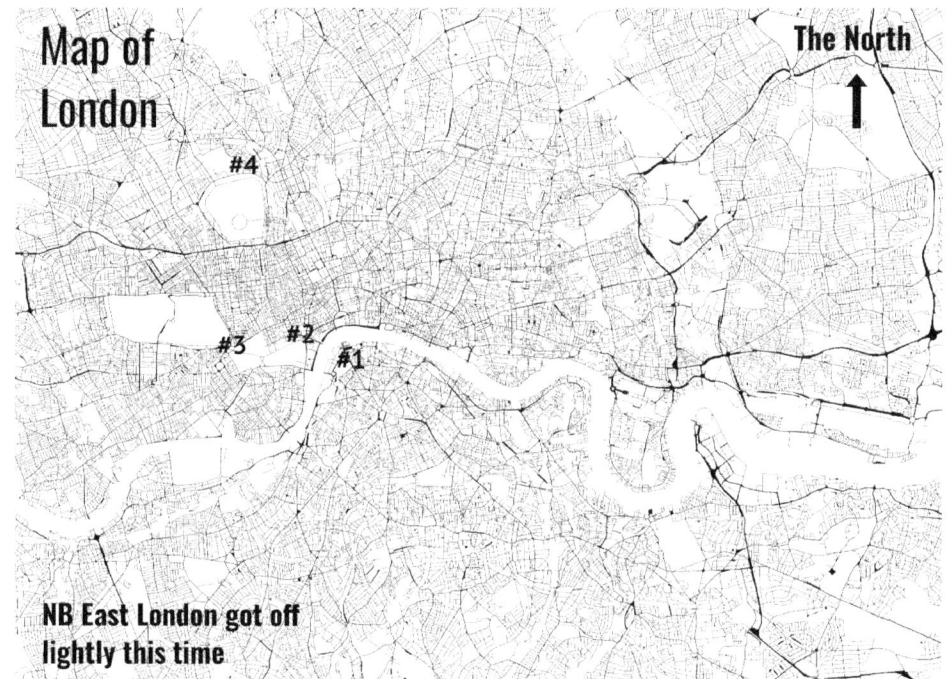

Sites you might find of interest

#1 Southbank Centre, South Bank of the Thames

The Southbank Centre is a complex of artistic venues in London, England, on the South Bank of the River Thames (between Hungerford Bridge and Waterloo Bridge).

It comprises three main performance venues (the Royal Festival Hall including the Saison Poetry Library, the Queen Elizabeth Hall and the Purcell Room), together with the Hayward Gallery, and is Europe's largest centre for the arts. It attracted 4.36 million visitors during 2019. Over two thousand paid performances of music, dance and literature are staged at Southbank Centre each year, as well as over two thousand free events and an education programme, in and around the performing arts venues.

In addition, three to six major art exhibitions are presented at the Hayward Gallery yearly, and national touring exhibitions reach over 100 venues across the UK.

#2 New Scotland Yard, Westminster

Scotland Yard (officially New Scotland Yard) is a metonym for the headquarters building of the Metropolitan Police, the territorial police force responsible for policing all 32 boroughs of London, excluding the City of London.

The name derives from the location of the original Metropolitan Police headquarters at 4 Whitehall Place, which had a rear entrance on a street called Great Scotland Yard. The Scotland Yard entrance became the public entrance to the police station, and over time the street and the Metropolitan Police became synonymous. The New York Times wrote in 1964 that, just as Wall Street gave its name to New York's financial district, Scotland Yard became the name for police activity in London. This building was acquired by hypermarkets operator Lulu Group International in 2015 and redeveloped into a luxury hotel, operated by Hyatt, which opened in December 2019.

The force moved from Great Scotland Yard in 1890, to a newly completed building on the Victoria Embankment, and the name "New Scotland Yard" was adopted for the new headquarters. An adjacent building was completed in 1906. A third building was added in 1940. In 1967, the Metropolitan Police Service (MPS) moved its headquarters from the three-building complex to a tall, newly constructed building on Broadway in Victoria. In summer 2013, it was announced that the force would move to the Curtis Green Building – which is the third building of New Scotland Yard's previous site (1890–1967) – and that the headquarters would be renamed Scotland Yard. In November 2016, MPS moved to its new headquarters, which continues to bear the name of "New Scotland Yard".

#3 Buckingham Palace, Westminster

Buckingham Palace is the London residence and administrative headquarters of the monarch of the United Kingdom. Located in the City of Westminster, the palace is often at the centre of state occasions and royal hospitality. It has been a focal point for the British people at times of national rejoicing and mourning.

Originally known as Buckingham House, the building at the core of today's palace was a large townhouse built for the Duke of Buckingham in 1703 on a site that had been in private ownership for at least 150 years. It was acquired by King George III in 1761 as a private residence for Queen Charlotte and became known as The Queen's House. During the 19th century it was enlarged, principally by architects John Nash and Edward Blore, who constructed three wings around a central courtyard. Buckingham Palace became the London residence of the British monarch on the accession of Queen Victoria in 1837.

The last major structural additions were made in the late 19th and early 20th centuries, including the East Front, which contains the well-known balcony on which the British royal family traditionally congregates to greet crowds. A German bomb destroyed the palace chapel during the Second World War; the Queen's Gallery was built on the site and opened to the public in 1962 to exhibit works of art from the Royal Collection.

The original early 19th-century interior designs, many of which survive, include widespread use of brightly coloured scagliola and blue and pink lapis, on the advice of Sir Charles Long. King Edward VII oversaw a partial redecoration in a Belle Époque cream and gold colour scheme. Many smaller reception rooms are furnished in the Chinese regency style with furniture and fittings brought from the Royal Pavilion at Brighton and from Carlton House. The palace has 775 rooms, and the garden is the largest private garden in London. The state rooms, used for official and state entertaining, are open to the public each year for most of August and September and on some days in winter and spring.

#4 Primrose Hill, London

Primrose Hill is a Grade II listed public park located north of Regent's Park in London, England, first opened to the public in 1842. It was named after the 64 metres (210 ft) natural hill in the centre of the park, the second highest natural point in the London Borough of Camden. The hill summit has a clear view of central London, as well as Hampstead and Belsize Park to the north and is adorned by an engraved quotation from William Blake. Based on the popularity of the park, the surrounding district and electoral ward were named Primrose Hill.

Amenities of the park include an outdoor gym known as the Hill Trim Trail, a children's playground, and toilets, all located on the south side near Primrose Hill bridge which connects to London Zoo and Regent's Park.

Like the Regent's Park, Primrose Hill was once part of a great chase appropriated by Henry VIII. Later, in 1841, it became Crown property and in 1842 an Act of Parliament secured the land as public open space. The name "Primrose Hill" has been in use since the 15th century – giving the lie to later claims that it was named after Archibald Primrose, whose premiership witnessed the rapid expansion of London underground rail network London.

In October 1678, Primrose Hill was the scene of the mysterious murder of Sir Edmund Berry Godfrey. In 1679 three Catholic labourers, Robert Green, Henry Berry and Lawrence Hill were found guilty of the murder (though subsequently exonerated) and hanged at the top of the hill. For a few years after the hanging, Primrose Hill was known as Greenberry Hill. In 1792 the radical Unitarian poet and antiquarian Iolo Morganwg (Edward Williams) founded the Gorsedd, a community of Welsh bards, at a ceremony on 21 June at Primrose Hill.

The canal through the area was completed in 1816, and the railway, running under the hill, was completed in 1838; this was the first rail tunnel in London. By that time, the area was considered to be a "prime development opportunity" according to one source. In 1840, Charles FitzRoy, 3rd Baron Southampton, sold the land that he owned and new villas were built over the subsequent years. Other land was still owned by Eton College but transferred to the government in 1841. The Crown drained and levelled the land after 1851 and began adding park features, to turn it into "park for the people". The park was historically split between the Ancient Parishes (which later became Metropolitan Boroughs) of Marylebone (now part of the City of Westminster), St Pancras and Hampstead (in the modern London Borough of Camden); with the hill itself a part of Hampstead.

As of 2020, the Primrose Hill Open Space is managed by the Royal Parks Authority.

Contents

Sites you might find of interest
Prologue
Chapter 1
Chapter 2
Chapter 3
Chapter 4
Chapter 5
Chapter 6
Chapter 7
Chapter 8
Chapter 9
Chapter 10
Chapter 11
Chapter 12
Chapter 13
Chapter 14
Chapter 15
Chapter 16
Chapter 17
Chapter 18
Chapter 19
Chapter 20
Chapter 21
Chapter 22
Chapter 23

Chapter 24
Chapter 25
Chapter 26
Chapter 27
Chapter 28
Chapter 29
Chapter 30
Chapter 31
Chapter 32
Chapter 33
Chapter 34
Chapter 35
Chapter 36
Chapter 37
Chapter 38
Chapter 39
Chapter 40
Chapter 41
Chapter 42
Chapter 43
Chapter 44
Chapter 45
Chapter 46
Chapter 47
Chapter 48
Chapter 49
About the Author

Prologue

There's one thing we have yet to touch upon. I've mentioned the Real, magic and what happens when the Realms collide. The mess it makes.

But I haven't really covered off one very pertinent question.

Why don't immortals and mortals get along?

Mythology is littered with accounts of Gods warring with their mortal followers, with immortals playing vicious tricks on the stupid short-lived folk, and seeking revenge for acts committed against their kin centuries past.

But you would think that after all this time, like neighbours arguing over a fence about whose goat ate whose prize vegetables, both sides would learn to set grievances aside and matters lie. Leave the past to the past, and move on with a less argumentative future. And less shouting.

But the fact is, neither side is suited to forgive or forget.

Gods and Goddesses down throughout the ages have performed miracles and marvels for their followers, raising them up and giving them their heart-most desires time and time again. Usually for the small price of their undying devotion, utter compliance to their commands and the odd sacrifice or two. Sometimes of their enemies, sometimes of their livestock, sometimes of their own kith and kin.

And time and time again, the fires of rebellion have been stoked and the immortals shocked when their followers rise up to shake their fists to the heavens and demand *enough*. Temples torn down, priests and priestesses disabused of their positions rudely and violently. The names of their once deities turned into curses.

On the other hand, mortals continue to be surprised when acts of benevolence are balanced by catastrophes and calamities. A beneficial harvest one year that is so bountiful the Gods are praised and sung to every night … but then the next year, a dire plague of insects strike that eat the crops and devour all but the most closely hoarded supplies. And the Gods are cursed, the mortals stunned that so bad a thing could happen. When there must always be a balance, a settling of accounts. Mother Nature herself abhors imbalance, and is currently rectifying the most significant one in terms of mortals populating her home and destroying all over life though Her actions are over the course of many aeons.

Partly the fault lies with the teachings passed down from deities to their followers, the knowledge that mortals are, first and foremost, before all other creatures. Raised up above the lamb and wolf, the goat and ox. Most immortals find it hard to derive meaningful worship from creatures that are only interested in their next stretch of grass to eat, the next bowel movement to ease their nature. So finding creatures of moderate intellect and language who can then be taught to follow, to praise them, begets a desire in the creatures who lives span millennia to make of these people something special. To tell them they are the chosen ones.

Tell a mortal they are chosen, and they will happily lord the fact over all others. Taking land from those that lived there first, setting themselves up as rulers over all as the *Gods have chosen them specially* for the task. Hunt and slay lesser creatures for sport or food, for these things are not loved by their Gods. They are not chosen.

After so many failed attempts by immortals, you would think they would learn. Stop making the same mistakes, understand that what they said actually has an effect on the people listening. But no.

Though immortals have had millennia to learn, they are like children at times. Trusting, carefree and oblivious to the impact they have on creatures whose lives come and go like a blink of their eye. And mortals, striving to reach the longest length of their tenure from squalling infant to wrinkled elder, feel that the Gods somehow *owe* them. That beings of immeasurable power and might are there only to make their lives better, to ease their burdens and deal with trivial matters like next door's goat eating their cabbage crop. Or that country's wealth being more than their own, and how unfair that fact is.

The simple fact is, immortals and mortals will never get on. One desires the other to be simple and compliant and to spend their meagre lives in adoration, whilst the other looks to the former to ease all their problems and make their short lives as glorious as possible without any payback.

It doesn't help that to most immortals, when they are crossed, their instinctive reaction is to seek payback. Like the man who finds his neighbour's dog has messed *again* on his prized and immaculate lawn, and then orders a truckful of manure to be delivered to the house next door's driveway. Immortals do not know the meaning of *measured response*, and that is why whole villages have vanished when a trickster was out-tricked, castles put to sleep at the prick of one young princess's finger for a single slight to the wicked fairy.

Mortals tend to forget that when the hero conquers the villainous ogre and steals back what was taken, when the youth climbs the beanstalk and steals the golden egg, that they are dealing with creatures of vast power and unchecked might. And very, very unforgiving natures. And usually some kith and kin kicking around who will take offence that their lord, father, mother or blood-tied relative of some kind is now hanging over the fireplace as a trophy.

No, mortals and immortals were made never to mix. Never to just get on and be happy with a peaceful and stable relationship. Tales of demi-gods, quasi-immortals and mixed lineages from the Real and Mortal Realms still are told, but you have to ask yourself, do they really sit down for a Sunday dinner together as a family and chat over how Aunt Ethel is doing, and what their week has been like?

Or is it thunderbolts and lightning, and silver forged weapons at every meeting, wolfsbane in the soup and faerie dust spiking the wine?

It is said that cats and dogs do not get along. But compared to mortals and immortals? Canines and felines are positively bestest of buddies, pals and sworn brethren for life. And that will be the way of things until the end of days, and someone is finally presented with a bill for the mess they've all made of the furnishings, and to cover the bar tab.

Chapter 1

We've talked about the main player, Artur Pendragon, in the Sword in the Stone mythology. But there were other players involved, for good and for ill, that contributed to how that story was told. I'll cover off a few of these in the following chapters – if only to help explain how things went so drastically and possibly comically wrong.

"Be you wakened, Morgan Black?"

A sing-song voice dragged me from the deep slumber I'd fallen into. A pair of vivid amber eyes flecked with emerald greeted me as I cracked open my own, bright with life and far too much wakefulness for this Gods-forsaken time of the day.

I'd spent most of the night trawling through online research sites and various books I kept around the apartment for when I needed background information on all things weird and supernatural. As much as Google was becoming the next God of the Internet … hey, I remember when *Ask Jeeves* looked like it was going to be the next thing, before it wasn't … there were times when it paid to have the original books written by people who'd actually encountered the creatures I hunted.

Either writing down their notes as warnings to keep away from the shit-scary beasts, or as hints and tips on how to defeat with them. Old-world cheat codes, sort of.

Anyhow, I'd collapsed around half three in the morning, having made sure Danny and Felix were safe and happy in the Land of Nod. The books I'd been reading were scattered around me, with scraps of notes I'd made fallen like autumn leaves from where I'd neatly stacked them.

I took in a face of pale green hue patterned with distinct leaf and vine motifs, with a faint touch of darker freckles and a questioning frown marring an otherwise youthful and attractive visage. One that could have graced any number of billboards advertising the latest fashion or trend for young women.

My eyes travelled downward even as I tried to work out what ungodly hour it was to have been woken up, covering the slim jawline and graceful neck, down past bared, well-muscled shoulders to …

I jerked straight upright, books falling off my bed to thump on the floor, cotton sheet falling down from where it had wrapped around me tight enough to suggest I'd been restless in my sleep. Immediately, I realised I was only in the bottom set of my sleep wear, not having bothered throwing on the top t-shirt before I stripped and crashed out earlier this morning.

"Uh, Goldspur. You're … Dammit, what are you doing in my bedroom? And why are you *naked*?" I growled at the dryad, jerking my eyes back up from her very bare and very feminine chest to stare into those golden-green eyes of hers.

And yes, I know my line of questioning needs better prioritization, but hell, I'd just woken up.

My brain desperately demanded coffee before I dealt with anything serious, but a stray thought started banging round my fuzz-wrapped mind. Since when did my house guest and homicidal guardian have breasts? The last time I'd seen her, she'd been child-like, though to be fair, still fairly psychotic what with the Shadow knives my sweetest granny had gifted her to protect our home. But definitely *not* a woman in shape and form.

"Good morning, Morgan Black!" The dryad slipped to one side of the bed, from where she had been straddling my sleeping body, leaning in way too close to stare at me. That had been what woke me, otherwise I was pretty sure I'd still be slumbering like the dead. "The sun is risen, your guests are stirring and … is there a problem with my attire? It is perfectly comfortable to me?"

She stood up straight, looking down at herself with one eyebrow quirked. If I wasn't imagining things, she had grown about two feet in the space of one night, from a child sized Real denizen to a young woman. Willow-thin, wearing a kirtle of layered material that hugged her hips and the tops of her thighs at what could be considered an indecent length for most mortals, she had those paired knives sheathed at her waist, hilts slanted for easy reach.

That was all the clothing she wore. And she *definitely* wasn't a child anymore.

"Is there a problem?" She asked me with a confused expression, hands pointing to exactly the place my eyes did not need or want to be drawn to. "If I am honest, these seem of little use to me. In fact they get in the way and affect my balance. But Father tells me they are natural and as such I should accept them. What do you think?"

I couldn't pick up anything from her voice other than genuine innocence, otherwise I truly would have thought the Morrigan had set this whole thing up as some sort of cruel joke at my expense.

Before I could respond, Goldspur bounced back onto the bed with inhuman agility, landing astride me and arching her back, looking down at me.

"What do you think, Morgan Black?" She repeated with that lilting voice of hers. "Are these *acceptable*?"

My eyes were filled with green curves, and I screwed them shut and made the mistake of reaching out to grab the tree-spirit to move her from my bed. I stopped as my hands encountered warm, soft skin, smoothly muscled under my fingers. Bare skin …

"A-*hem*." Felix's voice sounded from the doorway, and my eyes shot back open, taking in the young mortal friend as she leant against my doorframe and cocked her head at the scene she had walked in on. "I can come back later if I'm interrupting anything?"

Gripping Goldspur just above her waist, I gently but firmly moved her off me again and to the side of the wide bed I'd installed in my room. I hadn't purchased something so big with the normal bachelor expectation of sharing it with anyone, instead I just liked a big enough space to sleep on that meant no matter how I thrashed or moved, I wouldn't end rolling onto the floor.

"Felix, give me five minutes. And stop smirking." I growled at her as I rallied my brain cells. Rolling over to the *other* side of the bed, I grabbed up a loose t-shirt from a pile I'd recently washed, and tossed it one handed to the dryad. "Goldspur, please try wearing something like this from now on. I'm too old for half naked young women to be jumping on me first thing in the morning. In fact at any time, looking like that!"

The dryad plucked the t-shirt from the air, looking at the *Weird Fish* motif on its back, with two suited fish holding up a prawn and the logo *Natural Prawn Grillers* and her mouth opened to frame the question I knew was coming.

"It's just a joke on … oh never mind. Just put it on." I growled even as I pulled out another loose top and struggled into it. Felix sniggered, but quieted after I shot her a filthy look after pulling my head free of the t-shirt.

"Since you think this is so funny, and you've just about gotten through puberty, how about you explain to her what the problem is?" I snarked at my friend, shifting responsibility over to her to deal with. "Call it quits for letting you crash here."

Felix rolled her eyes at me but shrugged, then gestured for Goldspur to follow her out of my bedroom.

"C'mon. I'll explain what's got Morgan's knickers in such a twist, and you can tell me all about what it's like living with such a grumpy sod." She told the dryad, who smiled at the mortal woman and joined her. My happiness from handing over such an awkward conversation to Felix was deflated only slightly by the suspicion of what my friend might say to the Real creature, and what trouble they might agree to throw my way. As women, when they get together, are wont to do for sheer kicks and giggles.

The pair were replaced by Bear, padding into the room and coming up to me for a head rub. The massive trollhound leant into me, rumbling with base delight as I made a fuss of him.

"Yeah, I know. Breakfast is coming." I told him, eliciting a toothsome grin from the hound. The world could be going to hell in a handbag, but at least I could fix my companion food and arm myself with coffee before facing whatever shitstorm was headed our way.

Robert Knox, armed with the Harrowing. And behind the bastard, Morgana. Free from centuries-old incarceration and eager to begin reaping her revenge on pretty much everybody. Not to mention Jack the Ripper still lurking around the Mortal Realm, intent on payback after my friends and I had handed him his ass. Oh, and did I mention several other Real monsters my pack and the other lycan were still hunting, after Morgana freed them to wreak havoc and ruin this side of the Veil. A nice little bit of distraction to keep our eyes off whatever she had planned with her mortal puppet.

Yeah, nothing much really. I'm surprised I even thought I needed help with all that.

Washing away the dregs of my interrupted sleep in the en-suite, I shambled out into the living room to find Danny sat on one of the sofas. I instantly forgave him all his issues with me, seeing the large pot of coffee he'd placed on the table opposite, along with what smelt like pastrami and gherkin sandwiches, piled high. I almost started drooling.

"I figured it's the least I could do, after letting Felix and me sleep here last night." He told me, grinning with just a little hint of shame. I guessed he remembered unburdening himself to me before he fell pretty much unconscious, and I caught enough of his tangled emotions from the scents he was giving off to know the man was definitely feeling unsure and a bit awkward. "Your … ah … house guest is … uh … different? She been living here long? Only I didn't see another bed made up downstairs, so I hope we didn't take up her place?"

Danny's fishing was hilariously obvious, the guy having even less skill at subtlety than me. Which is saying something. I grinned and shook my head even as I walked around the sofas and made for the kitchen to rustle up some food for my walking bear-rug.

"She lives in the tree, mate." I poked my head round the wall dividing the kitchen and the living room, nodding to the massive gnarled apple tree that dominated the room. "Think of her as its guardian and daughter. Nothing going on there, so don't start getting all prudish on me. Sheez, she's like a week old, max."

"Uh huh." He eyed the tree dubiously, taking a pull from his coffee. "Never seen a week old *anything* looking like that. She often walk around, you know, dressed in not much?"

"No idea. That happened overnight." I finished depositing a large, fresh hunk of meat into Bear's bowl and set it on the floor. The trollhound had followed me in but now looked back at the table with its load of sandwiches then to his own bowl meaningfully. I shook my head, and he gave a hard-done by sigh before padding to his food and chowing down.

Leaving him munching away, I joined Danny again, slipping onto the other sofa and pouring myself a large mug of steaming goodness. He waited in silence as I took a long sip and closed my eyes for a moment, savouring the warmth and taste.

"I told Felix to have a word with her. Woman to woman." I finally replied, swallowing the warmth and reaching over to the plate of sandwiches that were practically begging to be demolished. "Hopefully set her straight without putting my foot in my mouth, as I'm wont to do."

Danny snorted a laugh, making me look across at him with a questioning expression.

"You asked *Felix* to give your … whatever she is, the birds and the bees talk? About men and women stuff? Oh, Morgan. You don't half choose them, and I can say that because she's my daughter!"

I took a large bite of my sandwich, almost groaning with pleasure at the taste, and mulled over his wisdom. Finally, I had to shrug and accept whatever consequences I'd be owed for my choice. Seriously, how bad could it be?

"So I'm guessing the *real* reason you called me before?" I mused, after swallowing. "Was coz Felix started doing weird shit?"

Danny jerked as if I'd slapped him, face paling as he took a breath then nodded. He was about to speak, when, of course, we were interrupted by the sound of stomping feet coming up the stairs.

Chapter 2

Merlin.

Also known as Myrddin, Marzhin or Merzhin depending on who you speak to. Thought to be the son of a mortal woman and an incubus, he inherited supernatural powers from his father – including those of prophecy and shape-changing, as well as his talents for magic. Apart from his involvement with Artur, and previously Uther Pendragon, Merlin has also been linked with the raising of Stonehenge, and also the older mortal king Vortigern who was renowned for trying to raise a tower over a like where dragons embodying the Celts and the Saxons fought for dominance.

After Artur's perceived death, Merlin vanishes from history. Tales are told of his weakness for the opposite sex, sometimes this being Morgan Le Fay, other times being a fairy named Viviane or Nimue. It is told one or more of his liaisons broke his heart, or grew jealous of his affections for other ladies, or spurned his advances in the first place. Whatever the truth, Merlin with all his mighty powers did not foresee his doom and was unable to avoid entombment within a crystal cave for the rest of eternity 'and that is where he remained, for never again did anyone see or hear of him or have news to tell of him.'

The footsteps heralded the return of the two women, but I'd caught their scent growing stronger anyhow, and guessed they'd finished their chat. Goldspur and Felix exchanged a look when they reached the living room, giving nothing away except the dryad nodding once as if something had been agreed. Then she walked softly over to the apple tree and slid inside.

I clocked Danny's quiet whistle of surprise and guessed he hadn't really believed my explanation about where she lived. I wasn't sure which bothered me more, him not believing me or the thought of anything going on with someone so young, so new to the world. Despite her having handed a Special Ops team their collective asses, Goldspur was still basically a child and I guess I felt protective over her.

Felix for her part simply vaulted over the back of the easy chair and slid into its cushioned embrace. Setting her feet on my coffee table, she grinned across at the both of us.

"Well, since you were going to start talking about me, reckoned you might as well hear it from the horse's mouth." She told me, whilst Danny just sighed and leant back into the sofa, cradling his coffee.

There was a challenge in her eyes that I couldn't miss – an obvious statement that she was not going to be talked *about*, even by her own father and a family friend. So I just shrugged, settling myself with the remains of my sandwich and looked pointedly at her feet.

"What?" She played dumb, but Bear came to my rescue at that moment. The trollhound could move silently when he wanted to for something so big, and he'd re-entered the living room and settled down amongst the roots of the tree without anyone but me noticing. Now he rose up, padding over to Felix and, with a care that spoke of him knowing just how strong he was, set his jaws on either side of her outstretched legs and pulled them off the table.

"Hey!" She jerked, going to jerk her trousers free from his teeth.

"I wouldn't if I were you. Not unless you like your clothes shredded in a very unfashionable way." I warned her, as Bear rumbled a deep growl in the depths of his chest. "Plus his drool is *impossible* to get out, and I'm not buying you a fresh set of pants. Best bet, just move your feet."

The firm set of her jaw said she wanted to argue, but even she realised the futility of wrestling with the massive hound. With a muted *whatever*, she slid her legs down and set her feet on the floor whereupon Bear loosened his hold and shook himself, grinning that wolfish smile of his as he congratulated himself. He walked over to me, letting me rub his thick skull, then slid to the floor again and immediately started a gentle, rumbling snore.

"You were about to say?" I prompted Felix to start talking, as she inspected her trousers and poked at a damp patch on her knee. "Weird shit happening?"

"Yeah, so you'd dropped me off at the café," She started, settling into her seat and closing her eyes as she remembered. "I'd called Dad … yeah, we've agreed it's too weird to keep calling him Uncle or Danny now. Anyhow, I'd called him as you said I should, and I was just waiting. All alone. Just thinking about what Gary had done. What he'd wanted."

She shivered, the memories far from pleasant.

"Thing is, if he'd tried to … well, you know, jump my bones, I think it would have been less weird, less *wrong* somehow. Like, that's what we're told happens, it's normal even if it's so fucking wrong?" She explained, opening her eyes and staring down at her hands. "But instead, he tied me up in that boat shed. Kept whispering things to me, telling me he had so much to show me, that I could be like him. *Free*. And then there was this feeling like something was soaking into me, like I was in water but it wasn't water. Oil, maybe, but hot *and* cold at the same time. It made me want to puke, spit the taste out my mouth but there wasn't anything there."

I remembered the downstairs of Gary's boathouse, enscribed with powerful wards and lines of Veil energy running throughout the space. All centred on and spiralling into where Felix had been tied up. He'd left her inside a circle of some kind, definitely a ritual of some kind but I wasn't the expert on such things, and after I'd collapsed the boathouse on us there was nothing left for me to take back for the witch to check. But the stench, the sensation Felix had felt, that was definitely the rottenness, the wrongness of the Veil. A Realm made over into a graveyard, now that I knew what Oberon and Madb had done.

"Anyhow, sitting in the café alone, all of it came back to me. The fear, the feeling of everything changing, of never seeing my Dad, my friends, my life again. All of it, swamping me. I couldn't breathe…" Her hands were knotted together, her forehead creased with the strength of the memory, and I caught the faint taint to the air, a thread of that magic Felix had called up outside the restaurant. When she had fried Baba Yaga. "And I just … I just had to scream and let it all out otherwise, I felt I was going to explode, you know?"

She looked up, and I was surprised to see tears glistening at the corner of her eyes. She smelt of fear, of pain, but also a grim anger, seething down deep inside her. A core of strength I reckoned she had only just learned she had.

"Next thing I know, that purple fire sort of went off like a firework. Blew a load of plates and stuff to bits, set fire to some napkins. I was so shocked I didn't know what to do for a second." Felix laughed then, a little maniacally, a shrillness that certainly wasn't the same carefree chuckle she used to have. "By the time Dad showed up, I'd cleaned up most of the mess, and when the police asked, I just said I'd gotten upset and thrown the plates around. They seemed to think that made sense."

"It happened again, when I got her home." Danny now spoke up, setting his cup down and shuffling on the sofa so he could be closer to Felix. He set one hand on her knee, and she leaned a little into him, obviously welcoming the closeness. "I guess I was treating her like she was going to explode, being over-protective and wouldn't let her do anything. Go anywhere, without me following behind. I just didn't think."

"He was just there everywhere I went, and then I needed to go for a pee. It was so stupid, but I just lost it." Felix shook her head, even as Danny winced. "I went to scream, shout at him, but …"

"I wasn't going to go in or anything! Nothing like that. I just … if I lost sight of her, I was afraid I'd lose her again. I still wasn't exactly thinking straight at that point." He admitted. "All I know is, she screamed at me then there's this loud noise, like an explosion, and the door to the toilet disappeared in all this purple fire. Felix was just standing there, with water and broken ceramics everywhere."

"I blew up the toilet. And the sink. Pretty much destroyed the whole room." Felix admitted, wincing herself at the memory. "I didn't *mean* to. Just got so angry."

I blew out a breath, memory sparking back to when I'd picked her up as she slept, aiming to put her to bed. I'd felt that same energy spark to life but had managed to calm her down without an incident. Now I realised the sort of bullet I'd dodged, given her newfound ability to wreck things.

"When we put out the fire and cleaned up the mess as best we could, I got Dad settled down and we tried to think what to do." Felix laid a hand on top of his own, letting him know it was ok. "Dad didn't want to call you, no matter what I said. But then I remembered the woman at your office. She helped me when you picked me up from the police station. Elspeth. She always said if anything happened, for me to call her. So I did."

"And she's been coming to see you since?" I already knew the answer, but it would be good to clarify what had been going on under my nose. I wasn't angry at Danny or Felix, or Ellie. I just needed to get up to speed.

"Sometimes I'd go see her, but yeah, normally she'd come over. We spent most of that night with her, talking through things. Just trying to understand stuff." Felix carried on. "She reckoned whatever it was Gary *did*, it's all linked to my emotions. I get angry, scared … whatever, it kickstarts this thing inside me. And then I make things go boom."

I nodded, since that made perfect sense. Felix had been scared at the restaurant when she had taken down a Real hag of fearsome strength. She'd been pissed at Danny when he had been mother-henning her at home. And I guessed she'd been upset and afraid at the café when she first went 'boom'.

Magic is weird. Elspeth had tried to educate us lycan on the nuances of what was basically the lifeblood of the Realms, accessible via carefully controlled rituals and practices that these days mortals called *spells* or equations, but also easy to tap into accidently. Wild talents, the way some stories told of wizards and witches throwing fireballs from their fingers and conjuring lightning from thin air, when the majority always spoke of wands or staffs needing to be used, key phrases and gestures to summon the craft.

I was no expert, but I was guessing either Felix was a wild talent that had been latent all this time, or the rituals Gary had used on her had somehow connected her to the Veil. As a once-Realm, it was theoretically possible the power still existed as a source of magic, as I'd seen Knox tap into it, and the fallen King of the Twilight fae when he almost brought ruin to the Beltane tournament. And now Felix was dipping into it when she got angry or upset, with obvious results.

"We tried a few things, to see what I can or can't do." Felix explained as she sneaked one of my sandwiches from the pile. I went back for a top up of coffee … the way this morning was turning out, I'd need the juice to keep me upright. "Like tests, natural exams she explained. Like some people are good at languages but crap at music."

"And?" I swigged the hot drink, letting the young woman take a bite of her sandwich before she answered.

"Turns out blowing up stuff, I'm really good at. Elspeth hid something, then told me to find it. I could *feel* where it was, so just pointed it out first time." She smiled at the memory, then shrugged. "Other stuff, I couldn't do. I was meant to stop some bean bags she threw at me, but just sort of blew them up instead. She made three stones look alike, even though one was a different colour and shape, and I couldn't turn it back or work out which one it was. Kids games like that, but she said it was important."

"You said you hear voices?" I prompted, seeing Dany start at that and guessed they hadn't shared *everything*. Not surprising really. Felix looked guiltily at her father for a moment, then nodded.

"Not all the time. And it's like someone singing to me, not speaking. But yeah, sometimes if I'm trying to do something, I hear words in the song that tell me how to do it." She admitted, then closed her eyes as a memory surfaced. "Like that … *hag* you called her? Baba Yaga. The song said how I could stop her hurting us all, so I just did it."

I nodded, not that it made much sense to me but just accepting the fact for what it was. Weird voices singing instructions to Felix when she used magic? It wasn't the strangest thing I'd heard, and I was far from an expert on how magic worked with mortals. That was Ellie's field of study, her area of expertise.

"And the hair?" I gestured to Felix's head, pointing out the albino elephant in the room.

"Uh, that sort of just happened." She tugged at one of her braided locks, yanking it round to look at the pristine white hairs. "After I blew up the toilet, the next morning I woke up to this. Scared me half to death when I first saw it. But Elspeth told me it's nothing bad. I haven't suddenly aged or lost my lifeforce or anything I was sure was wrong with me. She just says it's a thing that happens when people like me and … magic, well, get involved. Like a mark. Like those tattoos you've got on your hands now, I guess?"

"Ah, those are something entirely different." I shifted my hands from sight, realising Felix, sharp eyed as ever, would have noticed the change. "So. Shit happened. What's the plan now?"

The pair exchanged looks, then Felix nodded to her father. Danny shrugged.

"We've agreed to pull Felix from University, at least for the moment. I've spoken to her tutors and she can continue working on the coursework and just send it to them, but they agree she should take what time she needs after the whole kidnapping thing." He still winced at the word, the pain from what had happened to her a raw wound for him as well. "Your colleague, Elspeth, she's been helping Felix control her moods, and channel what she can do so there's less chance of it all building up and ... well, going bang again. Beyond that, mate, I ... we just don't know. This isn't anything I know much about."

"Yeah, no kidding." I agreed, settling back and munching on another sandwich as I chewed things over.

I may have said, but real life in the Mortal Realm isn't a *Harry Potter* story, or even *The Dresden Files*. A good series to read, if you ever fancy, with the sort of level of sarcasm I can really appreciate. Anyhow, there wasn't a magical school that Felix could suddenly attend, or a government of wizards and witches she needed to be introduced to. Ellie had given me the highlights when I'd asked ages ago.

Most witches belonged to a coven and worked with each other to share knowledge, bring in new members and basically keep a track of any offenders abusing their talents in ways that didn't merit us lycans getting involved. But like her, there were some witches who preferred their own space and worked mostly solo, specialists who still kept in touch with her sisters but worked on their own projects and answered only loosely to anyone else. Apart from their Goddess, the ultimate boss.

Wizards, warlocks or mages, they were less sensible, more problematic. Whatever you wanted to call them, they tended to be more isolated, less inclined to gather together. Male practitioners seemed to do better on their own, and only ran into trouble when they tried working in groups ... mostly because someone invariably wanted to be top dog of the pack, and think themselves better than the rest. That just led to in-fighting, squabbling and the abuse of talents. Like politicians from different parties sniping at each other, but with the ability to cause magical mayhem and destruction on top of their verbal insults. Never seemed to end well, so most men with the talent stayed as far as possible away from each other.

For their own safety and sanity. And to avoid freak explosions and surprising sinkholes.

It sounded like Ellie had taken Felix under her wing like any good witch might do with a newbie coming into their own talents. She'd be able to guide her and hopefully stop Felix from causing too much trouble until she had a handle on what she could do. Plus also help both her and Danny understand what it meant for the young woman's future, her life choices. Being able to use magic meant she would eventually have to learn about the Accords, the rules of the Realms and the laws she would have to abide by. And the consequences if she broke any of them.

And that meant learning about us, the lycans and our role in keeping the peace this side of the Veil.

The snarky part of me couldn't wait to see Felix's face when she realised what my *real* job entailed. But another part of my messed up psyche realised it'd most likely ruin our little game of taking the mick between us. A shame, really, as I did enjoy the banter we had going.

"Ok, that's me up to speed on the shit hitting the fan business." I spoke to them both, pushing aside my mug and leaning forward. Time to ask the serious question. "What I need to know is … what do you want from me?"

I held up a hand as Danny went to speak, knowing his knee-jerk response wasn't what I was after.

"Before you answer, let me say something." I took a breath, thinking how to put this without hurting either of them, but also giving it to them straight. "I'll be honest with you, I feel responsible for this. For what's happened to you, Felix. And what this means for you too, Danny. This is my world, and you've both been pulled into it without being asked, without knowing just how much this will change your lives. I get that you didn't get to say no, didn't get to walk away and stay safe. That was my job and I failed you both, as a friend."

"So, if you want, I can walk away. Let Elspeth pick things up and try to sort out this mess. She's great, and I trust her with my life so you are in the best hands." I explained, seeing mixed emotions in both my friends' faces, a riot of feelings there to be read in their eyes. "My life is *really* complicated right now, and hanging round me is liable to bring you more trouble, even possible danger. Like last night. So if you say you want me gone, I'm gone."

"But," I held my hands open, knowing that despite my words, if they did say they needed space, it'd hurt me. Hard. "If you want me involved, then I'll be here. I don't have all the answers but I can promise I'll have your back. That's never changed."

Danny and Felix exchanged a long look, leaving the sort of delay that gameshow hosts tend to use to drive the audience mad with anticipation … hell, I said I'd watched them, not that I *liked* them. Then Danny grinned across at me.

"Felix and I have talked, and we both agree. We're *family*, mate. Good or bad, you're part of our lives, and hell, we're part of yours." He told me, even as Felix got up and slid round the coffee table to drop onto the sofa beside me, grabbing my arm and hugging it tight. "I know what I said before, but I trust you. *We* trust you, and whatever the hell is going on here, we need you to help us get through it. At least in some sort of reasonable shape."

I bounced my head gently against Felix where she snuggled into my shoulder, feeling the strength of the emotions coming from both her and her father. It was like stepping outside, feeling the sun warm and bright on your face … it did me good to be wanted like this. No strings, no reservations … just the simple truth. It was how Jessica made me feel now, how my pack did. But Danny and Felix were mortals, and they had way less pack-mentality, more mixed emotions towards everything. Mortals tended not to be simple creatures, their emotions and feelings a tangle to have to unknot if you wanted to ever know how they were doing, what they were thinking. Especially the ones you just happen to fall in love with.

"Promise me one thing?" Felix muttered, raising up her head and I felt a lump in my throat to see the glitter of tears in her eyes.

"Shoot." I told her, giving her arm a squeeze.

"Don't let me go all *wicked witch of the west*. Please?" She asked quietly. "This thing, it … it scares me a little. A lot, really. I could hurt someone, like I did to that thing last night. But someone I know. My dad, my friends. Even you, but that's scraping the barrel…"

I mock-punched her arm to lighten things a little. As much as Felix always put forward such a strong, devil-may-care attitude, it was easy to forget at times she was still young. Still someone with strong raw emotions, and a deep well of feelings that left her open and easy to be hurt, no matter how well she tried to pretend otherwise.

"I promise I'll stop you before you get a thing for winged monkeys and ruby slippers, ok?" I grinned as she nodded and hugged me back. "Besides, green is *so* not your colour. You'd look hideous!"

Over her head, I caught Danny looking at us, and saw him mouth *thank you* to me. I just nodded, letting him know it was all ok.

The moment was a good one, a memory I wanted to lock in and remember when thing got worse. The three of us sat together, salving wounds before they grew too deep to heal. A small but powerful measure of happiness amidst all the hell and pain these past weeks.

Of course, this being the real world, it couldn't last.

Not even for five bloody minutes.

Chapter 3

My mobile pinged to life where I'd left it on the table.

Given my new partnership with OPS, the Office of Preternatural Security employed by Her Majesty's government to police the non-mortal side of law enforcement, and their habit of texting me moments before someone dropped a bomb in my lap, I was already bracing myself as I disengaged from Felix and picked the annoying thing up.

Checking the display, I found it was Jacob, my packmate and de facto leader of the enforcers within our pack. Jessica, our Alpha, utilised his skills at managing volatile and dangerous situations with a degree of discretion and finesse I could never match, making sure we dealt with any problems from the Real but remained out of the local or national news. Compared to him, I was a short-sighted bull in a china shop, high on coke and trying to dance the tango.

So I was surprised to see the text was a summons, but then my stomach clenched at the rest of the message.

Camelot School. Bird In a Bush Road. Primary school Peckham. Redcap hunting. Get here.

Crap. The Redcap, a Wyld fae with a peculiar and twisted need to soak his headgear in the blood of the young and innocent. Just recently released from prison by the big bad we'd discovered was Morgana – late of the Arthurian legends and something of a powerful sorceress or demi-goddess depending on what press you read about her. I'd thought we had the bastard cornered from an update sent to Jessica, but I guess he'd slipped free and was not wasting time in seeking his prey.

Children.

I checked the clock, seeing it was just quarter past seven in the morning ... Sheez, I'd had four hours sleep. No wonder my brain still felt like cotton wool. Anyhow, these days, I had no idea what time schools opened but guessed there was a window of opportunity here. Maybe only staff on site before the youngsters arrived.

And that reference to Camelot? The Ivory Court's castle and seat of power, and also linked to the legend of King Arthur? With Morgana behind all this madness, that *couldn't* be a coincidence.

Peckham was maybe 15 minutes' drive, with early morning traffic not being an issue if I could get out sharpish. Just gave me enough time to pick up my 'grab bag' of goodies, and make my apologies.

I looked across at my house guests, knowing my expression probably said it all.

"You've got to go?" Danny asked, and I nodded.

"Something's come up. You can hang out here as long as you want. I'm not expecting anyone, and Bear will enjoy the company." I told them both, then grinned across at Felix. "Of course, if you start blowing up any toilets, I'll have to bill you."

"Hah bloody hah." She snorted, then had a thought. "Do you know if Elspeth is ok? She was pretty messed up last night. Do you think she might need some company?"

Elspeth. Gregory. That was another mess I knew needed some attention. Ellie was not just someone I worked with, a contractor for *Good Deeds* with all her witchy knowledge and skills, she was also my friend. And she had lost the man she was convinced she was fated to love only last night, after they had started seeing each other for only a few weeks.

I hadn't had any missed calls from her but given how grief stricken she had been when I left her, I doubted she'd been back to the office. Probably instead curled up at home, handling her grief privately.

"Give her a call. See if she wants to come round." I suggested, knowing Felix's situation might be just the thing to take her mind off her own pain, let alone Goldspur's presence. I hadn't had a chance to share the fact I had a dryad living with me with the witch, but guessed how much she'd jump at the chance to get to know a creature so linked to nature. "Might be good for her, seeing you."

Felix nodded, showing her understanding and wisdom beyond her years, despite a fundamental lack of personal experience of heartache. Danny's daughter, to my knowledge, had not had a single serious relationship, no crushes or broken hearts to her count. She'd left enough young men and boys in her wake, but just had never been invested enough to commit to something serious when she had so much else to do, to experience and enjoy. I'd teased her enough times about the trail of crushed hearts and kicked puppies that mapped her explorations of her love life, but that just left me open for her rebuttals. And I was probably the more sensitive of the two of us, given the mess I'd made of my one serious relationship.

With Danny and Felix settled, I quickly grabbed a shower to wake myself up properly, and changed into work gear. Something similar to the clothes I'd worn last night to face off against Jack the Ripper and Baba Yaga, but without the rips and bloodstains. All my wounds from that fight had long since healed, but the clothes were a mess and probably deserved burning.

I'd lost one sword that Gregory, with his dying act to protect Ellie, had shoved into my half-brother's side before he was tossed into the depths of the Thames, so I grabbed a replacement from the small stock of weapons I kept near to hand. Bear caught the sound of my rummaging, and came padding from the living room to the bedroom, cocking his head and tail thumping with delight at the idea of joining me on the hunt.

"Sorry, bub. You've gotta stay here." I told him, seeing his ears droop and his ass hit the floor with a solid thump. He whined, pawing the floor to show his obvious disagreement and frustration. To be fair, I'd left him out of a lot of the chaos I'd been handling recently, when he would have been an asset I could count on. But all this was happening Mortal side, and I couldn't risk him being seen in his steroid pumped version of battle cat. It's from *He-Man and the Masters of the Universe*, an old cartoon that was so camp and silly, it still made me laugh.

He whined again, so I crouched down and faced him, ruffling his head.

"Hey, I promise I'll take you along the very next time we go Real side, and find you some nice crunchy trolls to hunt. But for now, I need you to guard Danny and Felix. Keep them safe in case anything comes calling. Can you do that for me?"

He grumbled, pawing at me and almost knocking me sideways, but I just scratched his ears until he yawned his acceptance and leant into the attention I was giving him. Bloody dog was more cat than hound at times.

Cat. That reminded me, I had one other character I needed to check in on. A certain Wyld fae I'd granted licence to hunt in the Mortal Realm for a year and a day, so he'd help me find my missing … whatever Sarah had been at that point. I needed to make sure the Bayun Cat wasn't causing too much trouble with his freedom, plus there was always the chance he could help track Knox down again.

Of course, the last time I'd asked him to do that, the fae had been ambushed by some pretty vicious imps, and had sworn to do several nasty things to me for the insult done him. So I wasn't sure he'd accept the deal without me offering something juicy for him to sink his teeth into. Literally. Hell, I'd cross that bridge when I ran into it.

The last task for me was to dial up a cab, confirming my destination and swig down another mug of coffee to settle my still-fuzzy brain. I was grabbing up a pair of the sandwiches Danny had made to eat on the way, when Felix stopped me. Her father had disappeared downstairs, probably to tidy up and clear away the bedding they'd used – I'd never known someone fuss about such things like him, but having seen his home, I knew he had a predilection towards neatness.

"Morgan, I just …" She began, then shook her head and looked me in the eye. I could feel how tired she was still, how afraid of these strange things happening to her, but also got a sense of excitement, a trill she felt from it all. "Just wanted to say, thanks. I know Dad ripped you a bit before, but he was just scared for me. For him. Hope we can still, you know …?"

"Don't worry," I told her, gripping her hand with my free one. "We'll get this sorted and go back to how things were. Me getting free food off your Dad, you giving me grief over it. No worries."

Felix shook her head, the feelings coming from a mixture of sadness and trepidation.

"Can they? Go back to normal? Like things were?" She asked, voice tinged with doubt. I could have given her the bull-shit line, could have pretended for her sake, but as I'd said, she was a friend. And deserved the truth.

"I honestly don't know." I replied with as much sincerity as I could muster, given I was still a semi walking zombie from too little sleep. "But we can try. That's about the best I can ask of you and Danny right now."

She nodded, leaning in and giving me a quick kiss on the cheek.

"That's for being so good to us. For looking out for us" She told me, her eyes large and full of sincerity. I'd never really noticed their colour before, not having spent ages staring into them, but now I noted flecks of bright violet showing amidst the cool blueness. Another change, I reckoned, from her exposure to the Veil.

Before I could answer, she then punched me hard on the shoulder.

"And that's for being such a cheapskate!" She grinned savagely. "Dad told me you own this entire bloody building! Why the hell are you grifting free food off of us?!"

Ah, dear old normality. I'd missed it.

Chapter 4

Guinevere.

Also known as Gwenhwyfar, Gwenivar and Gwynnever. Renowned foremostly as the wife of Artur, and a member of the tragic live triangle between her, her husband and the 'saintly' knight Lancelot. There is also a tale that she was seduced by Mordred, the bastard child of Artur and Morgan Le Fay.

Guinevere is less commonly known by her welsh origins, where her name translates as White Enchantress or White Fay/Ghost. Tales do no mention any supernatural powers ascribed to her, so this may have been more a title conferred for her luminous pale complexion, when most other mortals would have been heartier and ruddier in skin colour.

Following on from the events of Artur's fall, tales differ in what befell his Queen. In some, she is kidnapped and held prisoner for the rest of her mortal life, in others she takes vows in a convent and becomes its Abbess. One particularly brutal story is told of Artur himself sentencing her to death for infidelity and betrayal, either to be burned at the stake or torn apart by wild horses.

    Camelot Primary School resided near Our Lady of Sorrows Church, down the street from someplace called Friary Estate. It was opposite a large green space, Bird In A Bush Park, and comprised several large buildings of light brown brick, set behind a high fence of stone and metal with security gates and big letters painted on the roadway to indicate *School – Keep Clear*.

    It was about as different to the Camelot of the Ivory Court as could be, so I guessed the name had been something chosen by the mortals to make the place more appealing to their children.

    I'd checked their website as I sat in my cab, speeding through the backstreets from my home to Peckham. They'd even used the Lady of the Lake, delivering Excalibur from the waters, as their school logo. Thank Gods they never met the actual immortal, as I reckoned she would have been less than pleased of the reminder of her past. Of the Real relatives who had dumped her in the Mortal Realm and left her to rot in the mud and shit. And now used as a badge of honour for a school teaching young mortals. Yeah, she would have *hated* that.

I'd made good time, getting to the school within ten minutes of the taxi turning up. Just past eight in the morning, with not a single child to be seen either inside or out. The gates were still locked tight, so that told me we'd gotten ahead of the opening hours, but the clock was ticking.

As my cab pulled up, I saw Jacob leaning against the fence to the park, opposite to the school and indicated to my driver to stop by him. Scribbling my signature for the receipt, I grabbed my bag and hopped out to join my packmate.

"Not bad." He grunted, giving me a quick nod by way of greeting. He wasn't alone, I caught the scent of other lycan even as Emma and Markus stepped around the small entrance to the green space. Both shot me welcoming smiles, before I glanced across at the school.

"So, the bastard's inside? I thought Sean Boseman and his lot were handling him?" I queried quietly. Jacob grunted a chuckle.

"Slipped past them, the tricky sod." He obviously found the story amusing, but I guess I'd get the details later. "We picked up his scent, so he tried to lose us in the sewers before he backtracked through the Lows. But eventually followed him here, about an hour ago."

The Lows? That sparked a flicker of concern in me, not just from the memory of my last visit there, and what it had cost the ruling members of the place. I was surprised lycans had been allowed to hunt, what with Rous, partner to Molly, having been reduced to a shadow of his Rat God self or completely annihilated. I wasn't entirely sure which, and hadn't had a chance to go check. Or the inclination if I'm being truthful.

No, the *other* reason why hearing the pack had had to chase the Red Cap through that other domain was because it was also the haunt, until recently, of Robert Knox. The madman we *officially* weren't meant to be hunting, that the Office of Preternatural Security wanted instead. On their list supposedly for arranging the death of a handful of scientists, colleagues, to cover his own escape from governmental service. Armed with the knowledge someone had been stupid enough to trust him with, having tasked him to research a deterrent against the Courts, and anything that lives beyond the Veil.

The Harrowing. The death of immortals.

If the Red Cap had run through the Lows, I was instantly suspicious, since the Wyld goblin could have fled anywhere to get away from his lycan hunters. But him heading there, after I'd found that Knox was also employing Baba Yaga and Jack the Ripper to settle a score with me … well, that got my *suspicious bastard* bell ringing.

"And he's just, what, waiting inside?" I didn't think that sounded much like the Red Cap I'd read about. The goblin wasn't a planner, an ambusher. He was a vicious killer, a brute that relied on his great strength in fights, and his savagery to get him what he most desired. The blood of young mortals, to use as ink for his ragged and tattered cap.

"Probably thinks we won't go in if there's a risk we'll be seen. Reckon he's just holed up and waiting for the kids to come to him." Markus growled quietly but I snorted a laugh. "You reckon otherwise?"

"Red Cap doesn't strike me as the patient type. It's not his MO to lie in wait and surprise his victims. He always just bowled in and grabbed them, causing as much bloodshed as possible." I answered, shaking my head. "If he's here, before any kids are on site, I reckon he's after something else. Something to so do with his trip through the Lows maybe."

"Hmm. Knox?" Jacob clearly did the same mental one plus one, and saw what I was getting at.

I shrugged.

"I'm a suspicions bastard, can't lie." I checked my phone, finding time was definitely not on our side. "So what do we do?"

Our pack enforcer eyed the school carefully, clocking the layout one last time before laying things out.

"Here's the play. Markus, you circle round the back for any exit he might take, if he is after a snatch and grab. Emma, you're on front gate duty. Start stopping traffic, anyone approaching. You know the line. *Suspicious character seen on site. Police called, waiting for them to arrive.* Get them to gather in the park, use open ground so you can see any threat approaching." Jacob explained, both packmates of his team nodding.

I had no idea why he'd only brought two of his team, and why there wasn't any other lycan from the other packs. But if Jacob thought they were enough, he probably was right. This was what he did. Then again, he'd called me …

"Leaves us two." I commented dryly as he turned to face me.

"I'm going in the front." He told me, slipping a slim wallet out of his jacket. He'd dressed in non-descript clothing, not so obviously protective like my gear but I guessed it was the sort of outfit used by plain clothes security. Flipping the wallet, he showed me the ID contained within. "Get any teachers out and keep them from getting back in."

"Leaving me." I grimaced as he grinned.

"You're with me. If you're right and he's after something for Knox, you get to handle that. *Sir Knight Errant.*" I groaned at the reminder of my newly gained title with the Courts. Of course Jacob would choose this moment to have a dig at me. Silly of me not to expect otherwise.

The plan in place, we didn't waste any more time. Markus headed off at pace, moving fast enough to get round the school without drawing undue attention. Emma slipped out another wallet, a twin to the one Jacob had shown me and stepped into the road, settling so that she could see both routes in and react accordingly.

I followed Jacob, as he strode up to the gates. They were still locked, but I caught the glitter of lights within the nearest classrooms, so someone was home. Jacob jabbed the bell button set on the brick pillar, holding it down to make sure whomever was inside didn't ignore us.

It took a moment, but finally the main door opened and a middle-aged man came walking quickly towards us. I could scent the confusion coming from him even as he caught sight of two large adults outside his gates, ringing his bell without a single child to be seen. Probably thought we were tourists who had gotten lost, or potential applicants to get our child onto their books. Not that I would say Jacob and I look like we could be a couple, but hey, I'm not a good judge on who looks good together. I'd been stunned to hear Liv Tyler and Joaquin Phoenix had been an item for three years. Who would have called that??

The head teacher or whomever the man was obviously had a speech prepared for us, but Jacob didn't give him a chance to use it. Flashing his badge, he had the gates unlocked and the pair of us through within a matter of minutes. It took another five minutes for him to get Mr Robinson, the headteacher of the school, to agree to clear out the seven other staff members who were on site, and to pass us the master keys to the property.

Mortals. Sometimes I do worry over how easy it is to fool them.

We cleared the two main buildings without a whiff of anything Real, and had moved to the single level classrooms that had been built around a central quad of greenery, when my senses kicked in. It was the taint of rotten meat, the metallic tang of blood and an energy I was beginning to associate with the Wyld Court. Faint, already starting to break apart but definitely present.

Jacob nodded to me to show he'd gotten the scent too. Past the closed classroom doors and through what had to be the teachers' rooms. The difference was mostly less pretty flower pictures on the walls and cups of crayons and paintbrushes on the tables, more coffee jugs and wallboards covered in tacked messages that had multiple scribbles over them. Schedules of classes, attendance, that sort of thing.

The scent grew stronger as we passed through the central quad of green shrubs and small trees, and into what had to be the caretakers' abode. Corridors of boxes filled with stationery and office supplies, rooms stuffed with tools to keep the school tidy and safe for the children. All normal everyday clutter, nothing to be suspicious about. But the scent led us on.

Turning a corner, we found ourselves at the far end of the school building, with doors leading outside. But the trail did not lead there, but instead to a railing and a flight of steps that disappeared downward.

A basement. Of course. A goblin would be drawn to somewhere underground. Out of sight. Maybe I'd been wrong, and the sod had planned to lie in wait, make an ambush once the kids were running around the school. Who would miss one, quickly grabbed? Who would notice one scream amongst all the other loud noises?

Jacob must have had the same thought, as he motioned for silence, no spoken word now. Knowing the school was empty, I opened up my carry all and offered up first choice to my packmate. Not out of any sense of rank, just being polite. He eyed the choice critically, almost giving me a *what do you call this?* look before shaking his head and slipping free a cold wrought machete he must have had strapped under his coat. The weapon suited him just fine, short enough to use in tight spaces but with a good cutting edge to end any argument he got into.

Fine, I shot back at him with a roll of my eyes and slid free one of my last remaining short swords. Duly armed, we slipped around the railing and took the stairs down.

The basement was dark, cloaked in shadows even though the sun was already up and blazing down on the building above us. This must be where they kept the boiler, water tanks and such, given the large and bulky containers and mysterious pipes leading off like some metal octopus monster. There were light switches on the walls, but we left them off since our eyesight was good enough to pierce the gloom easily, and it wouldn't do much for the element of surprise if we started igniting bulbs around us.

The scent was stronger, but still fraying, as Jacob and I moved through the large room, checking around us on the off chance the Red Cap was lying in wait to spring out on us. But I didn't pick up any sound of breathing, no stealthy movement to warn of an attack. Besides I was getting a suspicion about what we'd find down here.

Passing through another doorway, we entered another large room but this looked to be for general storage. Objects had been stacked on every side, with sheets thrown over them to hide their identity or keep the dust off. Three things struck us as we stopped just inside the doorway.

Firstly, across from us, the far wall had been partially demolished. Broken through, with shattered brick and mortar lying all around. Whoever had done it hadn't had any plans other than *make a bloody big hole* which led off into darkness. Cold air wafted through the gaping rent, carrying the scent of *deep down* to us. Definitely not just someone wanting to peek behind wall number one.

The second *one thing is not like the other things* were deliberate and savage rents made in the remaining brickwork beside the massive hole. Someone had obviously been thoroughly displeased with this task and had vented on the nearest thing to hand. Beside the damage done, the perpetrator had deliberately carved thick letters in the brick, spelling out a short message.

Next Time Wolfs. Will Have Blood.

Seems the goblin had been expecting us after all and was nice enough to leave us a note since he hadn't stuck around to greet us in person. What a gentleman.

The last thing we noted was that a big space on the floor looked to have recently been cleared. Dirty scratch marks on the floor and even dirtier sheets thrown to one side to show *something*'s displacement. Whatever had been there was big, definitely of a size to make me wonder how it had been stored down here in the first place … but other than the sheets, and gouged lines leading to the gaping hole, there was nothing to identify what it had been. Except for a fading tang to the air, something I was growing used to finding, what with my exposure to it in Knox's rooms and now the Gardens of Ice.

Life energy. More bloody stolen life.

I walked over to the hole and sniffed, confirming my suspicion.

"He's been and gone. Through here by the smell of it and that nice little note of his." I told Jacob, nodding to the wall. "I'm just guessing, but whatever was on the floor and now isn't, looks like it went through the hole there too. And Red Cap is known to be pretty strong …"

"Huh. Follow the white rabbit?" My packmate commented dryly, slipping the machete back into its sheath beneath his coat. "And if I dropped you down that hole, you reckon you'd end up where? Wonderland"

I took a deep lungful of air, sorting through the scents and smells before I stuck my head through and tried to peer down into the murk. The Red Cap hadn't just broken the wall, he seemed to have used that inhuman strength of his to break down through the foundations and drop into some sublevel below the school. Probably an old access for the deeper sewer pipes or possibly even old underground lines that never were properly implemented. London is a honeycomb of old tunnels half made and old spaces built over then forgotten,

"If I were a betting mutt?" I mused, moving back from the hole and facing Jacob. "I'd say it leads down. Probably *all* the way down to an access point for the Lows. He was fetching something left in the basement of a primary school that just happened to be nicknamed after the Ivory Court's seat of power. Something big, that *maybe* the lunatic mortal pulling the Red Cap's strings had snuck in here for safe keeping whilst he was hiding from his old workmates. Like … oh, I don't know, another bloody container of life essence that he'd sucked from the children going to this school quietly over the many years so no-one noticed. But then, I'm just a suspicious mutt who *really* hates coincidences."

Jacob grunted, shaking his head and not bothering to point out the many assumptions I was making with my theory. Coz, truth be told, it was probably still true.

"Time to go speak to Mr Headteacher again. Maybe a good idea to see if he had any clue what was stored down here, oh and maybe if anyone's reported feeling tired, drained or the like recently." I prompted, earning a hard look from my packmate. "Oh, and if the name Knox means anything round here. Just a suggestion."

Jacob took one last look around the dingy room then turned his back and walked back towards the stairs. Heading back to the school's principle who was about to get the grilling of his life.

Chapter 5

Two hours later found the Scooby Gang back at *Good Deeds*, after we'd decided to reconvene there to update our Alpha on our findings, and incidentally greet the morning with more coffee and breakfast snacks which were always available.

Yeah, I know I'd already munched a pile of pastrami sandwiches, but I also know I've mentioned how the lycan metabolism burns way higher than a mortal's, so we get hunger pangs fairly regularly.

Jessica sat with us in the large meeting room situated to one side of the main office floor, having called us in almost as soon as we'd set foot in the building. Given the events of the past few days, she still managed to look her calm and professional self, suited in something light for the summer warmth but definitely bespoke and tailored. Somehow I reckoned she'd still put the rest of us to shame in just ragged jeans and a rumpled t-shirt, but that was so unlikely to happen, I left it as an idle thought.

In comparison, Elspeth was a shadow of her usual self, as she slumped in a comfortable seat and listened to us without comment. She had been in the room when we joined Jessica, so I guessed they'd been in a meeting which we'd somehow hijacked. Whilst the witch was still clad in her rich colours and gypsy-like attire, she'd added a thin dark scarf carefully wrapped close to her skin, and her eyes were tired and pain-filled.

"We checked with the head teacher, and he said he wasn't sure what had been in the basement, but the janitor had mentioned something about a *weird Victorian looking machinery* and *glowing lights* in his annual report. Thought it was an old science experiment but since it wasn't hooked up to anything, they just let it be." I wrapped up the report, since Jacob had covered off the actual events but left me with the revelation of what we'd found. "He's had reports of staff and pupils feeling lethargic, dizzy and not themselves over the past year or so, but he had the place inspected without anyone finding anything like a gas leak or pollution to cause anything serious. He thought it might just be a bug going round."

"Oh, and yeah, he recognised the name *Knox* but from a list of people who donated funds to keep the school open after it almost closed sixty or so years ago. They hold a place in their morning assemblies to thank all the donors by name for their generosity to the children of the area."

I'd had to bite back a seriously sarcastic snort of laughter when Mr Robinson innocently divulged that nugget of information. So not only had Knox set the school up as one of his feeding grounds, to steal life energy from young children to use in the most diabolical of ways, but he'd managed to get onto his victims' thank you list and his name praised each day.

I had to hand it to him, the guy knew how to play the mortals like an absolute pro.

Jessica steepled her fingers, closing her eyes for a moment before looking back across at the pair of us.

"Ah'm of a mind tae agree with yer assumptions. That this is linked tae Knox and his need fer the life energy of mortals." She shook head. "Ah am at a loss, though, tae understand what he needed the Red Cap fer, since the device was well hidden and most likely working as he intended."

Elspeth pushed herself up from where she was curled in the chair, tapping the desk with one hand to get our attention.

"I think I can answer that one." She told us, voice quieter than normal, without its usual edge of *I know more than you do*. Not that she was arrogant or anything like that, just the plain fact there were some subjects she was an expert on. Hence us paying her for her skills and services. "I very much doubt Knox guessed how events would unfold at Russell Square, when he loosed the Harrowing on Morgan and I. We destroyed his hideaway, and a substantial portion of the life energy he had stored there."

She tapped on the electronic keypad in front of her, and the image on the room's big screen changed from an overview of all the information we had gathered about Robert Knox, to the detail Cormac had shared with me. The six key London locations OPS had identified as linked to the man, with strange devices found at several of these already.

A red cross had been marked against the Russell Square location, with the history *Destroyed. Threat neutralised?* Which made me feel a little better, having almost burned down a very expensive area of mortal real estate in my efforts to save Ellie and I from the Harrowing. I hadn't particularly cared about the damage I'd done, but I was painfully aware how Jessica felt about any of her pack leaving gaping holes in London proper.

"The fact is, from the information given to Morgan on top of what we've uncovered, it's clear Robert Knox aims to attempt a ritual. A bonding between the body he's been building from his harvesting of mortal women, and Morgana's spirit." Elspeth detailed. "This is an *incredibly* difficult ritual from the little I've been able to research and what I've read in the notebook I took from his Russell Square residence. It requires precise incantations, and very specific elements relating to the spirit he is instilling in the crafted vessel. But most importantly, it needs a focal point, a location linked to both this world and the Real. Something symbolic to Morgana."

"That being the case," She continued. "If Knox has these six locations dotted around London, it's reasonable to assume that us disrupting one node severely impacts his plans. He obviously needs access to all the stores of life energy he has stolen, and his comments about *this needs to happen soon* must mean he can only bring what he thinks is his daughter's spirit over now, not delay and siphon more to replace what he lost. In such a case, using Red Cap to access contingent sources he had in place around London actually makes a lot of sense. No matter how much I hate the man, he's planned this event for many, many years and probably expected to run into trouble."

"Hnh." Jacob grinned a hard smile. "Don't matter much what he planned, *no one e*xpects something like Morgan here. He's a walking disaster at the best of times."

"Why thank you, buddy." I snarked a smile across at him. "Nice to see my efforts are appreciated."

"Whilst ah appreciate the humour, there is truth in Jacob's words." Jessica spoke up, moving the wall display on a slide. Here we'd listed off what we thought were Knox's objectives:

1. *Raise his daughter from the dead – not daughter, Morgana*
   1.1. *Use all the life energy stored to bring her to life*
2. *Keep them both safe from harm – how?*
   2.1. *Use Harrowing to cover escape? Harrowed unleashed in London*
3. *Avoid capture and disappear. Morgana's plan?*

We mulled over the depressingly savage list, given the outcome for the mortals, lycan and any Real residents in the vicinity if he went through with his plan.

"It's a stupid question, I know," I braced myself for the trolling I would normally get from Ellie, but the witch was lost in thought, expression grave as she stared at the large screen. Fine. "But what if we just go do what we did in Russell Square to all those other sites I've been told about? Wreck them as well. Wouldn't that just scupper any chance of what he's got planned ever happening?"

Jacob snorted whilst Jessica shook her head as if I'd said something particularly foolish. I looked over at Elspeth, loosing a sigh and giving my best *let me have it* look.

"It's not the *worst* idea you could have had," The witch acknowledged, making me feel just that little bit better. Then she continued. "But you're ignoring the fact we've just proven he probably has other stores of life energy stashed around London. If we go ahead and destroy the sites we *know* are his, most likely he will simple adjust his plans and use his reserves at locations we *don't* know about. And still target the same site for the ritual, which we still haven't identified."

"Uh, ruining any chance of OPS or us nabbing him if he slips up and shows up at any of those sites. Ok, I see the small issue." I admitted, knowing this was why Agent Cormac Smith had the locations under observation and hadn't already deployed his teams to search the places for more devices. "Leaving us what then?"

"*Officially*, we still have three convicts tae hunt. Black Shuck, Chimera and Red Cap, all still at large despite the packs' efforts tae contain them." Jessica nodded at the screen as she changed the display again. Someone had listed the escapees from the Ivory and Shadow prisons, and then crossed through those that either our pack or the other London lycan had dealt with. Or who had been dusted by a young mortal woman with unnatural powers from the Veil, I added to myself, seeing Baba Yaga's name marked off.

The hound, the goblin and the shapeshifter. None of them inherently dangerous, more just nuisances if left to their own devices. However, if they were under the control of Knox, who knew what sort of trouble they could and would cause.

Three … not quite.

"What about Jack?" I pointed out the elephant in the room, the last escapee that was untouched on the slide. "Are we just ignoring the fact he could still be out there somewhere, licking his wounds and plotting revenge? Or at least a rematch after last night?"

The words were out before I fully thought through their impact on our little group, and kicked myself hard when I realised the pain my flippant question might cause Ellie. But the witch just took a breath, jawline clenching as the only sign my words had hurt. She shook her head, managing a hard smile before she spoke.

"I was able to gather some of the Ripper's blood from where you fought him. Where … *Gregory* … ah, Goddess." She breathed slowly, pushing the pain aside with effort before continuing. "It was a simple enough task to use that to track him. Glean some knowledge of his whereabouts. What state he is in."

"And?" I didn't want to push her, but this *was* sort of important …

"He's a wounded beast, maddened from the poison of the cold iron sword used to pierce him through." She answered after a moment, voice cold. Hard like stone. "He is far from here, and in hiding, with little rational thought that I could sense. He was taught to fear last night, Morgan, taught how fragile his life is and how he almost lost it at the hands of creatures he thinks of as less than vermin. We'll need to deal with him eventually, but for now, he's not a problem we need to worry about."

A large part of me wanted to argue. To tell them all what a mistake it was to leave Jack the Ripper of all creatures loose and free to do harm. But neither Jessica nor Elspeth were ones to take unnecessary risks with our lives, nor those of the mortals in the Realm they called home. If they agreed he was out of the picture, at least for now, then the least I could do was trust them.

Didn't mean I wouldn't keep my eye out, in case the bastard tried to prove the witch wrong. A wounded animal could still be a threat to life … sometimes more so. So I'd keep a knife good and sharp, in case he came a'calling.

"What about Knox?" I moved the conversation on, facing my Alpha as this was her call to make. "Part of the deal with OPS was to let them handle him, whilst we cleared up the mess from the Real. We really going to play ball with them on that?"

Jessica met my gaze, smiling a small smile as she shook her head.

"The oaths we took were tae guard the mortals from harm, and I dinnae remember any fine print stating we are beholden tae anyone on what that means and who we hunt." She answered, earning nods from the rest of us round the table. We were too invested in finding this particular bastard to back down now, we'd lost too much to walk away without seeing it through to the end. "But we will need tae be discreet. Be seen tae let this mortal office take the lead and hunt him. Share what we know, whilst we go those places they cannae. Speak tae those they will not."

I got that sinking feeling in my stomach, guessing exactly who OPS might struggle to interact with, given their mortal status. And who I had tangled with too many times recently for my liking.

Jessica laughed, shaking her head

"Nae, Morgan, ah think you have burned enough bridges with the grimalkins and those of the Lows tae last one lifetime." She read my mind like I'd spoken out loud. "Jacob, ah'd like you tae take the lead on hunting the Lows fer any sightings of Knox. The Red Cap most likely returned there with the stolen equipment, so ah shall ask Rous and Molly fer permission tae hunt there once more. Meanwhile, you should organise a token response tae hunt these Real prisoners, and ah will speak tae the rest of the Alphas tae see if we might borrow some kin tae make it look like we are focused on that task alone."

Jacob nodded once as he was given his orders, granite brow furrowing as he turned his thoughts to planning the separate hunts well enough to fool any watchers.

"Elspeth has agreed tae continue her research of the articles taken from Knox." Jessica continued, nodding to our resident *all things spooky* consultant. "She has already gleaned details of the ritual he plans, and other matters that may help us narrow down the location he intends tae use. But that will be of little help if we cannot know *when* he seeks tae bring Morgana through the Veil, tae her new body. Knowingly or not."

I glanced at Elspeth, surprised that she was still so engaged in the hunt, given what had happened last night. But then, I guess, this was just her way of dealing with the loss of DI Allen. Not focusing on life without him just yet, instead putting all her energy into the ones ultimately responsible for his death. Put like that, it made perfect sense.

"And me? Where do you want me?" I had to admit, I was relieved I wasn't heading back to try to talk to the grimalkin, or to see whether Rous still lived and ruled the undercity of London proper. I hadn't been making many friends this side of the Veil recently, and I knew I was in for a tough time once all this madness was over, to rebuild any sort of network of contacts I might need to hunt normal prey.

"Ah think we need tae explore every possible lead, anything linked tae Knox and his *activities*. With Talen and Sal nae longer with us, I cannae enquire of their dealings with the man, nor tae give us any insights into his whereabouts." She told me, then shrugged. "However, with them gone, Knox will have had tae reach out tae those they dealt with directly. Tae replace what was destroyed in the Lows, tae complete his work."

She smiled that grim smile of hers.

"And ah can think of three such low-level miscreants who would have nae problem dealing with Knox, but are tricksome enough tae learn more than they should about him and his plans."

I sighed, seeing where this was going now.

"The brothers Bung. With Morgana on the loose, Knox planning Gods know what chaos, you want me to find three thoroughly disreputable trolls who aren't even loved by their own kin. The bastards who dumped a barrel full of half cooked seagulls onto me, after kidnapping mortal women to trade? Those little shits, right?"

My Alpha nodded.

"In their line of work, ah am sure they will have learned more than Knox might want of his business, if only tae have something tae bargain with if they are caught." She told me, pointing out the obvious fact. "Criminals are all alike, and predictable in many ways. Tis just a matter of knowing how hard tae squeeze them fer what they know."

I rolled my eyes even as Jacob grunted a laugh and a quiet *kitten finder* at me getting the least dangerous of the assignments.

Problem was, I'd already put out feelers to find those three arseholes, after my run in with them. But either they'd caught wind of what had happened to the Nighters, or I'd scared them enough that one morning that they'd literally dug a hole and vanished. Whichever, they had done a pretty good disappearing act, and I had come up empty and frustrated from my efforts in tracking the sods.

But I did have one last card to play, one lead I was fairly sure would work. I was however *also* pretty sure Jessica would not approve.

"Fine, but then I gotta ask a favour." I shrugged as my Alpha eyed me coolly, seeing how it wasn't standard for any of her pack to negotiate a task given by her. "The three sods have gone to ground, and my usual contacts haven't been much use in locating them. But there is *someone* who might know where they'd hide. He always had his hairy ear to the ground and knew where to look for anything I asked for."

"Ah don't see the problem in asking this contact of yours tae assist, then?" She prompted and I spread my hands. "Ah don't expect you or any of the pack tae have tae ask permission for such decisions, you know this, Morgan."

"Uh, the problem is, he's locked up. We handed him over to the Furies for his part in the whole Mistress shitshow at the Natural History Museum. Terrigyle Munstrum." I reminded her. "He was the one who got the old sea mine working again for her, and was ready to blow up the place just for the fun of seeing it go off."

"And you think this gnome weapons merchant would know where tae find these trolls?" She queried with more than a dollop of doubt in her voice. But I nodded, knowing it was a pretty safe bet. "That seems tae be a bit of a reach, even fer you?"

"Teri's plugged into the troll community, and if anyone's doing anything dodgy or skirting the rules, he'd know about it. I don't think he'd be involved in trafficking mortals but he'd certainly know where I should look to dig out the little shits."

My Alpha kept my gaze for a long moment, obviously thinking through her choices. Finally she gave me a nod.

"Ah will approach the Furies after this meeting and ask fer this gnome tae be released into our custody tonight fer this one reason, and this one reason alone. He is still an Accord breaker, who put mortal lives at risk. This is *not* a reprieve of his sentence."

"Any chance I can wangle a reduction on his eternal suffering for good behaviour then? I kinda need to offer him something so he'll talk to me?" The fact that the gnome had played me, been working with the Mistress and almost blown me, the pack and Sarah to kingdom-come with his insane desire to see an explosive device *be all it could be* only partially coloured the fact that he'd been a great source of information for me before, and had come through when I needed him.

If he'd learned his lesson from whatever torments the Furies had put him through already, I reckoned having him back on the street was more beneficial to me than him spending an eternity roasting over an open fire.

That is, if he'd get passed the small issue of me turning him into a troll-popsicle after he attacked me.

"Ah will put it tae the Furies, and see if they will consider yer suggestion." Jessica shrugged and added with a shake of her head. "Dinnae hope too much fer leniency, Morgan. The gnome *did* try tae blow you up, as well as a large number of mortals. The matter is clear cut."

"*A momentary lapse of judgement brought on by events beyond his control.*" I quipped, a line used oh so many times in mortal courtroom dramas to make excuses for why the accused had gone postal and done something incredibly stupid. It was used so much, I was surprised someone hadn't named a law after it or something. "And, besides, I still reckon the Mistress somehow is to blame for his involvement and actions. Teri might sell weapons of mass destruction, but the *last* thing he ever would do is risk his hide so stupidly."

With that agreed, I sat back, thoughts turning to the task ahead. Troll hunting … I could *almost* pretend things were back to normal for a moment.

Just your average run of the mill job for a lycan and his hound this side of the Veil, even if the little smelly bastards were rank as hell, probably tasted of sea gull, and I needed to keep at least one of them in reasonable shape to learn what they knew of Knox.

Still, Bear was going to do backflips at the chance to go hunting his favourite chew toys.

Chapter 6

Lancelot.

Also known as Launcelot, Lanzelet and Lanslod Lak. A knight sworn to Artur's cause, usually depicted as the greatest knight of the Round Table and touched by God. This character is known to have been able to heal wounds through prayer, even restoring life on one occasion.

Other than the infamous affair with Guinevere, Lancelot is renowned for having bested dragons and giants whilst serving Artur. The knight fought the Saxons and forced their witch-princess Camille to surrender when no other could face her.

Less well known are tales of his fits of madness and a darker, more violent side that the knight unleashes whilst incognito as either the Black or Red Knight. Despite this, Lancelot is recorded as having sworn that 'for all the knights in the world he was the one most unwilling to hurt any lady or maiden'.

"Morgan, can I have a word? Please?"

We'd wrapped up the meeting shortly after Jessica handed out our assignments. Not much more to be said, work to be done and all that stuff. Jacob had waited for her to leave first before hustling out to go organise his teams with Emma. With two packmates down, it left holes they'd need to fill soon enough … but for now, they'd make do with the lycans they had to hand. Or paw.

I wanted to hang on, as this was the first chance, I'd had to check on Ellie and see how she was coping. Give her a chance to rail at me for letting Gregory come along, get in the way of Jack if that was what she needed. Or whatever. But she had slipped out of the room almost on the heels of Jacob, so I guessed she hadn't been ready to talk.

But I'd only just stepped out of the meeting room when I sensed her nearby, that *rawness* of her pain so present and real, overlaying her usual scent.

Elspeth was standing by the nearest large display of office plants, one of many that Jessica had included when fitting out *Good Deeds* to make the place less gloomy and grim, more natural. Large green leaves flopped in all directions, with thick stalks carrying white tubes towards the ceiling and scenting the air with faint notes of lemon and lime.

And hey, I may not be able to tell you what a particular plant's name is but I have never professed to having a green finger, thumb or any digit you care to mention. Plants are generally smaller than trees, trees are things Bear pees against, and weeds are anything that grows where it shouldn't. That's about the distinction I make. Live with it.

As I turned at her voice, she stepped closer to me, her pose a little hunched, turned inward as if the pain she was carrying was weighing down on her. Which it probably was. All I wanted to do was enfold her in a massive hug, tell her things would be ok somehow. Lie through my back teeth if need be. But I wasn't getting the feeling that was what she needed right then, so I hung back, giving her space.

The next moment, she was wrapped around me, red hair falling over my shoulder as she folded around me. A small sob escaped the mass of fiery braids and tresses, and I closed my eyes and laid my cheek against the top of her head. Holding her tight just for that moment.

Yeah, I know. Got that one *completely* wrong.

After a moment, Ellie gathered herself, stepping away and swiping at the tears that stained her face and, conversely, my shoulder. Drawing a breath, she gave me a smile of honest thanks.

"We haven't talked since … since last night." She began, and I bit back the urge to jump in, tell her she didn't need to say anything, to explain. Just too easy to say the wrong thing here, so instead I just nodded and let her speak. "Now's not the right time, but I … I want you to know, I don't blame you for what happened. It wasn't your fault he came along, and what Jack did. You *need* to know that."

I shrugged, shaking my head as I thought back to the conversation we'd had, Gregory Allen and I. How I hadn't stopped to think, telling him Elspeth was in danger, and where she'd be. No matter what she said, there *was* a responsibility I would carry, just coz. But I wasn't going to argue with her about it, standing in the office. Things were all too raw and real right now.

"Anyhow, that's not why … Look, can you please come round mine tomorrow night? I need help with something. Not the case, but it's important." Elspeth asked, refusing to meet my gaze, the sense of her pain and loss still wrapped around her like a second skin. "Just you. No one else."

I didn't even bother asking for details, knowing I owed my friend too much already not to help wherever I could.

"Sure. I'll have this stuff with the trolls wrapped up, then I can bring round pizza and wine, if that's ok?" I gave her as normal smile as possible. "I'll even make sure one's a Garden Party that you like, just this once. With double pineapple, though it's a crime against pizzas."

She smiled wanly back at me, then nodded towards the rest of the office.

"Can we keep this between us? It's just, I don't want anyone else involved. If you're ok with that?" She queried, and I shrugged. It was sounding like whatever the favour was, it wasn't a simple case of helping move a sofa for the witch, and most likely somehow wrapped up with Gregory Allen's death. But if she needed me to keep quiet right now, I trusted her enough to reckon that was an easy ask.

Besides, this was sensible, stable Elspeth. What sort of *real* trouble could she be in?

"Thank you, Morgan." She leaned in close and gave my arm a quick squeeze, then turned on her heel and headed off towards the front door. She had her research to focus on, whilst I had some smelly trolls to find. With or without my old mate's help.

Jessica's promise to talk to the Furies in no way meant they'd agree to my request, just that she'd ask and hopefully use those legendary powers of persuasion of hers to get me my contact back. The Furies, well, they were absolutes in a world made up of margins, black and white against everything grey. It's what made them perfect for their role as ultimate arbitrators and enforcers of the Accords, but about as easy to deal with as juggling chainsaws. Whilst blindfolded and drunk.

And about as painful when it went wrong.

Probably past time I explained a little bit about these particular immortals.

To my knowledge, there were three Furies who oversaw the punishment of Accord breaches, with a side-line in handing out vengeance on oath breakers and particularly obscure crimes committed by Real denizens. Alecto, Megaera and Tisiphone. *Endless Anger, Jealous Rage and Vengeful Destruction* in the old tongue.

And they perfectly suited their titles, I can assure you.

The binding oaths sworn by the lycan packs to work for and report to these immortal hellions had been made centuries ago, back when the ink of the Accords was still drying and no signatory trusted the others enough to police them effectively without a neutral element involved. So far back I don't think any of the Alphas from that time were still vertical to explain how we drew the short straw. Attrition and wear and tear, or just plain stupidity if you look at what happened to Talen and Sal of the Nighters.

My personal suspicion was the Accord signatories had gotten the Alphas drunk and just fobbed them off with the duty, probably as a *temporary situation to be better managed as and when better resources could be identified*. Some sort of bullshit like that.

Only Alphas met with the Furies, as part of the contract. We, the pack mutts, might chase down and secure whichever Accord breaker we were after, but the protocol was always to offload the unlucky prey to our pack leader, step away and go run for cover before whichever Furie arrived to take charge of the culprit.

Oh, and mortals never, ever got to deal with them. Whether the rulers of the Realm, their governmental offices like OPS or even whomever had been the signatory of the Accords. The Furies despised mortals, from a history of dealing with them that you can read all about in Greek mythology, and were not shy about making their feelings clear about them. Which was funny, given their role in keeping the Realms safe, the creatures they hated free from harm. Just goes to show, you can be immortal and *still* have completely illogical prejudices.

I'd once asked Jessica to describe the Furies, just so I had a point of reference when explaining why I avoided them. Her answer had been typically Jessica-esque.

"You wish tae know about Furies?" She'd replied, stopping for a moment to think before nodding. "Well then. Imagine if yer will. You have nae fed your trollhound fer a whole day, ignored him and made him feel unwanted. Unloved. Then you finally prepare his most favourite of treats, the juiciest of steaks and sausages, so that his mouth waters and his tail wags uncontrollably. But then, just as he goes tae take a bite, you snatch the food away and throw it in the bin. The look on his face, the pain, the betrayal? That is nae a Furie. Now imagine the same, but instead of Bear, you had done so tae the smallest, the cutest of cats. Just before it claws your arm off and scratches yer face tae utter ruin? That look of utter, crazed and demented rage in its eyes ... there you have a Furie at her most calm. Better you nae ever have need tae meet one."

I'd done some of my own research, but mortal artists had a wide and varied view of what the three looked like. From simple women bearing angry expressions to winged demons of utter destruction, with talons and sharp teeth used to tear their prey apart.

Having met some pretty horrific and terrifying creatures Real-side, I was betting that no matter how bad I thought they were, in real life they would be much, much worse.

One thing was for sure. Those we handed over to Alecto, Meg or Tisi were bound for truly horrible torment. The Gardens of Ice and the Burning Halls of the Courts were bad, but in comparison to what the Furies did to Accord breakers, they were a slap on the wrist and a kick up the backside before the offender was sent merrily on their way. Stories told of those the Furies judged being staked out over hot coals, their insides slowly drawn out through precise cuts and cooked as they watched. Of prisoners having their bones ripped one by one from their living bodies, inch by inch, dragged out through their flesh only to be inserted back in with the same careful torture. And then there were the tricks they played with their charges' fears and terrors. The Furies were able to sense just what would break a creature put in their care, how far they could take them to the brink of oblivion ... to then draw them back and start back all over again.

Mortal inquisitors and witch finders of olden day would have worshipped the Furies for the sheer level of cruelty and nastiness they employed on their prisoners. Except for the fact, them being mortal, the Furies would have probably ripped the skin from their bodies for their audacity.

Another fact about the Furies was that, much like mortal police authorities, they were bound to *only* have remit over those that had committed their acts already. Despite being creatures of mass destruction and with the sort of power to make the Lord of the Ivory Court shake in his shiny boots, the sisters had no power to enter the Realms and stop bad things *before they happened*. Punishers of the guilty, they were bound by the very laws they protected to only get involved after the bodies had fallen, the blood was spilt.

Someone really messed up the fine print there, but it made sense why they employed us lycan to try to stop breaches in the Accords in the first place. Otherwise I reckoned the landscape of the Mortal Realm would look a lot different these days. Smoking craters, wailing mortals and body parts littered here and there.

It was safe to say I had *no* wish to mix with the Furies, happy instead to let Jessica handle them. Instead, I figured there was no harm hedging my bets in case they denied my request to hand over Terrigyle. I didn't have another gnome on tap with the sort of connections he had. But what I did have was another chance of tracking the three smelly little kidnappers, one I hadn't tried to date only because I hadn't felt it necessary to poke that particular bear. Or cat. But now? I had my pokey stick out and reckoned it was past time to use it.

With what I was thinking, I didn't fancy making the attempt in the office. First off, I wasn't *entirely* sure I wouldn't trigger the alarms set up by Elspeth even though *technically* I wasn't breaching the Veil. The creature I sought had to be hanging round the Mortal Realm still, given the free pass it had won from me when I was desperate. Secondly, as a thing of the Wyld, I'd have more chance attracting its attention if I called for it in its natural surroundings.

So, off to the park it was.

I may have mentioned it before but *Good Deeds* sits opposite one of London's largest and most glorious offerings of outdoor and natural expanse. Hyde Park is one of eight Royal parks scattered around the capital city and covers an incredible three hundred and fifty acres of grassland, trees, cultivated parks and gardens. It's split by the Serpentine and Long Waters lakes, and has been a place for mortals to visit and relax since the early sixteen hundreds. Before that, good old King Henry *I can't make my mind up who I want to be my wife* the Eighth used it as a hunting ground, having requisitioned it from Westminster Abbey … as Kings are wont to do.

I'd read this all in the leaflet from the park office, one day out of sheer boredom.

Three things made Hyde Park perfect for what I wanted.

Firstly, the size of it meant that even on its busiest day, with a summer's sun beating down and mortals out in their hundreds to fill the place with noise, smells and emotional baggage, I could find my own little patch away from prying eyes and nosy people who might stumble into my ritual and end up running away with their childish version of *Alice In Wonderland* forever spoilt. If they were lucky, and got to walk away at all.

Secondly, despite the fact mortals had ringed it with concrete and overlain it with pathways and ornamental structures to make it somehow *prettier*, Nature was unbroken and unfettered within its boundaries. I could always *feel* the difference as soon as I stepped off the path and into the park proper, like being able to suddenly draw a breath after holding it for too long. Here, the Wyld still had a connection to the Mortal Realm, and that made ringing one of its courtier's bell all the easier.

And finally, that little fact about how King Henry the Eighth had used the grounds for hunting made this place perfect for tracking down *this* particular Wyld. The thrill of the chase was in its blood, its reason for existing. All it thought about.

I'd snaffled a couple of choice items from the office kitchens before I left, as well as a rug and my kitbag of handy tools that these days I took everywhere, for every occasion. Fact was, I wasn't sure how the Bayun Cat would react to me summoning it, and what mood it might turn up in. So me taking a few precautions to keep my hide intact only made sense.

Look at me, adulting!

Placing the lumps of prime steak, bloody and fresh, on a clean plate, I settled onto the rug I had laid out like I was having a gentile picnic. Just in case anyone stumbled off the beaten track, managed to get through the clump of trees and bushes and then made it down the sides of the small dell I'd chosen to use for my summons without me noticing.

Likely? No. But with mortals, you just never know.

"Bayun Cat, by oath given, by Herne the father and by the blood I call as his son, I call on you." I called out, tapping my connection to the Wyld and drawing energy from it to strengthen the summons. The times before, I'd had to repeat myself three times to get the fae's attention *and* get it to obey, but that had been down to both my inexperience with this sort of thing as well as the sod's bloody mindedness and stubborn desire to piss me off.

This time, I felt its attention catch the first time, and got a sense of its mood through the connection. Mild vexation, the sort you feel when you are doing something and your phone rings, but with a spark of actual interest. Less of the screaming fury and arrogance I'd expected from this fae, which came as a mild surprise.

The air above the plate of steak shimmered like oil on water, and the meat suddenly flicked up like a fish on a hook. Blood pattered down as chunks of it disappeared in quick bites until everything was devoured. Only then, with the meal done, did the Bayun Cat slowly fade into sight. As ever, it started with that massive gaping maw filled with sharks' teeth and those glowing amber eyes, lit like a predator gazing upon its prey. The body slowly filled out, its crest and spiky fur rippling with many hues and that barbed tail calmly lashing the air as the Wyld fae lazed about three feet off the ground.

"Well met, Morgan Black." The fae greeted me with a sardonic twist of its lips. "What madness are you engaged in now, and who do you wish for me to devour?"

Chapter 7

"Hey 'Cat." I nodded back at the Wyld fae, noting its good mood and not believing it for one second. The creature seemed almost happy to see me. So instantly I distrusted what it was selling. "Been up to much?"

"Oh, a bit of this, a bit of that." It replied with that quirky smile, slowly extending one talon from its paw and wiggling the sharp point between two teeth to free some shred of meat. "A year and a day you gave me, with no boundaries or chains to bind me. I vowed to make the most of your lapse of judgement, and so I have been doing."

I grunted, accepting it's point. The Morrigan had gleefully explained my mistake when I rushed a bargain with the fae, to get it to hunt and find Sarah. The fact that it had done so, and probably saved her life from even more pain and suffering at the hands of Talen Orben after I renegaded on our deal helped balance things in my head.

Still, I *had* kept a check for sighting of the Bayun Cat, any hints it had been causing the sort of trouble to draw attention to itself. That was the last thing I needed, having Agent Cormac Smith and his OPS on my case for actually breaching Accord rules. I had the sense to realise if the deal I'd made with the fae came to light, and bodies turned up as a direct result of my decision, then I wouldn't be walking out of any interrogation room nor waking up on a park bench, having been drugged for easy transportation. No, I'd find himself in a hole somewhere far from daylight, far from my life and friends. For real this time.

Still, no use worrying over silly little things I had little or no control over.

The fae eyed me, rolling slowly in the air like it was in zero gravity and playing the fool, before giving an exasperated sigh.

"As much as I do enjoy seeing the concern writ on those lumpish features of yours," It drawled, tail twitching. "You can rest easy this one time. Though the temptation to leave a trail of wretches leading back to your door did indeed cross my mind, I have decided to use my time in this Realm *wisely*. So if there are any bodies, I have made sure none shall ever find them."

"That's, uh, reassuring." I lied.

"Tsk, I taste the doubt in your words like the bitterness of spoiled meat." The Bayun Cat hissed, amber eyes narrowing. "Do not make me change my decision, as a lesson for you to take me at my word and not mock your betters. You will not like where that will lead."

"Ok, ok!" I held up my hands, knowing if I pushed too hard, the fae could easily make my life way more complicated. "It's just … look, you're a hunter. You hunt, and mortals are prey. You're in their Realm which to you is like an all-you-can-eat buffet that's just slapped an *everything for free* sign up. But instead you've decided to do … what exactly?"

The fae growled a decidedly un-feline noise, shaking its great head.

"You would not understand. And I shall suffer no mockery. Now, let us talk instead on why you have summoned me here? So I can disappoint you and be on my way."

The Bayun Cat was hiding something. Despite the fae generally being as slippery as oiled eels and twice as tricky with their glamour and craftings, even a lump like me could tell this one was hedging, trying to change the subject. And yet, I got the strange but distinct impression it also wanted to tell me.

The sensible route would be to give up, let it be and get on with bargaining for its aid in tracking the Brothers Smelly. But then again, I'd done my adulting for the day. Too much, and it might start rubbing off on me.

"C'mon. I won't mock. promise." I smiled and held out my hands in the universal gesture of *trust me, you want to buy this car from an honest guy*. "I can only imagine how tough it was, deciding not to take advantage of my stupidity. And I *really* appreciate it. So what is it then?"

The Bayun Cat yawned, showing those jagged arrays of teeth filling it's too-large mouth. It rolled in the air, turning a full circle then looping into a figure of eight as I waited patiently, letting the silence fill the space between us. Outside the dell, the sounds of mortals going about their chaotic and noisy lives filled the air, along with the muted roar of traffic and the very rare sound of bird song chirping as a counterpart to bellowing shouts and high-pitched screams.

Finally, it spun to face me, yowling a heavy sigh.

"Oh, if you must know?" It rolled its amber eyes, and I nodded encouragingly.

"Mortals fill me with little joy these days, hunting them is just so *easy*." It complained, shaking itself as its fur spiked. "They are noisy, self-absorbed things. Too focused on themselves and the prisons they make for themselves to ever truly challenge me. I find little or no pleasure even thinking of them as prey anymore."

"But, oh! The things these moronic, noisome creatures can do with a little water and a dab of coloured paste. With cold marble and heated copper. The *vision* they craft from utter nothing, with their spindly, weak hands. *That* is a true marvel, and what I find myself drawn to." The Bayun Cat let its eyes close with pleasure as it slowly spun in the air, images filling its predatory mind. "They lock up these treasures in dark places, behind ropes and glass and metal, hiding them away and seeking to keep these wonders to themselves. So I hunt these things, these magnificent, glorious creations. No matter the darkest hole they choose, no matter the most secure fortress they build. I go where I will, and take what I want. Leaving them a suitable replacement for their greed and folly."

"Huh." That was all the response I could come up with right there and then.

I ran everything the fae had said through my brain a second time, just to make sure I wasn't mistaken. Had I really just heard the Bayun Cat admit to being …

An art enthusiast?

Surely not.

"Uh, I just need to ask … and please note the complete lack of sniggers or sarky comments," I caveated heavily, seeing the fae's eyes ignite with fury as its neck spikes flared up in warning. "Instead of doing what the

Wyld Hunt is legendary for. Hunting down mortals who've committed any sort of transgression – be it a mortal law broken or a slight against those of the Real – instead of that, you've been breaking into their private vaults and collections, and stealing their art? That's what you've been doing with your time here?"

The Bayun Cat swished its tail viciously to show its dislike of being questioned, but thankfully it didn't seem to find any fault with my line of enquiry, no mockery for it to take offence at and thus have the right to savage me. Instead, it cocked its head then nodded, once.

"*Stealing* would mean I believed what these mortals had locked away was theirs and theirs alone." It countered with a shark's smile. "But the beauty of what they hoard is not for them, and them alone. I desire it, and so I take it. And leave them a pile of steaming excrement to show my vexation that I had to expend effort doing so."

"Oh, so you don't *just* nick their prized possessions, you also shit in their collection. Nice touch." I snarked, shaking my head. "What do you do with this beautiful art once you've freed it from the naughty mortals. You have a showroom set up someplace where others can come and enjoy it too?"

Now, I'd only known this particular fae for a short while, and in that time, I'd mostly either been in the middle of bloody combat or bouncing between the Realms on a hunt. But in that time I'd gotten used to its imperious nature, its dripping sarcasm and smugness. All fitting for a master predator, a killer that had stalked the mortals since the dark times and was a thing feared across the continents of Man.

One thing I had *not* come across, which I faced now was …

Embarrassment.

"I eat them."

"I'm sorry, I missed that mumble. Could you try that again?" I queried even as the jagged fur outlining the Bayun Cat's face took on a decidedly rosy shade. "It almost sounded like you said …"

"I eat them!" It snarled then shook itself as if plagued by something intolerably irritating. "I just can't help myself! The paintings, the sculptures

… they crunch like bone, but explode in my mind like … like flowers! Every bite is different, every taste something I have never had before, nor will again!"

"I. Can't. Help. Myself!"

It panted, lowering itself to the ground and curling around itself so that I faced a rosy-hued bundle of spiky fur, with stubby ears and amber glowing eyes peeking at me from behind its own arched back. If I'd tried to twist that way, I'd have dislocated most of the joints in my body. Bloody flexible felines.

"Ok, ok." I could see the fae actually *trembling*, the strength of the emotion running through it as it voiced it's weird-as-hell addiction. An eater of all things beautiful, I would never have pegged it. "Look, I'm not judging you. If you get the munchies seeing an old Van Gogh or marble bust of David, it's not my business …"

"I blame you." The fae snarked at me, grumbling. "If you hadn't been foolish enough to grant me my freedom here, to let me loose without the chains to bind me, I would *never* have discovered this need inside me. Fah, I should have expected nothing less from a son of my Lord. You are all the same. Trouble."

I wanted to argue, but the plain fact was, the only other son of Herne I had met was Jack the Ripper, and he was about as Trouble as Trouble could be, with a capital Troub. Right now, the best thing I could do was take the Wyld fae's mind off its own problems, with a nice simple job tracking some smelly trolls.

"Look, I have a favour to ask. Something you can focus on, to help you forget about your thing." I told it, seeing its ears twitch in response. "A hunt."

"The last two *hunts* you have asked of me, have been for mortals." It hissed spitefully, reminding me of the failed attempt to track Knox and the more positive tracking of Sarah when she was kidnapped. Little good it had done her. Or me. "I have made it clear my feelings on wasting my energies on them. You have a nose, learn to use it."

"It's not mortals I want hunting this time." I replied, biting back any number of sarcastic quips that sprang to my lips. That wouldn't get me what I wanted here, just a headache if I was very, very lucky. "Three trolls. Brothers, they go by the family name Bung. Outcasts from every tribe this side of the Veil, and probably every other one Real side. I need them found, so I can question them."

The Bayun Cat slowly unwound itself from the huddle it had formed, stretching lazily as it stalked back into the air then settled down, facing me. It yawned then shook its head.

"I see no challenge in this for me, and I know of nothing you can bargain for this to be worth my time. No. Take your hound and hunt them yourselves." It told me bluntly. "In point of fact, I am considering returning through the Veil and never setting paw in the Mortal Realm again. It has become … *tainted*. Not a place I care to be."

I growled out an exasperated curse, wanting to grab hold of the fae and shake it, but knowing that would just end up with me minus several fingers.

"Then why the *fuck* did you answer my summons, if you were thinking of simply running off Real side like a frightened bunny?!" I growled in reply, feeling the tattoos on my hands thrum with latent might, all too ready for me to summon and use. Far too easily for my peace of mind these days. "You fought me tooth and bloody claw last time I called on you, but now, you practically jumped into my arms for a belly rub. What gives?"

"Fah, if you try to get anywhere within touching distance of my belly, I shall make you rue the day you were born." The fae replied with a savage grin. Then it turned in the air, coiling around itself like some furry serpent. "But I shall answer your question."

"I came, for word had spread how you faced your half-brother, *Wicked Jack*, and survived to stand tall whilst he now flees in fear." The Bayun Cat drawled as it slowly arced through the air, forcing me to get to my feet and turn to follow it. "I wished to see for myself if these were lies, or if you had indeed bested him. And I see the truth, the changes in you. Where before I saw a shallow and lost pup, now I see … well, *potential*. You have found your roots, Morgan Black, and now you can grow. Lycan, Alpha, Knight Errant. Who knows where you may end?"

Alpha? I choked back a laugh, knowing despite my family heritage, I was far from being pack leader material, let alone as strong as Jessica and the rest of them. That was just ridiculous.

Wasn't it?

"I answered for one other reason, bringing words from your father. The Hunter. Our Lord." The Bayun Cat continued and I sharpened my attention back on it. But it fell silent, watching me with that hungry smile as the seconds ticked by. Eventually, I gave in.

"What. Words?" I asked, biting down on that urge again to shake the bloody fae out of sheer frustration.

"The words I bring, Morgan Black, are …"

At that moment my senses lit like fireworks, as a scent rolled into the small clearing. The strong musk of an Alpha lion, the sly whisper of a wolf tracking its prey. The deep drumbeat of a pounding heart, strong and overpowering. I'd felt this before, and felt my body burn with Wyld energy as it responded to the presence I felt join us.

"*Turn. Around.*" The Bayun Cat hissed, amber eyes blazing with joyous light, flaming in their sockets.

Drawing a steadying breath, I slowly turned to face the newcomer, its power so strong that it felt like the sun beating on my skin. Be calm, I told myself, as my fists clenched instinctively. At my feet, I nudged the grab bag I'd brought with me, making sure it was within easy reach as I settled on my soles and faced him.

Herne the Hunter.

Lord of the Wyld Court.

My father.

Chapter 8

Uther Pendragon.

Sometimes known as Uthyr Pendragon, Uthyr Bendragon or simply King Uther. This 'father' of Artur is famous mostly for his seduction of his enemy's wife, the Lady Igraine, by means of a spell cast by Merlin to make him look like her husband, Gorlois. This act was known to have produced Artur Pendragon, whilst Igraine and Gorlois remained the mother and father of Morgause, his half-sister.

Things did not improve by Artur siring Mordred with Morgause later on, which led to his ultimate downfall and death at the hand of his child.

"Greetings, son."

Herne's voice was thick and throaty, a rumble of a large predator. Savage tones ran off every word, and I half expected him to let loose a sudden roar, so animalistic was the sense I got from the Lord of the Wyld.

He stood, leaning on a carved spear of bleached oak, runes running along the wooden haft and circling the sharpened bone head. He was tall, though not as overpowering as I remembered him at the Beltane Tournament, and I assumed he must have adjusted his height as some sort of attempt to appear less threatening, less shit scary.

It made me feel all warm and gushy inside, him making the effort. Not.

He was clad in leathers and rough cloth, dyed the colours of the deepest forests mixing with the stains of deepest shadow so that he seemed to blend into his surroundings. A piece of the wilderness broken off and given form. He was bedecked with worked materials taken from his prey, horn and claw threaded and bound to him as trophies of the creatures he had conquered. Put me in mind of the *Predator* aliens from the movies, if they had been given an 18+ rating.

Herne still wore his hood, hiding his features except for those amber eyes which glowed from the shadows, but his horns curled up and glinted in the daylight like those of some elder stag. I noted small charms bound to the tines, and the dark stains which I could only assume was dried blood blackening their surface.

All in all, *not* the friendliest father figure I could imagine, wanting to come clap me on the shoulder and tell me everything was going to be all right. That he was proud of me, and give me a manly hug before offering to join me for a pint down the pub.

The weirdest fact, though, was that the noise of his words had not come from the depths of his hood, mouth hidden in shadow. No, they'd come from behind me.

I turned around, finding the Bayun Cat grinning at me with that sardonic smile. It slowly drifted through the air, circling me, until it rested beside its Lord.

Ok, not creepy *at all*. I looked at the pair, from Herald to Hunter, and accepted the simple fact this was not going to be a normal conversation.

"What are you doing here? Trying to breach the Accords for kicks?" I growled, even as I let my connection to the Wyld lend me strength. Just in case he tried that *bow to me* crap again, and I had to fend off his will.

"Cannot a father simply visit his son?" Herne's voice rumbled from the Bayun Cat's mouth, the feline's lips parting and framing the words. The Hunter's eyes flashed at my sharp tone but I just shook my head, holding up my hand and counting off fingers.

"One, you dumped me in the Verdance when I was a baby, coz you couldn't handle bringing me up without my mother. Two, you've known I've existed for too many bloody years and done fuck all about it. Three, when we do finally meet, you try to pull some macho-shit on me instead of letting me know who you are. You try and make me *kneel*." I counted off, almost snarling each point. I didn't care that I faced an immortal supremely more powerful than me, who could literally *force* me into my beast suit and make me serve him as a bloody hunting dog if he so willed. No, I was *pissed*. "So, no, you don't get to just turn up and give me the *hey son, been a long time. Fancy a catch up?* speech."

Beside him, the Bayun Cat hissed and lashed its spiked tail, its displeasure at my tone obvious. But I just focused on Herne, ignoring the lesser fae this one time. Of the pair, the Hunter was definitely the one I wanted to keep my eyes on.

For his part, Herne simply shook his head once, but it was enough to make his Herald and Knight subside down to the sort of muted grumble you know all cats give when they've been warned, and are pretending to quieten down and listen to you. Whilst they plan bloody vengeance … or to piss in your shoe.

"Word of your contest with Jack reached the Court. I wished to see how you fared." Herne replied via his Herald after quietening it, those inhuman eyes of his burning within the shadows of his hood. **"My other son was always troubled, but the monster he has become … that is a beast which cannot remain free. He must be hunted and bested once and for all."**

"Yeah, well, you're welcome to go kick his arse back to prison anytime. Tangling with him already cost someone I care about too much, so you'll excuse me if I don't volunteer a rematch." I quipped back, the memory of DI Allen sprawled on the floor, blood pooling around him and Elspeth cradling him in her arms all too raw. But then I rethought my specific words. "Just, you know, don't take that as me giving you leave to Hunt here. I've already fucked up allowing one of you lot over here without a leash."

Herne gave an all too human sigh but forbore to reply. Showing him to be the bigger man of the two of us, probably. Given he still topped eight feet in height, I wasn't too bothered.

"You've seen me. I'm still standing. Anything else to impart before you can bugger back off to the Real?" I knew I was sounding a little petulant, but for Gods' sake, I was still coming to terms with the fact he was my *father*, and someone who had abandoned me as a baby. Neither fact was sitting that well with me. "Coz otherwise I'd say we're done."

"I bring warning, son." He answered me, taking a step forward to halve the distance between us.

Up close, his scent was even more brazen and overpowering, but it wasn't just that ... the *sense* of him was like a hammer blow, the immortal's power wreathing his body like a storm cloud. I was getting used to being around the Morrigan, the ice-cold threat of her nature, and the blazing sun that was Oberon's presence. Titania was a gentler touch than her partner and Lord, but that just cloaked the sharpness of her power when she wielded it to wreak utter ruin. As for Madb ... the child Queen of Shadow, she simply scared me half to death every time I was around her.

Herne was different. His presence awakened that link inside me, my connection to the Wyld. No matter how much I might be pissed as hell towards him, I couldn't ignore the bond between us. In some ways weaker, in some ways stronger than the bond I had with my pack, with Jessica as my Alpha. But still all too real.

"Warnings. Oh joy, *just* what I need." I growled but knew with good sense I could ill-afford to ignore him. Stupid behaviour like that cost people around me, sometimes with their lives. "Ok. Lay it on me. What anvil is falling my way now?"

The Hunter settled his spear into the crook of one arm, and reached into a fold of his armour. Grasping something, he casually tossed the thing through the air between us. I caught it by reflex, looking down to find a small cloth and twine doll in my hand, Black hair, hopefully of string but it did look far too *lifelike*, hung from its head, and its face was simple in design. Two small crosses for eyes and a thin line for a mouth. The thing was old, the rags used to make it stained and torn, the whole thing looking like it had been washed down the sewers a few times.

"Uh, I'm a little old for dolls, let alone the fact I never really played with them as a kid." I looked up into those burning amber eyes, trying to figure out the meaning of the strange gift. "Are you telling me I gotta watch out for falling dollhouses or possessed kid's toys? I've seen Chuckie, you know."

Herne gave an exasperated grunt, shaking his head and pointing to the doll. The Bayun Cat grinned even more savagely as it spoke the next words.

"Morgana. Those are the rags she wore, the hair from her head. The blood from her body." Herne told me with grim certainty, as I forced myself not to throw the disgusting effigy across the dell in disgust. I mean, what the fuck?

"Where the hell did you get …?" I started to ask but then stopped.

Of course. How else would the Lord of the Wyld be able to lay his grubby mitts on such intimate substances taken from Morgana's old body. Except from his dear sweet mother. The Morrigan would have had no trouble returning to the Gardens of Ice and salvaging all the necessary stuff to craft this creepy doll, from the mess left after Madb had thrown her toys out of the pram and literally torn both Morgana and Mordred apart. Except of course, her sister had already done a runner, leaving the body behind and escaping as a pure spirit.

Mordred hadn't been so lucky. I still couldn't get my head round Morgana leaving him behind, at the mercy of Madb. Despite her words, saying she despised him for his weakness … she had been her *son*.

"Ok, so that's possibly the grossest thing I've ever received." I eyed the doll in my hand, trying hard not to remember the ice exploding through Morgana's body and shredding it And failing miserably. "And completely bloody useless by the way, if you were thinking I can use this to track her or ward against her somehow. She ripped herself free from her body ages ago, and the meat sack she left behind had no connection to her anymore. Even before Madb blew it all over the cell."

"**She is unlike anything you have faced.**" Herne told me solemnly. "**If you try to trick her, she will kill you. If you fight her, she will kill you. No matter your tricks with Shadow, with Ivory … she *will* kill you.**"

"**My warning is … look not for aid from the Courts. From me. We cannot fight this battle with you.**"

"Huh." I eyed my father in the eye, cricking my neck as I scowled up at him. "How's that again?"

"**Oberon will not enter this Realm to face her without invite. Madb will remain where she is strongest, and await her there. None of the Courts will risk breaching the Accords, acting in the Mortal Realm before their aid is sought.**" My father answered, shrugging his massive shoulders. "**None of the mortal rulers are foolish enough to request their aid, for they do not trust the Courts. Why should they? Doing so will only grant Ivory or Shadow power over them, the right to ask for whatever they wish. Asking for aid will put mortal lives at risk, as in times of old.**"

"And you? What about the Wyld Court?" I asked him, feeling cold anger temper my disgust. Realising the simple truth of his words. The Courts never did anything out of the goodness of their hearts, given how old and wrinkled the things probably were. No matter the fact they were to blame for why Morgana wanted vengeance, and was so hell-bent on destruction and bloody revenge.

"**I? The mortals still remember when I used to hunt them for sport. When *I* was the executioner for wrongdoers and villains.**" Herne shifted his spear, running one hand along its carven length. What I had taken for runes wrought into the wood, I now could see were figures. Large, small, animal … and man. Intricately carved, a tally of the countless prey Herne had hunted, had slain. "**No, they will not ask aid of me either. With good reason.**"

"But that's just fucking stupid!" I snarled, clenching my fist around the doll without thinking, feeling it squish in an unpleasant way under my fingers. "She's your bloody problem!"

"Stupid. Yes, that sounds about right." Herne nodded once, as the Bayun Cat sniggered beside him. "**Stupidity is the chewing gum which sticks the Mortal and Real Realms together. It is what was used to write and seal the Accords, when mortals and fae had fought to a bloody and exhausted stalemate. The Accords prevent the greed of Ivory, the avarice of Shadow … the hunger of the Wyld, to ever threaten the mortals. On the other hand, it means we are unable to take action here unless formally invited. Hence, stupid.**"

"And let me guess, by the time anyone agrees to bring in the heavy guns to tackle Morgana, the Mortal Realm will be a smoking ruin and just ripe for the Courts to jump in and set up shop. It's a win-win for the bastards." I surmised, seeing Herne nod once. "You know, you are *awfully* verbose compared to the last time I met you. Then it was more of a *one grunt for yes, two for no and three to splat you* kinda thing. What's changed?"

The Bayun Cat made a ghastly noise, that disgusting sound all felines are capable of just before they spit out a lump of fur and other gross stuff onto the pristine carpet. It shook its head, then replied in its own voice.

"Your father is an elemental, a force of Nature herself. Normally he does not need to use such vulgar ways to communicate." The Cat told me smugly. "However, as the message was of such importance to him, he felt the need to sink to your level. And so I speak for him."

"Yeah, and you *never* shut up." I snarked back at him, seeing the fae's eyes narrow as I scored my point. But Herne hit the ground with the end of his spear once, a thud that echoed round the dell and caused the ground to shake. The Bayun Cat gargled again horribly, and its voice switched once again.

"Enough. I did not bring you together to squabble like yapping pups." He verbally slapped us both down, as he pointed the spearpoint to the pointless doll in my hand. **"Take my warning. You cannot defeat Morgana, not with all your pack, your witch and all the tricks you've learned. You will not best her through combat or trickery. Her arrogance is her weakness, and you shall have your chance only when all seems lost. Till then, I advise caution."**

I was about to reply how much chance I had of being cautious, when the sound of rustling undergrowth caused all three of us to turn quickly.

"…Yeah, just here. No-one'll disturb us here, babe …"

A young man and a young woman staggered through the trees, coming to a stop as they locked eyes on the three of us. They were dressed for the summer, the guy in designer distressed jeans, in other words looking like a moth with a chainsaw had had a go at them, and a tight-fitting t shirt to show off his physique. What little there was of it. The girl was in a strappy blue dress, one aforementioned strap already slipped off her shoulder and hanging loose.

A thin, hand-rolled cigarette hung from the guy's lips, and from the smell of it wafting into the dell, I knew that the pair weren't burning simple tobacco.

The moment held for a long moment, before the guy, taking a long drag from the spliff and handing it across to his partner, spoke up.

"Uh, hey. Uh, is your cat, like, floating? And what breed is that? He's *huge*!"

The girl giggled as she took a deep breath, pulling in a lungful of burning weed.

"He's so *cute*. Is he friendly? Can I stroke the cute kitty's tummy?"

I was already moving, putting myself between my conversation partners and the two partially stoned mortals. I'd picked this place to be as far away from interruption as possible, but as I may have mentioned, mortals have this uncanny habit of stumbling into exactly the wrong place at the wrong time. And then acting as if they belonged there.

And whilst the Bayun Cat had admitted finding no joy in hunting mortals these days, there was literally no way the pair of them were walking away from witnessing a non-authorised intervention by Herne of all fae. And they'd called the Bayun Cat cute, let alone suggested fluffing it like some common house pet.

Those type of words ended in blood.

Herne seemed to be of like mind to me, as his Herald hissed and its eyes blazed with rage. Before it could spring at the pair, who seemed to have the survival instincts of suicidal lemmings as they stood laughing and giggling at us, the Lord of the Wyld levelled his spear at them. I had visions of him running either of them through, holding the spitted mortal up and letting their blood flow as their partner screamed with the reality of what was happening to them …

Ok, even I have to admit that was a thoroughly disturbing place for my mind to go.

"Don't!" I tried to warn both Herne and the mortals, hoping the idiots would make a run for it.

Something flashed through the air, sparking from the Hunter's spear to the man and woman. They managed a single, startled scream that was choked off ... as their bodies twisted and shrank, clothes falling to the grassy floor as they were suddenly emptied.

"You didn't have to bloody well kill them!" I snarled, wheeling back to glare at the Hunter. It was always the way with the fae, how they mishandled mortals so badly. No light touch, no sense of handling a situation with delicacy ... just overreacting and lashing out without stopping to think.

It's why so many amazingly detailed statues used to litter the landscape of the old Mortal Realm when the artists of the day still struggled to stack blocks atop each other. That and why so many ruins discovered by archaeologists or anyone with a spade appeared to have suffered some disastrous catastrophe when history somehow missed the pertinent details.

Herne snorted, and waggled his spear pointedly back at the pile of clothes.

Which were moving.

As I watched, the clothing was pushed aside and two very fluffy, pink nosed and long eared rabbits scrabbled to freedom. Sides heaving from the effort of escaping their cloth prisons, the pair of bunnies scrambled onto the grass ... then froze as they saw us.

The Bayun Cat gave one sharp, yowling cry, and the rabbits-that-were-mortals immediately sprang away, tearing back through the grass and brush, disappearing into the treeline. Then that familiar coughing rasp heralded a response from my father.

"I kill only when I must. When the hunt is to the death, or I am challenged. Not like your mortals, who take life on a whim, without thought." He mildly reproved me. **"Those two shall return to their natural form once the sun has set, but with no recollection of what they saw here. Consider it a more fitting gift, from father to son."**

"I'm guessing they'll also find themselves butt naked in the park, which won't do their credibility much good if they *do* try to tell anyone anything they remember." I nodded to the two small piles of clothes they'd left behind. "Nicely played, *dad*."

Hacking up another cough, the Bayun Cat hissed its own comment.

"That merciful side of yours is going get you killed," It told me with a smug grin. "You bested Jack, and that tale will keep the knives from your back a while, but you're going to have to start making the hard choices. Mortals, they aren't worth the pain they'll cause you. Especially when Morgana will see that weakness in you, and use it to bury you before you even blink."

I shrugged. I could spend days arguing with fae about whether mortals matter, and why it was wrong to consider them at best an annoying inconvenience, at worst a plague that needed to be cleansed. And I'd only get a headache for my efforts.

"We done then? No more warnings to impart, and no chance you can talk your Herald into finding the trolls I'm looking for?" I had to try, but Herne shook his head once as his Herald replied for him.

"Nice try, pup, but you ask for my aid, I've told you no. Your father cannot compel me to serve you, otherwise it negates the accord between us. And he'd owe me as well for trying to coerce me against my will." The Bayun Cat explained with languorous smugness. "This isn't the Ivory or Shadow Court. The Wyld plays by different rules."

Herne gave one final nod, before stepping back and fading. The sense of him dissipated on the air, until the space where he had stood lay empty, grass untouched beneath his feet. The Bayun followed suit, pulling its disappearing act so that finally, only its amber eyes and grinning mouth hung in the air before me.

"One last thing, pup." It told me with a mocking twist. "I offer my advice this once for free. Morgana is way out of your league. Don't stand in her way. Let her do what she wants and leave it to the Powers to handle her … when they see fit. Find a hole, jump in and pull the lid over you. It's what I intend to do."

With that, the Wyld fae vanished, leaving me alone with my frustration.

Oh well, scratch using the Cat to find the Brothers Bung. I'd exhausted most of my normal leads and had little faith in striking it lucky with those that remained.

It now all hinged on *if* the Furies would agree to my request. *If* they would return Terrigyle to me. And then *if* he'd agree to help me locate the smelly bastards, and *if* he knew where to find them.

Lots of *ifs*, and lots riding on a pretty thin hope. But it was the best I had for now. No use me standing around twiddling my thumbs, so I reckoned I might as well head back to the office to see if I could lend a hand with the hunt for the last three escaped prisoners. Something to take my mind off the clock ticking away in my head, until Knox wrought ruin and destruction to the Mortal Realm as he mistakenly sought to bring his dead daughter back to life.

That hole, the one the Bayun Cat suggested?

It was looking awfully tempting the more I thought about it.

Chapter 9

I've found it's a common misconception that trouble always comes in threes.

In my personal experience, trouble seems to come by the truckload, and only stops piling on me when I hunt down the driver and hit them till they fuck off. That might not be an eloquent or sophisticated way of handling my problems, but at least I knew it worked.

So when I stepped back into *Good Deeds*, grumbling still from my failed attempt to elicit aid from the Wyld fae, it came as less a surprise than it ought to, to have a particular scent fill my nose. One I unfortunately knew far too well, and that spelled trouble with a capital 'C'.

Or 'B' if I ignored Elspeth's prohibition of the word used to describe female canines.

I stomped up the stairs, nodding to Charles who was manning the desk. Before he even could get the words out, I shrugged and mouthed *I know* as I passed, There was no use trying to duck out, go chill out in the park under the hot sun until the unpleasant visitor went away as I knew she'd keep coming back until she got the pound of flesh she wanted.

Cerce was standing at one of the nearest desks, arms crossed and forehead furrowed with a deep frown as she tapped her foot impatiently. She was dressed in another Italian designer suit, cut to fit her figure, and her long flowing hair had been piled up and set in place with intricate pins. I hated to think the uses she put those foot long spikes to when she wasn't making her hair look like a voodoo doll for someone particularly obnoxious.

"There you are!" She exclaimed as I crested the stairs. Across from her, at the desk, Daniel rolled his eyes and dragged himself out of the seat. Obviously pleased to be rid of her, he shot me a wide grin and a thumbs up before heading off to go find coffee, food or someplace to wash the harsh ringing out of his ears. Cerce had a particularly … *strident* voice, let's just say.

"Oh for fucks' sake. Just what I need." I growled, making to push past her and follow Daniel in search for all things caffeinated. "If you want someone to yell at coz the mortals are still investigating your thoroughly dubious and morally corrupt activities, take it up with them. I ain't interested."

"We both know the *only* reason the Carteloni family had investigations opened on them by the mortals is because of *you* and your Alpha." She shot back, reaching out to grip my arm. "But that is not why I'm here. As hard as this is to say … I need your help."

Alarm bells immediately started clanging in my head. If Cerce, who had sworn terrible vengeance on me, had threatened my friends and generally made it clear she'd be happy using a spoon on me the way Alan Rickman had described in *Robin Hood: Prince of Thieves* … if she suddenly wanted my help, then it could be for no good reason.

"Look, as much as I would love to help you deal with whatever little problem you think you have, it's just not happening." I told her, trying not to feel a small stab of satisfaction as she scowled even harder and … I do not joke … stamped her foot in anger. "We've got a lot on, so if you could just, oh I don't know, come back next century, we might be able to lend a hand. But that's a big maybe."

"That is just not good enough!" She waved a finger under my nose, uncaring that I outweighed her by about three times, and could do very nasty things to that digit if she kept sticking it in my face. "Someone has *robbed* me, and I need you to find who it was. And get me my possessions back."

"You've been robbed? Who would be stupid enough to …?" I started to ask, then shook my head. I was getting involved, when I had far more serious things to worry about. "Forget it. Go speak to the police. They deal with robberies all the time. Just tell them what was stolen, and I'm sure the lowly mortals will be able to assist you. Or at least care more than I do."

Cerce scowled, but the anger faded a touch, replaced by what I sensed was hesitation. Not quite guilt but definitely uncertainty. It was immediately obvious that she didn't want the mortal authorities involved, and that unfortunately tweaked my curiosity. Damn it, I was too easy to reel in.

"They wouldn't understand. I need someone from *our* Realm, someone who will know the importance of what they took." She shook her head as I went to argue. "The mortals will not see this thing as anything important. They'll poke around where they shouldn't. Get distracted and not take the theft seriously. No, I need *you*, Morgan Black. You involved yourself in my business – now you get to pay the price."

I groaned, having a premonition I wasn't going to be able to shrug this one off.

"Do this for me, find what they took, and I will consider things as settled between us. You and your friends … Daniel Price and Soshana … ah *Felicity* will be officially persona inviolate. Untouchable by any of the family or associates. Off our books, never to be troubled again." She added, smiling that cold curve lacking all trace of warmth and humour. The one only creatures who had been alive for centuries could manage. "Isn't that what you want?"

"Uh, I thought you'd promised to leave them the fuck alone already?" I growled, but she just smiled even more coldly. "Uh huh, yeah, I thought so."

Dammit, she knew I couldn't turn my back on an actual promise, if it meant Danny and Felix were given guaranteed immunity from the mortal mob. The family he'd stolen their daughter from. I had to hope that the family and associates were aware what happened if they tried to cross someone like Cerce, and were scared enough of her to listen to any command she gave.

Then again, she had the current head of the family eating out of her hand, literally, after dosing him with one of her concoctions. Charles Carteloni, if I remembered it right, was more snake than man now, and definitely under her total control. If she said that helping her out would get Felix and Danny forever protected, who was I to piss that away just because being near her made my skin crawl?

"Fine. I'll need to run this by Jessica, and I wasn't kidding. Your timing is shit, we are *seriously* buried with stuff." I shrugged, grabbing up a pad and pen from the nearby desk and flipping to a free page. "But tell me what was stolen and from where, and I'll see what we can do. Best I can promise."

"The where is easy." Cerce replied, her smile curving like a knife, as I caught the smug self-satisfaction rolling off her. I'd given in, and once more proved she could get what she wanted when she wanted. "My private residence. You should be familiar with the location, given how much trouble you and your muscular packmate caused last time you were there. I have a suite on the top floor, and a safe where I keep certain keepsakes. That was opened without my knowledge, all my charms and security bypassed, and certain items taken from my private collection. Whomever broke in left no trace of themselves, I can assure you."

"Your private collection, huh?" I grimaced as a suspicion made me shiver. "*Please* don't tell me someone nicked your favourite sex toy? Or found your stash of pornography? I *really* don't need to be chasing around learning your centuries old fetishes."

"As I have alluded to before, you would be considered very lucky to ever be involved in that aspect of my personal life, after the time I have had to hone my skills and desires. However, I doubt I shall *ever* be that desperate. Besides, toys are for amateurs. All *I* need to reduce any man to a gibbering wreck are these … oh and maybe a little ice." She snarked as she wiggled her fingers and brushed her lips with them. "No, the items in my collection are tools I keep for rare experiments and certain items I have felt drawn to over the many long years. Plants that are … *not completely* legal to own this side of the Veil, but which are very useful in my work."

"If you are suggesting someone nicked more of that bloody sleeping poppy we found in your lab, we're going to have a problem." I growled, recalling the plant which Knox had been seeding wherever he worked. Used as a base for his crafting that stole the life energy from unsuspecting mortals. And Cerce had just happened to have the stuff under lock and key, when it *should* only be found in the Verdance, within the Real. "If you kept back samples, that means you lied to us."

"Don't be so naive." She shook her head, irritated at my suggestion. "I agreed to destroy all samples of that flora, and so I did. No, the thieves took my stock of *Betel nut*. A powerful substance that enhances whosoever ingests it. Whether physically or spiritually, bolstering any crafting they might be working on a hundredfold. Sometimes more."

Ding went that suspicious bell in my head. Who did I know that might need something to give him a magical boost, to help with a powerful ritual he was planning? Now let me think …

"The thing is, the nut will decay now that it has been removed from where I had it stored, as it requires very specific handling to keep it potent and the thieves were not delicate in their removal of my sample." She complained, oblivious to my suspicions. "At best, it will remain useful for five days, maybe less, before it crumbles to ash. And another nut from the *Betel* tree won't be ripe for harvesting for another hundred years."

I scored a line under that little fact, fighting to hide a sudden hard grin. Five days, maximum. Suddenly, we had a timeframe, something better than *soon* for when Knox was planning his madness. Of course, I was still assuming this was linked to him, but the coincidence was just too damn big for me to ignore. Like Godzilla rearing over the skyline of Tokyo.

"Ok, so you have some missing juju nut extract. They take anything else?" I queried, then looked up as silence answered me. Cerce cast a glance around the office, seeing if anyone was within listening distance … which given the place was full of lycan meant *no* conversation was ever truly private. But I wasn't going to remind her of that fact.

"Cough it up. What else got nicked." I prodded the witch, and she bit her lip before answering.

"There was one other item that was taken. Something I obtained *possibly* without the full authorisation and writ to have done so. But it is a piece of history and had been left to rot in a dungeon for decades. I simply discovered it's whereabouts and used my contacts to obtain it." She explained, her voice lowered several notches. I'd said that she had a strident tone, so it was a pleasant change when she hushed up, not having to fight the urge to wince at every word. "But it makes no sense. I *know* all those parties interested in the item, and none of them would dare steal it from me. And it is … in a way … worthless. Useless for anyone, unlike the *Betel nut*."

"Then there is no harm in telling me what you had stashed in your safe, is there?" I tried logic, not wanting to draw this out any longer than I needed to. "C'mon. You want me to find these things, so I need to know what I'm looking for."

"Fine." She took a breath, calming herself before leaning in.

"The only other item stolen from my vault was…the Stone."

I waited for a moment, for either a revelation to occur or the witch to add further detail, but she just settled back in her seat, eyes narrowed and fixed on me.

"The *stone*? As in … the Philosopher's Stone? Like from Harry Potter. Or the stone tablets used to record the words of God, according to quite a few deluded mortals?" I queried, tapping my pencil over the word. "What am I missing?"

"As ever, almost everything." She replied, then quickly snatched the pencil and pad from my hands. She sketched something quickly on the page, then placed them on the desk beside me. "That *stone*."

I looked at the drawing. It was fairly simple. A straight line sticking up from a rectangle, with another line drawn near the top of the vertical. A cross, but not a cross. What else looked like that? Then my brain fired up, memories of a few weeks back and sitting in Dukes Hotel with Jessica, as she made me read out a simple poem.

Not a cross. A sword.

And beneath the sword, a block. Or stone. As in the sword in the stone.

"You mean to tell me, you had the stone that *Excalibur* was stuck in, from that whole *'who so ever draws this sword from this stone shalt be King of England'* farse the Courts tried to pull with Artur Pendragon? That stone?!" I wanted to burst out laughing at the sheer randomness of it all, all landing in my lap. "That's what has been nicked?"

"Yes, I obtained the original stone pedestal into which the portal key was set, and which was then cast aside and considered lost when Artur and his entourage returned beyond the Veil." She admitted. "And now someone has stolen it from me. I want it back."

First I'd had to hunt for Excalibur, that most famous of swords, when it was nicked from the Ivory Court vaults and almost used in an attempt to wreak bloody revenge on Oberon and Titania by a vengeful once-Lady of the Lake. And now, someone had waltzed off with the chunk of masonry that had been a prop in their failed attempt to rule the mortals.

I knew without a doubt Jessica would want this investigated, in fact would brook no argument on the matter. I had no idea how it tied into Morgana's escape, and her plans to be reborn but it did. Somehow.

It's a fact I hate it when coincidences lined up like this, as all they ever led to was trouble and pain, leastways for me. But I could do nothing else than nod to the witch, rip the page off the pad, and go have a word with my Alpha as Cerce settled comfortably into a chair to await my return. Whilst I gave Jessica the good news, and added this latest tidbit of insanity to our complicated *'what the hell was going on'* slide deck.

What next? Maybe the Knights of the Round Table would pop by for a spot of tea and dragon bashing. Or Merlin might pop out of the woodwork, still alive, and start giving Disney a right bollocking for the comedic cartoon image they'd made him into.

The way things were headed, anything was possible.

Chapter 10

Morgan Le Fay.

Oft times also known as Morgause, Morgaine, and Morgana. A powerful sorceress who at times aids her half-brother and his Knights, at others is in direct conflict with them. Most especially after the birth of their shared child, Mordred. Morgan Le Fay is known to have had liaisons with Merlin as well, though tales speak more of her thirst for his magic than any other reason or desire.

What most stories agree upon is Morgan's jealous of Artur's rule and power, and her constant attempts to elevate herself to be his equal. She is known to have married King Lot and fathered other sons, including the Knights Gawain and Gareth, all who served her half-brother. She was known to be quick to anger, and willing to use her magical talents to punish any she thought had crossed her, or thwarted her plans. She set a sorcerous conjuration, the Green Knight, to test Artur knowing the warrior is unkillable, but it is her son, Gawain, who faces him down and proves the worthier of the two.

Tales do not tell how she dealt with her son's actions.

Well, at least I'd guessed right this time.

Jessica had listened patiently as I described the meeting with Cerce, the robbery and what the immortal witch had been keeping in her vaults. And the simple fact the enchantress saw this as a debt I owed her, and would settle everything between us if I took the case.

"I *did* explain we have a shitload on our plate right now, and sort of politely asked her to take this to the regular mortal police." I explained, earning a snort of laughter from my Alpha and a shake of her head. "Well, as politely as I could, given who we're talking about."

"Ah'm surprised I did nae hear her reply tae your *politeness*," Jessica replied with a smile, before drawing a breath, thinking. We were sat in the main boardroom, the slide deck still up on the big screen showing all we'd surmised about Morgana, Knox and their plans. "Ah am sorry, Morgan but I cannae argue that this is somehow linked tae those we hunt. An artefact of Arthurian legend, even one so simple and harmless, being stolen at this time makes me very suspicious."

"I was wondering." I admitted, hating the fact I'd been drawn into this little mess on top of everything else but agreeing with Jessica this couldn't be a coincidence. "Elspeth said something about the ritual Knox is planning. That certain things were needed. Could this be one of them? I don't remember Morgana ever being linked to Excalibur, but maybe…?"

"Ah was thinking the same thing. Tae my knowledge, Morgana and Mordred were involved only later on in that sad tale," My Alpha confirmed, her breadth of ancient lore far exceeding the bedtime reading I'd been doing of late. "But that does nae mean there is nae connection between her and the stone. This needs looking into."

"Any chance you can give this to someone else? Given the history between Cerce and me?" I gave it my best shot, not wanting to spend any more time around Cerce than I had to. Ok, it was *slightly* unfair dropping one of my packmates into the shit, but I could make it up to them later. Somehow. "Maybe I can help out Jacob, or give Elspeth a hand with the research?"

Jessica shook her head, smiling at me to show she understood my reasoning but it wasn't going to fly.

"Nae, Morgan. All your brothers and sisters are busy with tasks elsewhere, and Jacob has his team already managing both hunts most capably. You would just be a distraction." She told me bluntly. "As fer Elspeth, I cannae speak tae her need of help with any research, but she has nae complained tae me that it is too much fer her. As such, ah think you are best suited finding any connection between this theft and Knox's plan. Even knowing this may help some."

"I figured." I rolled my eyes and sighed theatrically. "Ok, I'd best go check out the witch's lair and see if there's a handy bucket of water I can throw over her. By pure accident, of course."

"Ah would expect nothing less." Jessica smiled, then stopped me before I got up to leave. "Ah have one piece of good news … well, its news at least. The Furies have agreed tae bring your gnome contact tae the office later this evening and will release him tae yer keeping."

She held up a hand as I went to thank her.

"There is one proviso. It is against tradition, but they will only do so if you will meet with them. They wish tae see you, speak tae you and judge whether this is the right thing tae do before they commit." Jessica told me, her smile slipping a notch. "It tis within their right tae do so, though they have nae asked tae meet any lycan other than us Alphas in all my memory."

"Will you do so?"

Bugger. The Furies wanted to meet me? I'd assumed Jessica would handle that side of things as normal, that they'd simply trust her enough to agree to the request. But them wanting to meet me definitely put my favour at serious risk. Could I be trusted not to fuck things up? Make some wisecrack and insult creatures who made the immortal rulers of the Courts step lightly and behave? The potential for me messing things up was *monumental*.

But then, this really was my mess, my problem to solve. Terrigyle was my contact, and I'd been the one to lock him away in the first place. Made sense that I was the one to put the argument to his jailers to let him out, even if for only a short while.

Damn I hated logic.

"Yeah, I reckon it's the least I can do." I nodded, then grinned at a sudden thought. "It'll piss Jacob off no end, the *kitten finder* of the pack meeting the Furies. Oh, this might actually be fun!"

"Ah do so hope you get the chance tae enjoy, but ah would advise tempering that pleasure until you've actually had an audience with them, and walked away after." She told me with a gentle reproof.

With no chance to help out Jacob, lend a paw to tracking the three at-large Real escapees or to bury myself in books with Elspeth, there really was only one place I could head next. And dragging my heels would just make the experience last longer, and be more painful.

It turned out Cerce had had her chauffeur wait for her outside the office, certain in the knowledge she'd be getting what she wanted, so I was treated to a ride back to the Carteloni's residence in relative luxury. The car was something American, built to take up as much of the road as possible, and fitted out like a presidential vehicle on the inside. The driver upfront was completely portioned off, whilst the space in the back was large enough to have a good size party in. Plush seating facing back and front, a drinks cabinet stocked with various beverages and even a small flat screen television and what I thought was a games console of some description. All the perks crime could buy.

The ride was made in silence, the witch obviously not keen to engage with the hired help now that she had gotten me to take the case, and I had enough going on in my head to keep me occupied.

I kept turning things over and over, trying to work out what Morgana's long play was, and how we could stop it from happening. She'd elicited Knox's help, obviously, by pretending to be his dead daughter and deceiving him into agreeing to 'resurrect' her into a new body. Based on whatever guilt he had over the young girl's death, most likely. It was her way out of prison, even though she'd escaped her own body all by herself … but the presence of life energy in her cell made me think Knox had had a hand in that too. Maybe the fae had needed all the energy to sustain her, when she was not inside her old body or something.

I'd leave the details of *that* to Elspeth to figure out. It was what she did best.

Fact was, Morgana had gotten free, but not before swearing bloody vengeance on the Courts, Artur specifically and pretty much anything that had ever looked at her funny, or not grovelled at her feet properly. Meaning pretty much everything in the Realms. She'd also staged prison breaks for various nasties from both Ivory and Shadow, forcing the Courts to close the Ways between Realms, and sowing chaos and confusion when maybe, if people had been thinking straight, they'd have had a chance of stopping her whilst she was still in the Real.

But that was where it all started to unravel.

Morgana must have fled the Real, and was most likely lurking in the Mortal Realm, sustained on life energy until Knox could slip her into his

Frankenstein-style creation like a new prom dress. But that left her vulnerable, without allies or a Court to protect her. Knox himself was hunted by the mortal security services, let alone by us for his actions and the small fact he was running loose with the ability to kill immortals.

And that little nugget. Knox had the Harrowing, a thing from ancient times, which he'd mistakenly been assigned to investigate whilst working for the same government that now wanted his head. Yet instead of using it as the weapon it was, and doing what most mortals do when given weapons of mass destruction i.e. go mad, take control and become top dog themselves - he seemed to actually be fighting the thing, sealing inside himself and only letting it out when he was most threatened, or to remove complications. Like power-hungry lycan who had made one too many mistakes and revealed their treachery. It was like he was keeping hold of it, saving it for *something*.

That was a particularly troubling thought.

And not to forget Morgana had sprung the remaining fae of the Twilight Court as well. That sister or brother or whatever you called it to Ivory and Shadow. Destroyed by Madb and Oberon, made over into the protection which sat between the Real and the Mortal Realms, filled with monsters that once had been their kin. Three of them, the Norns, had had enough combined power that Oberon had ripped out their voices in an attempt to weaken and nullify them. But Morgana *just so happened* to have a mortal doctor trained over several centuries, with the ability to build a body from spare parts and keep himself alive by renewing himself as well from kidnapped men and women. What did she need them for?

Oh, and finally, to actually get Morgana back into a new body, Knox had to perform a powerful ritual, using whatever stored resources he still had left as well as bolstering his skills with … and here I was guessing … stolen juju. But that left him vulnerable, given he'd been stupid enough to mark out locations around London that all pointed to a central location where the resurrection would take place. Giving the mortal forces, us lycan and anyone else who might be interested more than enough time to get in place and stop the thing.

When you're planning a magical event which you know other parties will do their utmost to stop, you *don't* hand them a map with a big X marking the spot where it would all take place. That just seemed idiotic.

Unless it was a distraction. A play, to get everyone hunting Knox, Morgana, looking in the wrong place. Or gathering them together for a trap to be sprung on them instead. Like loosing the Harrowing on them, maybe?

Round and round the thoughts and suspicions in my head went, as we drove through the London streets towards Mayfair. Towards the Cartelonis, and a place I had never ever wanted to see again.

We pulled up outside the grey stone building, and I felt the prickle of the protective wards Cerce had in place flare in recognition. Two goons stood outside the front door, not the idiot I remembered from the last time, the man who had also spied on my home and possibly on Danny's as well the same night Felix was kidnapped.

Instead, two thick necked and fully suited goons guarded the steps. One moved in and opened the door for Cerce, who slid out with almost liquid grace whilst I shuffled my arse across the seat and unkinked myself out of the door and onto the street. I felt the weight of the guard' stares as well as the unseen but definitely present cameras focus on me and could only imagine the conversations going on right now.

As the witch passed them, both men slid together to block my way forward. Expressions closed, muscles already bunching for a fight. The sense coming off them was akin to attack dogs, hackles up and snarling.

Cerce didn't stop, stalking across the pavement and up the stairs, her heels clicking hard on the concrete. It was only when she reached the front door and found no-one there to open it for her did she stop and turn, taking in the scene of me still standing beside the car with the two goons facing off against me, in my path.

I held up my hands, seeing both men twitch, one reaching for something bulking out the inside of his suit jacket. In broad daylight, no less.

"Uh, you want to call your boys off before I make a mess on the street?" I shouted out as politely as I could.

Cerce, turned and sighed as the pair reacted as I'd expected. Uttering very animalistic growls, they stepped into my space, the one of my right's fists swinging. But they froze as the witch gave one sharp clap of her hands, loud and echoing oddly round the street. Sharp and violent like a firework.

She didn't even bother uttering a command ... the single clap enough to have the pair immediately lowering their fists and stepping back. One stopped by the stairs, relaxing into that familiar stance that spoke of military service, of spending hours standing to attention and not wavering even when one's bladder was full.

The second guard mounted the steps and grabbed the door, swinging it open for her.

"Coming?" She asked as she walked through the open door without even sparing a glance at the mortal holding it open for her.

"I'd rather not." I mumbled to myself, but knew I had little choice. Jessica wanted this investigated, and I wasn't going to be able to do much from the pavement.

I was waived past the metal detector and inhouse security, and with a small escort of muscle, Cerce and I made it to the lifts without incident. One of the goons pressed the button for us both, earning not even a nod from the witch so I shot him a smile for expending so much energy on our behalf. Of course, I got a blank look back, each and every one of the team already altered by Cerce's experimentation to make them more than just simple mortals ... but also less in more than one way.

Only Cerce and I travelled up, the guards left behind in the entrance hall. Once inside the lift, the witch stabbed the uppermost number on the electronic pad, but then held her finger against the screen for far longer than was necessary to choose a level. Finally, the display flashed red, then a single 'P' appeared. This Cerce then pressed, and the lift smoothly slid upwards.

I probably should've felt at least a little awed that we were headed to the penthouse of the Carteloni building, but since I lived at the top of my own block, I wasn't that impressed. I was more interested in the security measures in place, guessing the lift's pad was fingerprint locked to stop anyone but Cerce or those she chose from gaining access to her apartment.

And yet someone had gotten in to steal from her vault, and then exit without raising any alarm. The question was, how?

Finally, the doors slid open, and we stepped into Cerce's inner sanctum.

Chapter 11

Mordred.

Famous as the illegitimate son of Artur and Morgan Le Fay, this Knight is also called the Usurper for his part in the downfall of Artur and attempts to have himself named King of Britain. Merlin warned Artur that a newborn babe would threaten his rule and so the High King ordered the death of all children just born to the world. This massacre of helpless babes was named the May Day massacre, and was a black mark against the King.

Especially as Mordred survived and was raised with the knowledge his own father had tried to kill him.

Mordred grew to be knighted, and gathered a host under his banner as he sought to challenge Artur's rule of Britain. There are mixed stories of that epic confrontation, some saying he slew Artur whilst others suggest he himself was slain but only after mortally wounding his father.

It was a little bit of a let-down, if I'm honest.

I'd expected … well, something to reflect that an immortal lived here. Archaic pillars and tapestries, monstrous skulls or burning torches in brackets. Bones of her defeated enemies artistically displayed for her to view whenever she chose. Typical tasteless stuff like that.

Instead, Cerce's apartment was *shiny*. Chrome and glass, polished so that every surface shone with reflections from inset overhead lights and floor to ceiling mirrors. Elegant vases stood on plinths, filled with large displays of vibrant flowers of every shade and shape, and countertops of darkest obsidian held a few large gemstones and small rock formations artfully arranged. I thought I spotted a chunk of coral like a complicated net, set beside a purple veined chunk of what I guessed was something more expensive and rarer than quartz.

A large flat screen television, of a size to rival the one in our meeting room back at *Good Deeds* was on and currently showing slowly shifting scenes from places round the world. Deserts, forests, even deep oceans, pinprick perfect and in ultra-high definition so that the effect was more a window into the world beyond the four walls, than a simple display to break up the monotony of a wall.

"Well, this is nice." I commented dryly, stepping out onto pristine white carpet that I immediately slightly sank into. Luckily my boots were fairly clean, but I really did wonder how the place was kept so clean. Cerce probably had bound some lesser fae and had them waiting in the walls to sweep up any mess as soon as she or any visitors left.

It's a known fact from mortal mythology that if certain fae … Brownies, Boggarts and the like … take up residence in a home and begin managing the task of keeping the place clean and tidy, they do so only when the mortals in residence were asleep or away from home. If they were ever caught at their tasks, it was said they would immediately fly into a rage and break anything within reach, destroying all their good work before vanishing, never to return.

The actual fact was, those fae had realised that mortals, if ever they found something supernatural cleaning or tidying for them, could not help themselves but point out things that hadn't been done right, or up to their standard. And nothing pisses off a fae more than being told they had missed a spot after they'd just turned a dirt-encrusted hovel into a shining, pristine palace.

Anyhow, back to the penthouse. Cerce walked on ahead, obviously expecting me to follow obediently behind like a good little lycan. Instead I dragged my heels, stopping to look at the large open plan living room with another massive screen, cream white sofa set that looked new from the warehouse and a coffee table chromed so much that it practically glowed. No mug ring-marks on the glass top, no scuffs on the sofa material that, say, a large trollhound had caused by rubbing an itch against the nearest surface. The place was practically untouched.

"If you've finished gawping, the safe is this way." Cerce told me sharply, as I poked at a delicate display of song-grass, a plant from the Real.

Each blade produced a single note, and Wyld fae could often perform complex musical scores by simply dancing through swathes of the stuff.

Shrugging, I cast one last look round the pristine, unmarked and soulless home, then followed Cerce through another hallway and down some steps.

This led me into a large open space, with a wide square floor set with sofas at the centre, and wall sconces set with individual pieces of art, lit underneath and overhead. Statues, paintings, even some broken and fractured weapons that I guessed were from ancient Greece by the look of them. This part of her home had a feel of a museum, those seats set to view the various items on display from as comfortable a place as possible. I noted a small drinks cabinet set discreetly to one side, filled with bottles of what I guessed were expensive champagne and spirits. Nothing like my stock of good quality red wine, this was definitely tailored to a different palate.

Cerce stopped by one section of wall that looked no different than all the others, and pressed her palm against the pristine surface. A light glowed red under her skin, and rapidly outlined a large section of the wall taller than either Cerce or me. The panel-door then slid to one side, revealing a vault door of more traditional design, with a massive airlock style wheel and another keypad. A red light blinked on this, obviously awaiting a code to be input.

"As I said, there were no clues left to identify whoever gained entry to my safe and stole from me." The witch told me as she gestured around the room. "As soon as I was aware that items had been taken, I reviewed the enchantments I have woven here to trace the intruders but discovered nothing. They were obviously prepared and used powerful protections to keep their identities hidden from me."

"Or they were already familiar with your setup." I mused, looking around the place. "Drinks cabinet, comfy sofas and handy access to your safe. I'm guessing this is where you entertain business associates, maybe suppliers of items you can't source by traditional means or through the lawful channels?"

Cerce stared at me with those hard green eyes of hers, jaw set in a firm line.

"Your point being?"

I didn't bother answering, instead just started walking around the room, letting my senses feel for anything out of place. The smallest detail that could explain what had happened here. Something that Cerce would probably ignore with her arrogance and supercilious attitude.

And I found it tucked under one of the sofas, thoroughly out of place against the pristine décor. I plucked the strands from the thick white carpet and held them close to my nose for a quick sniff. Urgh, definitely distinctive and pungent. I'd smelled that tang in an alleyway where I'd found a schoolgirl's satchel, and then in a work shack where I'd traced that girl through the sewers of London.

Troll hair, and from a particularly smelly and loathsome creature.

Have you been dealing with a trio of trolls lately? Go by the family name of Bung. Clanless, and with serious hygiene issues?" I queried as I cast my eyes round the room. "I mean, more than normal for their kind."

"I do *not* associate with such creatures." Cerce replied haughtily. "Trolls do not move in the same circles as do I, and the items I often require are not the sort I or anyone would obtain from their kind. Is that who stole from me?"

"I'm guessing so, since otherwise why is their fur here?" I spied what I was after, a small vent at the base of one wall, barred and too small for anything larger than a child to make use of. But trolls could get anywhere, much like grimalkin, and could squeeze through cracks and holes far smaller than they should fit through. I checked the vent and found a few more threads of coarse stinking fur just inside the grill, out of sight for anyone too arrogant to think to check. "I'm guessing your vault also has air conditioning fitted?"

"Of course. Certain items I store need a steady temperature to keep them potent." She replied, but then shook her head. "That might explain how they got in, but the items they took? The stone itself would not fit inside the air vents, nor the containers I had the nuts stored in. How do you explain their departure with what they stole?"

"Sheez, you don't please easily do you? I just told you the identity of your thieves, which you missed." I growled but swung my attention away from the grate and back to the rest of the room. "Your enchantments. What triggers them?"

She gave me a long, cool stare but I just shrugged.

"Hey lady, you asked me to butt in. If you don't want to tell me, I can't help you." I replied bluntly. "I've identified the thieves for you so I can happily sod off now. Job done."

"Fine. But if I discover you have shared anything of what I tell you now, I *will* consider it a breach of our agreement and seek restitution." Cerce informed me with vehement finality, before continuing. "The wards awaken whenever I leave the apartment, and will sense the presence of anyone entering this space without me. They will record whomever it is, and the time they entered or exited. Much like the mortals *cctv* but far more reliable when dealing with those of *our* sort."

I checked around the open floor, looking for any more fur, marks that could indicate a ritual had been drawn on the floor to allow the thieves to exit without being seen. None of the windows had been forced, to allow them flight out that way and besides, they were all small paned glass. The carpet's fibres would not have held chalk in a firm line, and paint would still be visible. So, they hadn't used those routes out, and the vent was a no go. So how …

Unless they'd simply gone out the front door.

"Uh, that enchantment of yours. Does it log when you return, or simply switch off when it recognises you?" I queried, not being familiar with the intricacies of all things witchy-woo. The stuff I could do with my link to the Shadow Court, and my summoning of strength through my newly awakened Wyld heritage, neither of those took much effort or followed any rule apart from *think it, do it*. Nice simple magic.

I'd leave the more complicated stuff to Elspeth.

"The ward is keyed to my essence, and simply returns to slumber when it detects me. Why?" Cerce replied tersely, tapping her foot on the carpet. "I told you, it did not detect any new presence …"

"Did you check if it froze anytime that didn't seem right? Like, I don't know, when you definitely weren't around?" I cut her off, seeing her expression grow more pinched, vexation plainly writ in the furrows on her face. "Humour me."

The witch stared at me for a breath, then shook her head and made a complicated gesture with one hand. Fire glittered in runic script around her fingers as she manipulated the crafting, tracing through one after another sequence without stopping.

Then she froze.

"That is … odd." She spoke up, plucking the glowing icons out of the sequence and staring at them intently. "It would seem your suspicion was right. This one time. The ward reacted to my presence late yesterday afternoon, entering a null state as it is meant to. The problem is, I was at work in the laboratory at the time, and only returned here in the evening."

"And I'm guessing if you call your pit bulls downstairs, they'll tell you they saw you leave the building." I hazarded a guess, having to fight a wry chuckle at the sheer audacity of the troll bastards. They'd known they couldn't get their stolen goods back out the way they had come in, so had decided to do the one thing no-one would expect. Waltz out the front door under the nose of everyone. Old school Vegas-style.

Cerce was definitely angry, but for a change her wrath was not directed at me. She stormed off, heels digging into the carpet, and grabbed up a handset fixed to the wall across from the both of us. She didn't even bother punching in any code, so I guessed the line was automatically routed to the central security office. Instead, she just whispered tersely into the phone and I politely hummed to myself to stop myself listening in. I'm nice like that.

Finally, with a sigh escaping gritted teeth, she hung the phone back on its bracket and turned back to me.

"So, was I right?" I asked innocently, fighting the smile that wanted to spread itself across my face.

"Not only did the guards think that I stepped out of the building at ten to five yesterday afternoon, but they even assisted *me* with a large package that I required loaded into an unmarked vehicle that was awaiting me on the street outside." She told me with hissing, vexed tones. "The guards' report is of an object of approximate size and weight of the Stone, but they believed it was some produce I had prepared for my distributors. Supposedly *I* required six of them to carry it to the vehicle, then return to their posts and not speak of it to anyone. One guard *did* think my voice sounded odd, but their conditioning prevented him from acting on it."

I *really* wanted to laugh now but knew it wouldn't help here. Of course, I couldn't resist the urge to have a small dig at her expense.

"So your modified attack dogs are so well trained, they can be fooled by someone impersonating you and who knows how to act like you, even if they sound a little off?" I commented, seeing her eyes flash with fury. "I'm guessing, but I think the person who sent the trolls to steal your Stone and nuts also supplied them with a simple charm to alter their appearance. Good enough to fool your wards inside and out, as well as the mortals dotted around this place so they must have known your setup quite well. Someone you let in, someone you dealt with so they could sense what sort of craftings they'd face."

"You let them in."

Cerce went to speak, but I cut her off, my voice growing hard as the odd shaped blocks fell into place.

"The fact is, I've recently faced a changeling and a bunch of homicidal knights armed with Wolfsbane in the Real, who wanted to terminally end my involvement in a complicated plot aimed at the Ivory and Shadow Courts. I've also faced mortals using hexen-charms, who also manage to get their hands on Wolfsbane and use it on me. They also intended to do me harm. Oh, and my packmate and I were threatened on these very premises by your trained chump guards, also with supplies of Wolfsbane, stocks of which you then surrendered to us under the rules of owning and utilising proscribed substances within the Accords." I counted off, as Cerce stilled opposite me. "The last one, hey, doesn't tie in with anything, but the first two? Those are linked to one mortal. Someone who is up to their ginger eyebrows in Real madness, working for a real nasty immortal and who a bunch of us want to find and stop from causing a shitload of pain and stupidity."

"So I guess my question is," I faced her, expression grim and stance set for trouble. "When was the last time you had Robert Knox up here, and what the fuck were you doing, dealing with the bastard?"

Chapter 12

Cerce stood opposite me, eyes grown cold, that fury banked and settled away. Now she was in firm control of her emotions, and making sure I read *nothing* that she didn't want me knowing from her.

"Robert Knox? Robert ... *Knox*." She tasted the name, before shaking her head. "I'm not sure I know who ..."

"Oh cut the bullshit. You invited me here, remember?" I cut her off again, certain that my suspicion was right. "If the name doesn't ring a bell, then I'm talking about a mortal man. Looking to be in middle years, ginger haired and wearing what I think you'd call vintage attire. Got one manky eye, glasses, and has scarring all over his face." I detailed out, watching for the tell from the witch, the twitch of her eyes as I described someone she knew. And there it was, just a slight one but enough for me. "Oh, and I doubt you got that intimate with him, but I'm not judging. If you'd seen his skin, you'd see he has scars all over his body where *he's used kidnapped mortals to replace his fucking body parts*."

Cerce took a calming breath, then slowly nodded. Just once.

"He used a different name, but his description fits a mortal I was approached by through my usual contacts, seeking information about rituals. Old world magic, the empowering of a disembodied spirit to keep it vital through the sharing of energies." She told me with no trace of regret, no shame. Just simple fact. "He sought to understand what truth there was in some texts he had obtained, theories taken from research into the passage *back* of a mortal spirit from beyond the Veil. Returned into a vessel. I believe reanimation or resurrection as the mortals describe it."

There are moments in time when all I really want is to step to the nearest wall and bang my fist or head against it. Not to solve a problem, take my mind off a thing or do anything particularly beneficial to me or anyone else. Just simply to release the frustration I was feeling at that exact point.

This was one of those moments.

"And I guess you were just oh so happy to help him with his research?" I didn't even need her answer, given what Knox was up to. The certainty he had in achieving his goal. Morgana might have been whispering in his ear, convincing him of the rightness of what he was doing and how it was all possible, but Knox had been the typical mortal and doubted. Wanted to verify his facts and get some reassurance from a knowledgeable source. And Cerce, being what she was, had been on hand to do exactly that.

"He paid well, and his checks came back without any red flags." She replied with a shrug. "I am, first and foremost, a businesswoman who relies on a reputation in providing what clients ask for. Whether that is a tailored child with certain personality traits or physical defining features, or knowledge confirmed or reputed for its authenticity, and guidance for those wishing to explore the arcane arts. This man, Knox you say, he had obtained reputable materials from sources I believe are locked within the mortal's Black Library. As such, I was only confirming details to someone with the appropriate access to know such matters."

"Well, congrats." I told her, not even bothering to keep the anger from my voice. "Not only did you help a mortal understand that his plans for butchering young women to build himself a new body for what he *thinks* is his daughter's spirit was possible. Not even that a ritual he'd found to draw that spirit through the Veil and into said body was possible. But you *also* showed him your valuables and where he could get some necessary ingredients for his fuckery. The nuts are for Knox, and as for the Stone, I'm guessing it's linked to the spirit he's working to bring over somehow."

Cerce stared at me, obviously trying to work out how much of what I was saying was true, and how much trouble she was now in. I helpfully kept my expression as open as possible, not hiding a thing. Knowing Cerce with all her wiles and craft, her skills learned from so many centuries being alive, would read me like a book.

One with plenty of swear words in it.

"This spirit? You know its nature? Its name?" She asked quietly, wheels turning quickly in her head now.

"Oh we do, and it's a doozy." I replied. We'd made an agreement, the Alphas and all those involved in the Courts' jail-breaks, knowing the truth of what we faced. Of who was behind all the weird as shit craziness we'd been facing. The promise - to keep a lid on the shitstorm headed our way until we'd at least tried to stop Knox and Morgana. There'd be the argument that maybe this was bigger than us, that we'd past the point where the lycans and whatever allies we'd scraped together passed this mess over to the proper authorities and let them handle it.

And as always, we'd decided that the *proper* authorities couldn't generally find their arse with their elbow, and as such, we might as well try to avoid the localised apocalypse from happening on our own.

I'd had been given leave, however, to pass on word to Cormac shortly after I'd gotten back from the Gardens of Ice, through the traditional method of scribbling the relevant details down on the nearest piece of paper and paying a taxi driver to drop the message off at the Tower of London, addressed to *Agent Cormac Smith with a 'C' - care of Her Majesty's Keeper of the Ravens (PS Yes he does work there). If in doubt, find Agent Evelyn Jones with an "E".* I figured someone would get the reference and make sure it was delivered, as I hadn't been given any other way of getting news to him.

However, Jessica had told me that it was down to my discretion if I felt someone needed telling what exactly was headed our way, if it greased the wheels or got a result I wanted. And I *so* wanted to see how Cerce handled the news.

"Yeah, we know who'se behind Knox and the shit he's been pulling. That spirit? It isn't his dead daughter." I replied, watching her face carefully. "It's Morgana. Sister of Madb. From Arthurian legend. Free from her prison and intent on wreaking revenge on pretty much everyone and everything she can once she's installed in her new body. Now do you understand just how fucked up things are, and how wrong it was to help that sonofabitch?"

Cerce's hand went to lips as her face whitened, her eyes flaring wide. The name eliciting the exact response I had expected from her. No attempt to hide the sudden fear, as she immediately looked back at her vault.

"Yeah, and you had a hunk of a relic from her time stored in your collection. I'm not sure what she wants it for, but Knox obviously was instructed to grab it." I told her coldly.

"No-one can blame me for whatever action Knox takes. I am in no way responsible for how he uses the information he himself obtained. I only indicated the authenticity of it and explained some key points that he was having difficulty with. I in no way directed him to use it. Not on those mortal women, not for bringing across a Power like Morgana." Cerce tried to reassure herself as she spoke, obviously not caring what I thought. Almost practicing for the defence of a trial she envisaged she might be pulled into.

I was happy to burst that little bubble.

"Oh, don't worry. No-one's going to have a *chance* to blame you for the shit hitting the fan." I let that nasty smile of mine slip free, as I continued. "See, you might want to talk to Talen Orben or Sal Orben. Two Alpha lycan that Knox used to get stuff he wanted, and who he used to obstruct our investigations into him. They didn't think they were doing anything wrong, that anyone would blame them for their part in all this mess."

"Maybe I should …" The witch began to say, but I shook my head, overriding her with glee.

"Ah, silly me. That'll be a problem, coz they're *dead*. Loose ends tied up, and all that." I happily told her. "Knox didn't want anything leading back to him, so he arranged for them to release an altered version of the *Harrowing* on themselves. In fact, their entire pack. Turned them into a particularly nasty type of zombie, I've got to say. Talen was lucky, or a coward though. He didn't turn. So, Knox unleashed the real thing on him instead, and drained him of all his life. Left a withered husk behind, one even dental records wouldn't identify if I hadn't witnessed his death."

Cerce lapsed into silence, searching my face for the lie. And not finding it.

"Yeah, Knox has the Harrowing, and seems happy to use it to clear up every little thread leading back to him and this fucking ritual. Anyone involved … they're walking dead." I shrugged, looking around the expensive apartment. "Still, you should be perfectly safe in this secure fortress, guarded by your own special super soldiers. It's not like a bunch of *trolls* could break in, steal your stuff and waltz out the front door … with your guard dogs helping them!"

I'm not normally a petty wolf, I don't take pleasure in other peoples' pain or misfortune. But after dealing with Cerce for only a short period of time, and knowing how she had threatened Felix and Danny, let alone how she had acted around me in front of my pack? I'm sorry, but I couldn't have been more happy seeing the realisation take root behind her eyes. The simple fact she had fucked up, and fucked up big time.

"I want protection. I know things, things that can help you ..." She started but I waved one hand in negation, ending her offer before she began.

"Save it for someone who cares, sister!" I growled. "I've done what you wanted. Found out who stole your precious lump of rock. We're hunting Knox, so I expect if and when we find him, I'll find that thing too ... unless he's broken it up or something. I promise, if you are still alive and this side of the Veil, I'll return it to you. But I'm not going to waste any breath over it, or you. You picked your side when you helped him. So, either bend over and accept what's coming, or go running for the Real. I reckon Morgana and her pet mortal are going to be a little too busy to try too hard hunting for you, if you are gone. That's my advice."

With that, I turned on my heel and walked towards the lifts. Behind me, I heard the snarl of rage from the witch, a mixture of fear and fury blended, but I just kept walking. Let her try and hex me, and I'd show her just how pissed I was.

And what a mess an angry lycan could make of home furnishings.

I made it to the lift without incident, and jabbed the button, summoning the carriage. Behind, I felt the build-up of magic, and guessed Cerce was about to vent in a spectacular fashion. It might have been fun to stick around and watch, but I had bigger fish to fry.

Number one on the list was updating Jessica on what I'd found out here. None of it made much difference, but it at least confirmed a few things of us, and indicated we weren't being paranoid. Knox really did have the ability to draw Morgana's spirit through the Veil and house her in the body he'd been preparing. Signed off by Cerce, with footnotes to help him along his way.

The lift door closed just as I heard the first sound of splintering glass and felt the release of arcane energies like static on my skin. I remembered those delicate displays Cerce had on show, and reckoned if they were parts of a set, the remaining pieces were just about to get a whole lot more valuable. And rare.

I grinned the whole way down to the lobby, and was still smiling as I walked out the front door without anyone stopping me.

Chapter 13

Galahad.

Also known as Galeas or Galath, this knight was reputed to be the illegitimate son of Lancelot and Elaine of Corbenic. His claim to fame was that he embodied purity and gallantry, in an obvious effort to make up for the circumstance of his birth, and that he inherited the ability of his father to heal the sick and even cast out demons.

Galahad was known as the Knight who was destined to find the Holy Grail, as foretold by Merlin many years prior to his birth. So great was the achievement of this goal, and according to tales that he also met Joseph of Arimathea, that he was able to bargain with the angels of Heaven itself and be taken up by them to join the heavenly host. This was witnessed by his fellow Knights, Bors and Percival.

It was much later that same day. As evening drew in and the lights around London began flickering to life, to stave off the encroaching darkness.

And I was sat in *Good Deeds,* a steaming mug of coffee slowly congealing beside me as I gazed at our complex murder-board style presentation. Seeking answers.

The place was deserted, everyone else apart from me and Jessica already out and about their hunts or told to head home and take the night. Jacob, on hearing the Furies were coming to speak to me had simply rolled his eyes and pointedly cleared a few personal items he kept on his desk into a holdall and took one last look around the office. *Just sos' I remember what it used to look like*, he'd glibly told me before leaving, the sod.

Jessica was upstairs preparing for the visit, so I'd taken the time to update our map of all things Knox. When I'd informed her what I'd found out from Cerce, and her involvement however unbeknowingly, our Alpha had just shaken her head.

"Tis nae surprise Knox sought validation of his plans, and his choice of sources tae use were few, given *most* with that sort of knowledge would have alerted the authorities as soon as they knew what he sought." Jessica rationalised. "It matters little, and we have larger things tae worry about than that witch and her well-being. She is a survivor, so ah expect she will find a hole tae crawl into, tae wait out the storm. Ah'll place a watch on her, just in case though."

I guess I could have popped home, to check in on Felix and Danny if they were still hanging round my apartment, and to spend some quality time with Bear. But I would have had to come all the way back to the office again for my date with the Furies, and it didn't seem fair on my mutt or my friends to drop in then bugger off again almost in the same breath.

And ok, I wasn't particularly keen on them seeing just how nervous I was too.

These were the bloody Furies, after all. Creatures with a singular purpose, to punish transgressors no matter mortal or immortal, whether simple peasant or Lord of a Court. Rumour had it that no force was strong enough to overcome a Fury straight on, no craft or godly power capable of holding them back from their intended prey for long. A bit like the Grim Reaper, but way scarier.

And yes, I consider the Furies far more bowel-loosening and terror inducing than Death personified. The Reaper is simply a being without intent or personal predilections towards those it came to collect. It was simply performing its task, to ferry certain special souls through the Veil and to the great beyond. I wasn't entirely sure *what* defined someone as earning this particular merit, but I'd never seen It, never felt the chill touch of a presence I couldn't explain or see … and I, hand on heart, could say I'd seen a lot of folk start that one-way journey to the Veil. I'd even sometimes helped them on their way.

But the Furies? They took rather too much delight in the torment and torture they doled out for my taste, if the stories told were anything to go by.

So yes, I was a little on edge. Like someone sat in the waiting room for a job interview, knowing the people on the other side of the door might be nice, reasonable individuals - but also could be raving lunatics about to crush your hopes and dreams with casual indifference.

Given that fact, I'd decided to distract myself, to try and puzzle out not really the *when* the shit was about to hit the fan with Knox, but the *where*.

The thing was, I still couldn't believe that Knox, with all his centuries of planning and noted high level of intellect, would have been *dumb* enough to leave an X marks the spot style map to where he planned to do his thing. Dotting locations in specific sites around London sounded like the sort of thing a ritual needed, keystones for the magic blah blah blah according to the little I'd read on these things and the lot that Elspeth had tried to tell me about. But the man was clever enough to know all that his old colleagues would do is connect the dots and be waiting for him at that central point, with handcuffs, big sticks and probably something stronger than biscuits dosed with knock-out juice.

Ok, yeah, I still smarted over that small fact. Sue me for not liking the fact I'd been so easily duped.

The ritual *had* to be taking place somewhere else, but the fact it was a ritual meant Knox couldn't just choose any random location and set up his mystical version of a landing pad and guidelights for Morgana's spirit. The place he chose had to be linked to her somehow, and that *really* complicated things given one small inconsistency. When this particular immortal was kicking around, London … or Londonium as known by the Romans … was just a piece of mud and grass, peopled by sheep and goats. Jessica, from her research, had noted the unarguable fact that the Artur incident had occurred over two and a half thousand years ago, whilst London only properly became a known place five hundred years *later*.

Question was, where the hell would Knox find someplace that linked back to Morgana in such a strong way that she'd feel drawn to it? I absentmindedly picked up my mug of cooling coffee, going to take a swig then stopping as the solution struck me.

Of course, I knew someone who could answer that simple question. From the horse's mouth so to speak. A particularly arrogant and annoying horse, in my opinion, but the truth was … I knew Artur. The actual Pendragon-King-puppet the Ivory Court had tried to use to dupe the mortals into handing over sovereignty and dominion to them. And the fact was, the slippery weasel owed me big time for hauling his sorry arse out of a cell where he was being kept by his once-paramour whilst she stole

Excalibur. If Elspeth and I hadn't come along and found him, his future had looked grim indeed. Munchies for a particularly nasty shape-changer.

Despite this rather pertinent fact, I was pretty sure Artur would do everything in his power to avoid talking to me. We hadn't really gotten along, and I *had* handed him over to his sister to take back to the Ivory Court for a … reprimand? Slap on the wrist for being such an idiot? Whatever it was Oberon and Titania did to Court fae who messed up. And who was top of Morgana's hit-list to pay a visit to once she was reborn? The once and future King who she blamed for her imprisonment and torture.

Which meant Artur was, by now, probably hiding in the deepest darkest hole he could find, with as much purloined booze as he could steal and with at least some feminine company to keep him from getting too lonely. And I really didn't have the time or energy, or even patience to hunt all the way across the Real to find him.

Thankfully, I *also* knew someone else who was a past master … or mistress … of finding her errant brother and dragging his backside back into the light of day. And I figured she was more likely to help me in my newly appointed capacity as Errant of Ivory, given how she was the reason I'd been granted that bloody title.

Thinking this through, I reckoned a good plan of action looked something like … *Meet the Furies. Survive the Furies. Get Terrigyle and find out where the Bung brothers might be hiding. Speak to Manisha & get her to hunt up her brother. Go hunt the trolls. Speak to Artur. Get the info to find Knox and stop him.*

Nice and simple, just how I liked it. Unfortunately, life never really ever seemed to agree with me on that small point.

I sensed my Alpha before I heard her footsteps, that change to the room around me like someone switching on a light bulb. I set down the untouched mug and pushed myself up out of the meeting chair as she swung the door open.

"It's time, Morgan." She told me, standing in the doorway. "Are you ready?"

"About as I'll ever be." I admitted, taking a calming breath and forcing the nervous energy roiling inside me to quieten. At least a little.

Jessica nodded and waved me to head on up to the second floor, falling in behind me.

"Just remember the reasons you think you need this gnome released, and keep tae the facts." She instructed me as we climbed the stairs. "Nae humour, jokes or wisecracks unless you desire tae see *why* the Furies are feared so much."

"That's ok. I got my laughter fix with Cerce, so I'm all good for being serious with creatures that scare the shit out of Obie." I replied truthfully. "All I want is to get Teri, see what he knows about those bloody Bung brothers and go find them so we can crack on with finding Knox. Jokes can wait."

Jessica did not bother answering, but the silence behind me said enough about how much she doubted my ability to hold my tongue, and make light of any situation at exactly the wrong time. She had good cause.

Stepping up onto the second floor, I saw that whilst I'd been trying to figure out Knox's schedule, she had been equally busy.

The sofas and chairs had been pushed back against the far walls, and anything that could be considered fragile, including the crystal statue and the wall art, had been taken down and put out of harm's way. The rugs were rolled up, leaving the bare boards beneath our feet. Finally, she had laid out two large, simple mats, facing each other. Both had been carefully enscribed with warding circles and sigils drawn by Elspeth for these meetings, to protect whoever stood in one and to contain whatever appeared in the other.

Candles had been set around the larger of the two circles, ready to be lit. These were largely symbolic, an act to generate energy to help open the way for whatever was being summoned to the circle. Movies and books get it so wrong when they show the summoned creature loosed from its prison when the candles blow out. All in fact happens is the room you're in gets a lot darker, and creepier.

Elspeth had happily mocked enough of my favourite shows and reading material, based on that and other common misconceptions.

If you're wondering why Jessica hadn't simply drawn out the two warding circles herself, or asked Elspeth to do so, like you always see the characters do in television shows … well, two things really to consider. One, I'd seen how easy it was to breach a circle made of salt or such by accident. As shown by DI Gregory Allen when he scuffed the ward jumping to my defence. That sort of rookie mistake has been the downfall of many practitioners throughout the ages, and is the reason why so many summoned demons and spirits get loose to cause mayhem and chaos. The other was more practical. Have you ever tried to clean up chalk or scattered salt from the floor, after you've worked it into the wood or carpet surface? It's practically impossible to ever fully get rid of, and if Jessica did have any minor flaws, it was a predilection towards neatness and tidiness.

Leaving coffee mugs out on the desks downstairs, without stacking them in the nearby dishwasher, would often lead to the lycan responsible being assigned the least enjoyable hunt or task she had on her books. It was an excellent teaching method, given how no-one ever fancied a return visit to talk to the grimalkins or a hunt through the sewers clogged with mortal waste if they could help it.

And yes, I know I'd been in contact with those smelly goblins more often than not. Probably down to me not learning my lessons all that well. Case in point, I'd left the mug of cold coffee on the table in the meeting room …

Slightly more worrying to my mind, I saw that Jessica had set out several fire extinguishers so that they lay close to hand, and also a bowl of water and several folded bandages and first aid tools. Exactly the sort of triage that you might expect from someone planning to deal with major trauma and potential damage to the immediate surroundings.

I nodded to these, and Jessica simply shrugged.

"Ah have learned from long experience, there is nae harm in planning fer the worst." She answered seriously, as she drew out a vintage silver lighter and walked over to begin igniting the candles. "And who is tae say these are fer you or I? Yer contact, Terrigyle, has been suffering at the hands of the Furies these past weeks. I cannae but think his physical state may be less than healthy."

"Fair point." I admitted, realising I'd been actively avoiding thinking about just *what* state the gnome might be in. As I've mentioned, those we handed our prey over to were not known to be fair and easy on them. *Eternal torment and suffering* being key words to describe what anyone who broke the Accords should expect, rather than slippers, a fluffy robe and a gentle massage.

So yeah, most likely Terrigyle would be in a bad way as they'd had him for weeks. But gnomes, like any troll-kin, were known for their resilience. And he'd been more a stupid tag-a-longer than an actual conspirator and part of the Mistress'es inner circle. I had hoped the Furies had been a little more lenient on him than her.

"Are you ready, Morgan?" Jessica asked as she finished lighting the last candle. When I nodded, she motioned for me to join her in the second warding, stepping in beside me. The circle must have been keyed to her somehow, as I didn't see Jessica do anything but I felt the thing activate. It was like a rush of static electricity over my skin, grounding itself through my feet.

I held my breath, waiting for … something.

A moment passed, then another, so I loosed my breath and looked across at my Alpha.

"Don't you have to, I don't know, call them?" I queried, knowing how I'd had to summon the Bayun Cat and the Morrigan by naming them thricely. "Or at least flip the metaphysical sign to '*Next caller please*' or something?"

Jessica just shook her head.

"Nae need. They come. Prepare yerself." She told me, nudging my ribs as I saw the air around the other circle start to shimmer like a heat haze, or how oil moves on water.

The disturbance intensified, writhing in the air as *something* fought to break through an invisible barrier. Faces pressed against that wall, wretched and agonised as they screamed in silent torment, fingers stretching out to claw and scratch for any chance of freedom from their fate. The pressure built in the room, so that I had to grit my teeth against the blood pounding in my ears. Beside me, Jessica remained calm and seemingly untouched, but even I noted the slight narrowing of her eyes. The only sign she too felt any discomfort.

The disturbance boiled within the circle, until finally, with a violent eruption the air split. A wave of sound … screams and bellows and cries … washed over us, from every type of voice, formless and without words yet clear in the story of pain they told. Something flashed, like a magnesium spark blazing in oxygen. I shook my head, closing my eyes against the brilliant brightness, then realised the cries and screams had vanished. Cut off, as if a switch had been flicked.

Standing there, in the protective circle, in the sudden silence with my eyes closed did not seem the cleverest idea so I braced myself and faced the other warding … and looked over.

And beheld the Furies.

Chapter 14

Well, Fury at least. One of the sisters.

She stood in the warding circle, smoke rising from all around her as if she had stepped from a blazing inferno or just dropped through the earth's atmosphere. Which, given her appearance, was entirely possible.

I'd gotten used to recently seeing immortals blend in with the current look and feel of the Mortal Realm. Witches dressed as businesswomen in smart-tailored suits. Gnomes in waistcoats and tweed. Even grimalkin wearing what could be loosely described as a uniform. Even Oberon and Titania had modelled themselves off the perfection of mortal fitness and beauty, mirroring those lesser creatures.

So it was a slight shock to the system to find the Furies hadn't gotten the memo, or just didn't care.

She stood about ten feet tall, towering over us from where she had settled in the warding circle. A pair of hooked and scarred wings were folded behind her, rising above her head and terminating in a set of vicious long spurs set into the folded joints. The Fury was clad in dark armour, moulded to her body and consisting of a tight-fitting bodice and chest piece, flaring down over her hips and covering her thighs in graven plates of some sort of metal. Chains wrapped around her shoulders and back, fastening the plates to her and dangling down to drape her shoulders and legs with differing lengths. A belt of links encircled her waist, upon which was hung a pair of viciously curved hand scythes, gleaming in the light with wicked edges.

Whilst she was, in appearance, abundantly female given how little the top half of her armour concealed, the Fury exuded an air of menace and threat that rivalled that of Madb, the chill Queen of Shadow. She wore a close-fitting skull cap that covered her forehead and eyes, leaving her seemingly blind, and the locks that fell from her scalp were serpent-like and bound with rings of metal, barbed and hooked. I couldn't help but notice how crooked her fingers were as she rested her arms at her side, with curving talons like some ancient bird of prey, and that her legs slimmed down to end in sharp hooves, split and bound with more metal to make a kick from either foot equally lethal.

The Fury's skin was a ruddy hue, patterned with strange looking tattoos that constantly writhed and shifted about her body. The affect was made even more unsettling when I noted some of the wording change, becoming legible. Words like *torture, pain, rend, tear* and *shatter* appearing then slipping back into whatever other language the script was written in.

All in all, not only was the Fury *not* something I'd like to bump into down a dark alley late at night, but not anything I wanted to meet in the full light of day, in any circumstance. Her very presence unsettled me somehow, leaving me feeling weak and off-balance. And definitely more than a touch scared.

"**I SEE YOU, JESSICA WALKER.**" The Fury spoke, its voice rasping and filled with inhuman tones. Even though bound, her head swung round to face us, focusing on where we stood with pinpoint accuracy. The blank mask covering her eyes made it difficult to work out who she was looking at, but I decided the wise cause of action here was to stay quiet until I needed to speak.

"Ah see you, Tisiphone." Jessica replied, and I guessed this was a ritual greeting between Alpha and boss. "Ah thought we might be expecting your other sisters?"

The Fury shook her head, the bands of metal clattering and striking each other in a discordant, angry tone.

"**NO, JESSICA WALKER. MY SISTERS ARE DETAINED ELSEWHERE.**" The Fury replied, her voice the growl of rusted cogs grinding together. "**ONE ONLY OF US NEED ATTEND, FOR ALL OF US TO DECIDE. WHAT ONE KNOWS, ALL KNOW.**"

Then Tisiphone switched that unseeing gaze across, and I felt the weight of her hidden eyes settle on me.

"**IS THIS THE ONE WHO SEEKS THE BOON OF US?**" She asked as I gritted my teeth against the sudden unsettling feeling washing over me. It was like pins and needles all over my body, that not-quite-agonising but still painful feeling of blood rushing back in after you'd cut it off for a short while to a limb.

My Alpha nudged me, and I focused, meeting those hidden eyes as best I could.

"I see you, Tisiphone. I am Morgan Black, of the Walker pack …" I began, using the same greeting as Jessica.

But Tisiphone reared up, skin blazing with an inner fire and her tattoos writhing with greater fury.

"**LIES! YOU SHALL NOT UTTER UNTRUTHS TO ME OR MY KIN!**" The Fury snarled, and I took a step back, only remembering in time that I stood in a warding circle. I shot Jessica a confused look, and she shook her head as well, equally puzzled.

"Uh, I didn't think I *was* lying." I spoke back up, facing the smoking, crimson skinned immortal. "What did I say wrong?"

"**I TASTE YOUR NATURE, AND YOUR BLOOD IS NOT OF THE WALKER PACK.**" The Fury corrected me with that grinding voice of hers. "**BLOODKIN OF MORRIGAN NA CROB DERG. SON OF HERNE NE EACHTHIGHEIRN. CHILD OF THE WYLD. THAT IS YOUR NATURE. THAT IS WHO YOU ARE. SPEAK TRUTH IF YOU WOULD ADDRESS ME OR MY SISTERS, OR NOT AT ALL.**"

I forced myself not to roll my eyeballs in exasperation, remembering just how much store immortals high and low put in introductions and family connections. It had been *so* much easier when I was an orphan, adopted and without roots anywhere.

"Fine, I apologise." I growled out, barely gritting my teeth with a supreme effort of will. "I'll try that again. I see you, Tisiphone. I am Morgan Black, son of Herne and grandchild of the Morrigan. I come asking a boon of you and your sisters. The return of one handed to you for punishment."

The Fury made an all-too-mortal sounding sniff at my corrected introduction, but eventually she gave one single nod. I saw the colour of her skin fade back to its quieter shade, and the tattoos settle into the more lethargic rhythm, which I could only assume meant she had calmed down a notch.

Way to go, not provoking the scary as hell immortal!

"I ask that you release Terrigyle Munstrum back into my custody, so that he can assist with a hunt I am bound to." I soldiered on, realising how careful I'd have to be with my wording given my habit of fudging the truth or telling only half the story. I hadn't encountered anything like the Fury before, combining lie detector and executioner in one bundle of joy. "I also ask that you consider his sentence served, with this final act aiding our lycan pack hunt a much greater threat to the Accords and mortals. I honestly believe his involvement in the attempt upon the Ivory Court was not entirely his fault, or made with him not being in his right mind."

Tisiphone eyed me from behind that enshrouding helmet, cocking her head as she tasted my words and sought for any untruth or attempt to mislead her. Finally, she took a step to one side, remaining in the circle but revealing the other occupant who had until then remained unseen behind her.

Terrigyle sat on the cloth, his familiar smoking jacket, waistcoat and assorted scarves all replaced with a baggy sack-like garment, ripped and torn, with hanks of what looked like prickly hay barbs sticking out from the rents. If the thing was as stuffed with those as it looked, it would be an absolute torture having to wear something so scratchy and uncomfortable. Chains bound him at wrist and ankle, effectively hobbling him and keeping him from moving anywhere without extreme difficulty.

All in all, the gnome weapons-dealer and trader in information was as sorry a sight as I could imagine.

He finally looked up from where he had been gazing at the floor, taking in his surroundings and finally who it was who stood opposite him. I'd expected anger, a tirade of verbal abuse from the gnome given how I had been the one to capture him, freezing him in place with my Shadow Court gift as the only way to stop him attacking me. And I'd ruined a perfectly good sea mine he had set to explode … well, Jacob had done the ruining when he punched a hole through it and mangled the mechanism, but only after I'd asked him to stop the bloody thing. Given those facts, I wasn't expecting the gnome to be overjoyed at seeing me.

Just goes to show, I can't be good at everything. Reading people really wasn't my forte.

"Morgan! Me ol' mucka! Oh oi'm glad to see you!" Teri cried out, clambering with some difficulty to his bare feet. "You springing me from this 'ellish torment or wot?"

I noticed then that the chains binding him led back up to the other's belt, fixed amongst the links there to bind the pair together.

"**THIS IS THE ONE YOU WISH TO ASSIST YOU WITH YOUR HUNT?**" The Fury asked, her voice full of those unnatural grinding tones but even I couldn't miss the slight note of disbelief in her words. "**YOU ARE SURE?**"

"Oi!" Terri glared up at his captor, gnome features scrunching up as he squirmed in his chains. "If moi mate Morgan say 'e needs me, then 'e needs me. Don't go besmirching me good name, an' suggesting 'e's not thinking straight or some'at!"

Then the gnome switched his attention back to me.

"Now, wot is it you need 'elp wiv?"

I decided the best option was to speak to the Fury first and foremost, given that the gnome was still technically a prisoner.

"I need Terrigyle's knowledge of the troll underworld." I replied, again choosing my words carefully. "I'm hunting three loners, no clan affiliations or ties to any known criminal organisations. They've kidnapped young mortal women, maybe men too and sold them on for spare parts to a mortal buyer so *technically* they aren't breaking any Accord laws. Just a whole lot of mortal ones."

I nodded to the gnome, whose face had screwed up with disgust as he heard what the creatures I was hunting had been up to. He might sell weapons with little or no regard to how they were used and on whom, but the gnome did have some moral code.

"Teri knows where they might be holed up, especially as their buyer is cleaning shop and tying up loose ends leading back to him. Permanently."

As I said this, I realised just how crafty Knox had been. Skirting the Accord laws so that in theory his activity to date was still not worth the notice of the Furies, but by working through denizens of the Real, he also fell outside the standard mortal law enforcement's jurisdiction. Basically he'd arranged so that only OPS and us lycans would be the ones hunting him, and he'd played us both too bloody well.

"Oh yeah, oi can definitely fink of a few places that sorta scum might go t'hide." Teri spoke up, shaking his large head with a moralistic tutt. "You'll be wanting t' hit the seediest and filthiest bars in this 'ere place, and you ain't getting in any of 'em wivout someone loike me along. A bloody Redcloak knockin' on the door? They'll have kittens, well, if the filthy buggers ain't eaten 'em, that is."

"You see? Perfect gnome for the job." I told the Fury, who spared a single glance down at Terrigyle. The gnome quickly shut his mouth and hung his head.

"IT WOULD SEEM SO. I CANNOT ARGUE THE LOGIC OF YOUR CASE FOR THIS PRISONER." Tisiphone growled out, but then raised one finger towards me. "BUT MY SISTERS AND I ARE AGREED. TERRIGYLE MUNSTRUM MUST BE PUNISHED FOR HIS CRIME. HE ENDANGERED MORTAL LIFE AND PROVIDED THE MEANS TO THREATEN THE IVORY COURT. THAT CANNOT BE CHANGED."

The Fury gestured, and the chains wrapping the gnome gave an unnatural shiver, flexing like the coils of a metallic snake before unwinding and sliding back down his squat form and clinking up to wrap around her waist once more. Terrigyle gave a groan of pleasure, straightening from his hunch as he found himself suddenly able to stand without the hobbling restraints.

"USE THE PRISONER TO LOCATE THESE TROLL-KIN YOU SEEK. FIND THEM, THEN CALL ON ME AND I SHALL RETURN TO COLLECT HIM FOR HIS PUNISHMENT." She focused on me, and I felt the air around me heat under the intensity of her focus. "SHOULD YOU FAIL TO CALL ME, OR SEEK TO PERVERT THE COURSE OF JUSTICE, I SHALL JUDGE **YOU**, CHILD OF THE WYLD. WE ARE DONE."

Before I could even begin to think of a reply to that statement, the air split once more with agonised screams. The Fury vanished into that maelstrom of torment, the cries cutting off as the portal closed behind her.

Leaving Terrigyle huddled in the centre of the Warding, looking back at me a hopeful expression on his wrinkled features.

"'Ere, me mate. Any chance we can swing by me gaff 'fore we go huntin' these reprobates of yours. Just so's oi can pick up some of me ol' threads?" The gnome asked, motioning down at the sackcloth he wore. "A gnome's repootation is wot he lives by, an' oi don't really wanna be seen dead in this stuff, know wot oi mean?"

Chapter 15

Bedivere.

Known as the one-handed Knight of the Round Table, Bedivere fought alongside Artur against the giant of Mont Saint-Michel as well as a number of other giant-kin. He was referred to as 'the most handsome man in the whole world' whilst at court.

He is also famous for his actions when Artur was mortally wounded. Told to return Excalibur to the Lady of the Lake, twice he went to toss the sword into the waters but held back — thinking the artefact too dear to throw away. Artur is reported to have admonished him, and finally he tossed the sword into the waters, where the Lady took it and returned it to Avalon.

They say there's no rest for the wicked.

It's also fair to say there's no rest for a sucker lycan and his gnome sidekick, when there are disreputable trolls to find, and seedy troll bars and stripclubs to search.

Yeah, you heard me. Troll *stripclubs*.

After checking with Jessica, and being told this was my hunt, so it was down to me how I handled the gnome put into my safekeeping … with the full knowledge any mistakes and repercussions were mine to handle also … I agreed with Terrigyle to allow him a change of clothes and a wash, whilst I also picked up the one item I knew was mandatory for this hunt.

I just made a mental note never to let Bear know I'd considered him an 'item'. The sofa would not survive his very physical response to that sort of slip up.

I'd used one of our *special* cabs, those that were fitted to deal with sights even the most hardened London cabbie might not be prepared to keep quiet about. Oh, don't get me wrong, the 'normal´ taxis I booked through *Good Deeds* often were witness to me in various states of bloody and battered disrepair, or having me store suspicious bags in the boot that might make the odd sound when I squashed them in … but that was still fairly vanilla compared to them actually ferrying one of the Real denizens around.

This meant the cab driver was boxed in and separate from where we sat, with the screens all darkened and no cameras rolling for him record anything he shouldn't. The insides were also soundproofed, with the agreement that *if* the cab driver, at the end of the ride, found the vehicle in *any* state of disrepair, damaged or not usable for standard mortal fares, *Good Deeds* would be charged the full cost of a new car at the very least.

I always made sure to clean up the blood before I ever stepped out of the cab, and vented any bad smells into the London air well before disembarking. I costed the office enough in mobile phones and taxi fares, without risking Jessica's wrath if I ever did something so stupid as to not clear up after me.

Anyhow, we'd bounced from the office to Camden Market, where Terrigyle made a quick dash into his troll-hole via the tradesman's entrance. This was down to the market being closed, and his front door being located inside another shop that was firmly locked for the night. It was a matter of trust, me standing amidst crates of unopened stock, packaged weapons of every shape and form, whilst he rid himself of the scratchy prisoner's outfit and washed as much of the barbs off his skin before hunting up more familiar attire. But then, I was going to have to give him the benefit of the doubt at some point that night, otherwise I'd be expecting him to try to escape at every moment … and be jumping at shadows when I needed to focus.

I've been duped before, and trusted when I should have done otherwise, but in this instance it *felt* right to allow the gnome some small privacy, and to feel clean clothes that didn't scrape his skin like sandpaper. Guess I'm a bit of sucker, when it comes down to it.

Refreshed, outfitted in a tweed jacket, checked shirt, soft cloth waistcoat and rugged trousers with matching hobnail boots and a flat cap perched on his high forehead, Terrigyle rejoined me with a handful of dried meat to chew on, and one of those fill-for-free plastic cups you get at festivals with an attached straw. From the smell wafting from the container, he'd poured a large measure of whiskey and coke into the thing, and was industriously sucking down a mouthful as he followed me back to the waiting cab.

From there, I directed our driver across town to my home, to pick up Bear. It wasn't a short journey, but I knew I'd need the trollhound if anything went sideways with the hunt, and I'd promised to let him stretch his legs at the next opportunity. Besides … as trusting as I was being with Teri, I reckoned having Bear along *might* make him think twice about doing a runner … knowing I had the perfect hunting dog to track him down and give him a thorough ass-kicking for messing me around.

"Oi'm so glad you pulled from that bloody nightmare!" Terri admitted as we barrelled through the empty streets of London.

"Yeah, well, as much as I'd like to say I did it coz we're mates, you need to know it's about the hunt first and foremost." I answered him, eliciting a nod and grin from the gnome. "I still don't get how you were so stupid, hooking up with the Mistress and thinking to blow up the bloody Ivory Court and a bunch of mortals. It's not your style."

"You got me bang ter rights, mate." Terri replied, knocking one fist against his thick skull. "Dunno wot I was finking, but at the time, it were like it all made perfick sense. And that old naval mine were a fing of beauty, mate, I don't mind admitting. None of this modern muck with compewters and artificial intelligence, and all that guff. Straight forward an' simple, as it should be."

"So, it was bad then?" I shifted the subject away from dwelling on the explosive the gnome had planned to set off under the Mistress's instruction, seeing that glow he got in his eyes when he spoke about weapons. The last thing I needed was him getting fixated again about blowing something up.

"Oh, mate, you wouldn't credit it." Terri groaned, leaning back in his seat and covering his eyes at the memory.

"Spikes, knives, pointy things being introduced to you slowly and painfully I'm guessing?" I wasn't all that interested in the details of the gnome's torture, but the Fury's parting threat had me wondering just what I might have to look forward to. I know, I do wonder some truly weird stuff at times.

"Well, there were some of that but nuffink I ain't had done t'me 'fore by cheapskate customers tryin' t'cut a deal on me merchandise." Teri admitted with a shrug. "Someone always finks they can threaten me, 'urt me and oi'll give the stuff fer free. Bloody morons."

"Nah, dem Furies, they knew wot to do to me pretty soon after they'd poked me a few times and got nuffink." He continued, shivering at the memories. "Bloody awful creatures, they get inside yer head. Find out wot really messes you up, then lands you neck deep in it right proper."

Teri shook his head and lowered his hand, revealing his eyes. They shone with memories of what had been done to him, haunted and pain-filled.

"Made me wake up inna world full of bloody peacemakers, of all fings. No one fighting, no arguing. No conflict whatsoeva. No one needing merch from me, not even fer sentimental reasons. No one even wanting t'talk about weapons. All love, hugs and kindness. All that sorta crap." He shivered, shaking his head at the thought. "No one argued, everyone was each other's pal. It were frankly disgusting, and it just went on and on. Oi 'ad to attend *ferapy* sessions to talk about me 'problems' and share how oi felt. They kept giving me hugs and clapping when oi spoke, no matter wot crap oi spouted. On and on, till oi were ready to scream … then they'd smile an' start all over again. Ova an' ova."

The gnome looked me in the eye, expression grim in that moment of memory.

"Oi'm telling you, mate. Oi 'eard wot the Fury said but oi don't wanna go back there. Not to that sort of torture." He told me bluntly. "Give me needles, baseball bats … the works. Do me over good and proper, but not that."

I held up my hands, feeling more than a little conflicted right now.

"It's not up to me, mate." I knew what the Fury had said, how Terrigyle had to serve his time. But there had to be some sort of negotiation, some chance to get him a reprieve. Treating him like the Mistress or the offenders we'd handed over for eternal punishment just didn't seem totally fair to me. "I still can try to get you time off for good behaviour. If we can find these trolls, who knows? They might listen to me."

"Yer, mate. Let's go find these little shits and see if that makes the sisters re-fink me punishment." Teri didn't look like he had much faith in that outcome ever happening, but at least he didn't try to dive out the window and make a break for freedom. Yet.

At my home, I found Danny and Felix had already left, cleaning up after themselves. They'd left me a note, to just say they'd be heading home and working on Felix's control of her new gifts. A big thanks for still being around, and for me to give them a call whenever I was free next to head over. Danny promised to send round a batch of his pastrami, gherkin and rye with whatever special sauce he used that made them so delicious … and a last comment from Felix to say she'd tried to call Elspeth but the witch hadn't picked up. So could I let her know that Felix was thinking about her, and if she needed anything, to just call?

Simple stuff, the sort of message mortals left for each other all the time – a little island of normality amongst all the weird shit going on right now. It was refreshing.

Bear was only too happy to see me, meeting me at the staircase with his harness and lead in his mouth, eyes pricked up expectantly. I took a moment to catch Goldspur up on all things being ok, and that I'd be out with my mutt for the evening so not to worry if we weren't back till late … well, later.

It felt a little weird telling the dryad all this, since she had in no way demanded to know where I'd been, what was happening and why I was taking Bear away. In that, she was the perfect house guest, I reckon … but it still didn't feel right ignoring her or treating her like a thing, rather than a person. A green-skinned, somewhat well-endowed and murderously efficient person, maybe, but the point was still valid.

Hustling the trollhound down and only stopping to let him relieve himself on the nearby bushes, I pulled open the taxi door and manhandled Bear into the open floor space. Terrigyle had retreated to the furthest corner of the taxi, pulling his legs up and doing his very best not to be intimidated by the sheer size of the beast I was currently filling the floorspace with.

For his part, Bear simply took a long sniff in the gnome's direction, hackles rising a little until he cocked his head and shot me a questioning look.

"Gnome, mate. Not troll. He's off the menu." I instructed as I pushed his hindlegs and backside up and into the taxi. "Now settle down."

Huffing, Bear shook himself before turning a few times to crush down the imaginary grass beneath him then thudding down onto the taxi floor. I pulled the door shut behind me, and slipped into the free seat. I'd brought along my grab bag with suitable body armour and weapons that might be useful depending on the reception we got, wherever it was Teri ended up leading us to.

"Ok, so where do we start?" I queried, knowing the taxi would just sit outside my home idling until I pinged the driver our next location. Burning a hole in my company expenses. "If I'd hazard a guess where to find a deep troll dive? Obvious place would be Soho, but I reckon that's too full of mortals. Uh, Kings Cross?"

"Nah mate, you're barking up the wrong tree completely there! Soho's for the mugs, yer right on the ball there. Bloody High Court fae swanking around knockin' back cocktails wiv dem mortals. But Kings Cross? That's been *urbanised* or somesuch nonsense. Even swankier than Soho these days." Teri grinned nastily. "These trolls yer after. You said they're Clanless. How bad would you say they were, in terms of wiping the shit offa yer foot bad, or worse?"

"They were cooking Thames seagulls to eat as a stew, and smelt like they'd bathed with the dead birds beforehand." I remembered the three rag-clad creatures, the matted filth and sorry state the three of them had presented when I burst into the hut. "I'd say …. Worse."

"Roight you are then, guv." Teri nodded as I confirmed what he had been thinking. "There's only one place fer trolls that low. We gotta be where fings are truly mucky and dark. Where even the mortals 'oo hang around there are as moral as cockroaches. So it's Westminster fer us."

And you know what? That really didn't come as that much of a surprise to me.

Chapter 16

By the time we reached the heart of Westminster, with Big Ben towering off in the distance and the searchlight-lit Houses of Parliament hunkering down across a chunk of the skyline like a lethargic lizard clinging to a rock, it was late enough that few mortals were out and about on the usually busy streets.

Which suited me just fine, as I reckoned the three of us made an interesting spectacle to draw all manner of unwanted attention.

Me in dark combats slightly bulky in odd places where armour plates were carefully concealed, with a matching roll-bag clanking quietly over one shoulder. With Bear on a chunky and much knotted lead linked to his oversized harness, even at his mortal-friendly size towering over any other dog or animal out on the streets unless a bear had escaped from the nearby zoo. And then there was Terrigyle, waddling along with his stiff legged gait, flat clap firmly jammed on his head and chewing on some unidentifiable meat strip he'd picked up from home.

Not your average group to be seen strolling the streets of the capital, in one of the wealthiest districts filled to the brim with politicians, religious leaders and assorted mortals from specific backgrounds where they learned to speak through their front teeth and pronounce Westminster with an '*ah*' at the end.

At the same time, I had to remind myself this was *also* one of the most morally corrupt and debauchery-entrenched places in London. Where the sort of crimes committed were either on such a grandiose scale that local law enforcement wouldn't touch them with a very long stick, or were so devious and complicated that it was hard to tell which rules they actually broke.

As such, it really didn't surprise me to find the troll community had set up shop, and made their own gutter town out of the sewers right below the feet of the mortals. The signs were there if I looked hard enough … amongst the redbrick town houses and iron-gated gardens, I saw troll glyphs scrawled beside steps leading down to basement apartments, and sewer grates with enough scratches on them to show they were often moved. There was also a distinct lack of pigeons congregating on the street pavements, always on the hunt for something to peck at, or rats to be seen furtively scurrying within the safety of shadows and rubbish. This being London, rats got *everywhere* as Rous and Molly had so indicated, so the fact that I couldn't sense any of the vermin around us as we walked down the darkened streets told me something simple. That ever-hungry and not so fussy trolls were making the most of the delicacies to hand. Or claw.

At least it wasn't bloody seagulls.

In my time as a Redcloak, I'd visited quite a few bars and eating houses set up by Real denizens now settled this side of the Veil. They tended to be perfect places to hunt down leads, pick up the local gossip and occasionally hide away from the mortals when I'd had too much of their noise and chaos. I generally found the establishments to be a home from home for diners and drinkers alike, like the themed bars and pubs mortals frequented whenever they went abroad, for a little taste of home and something familiar. Even if it was all artifice and as fake as leprechaun gold.

Fae bars were usually filled with glamour and exotic otherness, with live bands playing discordant melodies and illusions spun to excite and thrill the audience. As a rule, the drinks and food on offer would be overpriced and served in odd looking glasses and on platters of beaten precious metal. There would be at least one poor sap slumped in a corner, giggling at something only they could see, given how the fae of either Court dealt in proscribed substances and delights that *should* never have made it to the Mortal Realm but somehow always did. As long as it was the locals who partook, and the enchanted dust or fairy glitter or whatever they were dealing never made it into mortal hands, the suppliers managed to stay out of our hunts and ignored by the Courts.

Most fae bars were actively spelled to repel mortals, with visual glamours to indicate the establishment was closed for a private party, or were only accepting members that night. Or by appearing closed, and dampening the noise from inside, or sometimes by appearing under construction and not yet open. Very rarely did they allow anyone not of the Courts or their kin in through the door, not only to avoid any *accidents* that would draw unwanted attention but also for the simple fact that as soon as you let one mortal in, a whole bunch of them would follow, and start complaining about the music, the price of drinks and the fact they weren't serving their favourite lager or cocktail.

Goblin bars were a different kettle of water-dwelling denizens, as the Wyld fae delighted in welcoming in mortals and playing innocent tricks on them. Often designed to look like dirty, grimy grunge-bars, the goblins would invent weird menus to test if anyone was brave enough or desperate enough to try to order the *swamp burger* or *bleeding heart mocktail*. They would also often let their glamour slip just for a moment, so that the mortals would see something out of the corner of their eye that didn't look right … a bulbous nose, green skin or long pointed ears … but by the time they focused on the worrying detail, the glamour was back in place and the local would act offended for the attention paid them.

I'd heard that in America, a lot of the Real goblins formed biker gangs, roaring around the long roads on their chrome hogs, and tricking unsuspecting mortals whenever they stumbled into one of their roadside bars for a quick drink and to use the toilet. I think it's where a lot of the rumours about the bikers being Satanists originate from.

Now, on the other end of the spectrum were the troll bars. On the whole, trolls aren't that social and don't get together for a chat over a pint or get the urge to prove whichever one of the pack has the worst singing voice by mangling popular tunes and calling it *fun*. Instead, trolls tended to congregate at their most miserabilist, finding company in other troll-kin when they were feeling the whole world was against them … which it generally was. Greater trolls, the mountain types that were more geography than anything else, and the smarter lesser trolls tended not to frequent such dives, either because they were simply too massive to get through the door, or the simple fact they too couldn't stand their miserable lesser kin who made up the establishment's regular cohort.

No, troll bars were by nature grim, depressing places filled with creatures who not only were the scum of their own kin's social hierarchy, but also the punching bags and kick-balls for pretty much every other Real creature around. Trolls ranked even lower than grimalkins in terms of being detested, spat on and used only for the worst possible tasks imaginable.

Plenty of fantastical tales begin in a grungy bar, with a surly bar-keeper, dubious beer on tap and the sort of mood lighting that would make a funeral look like a firework festival. If those tales had started in a troll-bar, however, the bar taps would have been connected to the urinals in the toilets … if they in fact had any … whilst any shape-changing elf would have found themselves on the menu the moment they took animal form, and the wise storyteller who chanced by to give the heroes their first lead would have turned tail and fled as soon as they took one look inside and breathed in.

It would be a very short, very grim story. With no happy ending.

But despite this, when trolls gathered together for a communal sulk and general life-is-shit session, there was one thing which kept them from all agreeing to greet the dawn hand in hand and be turned to stone to get it all over with. One glimmer in even the scummiest and most deviant troll's mind that gave them pleasure.

Beauty.

And not the superficial beauty of a glamour model or Instagram influencer, those fake sculpted souls air-touched beyond reality by mortals seeking to match the glamour spun by fae.

No.

Trolls are drawn to the beauty of artifacts crafted with care and skill, from the most precious of substances which shine and glitter no matter how old they are. In fact, the older, the better which was one of the main reasons the lesser troll-kin were so adapt at stealing, purloining and generally obtaining through illegal means high priced objects. Objects that mortals kept locked up and supposedly safe from the riff-raff and scum their owners considered the rest of their kith and kin. Otherwise they'd pay less for private security and probably sleep better at night.

So what came as a surprise to me, much to Terrigyle's delight, was an introduction to troll-kin's intermingling of both the artistic and sordid desire. I had, at this point, never been to a troll *strip-club*.

Bear, at this point, was proving his worth ten times over. The troll hound was having the time of his life, sniffing out the one species his entire kin were genetically keyed to hunt and doing it in the Mortal Realm.

Following the massive hound as he pulled me along the streets of Westminster, Bear dragged the pair of us to the back of a newsagents shop and to a downstairs flat that looked boarded up and abandoned … except for the sullen troll lurking in a side nook, who only challenged us when my troll hound sniffed him out and growled like rumbling thunder with his snout pressed to the bouncer. Who honestly looked like it was going to wet itself even as it challenged with a *'what the 'ell were we doin' scaring honest troll folk jus' doin' their job'*.

Terrigyle, to his credit, proved my need for him had been firmly based in reality. Where Bear scared the bouncers into almost catatonic submission, it was the gnome who got us through the door and able to search both places for the Bung brothers with only the barest of grumbles and complaints from the locals where they lurked and hid away in the shadows.

Two bars, two strikes. There were definitely one or two drinkers I'd want to look up when this whole shitstorm was over, but none of them the smelly bastards I was hunting for. So with muttered thanks to the sullen bar-trolls as they watched us suspiciously from behind the plank and barrels they were serving whatever passed for a drinks menu, we ducked back out of each drinking hole with only a few moments of struggling with Bear to get him to leave without taking a bite out of anyone.

The third place Bear sniffed out for us was at the end of Dacre Street, with the offices of New Scotland Yard looming as a backdrop as we walked down the paved roadway. One of London's most well-known law enforcement offices. And as such, perfect for trolls to use as a cover for their seediest drinking hole. And a personal education to me, as it turned out.

Down a flight of stairs, with cardboard boxes stacked up on either side and old takeaway boxes littered underfoot, we found ourselves standing outside a suspiciously serious-looking door. Heavily reinforced, with the hinges hidden away and a single slot in the surface for whomever was on the inside to check out whoever was disturbing them from the outside. Just the sort of thing you *didn't* expect to see at the bottom of a rubbish-strewn stairwell.

Terrigyle motioned for me to stand back, holding Bear who was panting heavily and straining at his leash. Then he stepped up to the door and rapped hard on the metal several times. Echoes rebounded from his knocks, as the gnome set his flat cap firmly on his head and squared off as we waited for the slot to open.

It did, with a squeal of rusted metal, and a single bloodshot eyeball stared out through the gap.

"Wot u want?" A voice growled out, the eyeball trying to peer past Terrigyle as he stepped up to the door.

"Wot anyone wants mate, coming 'ere." He replied with a grin. "A bit o' a drink, maybe some social chit-chat. Oh and an eyeful of true bootifulism, if you take me meaning."

The gnome reached into an inner pocket of his waistcoat and pulled out something that glittered in the dim light shed by a street lamp above us. Focusing, I saw that it was a heavy gold bracelet, of twisted strands. The sort you see on late night shopping channels on television, modelled by a mortal woman and described with words like *hue, purity* and *the sort of gift your girlfriend or wife will adore you forever if she receives this. And yours for only three payments of $99.99…*

This he held up, and carefully inserted into the gap in the door. The eyeball retreated, the cover slid back and then there was the unmistakable crunch of teeth on metal as the door guard checked the trinket's authenticity the old-fashioned way.

Terrigyle shot a glance back at me, whilst we waited for the guard to finish masticating the gold.

"Uh, mate, any chance oi can get a receipt from yer boss fer that?" The gnome asked hopefully. "Oi reckon oi won't be seeing that little fing again, an' if oi do, it'll be wiv some nasty fuckers' teef in in it."

I shook my head, knowing what Jessica would say about company expenses and trusting whether the gold bracelet in question was actually real or fake, and would disappear the next morning with a touch of sunlight.

"Oi reckoned as much. Oh well." Terrigyle turned back just as the grate opened up again and the eyeball reappeared.

"Yer all good t' come in." The voice grated, then managed to see over Terrigyle's head. "Oii! Is that a bloody troll hound? Nuffink doin', letting that fing in 'ere! And wot's with the other bloke? Whose 'e?!"

I stepped forward, shushing Bear as he bristled and started his growl deep in his chest. The one that was a short fuse just before he went off like a landmine and blew up everything in a twenty-foot radius.

"I'm nobody. And he's my seeing dog. See things that I don't." I smiled grimly at the eyeball, then nodded to the cast iron and very solid door. "Like he's seen just what happens if that door doesn't open and you don't let us in now you've taken the trinket. And it doesn't end well for you, or for the door."

Now, the troll *could* have kept the door closed, could have called for help to deal with a potentially lippy customer. Maybe a couple of heavy muscled trolls to put the boot in and vent some of their combined frustrations on, dealing with an idiot who thought he could bully a door guard.

It was all in the tone. Just enough threat to hold them, just enough control to make them think they really only had one choice. The one I wanted them to take.

The door made an ugly squeal as it slowly swung open. The troll behind it was about nine feet tall, but stooped over with thick muscles bunching up under its gnarled hide. It had multiple piercings, all non-toxic copper, studding its heavy eyebrows and thick lips. Both eyeballs now glared at me, then down at Bear, then finally settled on Terrigyle who stood in front of us, looking thoroughly innocent of bringing trouble to the troll's door.

"One drink minimum, an' keep yer hands ter yerselves. And that dog better not make no trouble." The door guard growled, then stepped back to allow us inside. "Ovawise, don't care who Mr Nobody is, 'e'll be picking his teef offa the floor an' taking the mutt home inna doggie baggie."

Terrigyle nodded, and motioned me to follow him into the shadow hall. I squared my shoulders, and with Bear close at my side, stepped inside.

Chapter 17

Tom a Lincoln.

This character from folklore is known to be the bastard offspring of Artur Pendragon and a young woman called Angelica. Raised by a shepherd, he came to court and was made a Knight of the Round Table but Artur did not reveal his parentage. Instead, Tom was sent on a quest to uncover the truth of where he came from, which did not end well for him.

After a sojourn in the Realm of Fairies where Tom sleeps with the Queen, he and his comrades come to the land of Prester John. There, the Knight defeats a dragon that is plaguing the kingdom, but then runs away with the king's daughter, Anglitora. She gives birth to his son, named the Black Knight, whilst they are voyaging home. They pass through the Fairy Realm, where the Queen has given birth to another son for Tom, naming him the Fairy Knight. Grief stricken that he has not returned for her, she casts herself into the sea and drowns.

When Tom returns to court, Artur finally reveals the Knight's parentage. Finding that Tom is illegitimate, Anglitora promptly slays him. In a fit of pique, Tom's spirit travels to his son, the Black Knight, and tells him what has happened. Enraged, the Black Knight then slays his own mother.

The tale ends with the brothers, Fairy and Black Knights, sojourning off together.

Inside the troll strip club, I took a moment to let my eyes adjust … and to shorten my breath, to stop myself taking more than a half lungful of the heavy musk that hit me like a punch to the face.

Whatever the original layout of the building had been, the trolls had excavated and enlarged on the existing floorplan. That or they'd cheated and used the sort of charm Terrigyle had on his own premises to make them far bigger than they should be.

Whatever, the door led to a short flight of stairs that descended down a wide corridor with fake plants in pots set on either side of the stairs. At the bottom, a curtain divided this entrance from what lay beyond, and above this had been scrawled something in trollish runes.

"Da Gutterz." Terr translated, stepping carefully so as not to stick to the noisome carpet underfoot. "*When all else fails, when you're at your worst … you can always find a welcome in Da Gutterz*'. And most likely company of an affable nature, if you know wot oi mean, mate."

"Great, so the troll version of *Cheers*, with hookers." I grumbled, as I went to pull back the curtain.

"'Old on, mate." The gnome stopped me, voice lowered. "Look, troll bars are one fing, but 'ere, well, I'm suggestin' you walk a little lightly an' let me do the talking."

He nodded to Bear, who was almost drooling as he focused on whatever he was picking up from inside.

"It's bad enouf you brought a troll hound 'ere. But the loikes of them that drink 'ere, well, you start flashin' your red cloak status an' we'll be neck deep in trouble. They'll smell wolf on you, but if you keep quiet and I ask around, de'll most likely think oi hired you fer a bit o' muscle."

Giving it a moment's thought, I shrugged, realising Teri was probably right. I'd specifically sprung him from the Furies for his knowledge and experience in this specific situation, so I'd only be a complete idiot if I chose to ignore him.

Nodding, I noticed him clutching something at his neck as he went to straighten his clothes and settle his cap more firmly on his head.

"What's that?" I asked, seeing him flinch before shrugging.

"Oh, this?" He held up a grimly little necklace, with a tarnished and worn locket attached. "Just me lucky charm, to keep me safe whenever oi find myself in 'arm's way. And around you, me mucka, no offense but dis is definitely dat."

He tucked it back into his shirt front, squared his shoulders and then with the pair of us following, ducked through and into the main hall.

Music filled the air, a dull, throbbing beat that anyone who has frequented certain bars that label their entertainment *artistic dancing* would recognise. We found ourselves on a broad platform, with steps down to the main floor. This was filled with rough-hewn tables and chairs, whilst four central stages formed a square at the centre of the room. These were circular affairs of wood, raised up to allow anyone a good view wherever they sat. Off to the right, a massive bar took up most of the wall with a large selection of dirty bottles stacked behind it. The barman was a tall, gangling troll wearing a dirty apron and a bowler hat of all things, its grey skin mottled with scars and burn marks from exposure to the sun at some point. Smaller, hairy trolls moved between the tables and those customers slumped at them, delivering platters of noxious smelling drinks in reinforced mugs, and collecting the empties with deft skill as the drinkers steadily drank themselves into oblivion.

And up on the four stages, moving as rhythmically as a troll could, four figures gyrated around the platforms. They were clad in strips of scarves, shawls and tattered robes which they slowly drew off with tantalising motions. But where for mortal dancers, the lure would have been of naked flesh, the trolls seemed instead to be slowly revealing an array of precious jewellery worn about their bodies. Torques of beaten gold glinted dully in the dim light, whilst fingers flashed with rings fitted with oversized gemstones … the kind you see in mortal children's make up boxes when they pretended to be adults. Furry ears were studded with golden rings and charms that shimmered with each movement, and even the troll's bodies seemed adorned with more rings and studs to catch the eye.

"See, it's loik this." Terrigyle whispered to me as we stepped down the stairs to the main floor. Bear padded beside me, keeping close but swinging his massive head slowly around as we moved amongst the trolls and other kin still upright at their tables, whilst others lay slumped amongst the dregs of their drink, slumbering noisily. "Trolls ain't good lookin' creatures to anyone, even their own selves. So's erotic dancing ain't gonna attract much *clientele* if all they'ze doin' is revealing more of wot repulses them in da first place. But jewellery? Gems, gold, silver … trolls are loik magpies. Drawn to anyfing that glitters. Don't matter if its cheap. Just gotta look shiny."

Up on the stage, one of the troll dancers gyrated too near the edge of their stage, flashing a hairy and gnarled leg adorned with multiple circlets of silver and gold, studded with what looked like green and blue gemstones. One of the patrons, worse for drink or just seeing a chance too good to miss, reared up and pawed at the dancer, latching onto the scarves it still wore and making an earnest attempt to drag … *her* off the platform and into its lap. To be fair, it could have been a male troll dancing, I had no point of reference to really distinguish the sex of the species. But my head went straight to *she*, and stuck there.

The drinker struggled with the dancer briefly, but then the barkeeper emerged from behind its splintered and stained wooden stockade. It held a heavy wooden club, more tree than bat, and with those rangy arms of its, didn't even need to get close before it slugged the patron over the head with a loud *crack*. The drinker stumbled, staggering as the dancer tugged her garments free and scrabbled back onto the platform. Then, with not even a glance down to where the bar troll continued to lay into the stunned drinker with that rough but very effectively weapon, she started her routine all over again.

Professional.

We wended our way through the tables, Terrigyle heading to the large bar with obvious purpose. I decided I might as well act the part he wanted me to play, glaring at anyone who glanced our way or looked to want to say something as we passed. Bear seemed to pick up on my mood, his ruff rising to stand up in spikes and a low throbbing growl rumbling in his chest. More than one troll seemed happy to start an argument with me, but then noticed my hound and did an immediate re-think and found something thoroughly interesting in the bottom of their mug, in the opposite direction to us.

We reached the bar without incident and found a patch that wasn't too sticky or stained with a mixture of alcohol, blood and troll puke from what my nose told me. Terrigyle stepped up onto the raised platform which ran along the base of the bar, bringing him up to an appropriate height to order or at least be seen by whomever … or whatever was serving.

The bar troll finally finished pounding some respect into the groaning, bruised drinker and hauled it back onto its seat. Mortal bouncers might have thrown anyone acting that way out of the establishment and slapped a ban on them, but I guess management took pity on anyone ending up in *Da Gutterz*, and considered a thorough beating enough of a lesson.

"Wot you drinkin'?" The troll barkeeper growled, stowing that big club out of sight but probably kept close to hand. "And we don' have no doggy bowl fer water. That fing can drink outta a mug like anyone else 'ere."

"Ah, guv, oi'll have a mug of Ol' Toby Gubbins, but me mate here and 'is dog won't have anyfink by ways of them being on the job." Terrigyle winked at the troll, slapping a hand down on the bar top with what looked like gold coins underneath. "Better make it a large 'un. I 'ave a mighty furst on me, like."

"Dat's too much even fer drinks for you all." The troll growled, even as it grabbed out a rough wooden tankard that in the gnome's hands would be more a jug, or possibly a small barrel with a handle. Gripping it one handed, the barkeep snagged a dusty and cobwebbed bottle that could have been found in some archaeological dig-site or at the bottom of some old shipwreck. Thumbing the top off, the troll poured a generous measure of the contents into the mug and splashed it down on the bar.

Judging from the smell coming from the mug, whatever Old Toby Gubbins was, it could double as a cleaning agent for any one of the gorier crime-scenes around London. Some of the stuff splashed out of the mug, and oozed on the wooden bar with almost a life of its own. Which, knowing drinks from the Real, it very well could have.

"Ah, that's the monkey's nuts!" Terrigyle awkwardly grabbed up the mug and took a long gulp. Then, wiping a mess from his lips on his sleeve, he nodded to the gold on the bar. "An' that there's fer a little bit of information, like. By way of paying fer your time an' knowledge in this specific need we find ourselves in."

"Wot sort of information?" The troll drew out a dirty rag from somewhere and began scrubbing at the wooden top as if mere cloth and friction could remove the ingrained filth that had settled there from the years and years of spillages. "Dis ain't no library. Is a strip club. Wot you see is wot you get. That simple."

"No, no. Nothing about this 'ere charming establishment." Terrigyle took another gulp of the noxious beverage before continuing. "Oi'm interested in a couple of yer regulars. Some trolls oi'd like to 'ave a word with. In private, like. Fer business reasons."

The troll grunted and pointed to a rough sign that had been propped up against several empty bottles and, disturbingly, a collection of neatly picked bones.

No grabbers, pukers, welchers or troublemakers - on pain of pain.

No snitches, tattle-tellers or squealers - on pain of confiscation of tongues.

Lawfolk will be eaten.

"Oh no, mate." Terrigyle held up his hands, sliding the mug to one side. "Do oi look like the law ter you? Me? Gotta be 'avin' a mucky chuckle ain't you?"

The troll grunted, obviously not entirely convinced but its rag enveloped the gold coins and quickly gathered them up before anyone else noticed them.

"Wot you want ter know then?" It leant in, hushing its voice even though anyone with normal hearing would have difficulty hearing anything over the heavy background music score. But then, anyone with anything normal wouldn't have been allowed in through the front door, let alone be trying to strike up a conversation down here.

"Oi'm after three trolls. Go by the names Bung. No clan, no gang." Terrigyle leaned up to stage whisper at the barkeep. "Oi'm looking ter do a little job, and oi 'eard they're cheap and good at getting in and outta places wivout drawing too much attention. So it's business oi want ter talk ter them about, is all."

"Uh huh." The troll grinned, showing dirty, broken teeth. "Well, yer in luck. Da Bung brothers have a room downstairs. Numba fifteen. They wann'ed their privacy. Came inna sum money, and bin livin' 'ere most hours fer the past fwee nights or so."

Something clicked in my head, the timing about right for the trolls to have found out something bad had happened to Talen and Sal Orben, and all the Nighters. A whole pack of lycan disappearing wasn't something we could keep a lid on, and the Bung brothers had been neck-deep with the Alphas trading mortals to Knox for his experiments. There was no way they couldn't have made the connection and started to think about their own protection.

But they'd pulled the job on Cerce, so they were obviously still linked to Knox and his plans, no matter the fact they *had* to figure he'd be coming for them next, to tidy up their loose ends and shut them up for good. Or so I hoped, given I was making a fairly big leap of faith that the three trolls would have *something* I could use, some tidbit of knowledge to help me track down that bastard and nail him to a wall before he brought Morgana fully over and the shit hit the fan in truly apocalyptic fashion.

And then things got just that little bit more complicated.

"Fing is, dose trolls are certainly popular." The barkeep commented as it scrubbed a particularly stubborn stain. "Yer not the first to come lookin' fer them. Second tonight, in fact."

"Is that so?" I asked, forgetting I was supposed to be the silent partner and to let the gnome handle the talking. "Who else came for them, and when?"

The troll squinted at me, suspicions flaring slowly like geological motions across time. But Terrigyle coughed, shooting me a sharp look, before slapping some more coins down on the bar top.

"As moi trusty guard asked, who else is asking after them there trolls? And any chance you know when they came by?" The gnome queried, capturing the barkeep's attention again. "Just fer interest's sake, yer know."

"A fella came by, not arf an hour past." The troll quickly gathered up the money, eyes lowered and voice hushed. "Came in asking for them, just like you. Had *two* guards wiv 'im. Not that 'e needed them."

"How so?" Terrigyle queried, and I cocked my head, scenting something new amongst the musk of the strip club. A thread that was out of place, but oh so familiar.

Fear.

"Well, is just ... I caught a glimpse of the fella. Hid 'imself under hood and cloak, all mistik like." The troll slowly explained, scrubbing harder at the bar top and refusing to look up. "Caught a peek, is all. Big, muscle type. Wyld fae, or I'm a bloody grimalkin. In a *red* hat, hidden unna 'is hood."

The fear suddenly made sense, as I leaned over the bar and dragged the troll by his apron so that he had to look at me. I heard grumbles and growls from behind me, and more than one chair scrape on the floor, but I ignored them.

"Where are the trolls? And has this stranger left already?" I growled with enough threat and my lycan nature to make the troll's eyes widen and his scaly, scarred hide to pale.

"Down dere. An' no, the Wyld still is down there wiv them. Now, let me go wolf!" The barkeep mustered up a little backbone as I felt the presence of other trolls looming in the shadows. It seemed no-one liked seeing their barkeep manhandled … trollhanded or whatever … and there were enough of the shadowy forms starting to loom in our direction to make me think we'd best be on our way and about our business.

"No trouble 'ere, guv. We'll just be on our way, and go see them Bung brothers." Terrigyle grabbed my arm, giving me a quick shake. Beside me, Bear was growling his low rumbling threat that always preceded violence. But we hadn't come here for a simple bar scrap with trolls, and if the other stranger who had come for the Bung brothers was who I thought it was, we'd have an altogether different fight on our hands.

I loosened my grip, and the troll leant back, hands grasping for its club.

"Yeah, we'll just be on our way." I told the troll, then looked around at the shadowy figures that were slowly surrounding us. "Just want to talk to the trolls, then we'll be out of here and will leave you in peace."

Leading Bear on a shortened leash, I backed slowly away from the bar, with Terrigyle staying close at my side. Past hulking forms that glared balefully at us but didn't dare come too close, just enough to threaten from the side-lines without risking a bite from the troll hound's powerful jaws.

We made it to the stairs leading to the next level down, carpeted in fading plush material that was so stained and soddened it was like stepping onto forest moss. Old and rancid moss, but still. Behind, the trolls had encamped by the bar, making an obvious statement that they were protecting their own and standing guard in case I tried to bully the barkeep again … or possibly hoping for free drinks given their show of solidarity against me. I was just happy I wasn't having to wade through them to get to the Bung brothers, or the bastard I reckoned had come for them.

Taking the stairs down, we found ourselves in a wide corridor, with doors leading off on each side. These had chalk marks on them, troll runes, but I reckoned I could guess their meaning without having to ask Terrigyle for a translation.

Number thirteen was towards the end of the corridor, through another archway and round a corner. We approached quietly, Bear now silent and alert. I picked it up at the same time as him … fear, thick in the air. That and pain. Whilst I guessed the trolls normally used these rooms for private dances, just like their mortal counterparts, I reckoned those two scents weren't normal for whatever went on behind the closed doors.

Then again, this being trolls, who the hell knew.

I stood outside number thirteen, letting my ears focus in on whatever was going on inside … but the door was too thick. Probably padded as well, to ensure privacy. Cursing my luck at finding the one shitty troll haunt that invested in decent hardware, I motioned for Terrigyle to step back and out the way. I slipped the grab bag off my shoulder, reaching inside the flap to extract the solid and very reassuring weight of a cold iron and silver blended shortsword. Then I held up three fingers to Bear, slowly counting down.

Two …

One …

And with a burst of lycan-fuelled strength, I kicked in the door, following it and into the room beyond.

Chapter 18

And froze as I let the shattered wooden remains fall to the floor around me.

The chamber inside was large, gloomy and lit by flickering torches on the walls in recesses. It was cluttered with half open crates and overflowing bags scattered around the floor in chaos and disorder. The contents looked to be an array of nothing special. Tattered rugs, half eaten foodstuffs, the stub ends of broken weapons. Broken glass figurines, shattered clay jars and at a glance what looked like Japanese dolls. Useless, worthless crap that only the lowest of the low would hoard, thinking that they'd make something, anything for the rubbish.

Away from the mess, a burrow of sorts had been thrown together by the simplest method of knotting scarves and blankets into a grimy, stinking mass. Discarded bits of meat and bone lay on the floor nearby, an obvious sign that the occupants had little or no regard to hygiene.

And why would they, given they were trolls.

The Bung brothers were huddled on their makeshift bedding. Well, two of them were, squeaking and whimpering, exuding very real fear into the air around us. The third was being held in the grip of two large, heavily muscled gnolls. Relatives of the goblin family, these were well over eight feet tall and had the bodies of Olympic heavyweight competitors or power lifters. Slabs of muscle on muscle, with bald stub heads sat upon massive shoulders. The incongruously large and slightly fanned ears were wholly out of place on their heads, sticking out like handles on a jug. Their skin was a mottled green and grey, scaled and hard, natural body armour over which they had then added plates of ceramic fastened with thongs to make them extra tough. Clan colours of a red hand, with a single eye above, marked them as one of the tougher Lower clans.

Muscle for hire.

And between them, crouched down at eye level with the squirming, wriggling troll, was the third member of their group. As the barkeep had said, the figure was wrapped in an all-concealing cloak, hood up and held tight but still it was immediately obvious the creature was massive in size and bulked heavy from the swell of shoulders and back. Though it was facing away from me, I could immediately sense its attention switch to me as I stood amongst the ruined door.

"Knock, knock. Room service." I grinned at the party inside, nodding to the gnolls. "If you gents wouldn't mind putting down that troll, we need to settle the establishment's bill before you continue any ... well, entertainment you have planned this evening. Hope you understand."

The gnolls shifted their bullet heads, dim red eyes squinting at me before switching to the third companion. Obviously their leader.

"Hnh. The wolf made a funny." The figure's voice was oddly high-pitched, so different from the rasp and growls I'd heard from the trolls upstairs that I almost laughed out loud. I truly hadn't expected the Red Cap to sound like it had been breathing helium. But then, you never know what you'll face with any of the fae until, well, you actually meet them.

The goblin slowly turned, and as it did, I got a good look at what it had been up to, and what toys it had brought to the party.

The third Bung brother was writhing in the gnolls' grasp, jerking at its arms and trying to bite at the hands restraining it. But its legs ... where they stuck of the filthy robes and blankets it had wrapped around itself ... one was a dull grey, matted hairs already broken off the limb and clawed foot thumping the ground with unfeeling solidity. The other, well, that one was a broken shattered stump, fragments of the solidified, petrified limb scattered nearby.

And the Red Cap held in one hand a large, very modern looking ultra-violet lamp, set with a narrow beam from its front bulb. The sort you see in crime scene dramas where the investigation team check hotel beds for all manner of nasty substances. The things no manner of dry cleaning ever remove.

Ultra-violet. Canned sunlight. Death to troll-kin, and certainly not healthy to the gnome standing in the corridor behind me. The bastard was slowly petrifying the Bung brothers, and breaking them whilst they still lived. Utterly sick, even for a creature of the Wyld with their bestial nature and animalistic savagery.

"Knox said you might come looking for these three." The Red Cap pointed a free hand to the trolls, even as it played the UV light across the third brother's legs, eliciting a whimpering gasp of pain from the creature. "Said I could deal with you if you did, coz I had to leave all those lovely little children behind at the school. All those fresh, tender mortals … all that lovely fresh blood."

"But yours will do, at a pinch." It grinned, as it slowly pulled back its hood. The cap that it was named for shone in the torchlight wetly, dipped in fresh gore. It was a skullcap of a kind, braced with thin bones that I guessed were taken from its victims as well, forming a lattice over its knobbled skull. The armour had been attached by toughened cord sewn into the fae's actual skin, fixing it tight to its hide. That also explained another disgusting detail about the Wyld fae … to bathe its cap, it would drain the blood from its young victims into an old pot, and then pour the liquid over its head. Almost as if it were showering in the gore.

These were the sort of details you *didn't* find in fairy-tale stories for mortal children these days.

The gnolls, at some unspoken command, roughly threw the wounded troll back to its brothers, where the three huddled together in a weeping, panic-stricken mess. Then the muscle for hire stepped up beside the Red Cap as it rose to its feet, slipping the rest of its cloak off to reveal a body even more massively muscled than the two thugs it had brought along. The Wyld fae wore leather armour studded with more bones, straps that bound its body in something like BDSM ware, for the kinky barbarian. Twin long and very lethal-looking daggers of bone were hung on its belt, and I saw the haft of what I guessed was an axe or club rising slightly over one shoulder, the weapon having been hidden by the cloak.

Red eyes, maddened with blood lust and a thirst for battle, focused on me as the Red Cap turned and casually set the UV light down on the ground, directing its light so that it formed a barrier, preventing the trolls on their bed from moving more than an inch unless they wished exposure to the deadly light. Then it stepped back, clenching and unclenching its massive hands, readying for battle.

"I don't suppose you'd like to just lay down on the floor and accept a few boots to the sweet spot before I bundle your ass back to prison Realside?" I offered with a grin, as I gripped my sword and eyed the three opposite me. "No? I didn't reckon so. Oh well, let's get this over with."

The Red Cap snarked a high-pitched curse and jerked its daggers from its belt. It barrelled toward me, with the gnolls following with twin roars behind, big fists raised, muscles bunching like ripe melons all over their bodies.

And it was then that Bear slammed *through* the wall beside the door, having waited till there was enough noise to cover the sound of the troll hound taking a good long run up. Jaws gaping, he hammered into the gnolls, sending them smashing into a pile of wooden crates in an explosion of crockery and glass. The two fae bruisers howled in anger and pain, whilst I closed with the Red Cap, already swinging for its head.

"Get the trolls!" I shouted to Terrigyle, who had waited outside in the corridor, and now poked his head in through the hole made by Bear. This whole debacle would prove to be a momentous waste of time and energy if the three buggers went and got turned into stone whilst trying to escape the Red Cap.

The murderous fae in question crashed into me, knives flashing to carve me apart, and I suddenly realised *why* the bastard was so feared beyond the Veil. I was hurled back from the brute power of its attack, sword ringing with the strength of its strike. The fae was *strong*, much stronger than it had any right to be. I wasn't going to be able to beat it one on one, but Bear was occupied with the gnolls and there was no way Terrigyle was an asset in this sort of fight. I'd held the gnome off easily when he went loco on me for messing with his sea mine, so the Red Cap would just leave him as a smear underfoot if they tangled.

Best I could do was draw him away from the three Bung brothers, and give my troll hound time to finish off the hired things. Then maybe I'd have a chance.

"So, let me get this straight." I snarled as a distraction, as I regained my feet and rolled my wrists to release the ache from the Red Cap's attack. "You break free of prison, jump over to the Mortal Realm without any restraints or bonds to stop you … but instead of going on a rampage, killing defenceless mortals and draining their children to colour your famous headgear, you start acting as a runner for one of them?! You become someone's *skivvy*? How's that work?"

The Red Cap snarled and swung again at me, eyes narrowed with a total lack of intelligence but a thoroughly feral desire to see me dead.

"You know *nothing*!" It hissed, battering my sword aside and lashing out, forcing me to back out of the door and into the wide corridor. Over its shoulder, I saw that Bear had already downed one of the gnolls if a ripped-out throat was anything to go by, and was savaging the second one's massively thewed leg as it howled and battered at my dog with its fists. Behind, I could see Terrigyle creeping around the fight, nearing the UV light and the three trolls. Given how the light would be as lethal for him as it was the three brothers, he'd grabbed up a length of ripped scarves to wrap around his hands and arms, shielding him from the deadly unnatural sunlight.

"Sure, nothing. Like I don't know Knox is trying to bring Morgana over and fit her inside a body he's built for her." I mocked, retreating step by step as I ducked a wild slash aimed to blind me, and hammered my sword into the fae as it left its side open for a strike. But as well as being inhumanly strong, the bastard was just as quick too, catching my blade on its other knife and turning the blow aside. "Like he's planning the ritual in a couple of days, and has the bloody *Harrowing* to make sure no one messes with his … her plans. I know nothing. Yeah, right."

"Ha!" The fae sneered as it barrelled into me, throwing me back a step and scoring a line of fire along my left side with a darting slash. "Wolf thinks he's so clever. Skivvy am I? *She's* promised to make me a Knight in her Court. Gonna be Sir Red Cap, and I'll *bathe* in the blood of babies every day!"

I bit back a curse as the knife cut through my armour and into muscle, drawing blood. But it was more for what I was hearing … Morgana had promised to knight this bloodthirsty cretin? And what Court was she going to rule?

"But you don't need to worry about all that." The Red Cap snarled in its high-pitched voice. "Coz you'll be dead."

I'd let it distract me, too much bouncing around my thick head. Too late, I realised the goblin had backed me into the corner of the corridor, limiting the swing of my sword. I had rushed in, not even bothering to Change, so was without my claws or even the ability to bite the bastard, as it suddenly charged in. I desperately stabbed at it like my sword was an oversized and unwieldy dagger, scoring a strike across its back and severing some straps so that the massive axe hanging there tumbled free. But the Red Cap just snarled through the pain, punching those ultra-sharp knives into my shoulder and lower chest before I could deflect the strikes.

I howled as the pain tore through me, trying to stab at it again with my sword, but it was inside my reach now. Loosing hold of its weapons, the goblin knocked my arms aside and latched those massive hands of its around my throat.

And squeezed.

Blood pounded in my head as I reared back, trying to kick the bastard off me, but it kept close to me, the centuries of experience it had earned through bloody conflict coming to play right now. Dropping the sword, I grabbed at its wrists, trying to force them up and off me with a move practised time and again with Jacob and his team … but it was like trying to shift solid iron girders, unyielding whatever I threw against them.

"Gonna squeeze you till you pop, wolf!" The Red Cap spat happily as it leant in, applying more pressure. "Then I might just go back and visit that school. Get me some young, innocent blood. My cap's starting to dry."

It's cap. The one surety I knew about the bastard was that its inhuman strength and speed was bound up in the cap it wore. Part of an enchantment as ancient as the hills, and from a time when blood magic was *the* thing to use on armour and weapons. To imbibe great strength, invulnerability, swiftness … you name it, mortals and immortals alike used the stuff. Until, that is, they found the drawbacks with such a source of power … firstly the fact that to keep the items enchanted, one had to continually renew the blood rites bound to them. Hence the Red Cap's continual drive to hunt and slay innocent children and drain them, as something in their essence made for exceptionally strong magic.

Secondly, the blood imbued items would also, over time, weaken the wearers or wielders to such a degree that they could only function whilst using the bound item. They created a dependency, like a parasitic symbiote that drained the life from its victim but kept it fit and healthy until its final moments.

Magic is like that, well there's always a price to pay. A balance of power. A sucker punch you just don't see until it gets you right between the eyes.

I managed to get an elbow between us, forcing the fae's head away, desperately trying to grab at that wet, stinking cloth cap atop its head. But the Red Cap snarled and sank its teeth into my forearm, worrying me like a dog as I felt the air burn in my lungs, my vision starting to blacken at the edges. I tried to call on my Wyld strength, my Shadow gift, hell, even whatever the fuck Ivory had bestowed on me with the new tattoo … but pain was swamping me from the two big knives sticking in me, the lack of oxygen and the fae's toothy grip on my arm, and I couldn't concentrate enough to focus …

Fuck, was this it? After everything, was this how it all ended? I gasped for air, feeling the last of it burn in my lungs, as blackness closed in.

Chapter 19

Thankfully not.

Behind us, as the Red Cap pressed harder on my throat and gnawed at my arm, I saw something move, emerging from the shattered doorway. For a moment I felt a burn of hope, thinking Bear was about to make a timely entrance. But the shape was all wrong. Far too small, and with only two legs.

Terrigyle.

The gnome took in the sight of me backed against the wall, being throttled to death by the Wyld goblin. With no hesitation, the little figure crept as fast as it could behind the Red Cap and, gathering its strength, leapt from the floor.

Onto the other's shoulders.

The Red Cap tore its teeth from my arm in a spray of blood, head jerking back in surprise and a cry forming on its lips. I managed a pain-wracked grin, feeling the tightness on my throat loosen and air flood down like ice water, as the goblin went to pull itself away and deal with this sudden attack.

"No. Fucking. Way." I coughed out, feeling like I was trying to swallow nails but still wanting to snarl the words. With blood streaming from my bitten arm, I grabbed and locked the fae against me, knowing I only needed a moment to hold it there.

The thing with gnomes is, they're small and kind of funny looking, with their waddling gait and big ears, and oddities like Terrigyle's cockney accent common amongst the troll-kin. They aren't renowned fighters like their dwarrow counterparts, and tend to steer clear of physical conflict with a passion, instead focusing on the finer arts and pursuits … which normally amounts to whichever criminal activity with the largest amount of loot they can get away with at the end of the day.

People often see them as weak and easily intimidated. The sort to be pushed around and tormented with impunity. An easy mark to manipulate through strong arm tactics.

That's a rookie mistake to make.

You see, gnomes are troll-kin, and as such have the strength of mountains at their core. Little used, not something they relied on to get their way much, a cornered gnome could still eventually rip the arms off an opponent that was unwise enough to get caught in its grasp. I'd had enough difficulty with Teri before that I'd had to freeze his ass to stop him.

And now the Red Cap had let the little sod get his hands on him.

Terrigyle locked his stubby legs around the thick goblin's neck and tangled his fingers in the blood-soaked cap sewn into the other's skin. He'd obviously heard the same stories as me, and knew the trick to beat this particular enemy.

"No!" The Red Cap shrieked, wrenching one arm free, desperately clawing at the gnome riding him like a bronco atop a truly scary stallion. But Terrigyle wasn't hanging around to arm-wrestle the goblin. With one massive jerk, he hauled on the cap. Skin stretched then split, the hardened cords ripping free as the bloody cloth came away in his hands. He tumbled off the goblin's shoulders, scrabbling away with his prize clasped tightly in his hands.

He needn't have worried.

"My cap!" The goblin wailed, even as he began to deflate and shrink like a balloon that had been just pricked. I drew in a whooping breath of air as the fae's remaining hand loosened from my throat, the creature writhing amongst its suddenly too big armour. It groped at its skull, skin flapping where it had torn, silver blood running from the deeper gouges, and wailed in agony and sudden fear.

The Wyld fae continued to shrink until it finally reached the size of a small child, with an oversized head, long gangly arms and splayed legs. Given its armour had been fitted for something of monstrous proportions, it was left entirely butt naked, its green-grey skin crisscrossed with scars from all its previous battles. Long talon-like nails scrabbled at its head, as it cowered back and away from me. Its eyes lit on Terrigyle, sat on his arse and still gripping the gory trophy.

"My cap!" The goblin shrieked again, and struggled to free itself from the fallen clothing, already reaching out with those knobbly fingers and claws toward the gnome.

"Not fucking likely." I growled, voice still rasping. And with no hesitation or guilt, I lashed out and booted the goblin hard in the backside. Wailing, it tumbled through the air and slammed against the far wall, crunching hard enough that I knew it wouldn't be getting back up anytime soon. With a wet slurping sound, it slid down the dirty and sticky surface to crumple on the floor.

"Bloody 'ell, mate. You oir-right?" Terrigyle asked, finally dropping the sodden cap and scrubbing his hands on his trousers. "You look loik shit, no offence."

"None taken." I rasped, stepping out of the corner gingerly. Bracing myself, I grabbed hold of the two hilts sitting flush against my skin and jerked the knives out quickly. Pain crashed against me, threatening to floor me, but I bit down hard and finally reached for the Wyld strength inside me. It surged up, stilling my breathing and pushing the pain back. At least a little. "Feel pretty shitty, if I'm being honest."

At that moment, Bear limped out of the hole he'd made in the wall. The troll hound was battered, walking gingerly on his front paw, but he looked in one piece. Which couldn't be said for the remains of the gnoll he had clenched between his jaws. Looked like most of the thing's head and one shoulder, the shredded remains of its chest dangling down to soak the floor in silver gore.

He stopped, eyeing me for a long moment before spitting out the gnoll onto the floor and giving himself a thorough shake. Noticing the crumpled body of the Red Cap, he gave a coughing growl and stalked toward the unconscious goblin.

"Don't kill him." I rasped, not that I really cared one way or the other about the bloody bastard. But he'd been lippy enough to reveal Morgana had plans for him, so might just know some stuff we could make use of.

Bear turned and huffed at me questioningly, but I just shrugged and shook my head. The troll hound gave another shake of his massive head, then promptly lifted one hind leg and liberally peed all over the goblin.

"Fair enough." I told my furry companion, as I felt the wounds in my side and shoulder start to knit back together again. It didn't feel like the Red Cap had dosed his weapons with any poison … the way my luck had been going, he would have had some Wolfsbane on him. But I guess he kept his weapons clean to use on his victims. Didn't want to contaminate the blood when he was harvesting, or some shit like that.

"How're the trolls?" I asked Terrigyle, as I stooped to pick up the blood-soaked headgear from where the gnome had dropped it. This I stashed away in a side pocket, until I had a handy fire hot enough to burn the fucking thing. The number of innocents that had died to colour it, the thing deserved to be ash.

"Oi saved yer loife, didn't oi?" Terrigyle muttered to himself as I staggered past him, still feeling a little unsteady on my feet. Bear joined me, head butting my thigh so I could scratch his ears. The gnolls looked to have bruised him up a little, but troll hounds were made to take the sort of beatings handed out by high trolls, and that level of punishment was far above what the bruisers could have dealt. Still, they'd hurt him enough to make him limp … unless he was just playing silly buggers and hoping for a treat

"Yeah, mate. If you hadn't come along, well, I don't want to think of that right now." I absentmindedly replied, fingering my neck as I looked back into the room where the Bungs had been staying. "So, the trolls ok?"

The room was a wreck, crates shattered and the debris from inside scattered around the shredded remains of the gnolls. A leg here, an arm there. Ribcages bent and broken. Bear had not been gentle on the two bruisers, but then they had been attacking me, with an intent to do me harm. I couldn't feel all that bad at their fate.

Poking my head through the remains of the door, I could see the three trolls huddled on their bedding. Two of them were cradling their damaged brother, who was curled up around his petrified and broken limbs. Near the doorway, Terrigyle had set the UV lamp down so that its beam cut across the only way out, effectively barring them from running.

"Yeah, dem trolls are ok. So … fing is, oi fink oi've done more than you wanted. Fought fer you. Saved your loife." Terrigyle spoke up behind me, and I slowly turned at the tone I heard in his voice. Hesitant but final, like the gnome had come to a decision. "So, you've got dem trolls, an' that there Red Cap an' all. So then … well, oi'll be going, oi reckon."

"Going?" I felt that lump in my stomach as I gripped the doorframe. Beside me, Bear picked up on my sudden suspicion, my switch in mood and began growling again. I reached down to steady him, leaving a hand in the thick ruff of fur around his neck.

"Yeah." Terrigyle was up on his feet, facing me. He was clasping that pendant, the thing he'd picked up from his home. I hadn't even bothered checking the bloody thing. "Fing is, well, oi reckon you owe me now. At least ter give me a sportin' chance. Ter get ahead of those bloody Furies. Oi said, I won't go back to them. Not fer them. Not even fer you, guv."

"It's my arse on the line if you don't come back with me, mate." I replied, but the gnome just shook his head.

"They'll get ovva it. Come fer me, not focus on you." Terrigyle gripped that necklace tightly and took one step back. Slowly. Carefully. "Guv, oi … oi just 'ave to. Don't'cha see that?"

He nodded back to the room behind me.

"Oi told them to start screamin' about foive minutes after it all went quiet." The gnome admitted. "Dat'll bring their mates down 'ere. Now, oi reckon you'll 'andle them ok, but you've got fwee trolls to get outta 'ere, plus that bloody gobbo. Won't 'av a chance to come after me. Not if you wanna get them outta 'ere."

"Oi'm sorry, mate." The gnome finished as he took one more step back. "Oi hope you'll forgive me, an' we can 'ave a drink an' a larf about this one day."

With that, he snapped the chain in his hand. Light sprang out, bright and hot, filling the corridor for a heartbeat. I threw my forearm over my eyes to spare my sight, hearing Bear whimper in surprise and duck down behind me.

Then, the light faded. Taking the gnome with it.

I took a breath, feeling all the pain from my forearm and body wounds, my near strangulation. There really was only one thing to say at that point.

"I'm going to bloody kill him." I told Bear.

It was at that point that three sets of troll lungs opened up with shrill screams behind me, filling the room and corridor with a Gods awful racket. It was quickly joined by the scrape of furniture above us, and the thud of footsteps growing louder. Coming down to us.

I sighed, cracking my neck and wincing as the muscles protested. Then I picked up my sword where it had fallen, setting it against the doorframe and within reach. I ducked inside the door, and picked up the lamp, cradling the unit as I set my feet firmly on the floor, facing the direction the trolls would come. Bear, full sized, padded over to stand over the fallen goblin, making sure that if the Red Cap even twitched, he would see it and bite whatever moved.

As the first trolls peered round the corner, I smiled a grim smile and nodded in welcome, waving the UV lamp so that its beam spilled across the floor in front of me in a non-threatening, nonchalant way.

"Ah, there you are. Would someone mind bringing a broom and bin? I think I made a bit of mess." I commented dryly. "Oh, and you'd best tell your barkeeper the Bung brothers are checking out. I hope they paid in full."

Chapter 20

Lanval.

Lanval is a Knight of Artur's court, who finds himself loved by a fairy Lady but must swear an oath to keep her secret. Unfortunately Lanval then attracts the attention of Guinevere, and when he spurns her advances she brings him before Artur and accuses him of shaming her.

He faces a judicial court, suffering for his desire to keep true to his vow and not reveal his mistress's true nature. Finally the fairy Lady appears with her handmaidens and sets the matter right, returning to her homeland with Lanval.

Getting the trolls out of Da Gutterz proved to be relatively easy.

Well. Easy compared to what I'd gone through getting my hands on them, that is.

Only one troll proved of a mind to mess with me. It got as far as almost reaching me with its claws before I lightly roasted it with the UV lamp. Not enough to turn it to stone, but enough to leave burn marks over its claws and forearms, forcing it to stumble back in agony. Yeah, I know, I was just copying the Red Cap but at least I was trying to warn the bastards off, not torture them for sick fun.

Thankfully there was mobile reception somehow at this level, so whilst Bear kept a watch on the rowdy, upset drinkers I dialled up the office. I cut through the usual banter from Jacob, when he picked up the phone, and tersely told him I had the Red Cap and three trolls connected to Knox, and needed picking up by a full squad. I guess the pain in my voice must've tipped him this wasn't the time for taking the piss.

Almost in record time, Jacob, Emma and three packmates were pushing through the trolls lining the stairs. All were armed for trouble, silver and cold iron weapons in hand and ready to be used to deal out a lesson on anyone stupid looking for trouble.

In swift order, we had the three trolls bundled up and restrained, and the still unconscious Red Cap firmly bound and locked in silver. The Bung brothers hadn't said a thing since I'd rescued them from certain death, clinging to each other like scared children … only shooting furtive glances at the Wyld fae as Emma picked it up and slung the inert body over one shoulder.

Then it was just a case of passing back through a crowd of now silent, looming trolls with our prisoners. At the top of the stairs, the barkeeper waited, its club held loosely in one paw.

"Whose gonna pay fer damages?" He demanded in a hoarse growl, but I just shrugged and pointed a thumb back down the way we'd come.

"I reckon these three had something stashed away down there for emergencies, and there's two dead gnolls who probably have their pay on them as well." I helpfully prompted. "Maybe enough to cover the mess we made, and then some. All yours, free of charge."

We moved out of the club to the sound of trolls trying to fight their way down the stairs, with the barkeeper yelling *What'ver you find, it's the House's!* as loud as it could.

Jacob remained ominously silent as we bundled the prisoners into the first vehicle, locking them behind the custom fit grating and into what was, for all intents and purposes a set of cages. We'd taken the design from some units used to transport large dogs around in the back of Range Rovers, then added our twist to make them fae proof. Cold iron and silver plated, with salt crystals glued to the metal to foil any glamour or charms those inside the cages might attempt.

With Emma driving that vehicle, and the rest of the pack piling in for support, I found myself in the second with our pack's lead enforcer, with

Bear happily clambering up into the back seat and collapsing across the entire thing. I stowed my bag of weapons, and the handy UV lamp down the footwell by him, and did my own mini collapse into the passenger seat as Jacob closed the door and started up the engine.

We drove in silence for a while, the weight of unspoken words heavy between us. It was obvious my packmate had something to get off his chest, but hell if I was going to do anything but wait for him to speak. I was too tired and sore to care much at that point

"So. You going lone wolf now?" He asked quietly, nodding towards the first vehicle and its cargo. "Playing Knight Errant and tracking dangerous fae without backup? Not clever."

"Uh, firstly, thanks for the pickup." I replied dryly. "Wasn't sure I could carry all those buggers out of there myself, that and handle the locals. As for hunting alone ... I wasn't. Had Terrigyle along to watch my back and get me through the doors without having to break them. Oh, and Bear, remember? And finally, I was after three little troll-kin, who even a mortal could probably take if they had a big enough stick and nose-plugs."

"The Red Cap *just happened* to be there? Like Jack *just happened* to stumble on you and Elspeth?" Jacob bounced back at me, not backing down. "Seems to happen a lot around you lately. Ever since this thing with the Courts. You being a Knight and all."

"Jacob, I'm about as much a Knight as you. Hell, you probably qualify more than me, what with *trial by arms* usually being a requisite." I grinned across at him but saw from his stony expression that my humour was falling flat. Fine. "Ok, spit it out. What's bugging you?"

My packmate didn't reply, instead he reached over and without taking his eyes off the road, dialled the other vehicle. Emma picked up, and confirmed the three trolls were still basically catatonic whilst the Red Cap had woken and started screaming for his cap again. Until Charles had *subdued* the prisoner, which meant he'd probably thumped him back into unconsciousness. Brutal but effective, and I had *no* love to spare for that bloody goblin.

With that check in, Jacob slowed our car and indicated, pulling into a slot marked for taxis, buses and the occasional unmarked mortal police vehicle. Coming to a stop as he flicked on his hazard lights, he took a breath before turning to face me.

"What's bugging me? It's you, Morgan." He growled, expression grim. "We're a *pack*. We face things together, handle our troubles *together*. We hunt *together*. There's a reason why lone wolves die early in the wild, and the same goes for stupid-ass lycan that think just coz they're in with the Courts and maybe have an edge or two, they can take on the world single-fucking-handed."

I went to snipe back, knowing I'd had Jessica's blessing to go hunting the Bung brothers with just Bear and Terrigyle, but Jacob shook his head.

"I ain't finished." He grated, so I settled back, biting on my words. "I've been keeping a tab on you. You're taking more and more risks, and sometimes it's only you getting hurt, sometimes it's those around you too. It ain't always your fault, but you *do* need to stop and *think*. People we know are hurting, hell, even fucking dying. So maybe, just maybe, I'm asking you to hold off before you go charging headlong into the next little problem. Ask for some help. Let one of us swing some punches and take the hits. Just bloody *ask*. That's all."

I checked my watch, seeing it was past one in the morning. We'd spent most of the night chasing down the trolls, then fighting with the Red Cap and finally getting my arse pulled out of *Da Gutterz* with my prize. I was tired, I'd been nearly strangled and stabbed twice, let alone bitten. All my wounds were healing but still the pain was a present reminder of the damage I'd taken. And on top of that, I'd let Terrigyle do a runner on me, landing me in who knew what levels of shit with the Furies.

All that rattled around inside me, as I fought the surge of Wyld strength that flared as my anger burned bright. I felt more than heard Bear stir behind me, sensing my mood. So I turned to Jacob, clenching my jaw, letting him see the anger in my eyes. The rage and pain I was feeling, but holding back from letting loose.

"You think I *want* this shit to keep happening to me?" I growled as Bear whined and butted my seat. "You think I wouldn't love to sit things out, let someone else handle every single punch and kick and bite that keeps coming my way? You think I don't *know* that Elspeth is broken coz of me? That Felix Price is fucked up royally, coz she knew me? I *know*."

Grabbing the door lever, I popped it open even as I hit the release for my seatbelt. Jacob went to raise a hand, to probably stop me, but I just ignored him. It had been too much for me tonight.

"I'll walk from here." I told him bluntly even as I stepped out of the car and popped open the side door for Bear to join me. The troll hound jumped down onto the road, butting against me and huffing as he stretched his sore paw. "See what you can get from the Bung brothers, and get that fucking goblin back to prison. Probably best I'm not around if the Furies show up looking to collect Teri."

Jacob shot me a look, expression closed, no scent of an apology or even a realisation why I was so pissed at him coming off the lycan. Just a solid, unyielding certainty that he was in the right.

"Oh, and you know what?" I shot at him, knowing my need to have the last word was not an enviable trait, but I didn't much care. "I preferred it when you just grunted at me and made kitten jokes. This shit? I don't need much. So keep it for someone who cares."

I slammed the door closed, cutting off any response from the other lycan as I guided Bear round the back of the large off-road vehicle. For a moment I thought Jacob was staying put, but then the engine engaged and he pulled back out into the road. I watched his tail-lights till he turned a corner and vanished from sight, then squared my shoulders and looked down at Bear.

"Sorry bud. You could've maybe stayed in the car. Got a lift back all the way." I lamely apologised but he gave a chuffing bark, shaking his massive shoulders then butting me to show me I was just being an idiot.

We'd been following the main road back from Westminster to the office opposite Hyde Park, but had only just passed St James's before Jacob pulled over. Looking around, taking my bearings, I found we were just a short walk from the Victoria Memorial and Buckingham Palace, rising elegantly against the skyline with parklands all around. Not a bad place to walk this Gods forsaken time of the morning, with the streets pretty much deserted and only a few cars and buses wending their way down from the Mall and into Pimlico or Belgravia.

With Bear padding beside me, I walked at a leisurely pace along the empty streets, finally stopping as we reached the wide plaza set before the royal mortals' palace.

It was a truly stunning piece of architecture, white stone glowing under the light of the moon overhead and the streetlamps set atop its large gates glittering like fireflies. Beyond the imposing barrier, I could see the red coated guardsmen on display, standing stark against the palace walls behind them. All too easy to spot, keeping the attention off the numerous other well-hidden guards that were ensconced out of sight but ever vigilant and watchful.

Admittedly, compared to the Ivory Court's home of Camelot, it was less fantastical, more functional. Against Madb's realm of glittering ice and sculpted shadows, the palace seemed squarish and blocky. But whilst the Courts had managed to erect abodes to delight the eye and bewitch those gazing upon them, Buckingham Palace was an altogether different beast ... it exuded a *solidity*, a sense of permanence and stability that neither Ivory or Shadow managed to convey. The Palace was a statement, where mortals came from all over the world to stand outside and marvel, to bestow their awe upon a single building and those who lived there. It was akin to the simple magic I'd described before, of hearth protection that most mortal dwellings offered against ill-will and harm. But this was on a grand scale, a blanket of protection spread invisibly over London. Whilst Buckingham Palace stood, whilst the mortal royals ruled from its marble halls, anyone wishing harm upon the Mortal Realm ... at least this island and those nearby ... would face surprising opposition.

That thought made me stop, letting Bear settle at my feet, as I faced the Palace through the cold forged iron bars of the wall surrounding the massive building. Suspicions and questions bounced around my head, the storm that had almost gotten me strangled by Red Cap and still raged inside my skull.

Why would Morgana choose to come here, having broken free of her prison, binding herself to a mortal body and a Realm limited by the Accords to allow only the merest thread of magic. Rather than the Real, where magic imbued every leaf, every blade of grass. Every breath taken.

It made no sense.

Something sparked my senses, a brush of coldness that had nothing to do with the faint summer wind. Bear sensed it too, rising up and his hackles stiffening as he rolled his head from side to side, searching.

I slowly turned, letting my eyes roam around me. Belatedly I remembered I'd stashed the weapons in the footwell behind my seat, leaving me relatively defenceless. Relatively, given what I was.

Something shivered in the air, movement like a current running through water. A taint, cold and rank to my nose. Whatever it was, this thing was no friendly sprite, no simple fae dancing on the threads of dawn light.

"Tag, you're it. Now show yourself." I growled quietly, motioning for Bear to remain quiet. I was very aware of the attention of the guards beyond the wall, and knew if anything happened here and now, I was going to break all of Jessica's rules, let alone a few of the minor Accords. Those about keeping the mortals unaware of our existence. And I already reckoned I had one very pissed Fury on my hands, let alone annoying my Alpha.

That sliver of *otherness* rippled through the air, then thickened as shadows pooled and drew together. Until a figure stood near the Palace gates, hooded in ragged cloth. It was tall but full figured, with the curves of an earth goddess like Molly, and seemed to bear no apparent weapon. Not that that usually meant anything, in my experience from encountering figures appearing from nowhere.

In fact, the more they seemed defenceless, the nastier they tended to be.

"Ok, now what?" I checked to make sure I had plenty of space around me, and that Bear was clear to engage if the newcomer started any trouble. But the figure just spread its hands, the robe's sleeves riding up. Revealed, a pair of slim hands, elegant even, and wrists and forearms tattooed with dark ink upon ash grey skin.

Shadow fae skin.

The hood raised, and eyes of deepest crimson stared at me, lit with far too much intelligence and cruel humour.

"Now? I would simply speak with you since you have gone to *so* much trouble already on my behalf."

A woman's voice, the same voice I'd heard speak last in the Shadow Court's prison, from the mouth of a fae shackled in icy bonds, pierced through with frozen shafts. Yet free all the same.

Morgana.

Chapter 21

"What do you want?" I growled, instantly suspecting a trap, looking around the open area. I half expected beguiled Shadow Crows to leap from where they hid, or the missing Twilight fae prisoners to show up, tentacles flailing. It had been that sort of a day. Week … maybe even a month. I was beginning to lose track.

"Just to talk, Sir Knight." Morgana slowly lowered her tattered hood, revealing a woman of uncommon beauty. Locks of silver and ebony framed her face, those blood red eyes set above heavy cheekbones and thin blue lips. Tattoos lined her skin, an elegant script that didn't look either Ivory or Shadow, but something more tribal and elder. If I were to make a guess I'd have said Nordic.

Seeing how I'd seen Morgana's body destroyed by Madb in a truly awful fit of pique when she found her sister had escaped, I knew for a fact that this couldn't be her standing in front of me. Just a projection, shade or whatever, kept alive through the stolen life that Knox was feeding her somehow. Otherwise why did he still need Arthurian artefacts for a ritual if she was here in the flesh.

Of course, it *could* all have been a massive decoy, keeping us busy whilst he actually performed the necessary magic unbeknownst to us, and Morgana might already be in the Mortal Realm in her new body.

Only one way to find out.

Knowing she was watching me, a crescent smile on her lips like the sharpest of knives, I carefully reached into a thigh pocket and drew out a small container filled with rock salt. Perfect for breaking any enchantment but also a simple way of proving if the being in front of me was actually solid.

"You mind?" I held up the container so she could see the contents, shaking it a little.

"If you must, then do so. Then we talk." She replied with a shrug.

Cracking the lid, I palmed a small amount of salt then tossed the grains through the air between us.

As I did, I remembered doing something similar to the Morrigan what seemed like an age ago though then I didn't ask permission first. That time, the fae had gotten away with just light facial burns, but if this was a conjuring from beyond the Veil, Morgana would light up like a Roman Candle firework. I wasn't sure how I'd explain that to the ever-watchful guards outside the Palace, but that was a problem for later.

The grains scattered through the air … and continued through Morgana, falling to patter on the cobbles underfoot without even a spark. She was not solid, otherwise they would have bounced off her, but she was also no conjuring either to be dispelled by the basic laws of magic. She was here, in the Mortal Realm. Bodiless, but present.

Guess Knox hadn't foxed us then.

"Now that you are certain of my nature?" Morgana commented dryly, reaching down to wipe imaginary grains of salt from her clothing. "As said, I wished to speak to you. Will you hear me?"

The sensible thing would have been to say no. Walk away, and not acknowledge the spirit. Not only would it look less suspicious, since I doubted she was visible to any of the mortals guarding the Palace but it also meant I wouldn't hear her reasons for what she was doing. Hear anything to make me want to sympathise with her. No chance to be tricked, like she had Knox, Oberon and countless others who had served her either unknowingly or for false reasons.

Of course, I am *renowned* for doing the sensible thing. Everyone says so.

"Ok, shoot. But keep it short. I'm on the clock and Bear will only wait so long before he starts trying to pee on your foot." I told her, nodding to my troll hound who, now that a complete lack of villains had failed to jump us, was resting back down on the cobbles. Almost but not quite snoring.

"Short. I like that. To the point." The Shadow fae nodded, and clasped her hands in front of her. "In short, I want to offer you this one chance. Walk away. Let the mortal Knox complete his task, leave him alone … and I will make sure none other are harmed. No further loss of life occurs, when you have already paid so high a price. Packmates lost, mortals corrupted. Your mortal love scarred by contact with your true self. Enough pain to last more than one lifetime, I would think."

As much as I wanted to laugh in her face, and tell her where she could shove her offer, I knew this was a once in a blue moon event. Actually getting to talk to her before the shit hit the fan. Jessica would have my hide if I didn't *try* to get as much information out of the spirit as possible.

Of course, Morgana would know this. So the question really was, who was better at this game?

"It's a nice thought. Walking away, keeping everyone safe and well." I replied after a moment's thought. "Of course, I can't very well just make the decision on behalf of my pack, my Alpha. Or the mortals chasing Knox, let alone your sister and cousins in Ivory who want you back on ice. All I can speak for is me."

Morgana nodded, her eyes searching my face, obviously trying to ready my intent.

"Of course. I do not intend to make such an offer to my sister, nor my cousins. They have what they are owed coming to them. And I expect your Alpha and pack to do the right thing, as all good followers would do." She replied, cocking her head. "But the offer is to *you*, for you are no simple follower, child of the Wyld. Nor are you to blame for what was done to me. Agree to leave me be, and I will protect those you care for from any further harm. The mortal child, touched by Twilight. The witch, suffering lost love and a broken heart. The mortal you too have lost, sent far overseas and beyond *your* reach. All these can be saved."

There's a thing you have to get used to when dealing with creatures of the Real, most especially the fae. They *love* to bargain. It's practically in their DNA if they actually have the stuff. Mortal folklore is full of instances where the plucky hero or heroine is offered their ultimate desire or dream, if only for some small thing, some trifling thing. Sometimes a little golden ring of no importance, or their firstborn child. Or the first living thing that will cross the bridge. Even a portion of their immortal soul, guaranteed not to be missed. Satan, the devil, whatever you want to kill the incarnation of all that is evil, it gets lumbered with a lot of the meddling the fae have committed throughout the ages. But I don't hear too many complaints from Damnation, so I guess that's ok.

Fact is, Morgana's offer was most likely solid. She *would*, if I agreed to walk away, do her utmost to keep those three people safe from whatever she had planned. But that was the rub. The fae obviously had plans to commit something they needed to be warded against. Others would suffer, would bear the weight of her wrath and vengeance. Like my pack, my Alpha. Manisha the Ivory Knight. Hell, even my actual father Herne, and my dear ol' granny the Morrigan. Let alone how many mortals Morgana saw as little more than ants to be crushed underfoot.

If, when the dust settled, those people I loved and cared about found out I had sacrificed a chance to stop the shit from happening just to save their skin? Well, I had to ask myself, would they thank me? Or would they tell me I'd been wrong, that they relied on me to fight till the bitter end, to *try*. Even if I failed. That was what mattered.

In the end, the answer was obvious.

"I'm flattered, but I reckon I'll have to pass on the complimentary cutlery set and cuddly toy." I replied, seeing the spirit's lips thin in exasperation. "Thing is, I can only think you're making this offer coz you know we're getting close. I know you stole the stone Excalibur was stuck in for Knox's ritual. We've blocked pretty much all the minions you freed to give us the run around, even those bastards Red Cap and Jack. The mortals are closing in on their miraculously 'risen from the dead' colleague, and the simple fact is we *will* find you. It's what we lycans do."

Seeing anger spark in her eyes, I let my most annoying grin slap itself across my face as I cut off her reply.

"Here's *my* offer. I don't *care* what you've been through. The beef you have with Oberon and Madb, the Courts? That's your own fault for fucking things up in the past, and you're paying the price for that." I ground out the words, adding a bite of my frustration and anger to my voice. "Go back to the Real. Face up to your own mistakes, take things up with the folk you have grievances with back there. Leave the Mortal Realm alone, and stop fooling Knox into thinking you're his dead daughter come back from the grave. Fuck off, and never darken this side of the Veil again. Then we'll leave you alone. That I can offer."

Morgana drew herself up, expression darkening as those strange tattoos of hers seemed to writhe and shift. Much like the ones I'd seen on the Fury's skin, but with more sinister undertones. Above us, the sky was brightening as dawn started to unfurl across the horizon, the sun stirring and pushing back the gloom of night. Yet for a moment, it was like a switch had been flicked, dimming the light and adding a biting chill to the air. Like we had suddenly stepped into shadow.

"Foolish, stupid child." She hissed. Those crimson orbs burned in their sockets. "You *dare* speak to me so? I who once strode this Realm and was worshipped with gifts of blood and flesh by pitiful mortals seeking my good will? I who singlehandedly brought Avalon to ruin, thwarted that fool Oberon and my sister Madb's desire to rule here for eternity? You speak to *me*, and dare offer *me* a deal?"

"Yeah, and it's the best one you're gonna get, lady." I blithely replied, forcing myself to not shiver in the sudden plunging cold. Big bad wolf, feeling a little chill. Out of the corner of my eye, I could see a policeman walking across the way from us, in that casual manner that meant he had spotted me, was taking note of how long I was standing outside the mortal Palace having an argument with myself and would soon intrude to check on me. All the while standing in glorious pre-dawn light, untouched by

Morgana's shadow. "So how about you take the offer, tell Knox the truth and go be a plague or extinction event or whatever in the Real, and not our problem anymore?"

"Knox? You think the mortal deserves the truth after all he has done?" Morgana hissed, slashing one hand through the air. "I found him, a broken soul searching for a way to make right a simple, undeniable wrong. The truth of Robert Knox? *He left his child to die*! A healer, a mortal learned in all ways to cure the sick, to treat illness in its myriad diversity yet when his own daughter grew weak and ill-humoured, he ignored the signs. Driven to prove himself the paramount in his field of study, he turned away from his own child and left her to the care of lesser physicians. When even his wife begged him to treat her, he refused, so consumed was he by his own work. And thus the daughter died, in pain and misery, whilst her mother wept at her side. But her father? He was far from home, lauding his accomplishments and daring any other mortal to prove him less than the most learned of them all. His *arrogance* is what drove him to lose something so precious as his own daughter's life, and is what drives him still. I have done little, except show him what doors to open, what paths to take, if he truly wishes to conquer death. To breach the Veil."

Well, that answered one question. Why Knox was so hellbent on raising his dead daughter, when he seemed perfectly fine with the rest of his family being dead and buried. Guilt drives mortals to do the craziest and stupidest of things, often for what they think are the right reasons. To make good on something bad, to correct a mistake made. But the route Knox had taken, it was littered with the bodies of those he'd sacrificed to achieve his goal. And after all he had done, it was still a lie.

"Oh, you *just happened* to find this wounded mortal, seeking to make right a mistake he made? And I'm betting out of the goodness of your heart, you thought to show him how to first extend his life, to use the life energies of others to stay alive long enough to research a way of not just finding his daughter but bringing her soul back?" I quipped sarcastically, trying to see just how many answers Morgana would give me in her rage. "Oh, and I'm sure those little whispers of yours in his head, how to use his skills to craft his daughter a new body from the bits of other mortals? Those were just 'suggestions', nothing you ever thought he would act on, right?"

Morgana glared at me, her anger like icy daggers stabbing at me from the cloaking shade.

"Your jibes are as witless as they are obvious." She answered with a hiss. "*I have broken no law.* All that I have done, I have done whilst keeping to the rules written by mortals, the bonds we immortals must bear to keep the lesser creatures appeased. Take your offer, save your breath and know that when the planets align, I shall be reborn by the stones upon which that fool Artur made his worthless and traitorous vows to me. And then? Then I will expect you to kneel, and I might consider sparing your worthless life."

She gathered the shadows like cloth around her, spinning to cloak her once more until all I could see were those crimson orbs, fixing me with her immortal fury.

"We are done. When next you face me, remember that I gave you one single chance. One way to avoid what comes. And you chose to ignore it, and instead insult me." She hissed, voice once more the vicious thing I had heard in the cell within the Gardens of Ice, as she addressed her sister. "For that, there will be payment due."

With those words, her presence shredded and vanished, the darkness cloaking where I stood dissipating like fog burned off by the sun. I let myself shiver, the clinging chill lingering despite the fact the spirit had obviously left, then finally let myself grin a little.

Right. A planetary alignment wasn't so common a thing that we couldn't track when it was due to happen. Morgana probably didn't realise just how good mortals had got at mapping the heavens, at what technology these days meant they knew. And her mention of the 'stones'? Excalibur had been in one, but she'd mentioned plural, that and the fact Artur had made some sort of promise on them or by them. Definitely meant I needed to speak to that particular fae arsehole, and find out what stupidity he'd done to so piss Morgana off.

I paced over to where the spirit had stood and knelt down on the ground. Frost still patterned the concrete, but that actually just helped me find the salt crystals I'd thrown through her, since they sparkled like little diamonds. And in a way, they were just as precious. Sweeping them up, I stashed them in an empty container. It was a very small chance, but I'd take it. Definitely needed to get them to Elspeth, and see what she could do with them.

Immortal Morgana might be, but she was just as arrogant as the mortal she was manipulating, just as blind in her drive to accomplish her goal. And maybe, just maybe, we could use that against her.

Bear huffed as he rose, straightening from where he had rested. I turned, already sensing the incoming presence, brushing my knees off as I faced the mortal policeman.

"Nice morning for it." I smiled innocently at the man, clicking my fingers for Bear to join me. And before he could start asking any difficult questions, I gave him a nod and started walking, troll hound trotting beside me.

I even started whistling, feeling *that* good, right then.

Bear huffed a complaint, butting me in the leg as a gentle request to stop, but I just didn't care.

Chapter 22

Dagonet.

Also known as Dauguenet, and the Fool. He is Artur's court jester but also a Knight in himself. Stories either have him as a loyal follower of Artur who the other knights use to perform practical jokes on their enemies whilst keeping him from harm, or as a butt of their own jokes, suffering humiliation and abuse whilst he suffers from madness brought on after his best friend abducts his new wife.

This shows the darker side to the famed Knights of the Round Table, as they regularly abused and scorned the man, and amused themselves with his humiliation.

It took the pair of us about twenty-five minutes to get to *Good Deeds*, meaning it was gone two in the morning by the time I reached the office. My little talk with Morgana hadn't lasted long, but Bear wasn't going to be rushed given how cooped up he had been recently in the apartment. Pretty much every tree and lamppost bore his scent by the time I stabbed my code into the front door of our office, and the neighbourhood cats were firmly lodged in the branches of the tallest trees they could find.

I'd noted the company vehicles parked out back as I passed, meaning both teams had made it in one piece, with no incident. Well, none that left any claw marks, blood stains or the like, which I tended to equate with incidents. Typically cynical of me, but hey, walk a mile in my shoes.

Reception was empty and unmanned, but I figured no self-respecting client would stop by at such a Gods forsaken hour of the morning, so there was little need for any of the pack to be behind the desk. With Bear padding behind, already scenting the air for doughnuts, I quickly took the stairs to the first floor.

Jacob and Jessica were just walking towards the main conference room, cradling steaming mugs of coffee. They both stopped as I crested the stairs, and I nodded to them both, but mostly to their cups.

"Any juice left? I've just been speaking to the mother of all our problems, and it's left a bad taste in my mouth." I explained, knowing the best thing I could do was debrief my Alpha and packmate as soon as possible, so as not to forget anything pertinent. Personal feelings towards one of the pair aside.

Jessica nodded but simply gave me her mug, the rich aroma of vanilla spiced latte filling my nose like a welcome home hug. I graciously accepted it, telling myself I was that much more in need of the caffeine, given how fresh and alert she seemed. Joys of being an Alpha.

"Ah've been speaking tae the trolls you detained." She told me even as she motioned for us to head to the meeting room. Jacob just shook his head at my little revelation, obviously thinking I'd proven him right again by having faced Morgana all on my lonesome. And I just didn't have the energy to argue with him.

"They say anything useful? Apart from asking for seagulls." I queried as we entered the room. Looking around, I was surprised to find it empty, expecting despite the late hour to find our resident consultant witch on site, already working on whatever they'd found out. "Uh, is Ellie around anywhere? I've got something for her."

"Miss MacElvy will be along later, but asked fer some privacy tonight. Ah believe she had some *personal* matters tae attend tae." Jessica replied to my second question, and I guessed those had to have something to do with her dealing with the loss of her love, DI Allen. We all settled down in the empty chairs, and she motioned for me to start. "Why don't you tell us what you and that ... particular fae had tae speak about?"

I shrugged, then launched into a quick retelling. Starting with me storming off after being picked up by Jacob's team, then Morgana's appearance outside the gates of Buckingham Palace. I was careful to refer to her as *that fae* or simply *she* because I didn't want to chance drawing

Morgana's attention to us. I had no clue where the spirit could or could not go, but having her listen in on our conversation was not something I reckoned was a great idea.

I wrapped up with the juicy bits of information I'd tricked from her, using the fae's own anger against her before settling back. Outside, I could hear Bear moving around the office, hunting for snacks, but otherwise the place was silent and still. Jessica and Jacob both sat, wrapped in thought, so I just sipped my coffee and waited for the first person to tell what I'd done wrong.

"Hnh. You really told her to go fuck herself? After she offered you a Get Out Of Jail Free card?" Jacob finally spoke up, his tone not one of doubt, more just plain surprise. "You know what she was offering, right?"

"Yeah well, I hate Monopoly. Only played it once with Sarah, and she wanted to stab me with a fork after five minutes." I replied glibly, then shrugged. "Yeah I know. She was telling me I could keep Sarah, Felix and Elspeth safe from whatever the fuck she's planning. All well and good, but that's quite a short list for all the people I care about. My *pack*, for one thing. Not that you'd expect that from me, given me being such a *lone-wolf* an' all."

I snarled the word, using Jacob's own reprimand against him, and the lycan sighed, brow furrowing and expression hardening. We both glared at each other across the table. I knew it was petty, but for fuck's sake. What did he want from me?

Jessica took note of the interplay between us, and leant forward, slapping her hand down hard on the meeting room table so that a sharp *crack* resounded through the air. Mine and Jacob's mugs jumped, almost spilling, as we jerked round to face her.

"Enough of this foolishness! Morgan, Jacob has told me of his words tae you." She explained, surprising me. I'd expected my packmate to keep our little chat private, given I knew he felt every word was justified and that I was wholly in the wrong here. Ok, so he *might* have had a few good points but still. "Ah will have this matter settled between you both here and now.

The Blooding is passed, and will nae come again in time tae settle this the traditional way. So instead, ah am intervening."

It was an Alpha's right to step into any argument or problem between members of their pack, forcing those involved to cede to their judgement. It didn't happen often simply because most Alphas felt it fairer to let the lycans involved sort out their own shit and be adult enough to do so without needing babysitters. But I reckoned Talen Orben had probably always forced his lycan to bow to his and Sol's decisions, to keep them inline and subservient. Jessica wasn't like that.

"Morgan." She addressed me first. "Jacob makes a fair point. That you have been dealing with more than yer fair share of Real problems recently, and have found yerself at odds with immortals beyond any normal lycan's abilities tae handle. There have been times you could have asked fer help from yer packmates, but whether from pride in yer own strengths, or fear of them coming tae harm, you have nae done so."

I went to speak, but she held up a hand, forestalling my obvious arguments.

"You will wait. Jacob is simply concerned you will come tae harm, and those around you will also. From a foolish sense of bravado and testosterone-fuelled bullishness tae handle everything on yer own. That yer recent advancement tae Knight of Shadow, and now Errant of Ivory, has led you tae believe you are more than capable tae handle these matters all on yer own." Jessica looked me straight in the eye as Jacob nodded his agreement, letting me feel what she was thinking, calming the anger flaring to life as she echoed my packmate's concerns.

I drew a breath, pushing down the Wyld rage, forcing it into its box where it belonged. Then I shrugged, not trusting myself to say something particularly stupid.

"Ah ask you, Morgan. Do you trust me?" She asked, and I guessed what she was about to say. What she wanted to reveal. I remembered the Morrigan's words of warning, but the simple fact was – this needed to be shared. And I trusted the two people in this room, even if one of them had *royally* pissed me off. So I nodded once again.

"Jacob." She turned to face the lycan enforcer. "Yer concerns are based on a simple misconception. Morgan is nae simply a lycan of our pack. He has learned the truth of his parentage, and has shared this information with me. And ah now trust this with you, not tae leave this room or be spoken about tae anyone without either his or mah direct leave. Is that understood?"

Jacob eyed me searchingly for a long moment, then just grunted his agreement.

"Good. He has nae spoken of his mother tae me, only of his father. And that being is well known tae you." Jessica spoke simply, expression closed but I could feel her own slight tremble at what she was about to say. Hell, it still scared me shitless. "His father is Herne. Lord of the Wyld Court, a High fae and son of the Morrigan. The Herald of Shadow. Knowing this, ah believe Morgan has acted as best he is able, with nae thought tae be heroic. Simply tae handle the task that is in front of him, as we all do."

My packmate stilled for a long moment, then finally released an explosive breath. He turned to stare at me, expression open and honest. The emotions carved there and plain for me to read.

"Geez, that's fucked." He finally spoke, shaking his head once. "So that's why …"

"Yeah, why the Morrigan keeps popping up like a bloody mushroom around me. Why I got dragged into sorting out Obie's mess, stopping him executing his Queen coz *that fae* was in his head and messing with him big time." I replied, listing off a few of the messier shitshows I'd been dropped in recently. "And why Jack came hunting me, given he's *also* Herne's son. Different mothers, but he still seems to really hate me. It's not like I'm asking the bastards to come at me. More like they know it's open season on me, and I'm wearing a big fat target on my forehead."

"Now." Jessica looked at us both, expression stern. "Ah will have nae more of this contest and discord between yer both. Morgan, nae matter your roots, you are of our pack, and the pack will protect you. Learn tae ask more fer help, and it will be freely given. Jacob, Morgan bears the weight of his parentage, and will from now on be drawn in tae matters beyond any lycan of this pack or any other might expect. Cut him some slack, and know he isn't just trying tae be a hero or any such stupidity like that."

"Never even crossed my mind." I added truthfully.

"This matter is settled. Are we agreed?" She asked us, and after a moment I nodded to Jacob, who grinned a hard smile and did so too.

"Just don't start treating me differently." I asked him. "As much as it might seem otherwise, I kinda enjoy the kitten jokes."

"Never even crossed my mind." Jacob grinned, repeating my words.

"Ok, now we're all friends again, can we skip the group hug? And you share what the trolls had to say instead?" I asked, feeling a knot unwind between my shoulders as the sense of pack settled back into its natural rhythm. No lycan does well when something so fundamental is off key and imbalanced, hence the Blooding being a great way to reset. Punching out our issues with each other.

Still, all it took was the love of a good woman to sort our shit out. In our case the Alpha we both cared about who could literally wipe the floor with both of us to put things right.

"A few useful things." Jessica replied with a hard smile. "Ah need tae clear up some details or ask Elspeth tae confirm some things but ah believe we now have clues tae the location of the ritual Knox will attempt, and the time it will take place. Not such a bad night's work, if ah say so mahself."

Our Alpha tapped a few quick strokes into the keypad in front of her, and the screen behind her lit up on a Google search webpage. She quickly tapped in *planetary alignment dates* and hit return. Several pages flashed up, but she focused on one of them.

… Jupiter, Saturn and Mars are due to align on May 11th as a conjunction of the morning planets takes place. Heralded by Venus, the evening star, aligning four of the planets in an event not seen since 1623. Visible from sunset that day …

"Ah believe this would be the alignment *she* spoke of, unless two such events are due so close together." Jessica commented dryly. "Which ah doubt. So, we know Knox must perform his rite in less than two days' time, unless he wishes to wait another four hundred years."

"Well, *that fae* has waited, what, fifteen hundred years to have her revenge." I replied, but then shook my head, remembering my brief interaction with her. "Then again, she didn't strike me as particularly patient anymore. So maybe not."

"Ah agree." Jessica tapped something into the pad, and a fresh google search came up for the times of sunset in May. With this detail, she flicked back to our slide on Knox and what we thought we knew of his plans. Our Alpha added in a new section, highlighting *sunset – 8:40pm on the 12th May.*

"And the other thing? The where?" I pointed out, and Jessica nodded. She tapped another query into the search bar.

"As ah suspected, the trolls were aware of the Nighters' demise and decided tae reach out to Knox directly. Tae do away with the middleman." She told me as she brought up a search of the Sword in the Stone myth. A plethora of sites popped up, including the Disney cartoon and Lego toy site but what made me laugh was the slightly random link to a psychologist's book *Arthur and the Sword in the Stone: Feminine Desire and Power in the Arthurian Tradition.* Somehow mortals always managed to link things back to sex.

"After the trolls realised Knox had sent Red Cap tae kill them, they were happy tae fill in the gaps. Knox sent them tae steal the stone in which Excalibur was set. From Circe's vault after she so unwisely shared her trove with him." Jessica told me, as she focused on one of the web returns from her search. A black and white picture from 1933, with the title *Archaeologist uncover stone in which Excalibur was housed.* It showed a large white masonry block, worked by unknown artists to resemble a large anvil. "But they also added this was not the *only* stone Knox sent them tae find."

I stared at the photograph, immediately noting one odd fact. Whilst the overall shape was artfully fashioned to look like a large anvil made of stone, where the front section should narrow to a point was rough and broken. Like a piece was missing.

"A second stone?" I asked a little late, my ears playing catch up. Morgana's words echoed in my head … *when the planets align, I shall be reborn by the stones upon which that fool Artur made his worthless and traitorous vows to me* …

"Aye, another stone. You've noted the broken end of the stone from Excalibur, and the trolls were instructed tae search for the end piece as Knox requires the thing in its entirety fer his ritual." Jessica explained. "Or so he let slip, and the trolls overheard. Whatever, there is nae record of where the missing end of Excalibur's stone might be, nor what happened tae it fer it tae be so important."

"Ok. We just need to find this second stone before Knox does, then we stop him from stealing it before this planetary alignment thingie and we win?" I summed up, but Jessica shook her head. "What's wrong with that?"

"Things are nae so simple, Morgan. Ah have searched the web fer the end piece's location but found naught. Nae story tae tell how it broke, nor what happened tae it after. Ah will ask Elspeth fer her aid when she arrives. We also need to know *why* the stones are so important tae Knox and *her* since us obtaining one may not be enough tae stop him. Yer task, Morgan, is tae speak tae yer contact in the Ivory Court and seek the answers from Artur directly."

"You're talking about his sister, right?" I queried. "The only one he seems to be in any way afraid of, or listen to?"

Jessica nodded.

"Once we knew more, ah think it is time we also appraised the mortal authorities of what we have found." She instructed, reminding me I was past due checking in with Cormac Smith. I hadn't heard anything from the OPS agent from my briefly scribbled note and wasn't even sure it had made it into his hands. But I guessed I'd have had a surprise visit or at least phone call by now if the mortal felt I wasn't keeping up my side of our deal.

"What do we do until then?" I checked the clock on the wall, finding it was close to three in the morning. My stomach gave a quiet rumble, reminding me how long ago it was that I'd eaten anything halfway like a meal, and the coffee I had stolen off Jessica was definitely wearing off.

"You go home." Jessica told me and shook her head as I went to argue. "Nae, Morgan. There is little tae do here, and a few hours of rest will do you good. Besides, ah plan tae ask the Furies tae take Red Cap off our hands tonight. He is nae technically an Accord Breaker but ah can spin his threat tae mortal children as close enough fer him tae be their problem. Ah believe it is best you are not on the scene when they arrive."

Oh yeah, that small wrinkle. I was down one gnome to hand back to the Furies as per our agreement, and Tisiphone had been very clear what might happen if I in any way welched on the deal.

"Ah will speak tae them and see if ah can explain yer situation. Or at least come tae some sort of agreement fer the matter of Terrigyle Munstrum." Jessica tried to reassure me, but even I could sense the doubt in her voice. You didn't mess with the Furies, unless you were ready to pay the price if it all went tits up. Which was what I was pretty much facing. "So ah suggest you head home, get some sleep and then commune with the Ivory Court from the safety of yer own home."

I finally nodded, knowing Jessica was just looking out for me, and trying to make the best of a bad situation. One that I was at least partially to blame for.

"Besides, ah feel there have been far too many *unscheduled* visitations at this location fer my liking." She added, quirking an eyebrow at me. "Ah will be asking Elspeth tae look at the wards and see about increasing their potency. Ah suggest you warn your *contacts* against attempting tae breach the Veil here from now on."

"They will nae find welcome."

Chapter 23

"Manisha Na Pendragon Cie. By the right gifted me as Errant of Ivory, I summon you."

I was sat on my sofa, having moved the coffee table aside to give, hopefully, the Knight of Ivory plenty of pace to arrive from wherever it was I was dragging her from. Also, I was kind of attached to the furniture in my home, and had seen it destroyed too many times recently to risk it weathering any further damage.

As per Jessica's instruction, I'd headed home from the office with my troll hound moping and dragging his heels behind. He obviously hadn't managed to snaffle enough treats to his satisfaction, and felt me taking him from the source of all things savoury and unhealthy was a dire liberty on my part.

We left my Alpha and Jacob to handle the handover of Red Cap to the Furies, and to deal with the three trolls we now had in residence at *Good Deeds*. It seemed the Bung brothers had realised just how much in the shit they were in, and were willing to make any sort of deal to stay safe. My Alpha had made it known that if they tried to run, she would use the lycan packs as well as my trollhound to hunt them down and drag them back, but if they stayed put in the office and refrained from stealing anything or in any way jeopardising her or my packmates, she would extend guest rights to them and keep them from any further harm until this matter was settled.

Cretinous and craven as they were, the three trolls hadn't wasted much time agreeing to behave and abide by her rules.

I'd made it back home with Bear before the clock struck four, giving the troll hound one final chance to stretch his legs and mark the territory around the apartment block before we headed inside. I was feeling particularly rung out, my wounds having healed over but the ache from them a lingering aggravation I knew would only lessen with rest. So, only stopping to check that Bear had water and food in his bowls and to grunt a *hi* to the apple tree and Goldspur, I collapsed on my bed and sank into blissful sleep. Without even bothering to shower or undress.

I'd woken from a restless sleep, dreams filled with unpleasant things with too many tentacles chasing me through a maze that seemed to have no way out, just leading me back into their suckered embrace time and time again. To find both Bear and Goldspur waiting patiently beside my bed.

It was made slightly less unnerving by the presence of a large mug of what smelt like coffee sat on my bedside table.

"I am told that individuals who share the same living space often have agreements in place, to avoid any confusion or disagreement." The dryad had told me in her sing-song voice.

She was attired in one of my t-shirts, hanging off her more like a tunic due to her smaller size, and leggings she had scrounged up from somewhere. If she hadn't been bright green and covered in highly intricate verdant tattoos as well as sporting the knives she never went anywhere without, Goldspur could have passed for a young woman now. Gone was the child I had seen on the camera, taking apart OPS's security team. Instead, she had quickly matured and now looked like a twenty something young woman, her hair intricately braided and woven with what I guessed were charms and wards gifted her by her charge, the apple tree. Even as I took all this in, Goldspur set down a piece of rolled paper beside my coffee. "If you would read this, we can discuss anything you disagree with whenever you are ready."

With that, the dryad had left the bedroom doorway, as my brain tried to play catch up on the last couple of minutes. I'd grabbed the paper, squinting at the tight, uncertain writing that I guess had to be hers.

Tenancy Agreement for the attention of Morgan Black (the homeowner), in the matter of Goldspur (the tenant). Firstly, Morgan Black shall swear not to take advantage of the tenant in any manner, physically, mentally or morally. Secondly, Morgan Black shall at all times wear clothing about the home, to avoid upsetting the tenant. Thirdly,

Morgan Black shall refrain from bringing home any member of the opposite sex and engaging in adult entertainment without first consulting the tenant and obtaining her approval. Fourthly …

I had growled, tossing the paper back onto the bed. Where the hell did she get all *that* from?

Then it had hit me.

This had Felix's name written all over it. I'd asked her to have a word with the dryad about not walking round my home naked, or jumping on me when I was only just waking up. Instead it seemed she'd decided I was due some payback, and had arranged *this* little package of fun for me to handle. I could almost see her laughing as she explained to Goldspur what to write.

Knowing I would have to deal with this on top of everything else, I'd made the sensible option to finish my coffee as I scanned the rest of the document. For someone who hadn't been alive for more than a week or so, and had had no instruction that I knew of how to use a pen, let alone legal training, it wasn't half bad. Then I'd tossed the agreement aside and went to go grab a shower and throw on a fresh set of clothes that didn't have Red Cap blood staining them.

I figured Bear needed settling before I got down to business, so gave him a quick romp around the apartment block, then settled into tracking Artur Pendragon.

"Manisha Na Pendragon Cie, by rights earned through combat, defending your back and you defending mine, I summon you." I growled out, feeling the connection between the immortal and I take hold. She obviously heard me, but for whatever reason wasn't responding even after the second repeat. That either meant she wasn't in the mood to chat, or something was going on that needed her full attention. And given she had recently been appointed Titania's personal guard, that did not bode well.

"Manisha Na Pendragon Cie, by the fact *you're* the one who got me named as bloody Errant of Ivory and so this is kinda *your* fault, I call on you!" I sent as much urgency as I could down the connection, to make the

Knight aware I wasn't just calling her up for kicks and a quick chat. "I ain't going away, so just bloody answer!"

For a moment, nothing happened. Then the Ivory Knight's voice echoed in the air of the living room.

"*Morgan Black, I'm a little … busy right now … Can this wait?*" Her voice was clipped, and I heard background sounds intruding through our connection. Faint cries, thuds and clashes of metal on metal that could only mean one thing. I'd definitely called her in the middle of something.

"Not really. I need to speak to your brother." I spoke out loud, feeling a little foolish but then, I was still getting used to this summoning thing. As I'd said, we lycan steered clear of magic and all things related to the art as a rule, since our own nature usually meant we couldn't use it like the immortals and mortals did. But also because it was normally much easier to simply thump whoever we faced rather than try to use magic on them. It's very difficult to keep one's focus and complete all the ritual actions when something is chewing on one's leg and making a spirited attempt to disembowel you. Just saying.

"*Fine, if it's that urgent, you'll just have to come to me.*" She replied and I felt a tug, like someone had grabbed hold of me by my t-shirt and given me a good yank.

The living room blurred as I was enveloped by the stink of the Veil. Greyness billowed around me, as I yelled and tried to jerk myself free but to no avail.

The next thing I knew, I was falling on my arse amongst lush purple grass. The crash and clamour of battle filled the air, as well as the stink of blood spilt, bodies ruptured. It didn't matter whether it was mortal or immortal, they all smelt the same after a few hits with something sharp or heavy.

Manisha stood before me, clad in her full Ivory plate armour. The maul she had won from an ogre Knight who had unwisely given her too much attitude lay on the grass nearby, and instead she held her familiar greatsword unsheathed and stained with silver gore. Her amber eyes blazed from within the confines of her dragon-crested helmet, and she cocked her head as she took in my inelegant entrance.

"Well met, Sir Errant." She spoke with just a trace of laughter in her voice. "Methinks I should have informed you of your destination, 'ere I brought you to my side. You clothing is, well, less suitable than normal."

I quickly clocked my surroundings, expecting the worst. And I was not disappointed.

We were atop a large hill, with grass covering its slopes and rolling down to cover the surrounding fields in swathes of whispering lushness. Far off, I could see the beginnings of what I guessed was the Verdance, that uncharted and unending forestland in which the Wyld made its home. As well as a host of other nasties, like giant spiders who dwelt in the trees, monstrous insects that burrowed under foot, and all manner of forest-dwelling predators that would happily devour any foolish mortals lost amongst the towering fauna. In there, leaving a breadcrumb trail was akin to providing the monsters with their own starter, before they dined on the main course.

My attention, however, was grabbed by what was taking place a lot closer to home. Down the slope, at the foot of the hill, armoured knights clad in both the off-white of Ivory and the blue-black of Shadow fought side by side against towering ogres and plate-armoured dwarrow. Bellows and roars filled the air, as the monstrous fighters slammed huge mauls and axes down upon their opponents, whilst the dwarrow sang a diresome dirge as they summoned roaring flames to burst from their cannon-like weapons to scorch any caught in their wake. Magic flashed and hammered both sides, or each side, as I was thoroughly confused as to whom was fighting whom here.

"What the hell's going on?" I asked Manisha, looking back at the Knight. "I thought the war between Ivory and Shadow was called off? By Titania? Or was that just the half time break for oranges, and it's all kicked off again?"

"You are remembering things well enough." She answered, eyes switching back to the battlefield.

Behind us, I saw a large tent had been raised, and under its awning I saw white robed fae working on the broken and battered bodies of fallen soldiers. Slim fauns, bearing stretchers one between four, brought in the wounded as quickly as their hooved feet could carry them, whilst sylphs and other sprites sat with the more seriously injured, their charms and powerful allure used to bewitch and deaden the pain of those they tended. Goat bearded satyrs seemed the stock of doctors and healers, deftly setting limbs here, sewing up a wound there with unnatural skill given their stubby hands.

"So, if the war is over, what the hell is this?" I gestured back out to the conflict waging around and below us. In the air, dark crested harpies cawed and shrieked as they dove and clawed at slender wyrms of scintillating colour, silver blood and feathers exploding from each hit as they sought to tear each other from the sky. "Someone start a bar fight or something?"

"This? This is far, far worse." She replied, even as she freed a hand from her swordhilt and made a gesture. I realised we weren't alone, as suddenly a score or more pixies joined us. Clad in embossed leather armour, these diminutive fae all bore massive bows topping their own height by at least three feet. Yet despite this, they drew those weapons with ease, fitting long shafts to the nook of each bow and sighting. In the next breath, they loosed and re-bent, fitting more shafts and sending them arcing through the air.

Shrieks echoed over the battlefield, as the harpies realised they had drifted too close to the hill too late. Each arrow found one target, spitting them through the eye or heart with pinpoint accuracy. Down the dark feathered corpses tumbled, as their brethren further away howled their fury but wheeled and fled beyond bowshot. The remaining wyrms, freed of their opponents, lashed the air with brilliant fire and darted onward, seeking more prey.

"So, you going to tell me what's going on?" I pushed, knowing Manisha to be close lipped for a fae but I needed answers. And I didn't have the time to be bouncing back and forward through the Veil, especially not if I was going to be dropped into the middle of any more battlefields.

"Better suit up. Answers can wait." The Ivory fae told me, as she pointed to where a large contingent of ogres were pushing hard against the line of Shadow and Ivory fae warriors. It looked like they were driving as a wedge, trying to split the blockade and reach the hill. Whether as a military vantage point over the battle or to attack the wounded and disrupt their enemies, I couldn't say. But that didn't matter. They were headed our way, and I was in jog pants and a t-shirt, with none of my kit I'd normally bring when tussling in the Real.

"Uh, as you already noted I'm a little underdressed for this party." I answered. I could Change, take my full lycan form which would give me speed and enough strength to tackle any of the ogres one of one, but there were over two score pushing through. All armed with spiked and sharp-edged axes and mauls that would leave me a flattened pulp if they got in a few good strikes. I needed my gear, to give me the edge over the bastards. Only problem was, it was sitting in my living room closet, a world away.

Manisha eyed me, then nodded to my right hand.

"You have not figured out your blessing yet?" She asked, and I realised she was indicating the new tattoo I'd been gifted by Titania when she elevated me to Knight Errant. The touch of Ivory, to match my Shadow brand.

"Nope, it didn't come with a user guide," I joked, but Manisha just shook her helmet-clad head. "You know what it does?"

"Yes, Sir Knight. As will you, I expect. Very shortly." She replied, hefting her sword as I heard a roar from down below. The line of fae soldiers buckled, and finally gave as the ogres surged through, bellowing savagely. The Ivory Knight motioned for the pixies to lay down covering fire, sending shafts after shafts into the massive monsters, but they shrugged off the assault, those arrows finding their targets only penetrating their armour and thick hide a little, mostly bouncing off.

"Fuck!" I swore, as Manisha stepped in front of me, greatsword readied. Two other knights I didn't recognise, their armour just as decorated as the Ivory champion, joined her and the three faced forty or more massive foes.

I tried to ignore the mountain of muscle and pain charging uphill towards us, and instead focused on reaching for the touch of Ivory. I knew the Shadow brand as something like a shard of ice inside me, just ready to flood through my veins and freeze whatever I directed it to. And Wyld was like an inner core of strength, for me to call on when I needed some extra juice in my muscles. But Ivory? I hadn't tried summoning whatever the brand bequeathed me, hadn't needed to.

Now it seemed like I maybe should have practised.

Delving deep, I reached out blindly, trying the same thing I'd done to awaken my first brand.

"C'mon, c'mon!" I snarled, opening my eyes as nothing happened. The lead ogres had reached Manisha and her two companions, engaging with the clash and crunch of swords against mauls. Despite the differences in size, the Ivory Knights held the line and squared off as they battered the ogres back one foot, then another.

But there were more coming behind, and only three Knights. Fuck it.

I let the Change take me, feeling my body surge and burgeon with familiar strength as my clothes stretched and ripped. As much as I try to wear baggy materials that stretch enough to allow me to switch suits, sometimes I'm just unlucky. Like the Hollywood werewolves you see in the movies, wearing rags. Or the Incredible Hulk in his seemingly indestructible shorts.

Anyhow, clad in the rags of my clothes, I let loose an angry snarl and slid my claws out from my bunched knuckles. Unarmoured I might be, but I was lycan, fast and strong.

And oh so ready to dish out some carnage.

Chapter 24

The first ogre to make it past the three Knights was in no fit state to fight, bleeding silver gore from multiple wounds. Only its stubbornness was keeping it upright, as it snarled and weakly swung at me with its hammer.

I sidestepped the blow easily, letting the creature crash down into the grass to bleed out. It was going nowhere, but I still kicked its weapon out of reach. I'd learned my lesson from turning my back on an enemy still armed. Then I squared off, taking the back line behind the three Ivory fae.

Manisha was a whirlwind of destruction, wielding that massive sword like it weighed nothing, hammering blows into the ogres as she splintered their weapons and carved through their armour in sprays of silver. The two other Knights were equally deadly, one wielding a cruel curved axe that trailed fire as the fae hewed its foes like a lumberjack does trees. The other wielded what looked like two flails of fanged metal, creating a storm of slicing death as it hewed at the ogres, carving chunks from their armour and flesh alike and eliciting howls of agony with each strike.

The three companions held the line and threw back all that came at them, until the warrior with the flails misjudged a strike and stumbled, weapons tangling around its opponent's weapon. With a mighty heave, the monster dragged the Knight into the path of another ogre, this new opponent crashing its hammer into the fae's side and sending it to the grass with a pained cry. The monster raised its weapon again, ready to crush the warrior beneath one final blow. Manisha and the other fae raced to protect their fallen comrade, but they were held back as more ogres pushed forward, intent on making the kill.

I, however, was free to act.

Howling, I leapt across the grass, blood pounding and Wyld fire blazing in my veins. The ogre turned at the sound, massive hammer shifting to come crashing down on me instead …

And I stopped astride the fallen fae, punching up with both fists to knock the blow aside. A bloody stupid idea, I know, as I fully expected to feel my bones break under the force of the ogre's smashing strike, given the thing outweighed me at least five times over.

Something bounced off my fists, shattered bits of hammer falling around me. Like someone had thrown a basketball at me and I'd punched it away. Definitely not what I was expecting, nor the ogre as it staggered back, suddenly off balance and disarmed. We both exchanged a surprised look, as I checked my hands for the damage done.

A shimmering gauntlet now clad my hands, much akin to the plate armour worn by Manisha and the Ivory knights. In fact, I realised the weird armour now fitted me from head to foot. Somehow it did not restrict my vision in any way, as I checked the close-fitting plates, tapping them with my claws and hearing them scrape against the magical defence as if it were solid steel.

My claws were sheathed as well, but I immediately noted a different in their colour. Where the mystical armour was of Ivory cream and white enamel, these shone with metallic brightness, wickedly edged. Cold iron mixed with silver, I guessed. I didn't know how it was possible but the brand had converted my fist daggers into deadly weapons against my current foe.

Grinning a nasty smile, I lashed out and drove my claws into the ogre's chest, cutting through its armour as if it simply wasn't there. The monster roared in fury but then choked off as the poison from my strike ate into it like acid. Bloodied foam burst from its mouth, and it clutched at its chest as blood, blackened and fouled, gushed from the holes I'd punched. Mortally wounded, it staggered back and fell back down the hill, taking one of its brethren with it.

"I knew you'd figure it out eventually." Manisha called across to me, her voice filled with wry laughter as she hacked through another ogre, sending it stumbling back, its lifeblood gushing from a stump where an arm used to be. "You wear our colours well."

The armour bestowed by the Ivory tattoo was weightless and did not restrict me in any way, but solid enough to withstand the direct strike of an ogre. I couldn't help but grin, idly wondering if anyone had a mirror somewhere so I could see how odd I must look. A lycan in plate mail armour? Not something you saw every day.

I reached down and carefully hauled the downed knight back to its feet, bracing it as it staggered a moment. But in the next breath, it recovered itself enough to give me a nod of thanks before turning back, flails already spinning.

"Come, join us Errant!" Manisha invited me as she kicked an ogre hard between its legs. "And let's throw these curs back. Then we can talk of my brother."

Feeling much better attired for the fight now, I shrugged and hurled myself into the charging ogre pack, claws hammering out at anything that got close.

With the three knights at my side, we faced the ogres as they bounded and leapt up the hillside, meeting and blunting their attack with grim determination and more than a little luck. If the thick-skulled bastards had thought things through, they would have split their number and circled round, coming at us from all sides and so overwhelming our meagre defences. But they were enraged, seeing their brethren beaten down by only four warriors, and each and every one sought to attack us head-on, and bring us down.

When the final monster fell, gnashing its broken teeth and frothing with rage, I staggered and almost slumped back onto my arse, feeling more than a little knackered. Despite my inhuman nature, and even drawing on my Wyld strength, I wasn't used to taking on an entire warband of heavily armoured and powerful foes in one day. The three fae all bore scars and dents on their armour from weathered blows, but all stood, breathing slow and steady, casually at ease despite the fight. The utter sods.

I focused on strengthening my legs, stumbling along as the three retreated back up the slope. Warriors down below surrounding the hill tightened their defence once more, swallowing the hole the ogres had made. Beyond this, I could see that the flow of battle was ebbing, the day almost done. I wasn't sure who had won or lost, but right now I didn't care much as long as they did it away from this hill and gave me a chance to catch my breath.

"Bravely fought, Sir Errant." The fae who I'd saved spoke up, stowing their flails at their waist and unbuckling their helm to reveal the fae beneath. "And you have my thanks for the fact I am still able to draw breath and rejoice in a battle won. That beast would surely have dented my head if you had not interceded."

The fae was a woman, the fact hidden by an intricately engraved breastplate hiding, well, breasts. She smiled at me as I took in her fox thin features, braided white hair falling down to frame intense azure blue eyes and a quirked smile made so by a scar hooking the corner of her mouth. Silver sparkled amongst her tresses, and she bore slashes of red ochre under her eyes like the warpaint mortal tribal braves used to wear to battle.

"Morgan Black, Errant of Ivory, I have the pleasure of presenting Sir Lancelot du Lake. Knight of Ivory." Manisha commented dryly, as she too freed her helmet and set it aside.

"As in *Knights of the Round Table* and *Camelot* Lancelot?" I queried, wondering if I'd hit my head and not noticed. "But wasn't Lancelot, well, a man? Given the whole thing with Guinevere?"

"You mustn't believe everything the mortals say was 'fact'," Lancelot laughed brightly, combing through her tresses to free them from the tangle they had made inside her armour. "Guinevere and I may have, ah, dallied once or thrice, but it was no great love story or tragedy as they tell the tale. She was a fulsome and broad-minded mortal, and Artur did not appreciate her for her charms as I did. But that was long ago, and as she is not here to talk of this herself, I think we should leave that tale for what it is. History."

"Uh, fine with me." I shrugged, not wanting to get into the intricacies of what an Ivory fae might mean by *fulsome* and *broad minded*. "And hey, don't mention the *me saving your life* thing. All in a day's work for an Errant, I guess?"

"Ha, indeed. It has been too long since our Court appointed anyone to that singular rank. For what reason, I know not." Lancelot smiled that crooked smile again then gave me a short bow. "I shall take great delight in seeing what troubles you uncover in your appointed duty, and keep my weapons close to hand."

"If anyone has an instruction manual or at least a job description, that would be a great start." I growled but without too much real ire. I was getting used to having to wing any and all duties granted by the fae.

I turned back to Manisha and nodded to the remains of battle taking place below us.

"You said this was worse than the Ivory and Shadow Courts being at war. So what the hell is it then?"

The Ivory Champion set a toe to one of the dead ogres, nudging its head so that it rolled to face upwards.

"This is Sir Duggan, one of the Ivory Knights who I had the honour to serve alongside." She indicated the dead monster, then pointed to another corpse. "And that is Sir Grummage. An Ivory Knight too."

"And this one," Lancelot nudged one of the dead ogres. "It bears the mark of Shadow, one of their Knights I presume."

"Sir Darkgallow." An icy voice intoned, as a fell wind whipped at the hilltop. I turned, to find the Morrigan standing behind us, leaning on a graven staff and clad once more in her leather armour and knotted garments. "A Knight of Shadow indeed, as are a number of these ill-fated warriors I see littered at your feet."

"Ah, I was wondering when you were going to show up." I told her, and she shot me a wintry smile. "Where have you been hiding?"

"Walking amongst the dying, as is my rightful place." She told me, then turned to wave at the battleground. "But to answer your original question, pup. This is but one of many battles being retold across the Real even as we speak, with brother fighting brother, sister set against sister. Mothers warring with their children, whilst their fathers lie bloodied and broken in the dirt. The Courts are riven, as warriors we once named comrades renege against their rightful rulers and claim to fight for *her*."

"Ivory, Shadow and Wyld. Courtiers, noble fae and their lesser kin ceding to Morgana's cause. It is utter and most delightful chaos, wrought to strike at my Lady's heart, and aimed at the Lord and Lady of Ivory too." She smiled that ghastly smile of hers, as she let the import of her words sink in. "*She* sought to set the Courts against each other and have her revenge whilst remaining hidden, but you foiled that particular plan through hapchance and dumb luck. Now it would seem she cares not who knows of her return, as her name rings out in battle cry across our Realm."

"She speaks the truth, Errant." Manisha added as she used a rag to clean crusted silver blood off her sword. "You remember Sir Braddum? The ogre whom I took that maul off? He and his warband ceded to *that fae*, killing a half hundred Ivory warriors before they escaped the camp they were meant to be guarding. Him and his ilk, plus many more of both High and Low caste flock to a banner that none have seen raised, yet still has riven the Courts as keenly as a knife cut."

I growled to myself as the seriousness of this particular shitstorm hit home. If the Real was in this much turmoil and the Courts faced a challenge of this size, we really were on our own having to deal with Morgana in the Mortal Realm. Despite Herne's warning via the Bayun Cat, I'd still held out a hope that Oberon and Titania, or even Madb, would swoop in at the last possible minute and deal with their errant sibling. Leaving us to clean up the mess Knox had made, which was big enough and nasty enough all on its lonesome.

But now? Not a bloody chance.

"Cheer up, Sir Errant!" Lancelot grinned, as she wiped ogre blood from her flails. "Ivory and Shadow remain strong, and I doubt not Wyld will weather this storm well enough too. Before long, we'll have this disagreement settled and you can take on your duties proper. It has been too long since we had a good dragon hunt."

"Yeah, that's exactly what I'm worried about, right now. Those poor dragons feeling all neglected and ignored." I replied, noting the Morrigan roll her eyes dramatically at my words. But she refrained from adding any sarcastic comment, instead beckoning for Manisha and I to walk with her.

Below us, the battle was drawing to a bloody end, with a few remaining scrappy fights being fought between those few opponents still able to swing a weapon. Lightly armoured gnomes, sprites and other lesser fae-kin moved amongst the fallen, checking identities and scribing on rolls of parchment and, on occasion, dispatching a wounded foe that was not quite dead yet with a quick dagger thrust. No mercy was being given, from what I could see, no prisoners being taken. This was a fight to the death, with the fallen only good for a light bit of robbery or *requisitioning* as the mortals called it.

Most of those still upright and not at risk from their stab-happy brethren seemed to bear the banners of Ivory and Shadow, with the odd Wyld sigil adorning a back-banner. Which meant I guess we'd won, though from the mournful pallor laying over the battlefield you would not think it.

The enemy, those that had sworn for Morgana, had only crudely formed markers to show their changed allegiance. A variety of materials, even skin from what I could see, had been used as banners but all were daubed with the same symbol. Something like an upside down trident head, the forks forming a stylised *M*. And either there had been a job lot done on silver paint, or they'd used their own blood to trace the design.

Apart from the ogres and dwarrow, I could see armour-clad high fae, like Manisha or Lancelot, as well as harpies, goblins and gnolls amongst the dead. It really did look like all three Courts were represented amongst those who had sworn to Morgana's service, all types of Real denizens flocking to her call. And if this was a representation of what was happening elsewhere, things were truly fucked up this side of the Veil. The Courts provided stability, and order. They enforced what went for laws here and kept the monsters from returning to their old ways, where mortals were simply a plentiful snack and nothing prevented them from breaching the Veil to go food shopping.

If things devolved back to pre-Accord ways, I didn't want to think of what sort of nightmare would be unleashed on the unsuspecting men, women and children back mortal-side.

I didn't want to, but I did anyway. It wasn't pleasant.

No pressure then, Morgan, I told myself. Knowing we had to stop a disastrous fate from happening to however many mortals living their normal lives behind the Veil, blissfully unaware of what was headed their way.

With me and my friends slap bang in the middle of it all.

Chapter 25

Culhwch.

Meaning 'sow run', this Knight was born to his mother when she is frightened by a pack of wild pigs. His life is eventful – after his mother dies, his father remarries and his stepmother attempts to force him to marry his step-sister. When he refuses, she curses him so that he can marry no one besides the beautiful Olwen, daughter of the giant Ysbaddaden. Through trial and tribulation, Culhwch finally gains the hand of the young giantess, after her father is beheaded by the last remaining son of a shepherd who once was lord of the castle in which the giant now lived.

The Morrigan finally stopped near a small palisade, where sprites had hidden behind wooden bulwarks to send deadly arrow storms on any foe that came within bowshot.

Now the small fae were out amongst the dead, reclaiming their arrows and, as I'd suspected, looting the fallen for anything interesting. I had no moral feelings either way seeing this, since it was common practice for lycan to search any stiff we encountered. Nominally for identification purposes but if we came across a full wallet, that went into the kitty for team doughnuts. It's a dog-eat-dog world, and none of us are completely squeaky clean.

With a wave, the Shadow fae sent the few remaining sprites off to join their brethren, giving us the space. She settled down on a wooden stump, resting her staff beside her. Then my fae grandmother cocked one eyebrow at me, taking in my early morning attire. The armour had vanished as soon as the threat I'd faced had been dealt with, leaving me once more clad in my comfy clothes.

"I wasn't expecting to be dropping in." I explained as I settled myself against the wooden fence posts that made up the defensive wall. "In fact, all I was really after was a conversation with Artur. We've found some details out that might point to where Knox is going to perform the ritual, but I need to clear up one little point of confusion."

"Only one point confounds you? I am truly amazed!" The Morrigan smiled coldly, as she delicately brushed some dried silver blood from her hand. "Much of what transpires beyond this Realm is of constant consternation to me. Such as the mortals' belittlement of what they term superstition and yet their almost blind devotion to the Gods they create for themselves out of a crippled need for there to be *something* more. And their strange need to dress their pet animals in similar clothing to their own, when the animals already have fur covering them. Why is this?"

"Uh, I'll have to check on that and get back to you." I shrugged, knowing that to immortals, the ways of mortal-folk often seemed crazy and without reason, and no matter how many times you tried to explain something as simple as allergy stickers on packets of nuts, they never really got it.

I turned to Manisha, who had remained standing, her sword sheathed across her back and her wolfshead maul casually held over one shoulder.

"Anyhow, before we get too distracted with the silliness of mortals, I really need to speak to your brother." I reminded the Ivory Knight. "I'm guessing he's not anywhere near here, or any front line by chance?"

Manisha snorted a laugh, setting the maul down and leaning on the weapon.

"Ha. You guess right, Errant." She shook her head, amber eyes flashing with mirth. "My brother heard the escaped prisoner has sworn vengeance on him, amongst others, and as such he petitioned Oberon and Titania to be allowed to remain safe within Camelot. He argued if he were to fall into *her* hands, then we might face another attempt to use Excalibur against them, or worse, the Knights of the Table forced to serve her instead. They ceded to his wishes, so I believe he now hides in one of the tallest towers, drunk out of his skull and probably disappointing some poor maid or another."

"Eh? What's that about the Knights of the Round Table?" I knew it was off topic and not anything I should be worried about, but hell, the mess with the portal key sword had been bad enough.

Manisha shrugged, but saw she was going to have to explain.

"As part of the whole *King Arthur* ritual to make my brother ruler of the mortals, six Knights of the Round Table swore allegiance and service to the High King. And since they swore this on Excalibur, the oaths still bind them. *Sir Lancelot du Lake, Sir Gawain Ethlelian, Sir Galahad Mor, Sir Bedivere No Ols, Sir Gaheris Na Indra* and *Sir Bors Eld Yodwin*. Six of the Ivory High Champions, one who you met this day." Manisha reminded me. "In theory, Artur can still call upon their oaths and so command them. He has never done so, knowing that they would not take kindly to any of his foolish whims, nor was he until recently in favour with the Court and any of its members. As such in no position to ask for anything. But if *she* were to capture and control him, *she* would most likely command those Knights to commit atrocities in her name, or even challenge Oberon and Titania. And so, my Lord and Lady granted his wish to stay clear of conflict, and avoid any risk to their persons as well."

"Ah, ok. So that's a no to handing Artur over to *her*." I concluded with a grin. "As tempting as it might be."

"Don't. The thought has crossed my mind on more than one occasion." Manisha admitted, a smile touching her lips also. "But that aside, what is it you wish to ask of him?"

I shifted, using the wood behind me to scratch an itch before I answered.

"It's something that *a certain fae* said, when I got her all riled up and …" I began but stopped as the Morrigan shot me a frosty look.

"You have spoken to her?" The Shadow fae asked firmly, dark eyes narrowed with suspicion. "When?"

"She dropped in to say hi and ask me to back the fuck off," I answered truthfully, and briefly gave the pair the cribnotes on my interaction with Morgana. "Yeah, I know it was her trying to bribe me, so I didn't take the bait. Just pissed her off more, and that's when she let slip a few details."

"Hmm, that is not her style, to be loose of lip." The Morrigan tapped a finger against her lips as she considered for a moment, then motioned for me to continue.

"So, as I was saying, she made reference to a particular event, a planetary alignment we've identified as happening two days from now. Ish" I explained, seeing my fae grandmother nod as if this was simple common knowledge. "We figure that's when Knox will complete the ritual, something about the alignment being key to its success."

"It is a simple truth that most who work with magic know," The Shadow fae commented dryly, and once again I felt like the stupid child in the classroom, having the teacher explain things *really simply* for my benefit. "The movement of celestial bodies directly influence rituals, either to positively charge them with power or to block and prevent them from occurring. That is why even the wise mortals of old used to track the stars and planets, and keep a record of events that would embolden or inhibit their craft. Your Knox, I would assume, is learned enough to recognise a conjunction and will seek to use it to bolster his own strength."

"Yeah, what she said." I forced myself not to roll my eyes, knowing the fae couldn't help but treat me as the naive child. If I'd been kicking around for however many centuries, I'd probably act the same way to someone not even breaking forty years yet. "That said, we think we have the rough time nailed down. But she also mentioned using 'the stones', where Artur made some promises to her he didn't keep. We figured one of them is the hunk of rock Excalibur was stuck in, seeing how Knox got some trolls to steal it just the other day. But we only have a suspicion about the other one, so need your brother to remember his idiocy with *her* to help narrow things down."

Manisha sighed deeply. It was the sigh of someone who had spent forever making up for the shortcomings of their younger sibling, dealing with the damage he had done to their family name and generally making their lives way more complicated and unpleasant than they needed to be.

The sigh of an older child who had finally made good on things, set them back on the right path. Only to find out something else the younger brother had done was speeding towards them like a runaway train of muck and shit.

I couldn't exactly blame her. This whole mess, from the theft of Excalibur up to and including Morgana's escape from prison and bid for freedom, all kept coming back to Artur bloody Pendragon.

"No, I cannot help you with that particular topic." The Ivory Knight shook her head after a moment's thought. "I kept as far as possible from my brother's side whilst he acted his role for the mortals, and whilst I knew of his, ah, *dalliance* with this person, I know nothing of their intimacies."

"Guessed as much. Reckon I need to ask the man himself." I squared my shoulders, pushing myself off the fence and looking between both fae. "Either of you ok to give me a lift to Camelot, so I can get this over with and hop back Mortal side?"

"There is no need." Manisha told me with a hard smile. "Though the wards of the Ivory Court are raised, as Champion to my Lord and Lady, I am allowed certain privileges. One of which is to summon any fae of the Court, other than my lieges, to my side in times of need. Perhaps, say, if the Errant of Ivory were to formally ask my aid?"

I grinned, loving a loophole when it actually did me some good.

"Well then. Manisha Na Pendragon Cie, I formally request that you summon Artur Ne Pendragon Cie. That he might answer an Errant's enquiries on a matter most urgent." I tried hard to be as formal as possible, which is a bit tricky when both Manisha and I were fighting ourselves not to burst out laughing.

The Morrigan sighed, settling herself more comfortably on the tree stump.

"Children, please. A little decorum is warranted here, even if it is only for appearance's sake." She reprimanded us, but that just made me want to laugh all the harder.

"As is my duty as Champion of Ivory, I cede to your request, Errant." Manisha told me, then made a complicated gesture. Magic surged in the small air around us, making my teeth ache. Then with a sharp pop, a tangle of pillows, bed throws and arms and legs appeared on the grass before us.

"Wha … what the …?!" Artur's voice, only slightly slurred, sounded from within the mess of bedding, whilst another much more high-pitched cry of surprise came from close by. "Lord and Lady, where am I?!"

"Brother, I have summoned you to speak with the Errant." Manisha stepped closer to the mess in front of us, shoving aside several cushions to reveal Artur Pendragon. Butt naked, a cup of wine dripping down his bare chest from where it had spilled. Another fae, *definitely* female and just as naked, took in her surroundings with large, startled eyes before giving another shriek and diving under the protection of a multi coloured throw. "If you would answer his questions, we can return you to your *pursuits* forthwith."

"Be damned will I do any such thing!" Artur swore, staggering upright and dropping his cup. "Do you know who I *am*! How dare you …"

"Brother!" Manisha's voice snapped out, all trace of humour gone. Instead, her tone was one of command, cutting him off in mid rant. "Stay your tongue. You stand before the Errant of Ivory, who wishes some answers from you. You *will* give them, to the best of your ability or you and I shall have words."

"Plus, if you hadn't already noticed, you're standing butt naked in the middle of a battlefield with pretty much everything on show." I added helpfully, stepping forward so that his eyes fixed on me. "The sooner you answer my questions, the sooner you can be back safe inside the castle and out of harm's way."

Artur's eyes darted around him as the reality of where he was sank in. His rage dribbled away like wax under a flame, replaced with dread that paled his skin to almost a corpse-like pallor. He flinched, jerking around and snatching at the throw his paramour was hiding under. A tussle ensued, with

Artur finally cursing and loosing hold of the blanket, snatching up a pillow instead and curling around it as best he could.

"I can't be *here*! What if … if *she* finds me! You must send me back, sister!" He whined, and Manisha gave that heartfelt sigh again. Family, you can't choose them and no-one will ever take the bad ones off your hands, no matter how much you offer.

"Artur!" I clapped my hands, jerking his eyes back to me. "Questions first, then off you go. Deal?"

"You're the Errant?" He sneered, looking me up and down, and evidently finding me wanting in about every single way. "I'd heard that our Lady had made some odd choices recently, but still? You're just a Redcloak! A *lycan*! What was she thinking?"

"Beats me." I growled, so used to High Court fae looking down at my kind that it was almost refreshing to have him act normal around me. "But unless you want *me* to beat *you*, I'd answer my questions with as little lip as possible. We understood?"

Artur tried to rally some dignity, which to be fair was quite the effort given his nakedness and stupid posture, clutching the cushion to his privates, but Manisha just gave an angry, exasperated hiss and he slumped, nodding once in defeat.

"Fine. Ask your questions and then send me … *us* back." He belatedly remembered to include his partner hiding beside him, which spoke volumes to me. But I wasn't here to judge.

"Ok, let's keep it simple. It's about the stuff you got up to with*, a certain fae* who's the cause of all this trouble." I nodded out toward the battlefield, the numerous corpses piled one atop another. A tableau in death.

"You mean Morg…" He went to name her, the idiot, but I cut him off.

"Yeah, her. Call her *that fae* or whatever, but don't use her bloody name." I growled, and he blinked as he realised what he had almost done.

"Anyhow, she spoke of some stones, ones that you would know about. You supposedly swore some oaths on them? What are they?"

"Oaths ... Me swearing oaths to ... *her* ..." Artur almost crossed his eyes, obviously struggling to remember details. Ok, so it had been fifteen hundred years ago, but fae were dependably accurate when it came to details of things they'd done. If only because it helped them win argument against lesser creatures like mortals, and to seem all knowing and wise. "No, I'm not getting any recollection ..."

"Oh for gods' sake." I snarled. "*She* said you made some oaths to her on these stones. Oaths you then did not fulfil. What did you promise her?"

I suddenly saw his eyes narrow, forehead pinching as a thought struck.

"Ok, what was that you just remembered?" I pushed, seeing him shake his head.

"It's just ... look, *that fae* and I, we got rather friendly this one time. After we'd beaten the mortals at some battle or other. We celebrated, drank spirits and well, one thing led to another." Artur half whispered, a faint blush sparking on his cheeks. "And maybe, I *might* have said something along the lines of ... well ... that I might make her my Queen, that she would have a Court of her own. Countless servants, wealth, you know the sort of thing you offer in *those* situations?"

From beneath the blankets and cushions, there came a quiet but very disgruntled hiss. The sort of sound someone might make upon hearing the very rhetoric they had listened to, maybe even believed a little, turn out to be just a pile of deepest shit. I got the impression Artur was in a world of trouble once this little matter was done with.

"Fine, you promised to show her the world, just as long as she got down and dirty with you." I shook my head, as ever unamazed at just what levels some of the fae would sink to, and just how *similar* to mortals they could be. "What about the stones?"

Artur bit his lip, looking between me, his sister and the Morrigan.

"Is it *really* necessary to speak of this?" He wheedled, obviously not wanting to dwell on the details but I just growled and nodded for him to continue.

"Fine!" Artur hissed but then calmed himself, drawing a breath. "As I said, we had been drinking and … *that fae* seemed to think it would enhance our cojoining if we made out upon the very stone that Excalibur had been set. The one the mortals believed had been sent by their God. *She* it was who did drape herself most sensuously over it, inviting me to unsheathe my own sword and …"

"Ok, ok enough with the details!" I held up a hand, feeling my stomach start to churn a little. "So you both got kinky on the stone. Fuck knows, you could have chosen something more comfortable but I'm not going there. Why did she say *stones*, as in plural?"

Artur gave a short bark of a laugh, remembering.

"Oh that is right! As we frolicked, part of the original stone broke away. A smaller section, one that we had been using for handholds." He grinned, his shyness burning away for a moment as he remembered. "We were unable to fix it back afterwards, so instead told the mortals that this was a second stone, also sent by their God. That whosoever touched their sword to it, could lay claim to be King of England after my time."

"That is just *so wrong* in so many ways." I tried to stop the images Artur's retelling was conjuring up, with only a certain amount of success. Instead I focused on the detail. "So this second stone, what happened to it?"

"I know not." Artur shrugged, even as he sat back down amongst the cushions, trying to tug the rug back over his nakedness. His companion hissed, obviously displeased and in no mood to play. "There. I have answered your question. Please, return *us* to the castle, as you promised."

"I got one more, then you can frolic back to Camelot and make good with your companion." I told him with an edge to my voice. The responding noises I heard from underneath the rug made me think Artur was not going to get lucky anytime soon. "We also need to know if anywhere in London was special to her. A place, some home she had or anything that might provide a link to her. Think, this is important!"

Artur cursed, shaking his head as he darted nervous glances all around him.

"Your beloved city was just a collection of mud and stone huts in those days, with mortals sharing their dwellings with their pigs and other farm stock! Hardly anywhere one might call home, or bond to." He shot back at me. "*That fae* had no link to the land then or the place it has become. The only thing that might be called special to her was the river. She loved the water, the sound of it, how it was unstoppable, all enduring. She and the Lady found affinity with that, which did not please Oberon. Now, I have said all I will say! Return us!"

I snarled a curse but knew the fae was right. He'd answered what I'd asked of him, and we had made that deal. So I nodded across to Manisha, who stepped up to face her brother.

"Stay safe, my sister." The once and future King told her, a moment of seriousness cutting through his normal sardonic and self-centred nature. Let alone his inebriated state. "You are all the family I have left."

"Go get drunk, brother. Someplace safe where no-one will find you. It's what you do best." She answered with a note of sadness, then gestured.

With another rush of displaced air, the fae and his companion, plus their assorted bedclothes and pillows vanished.

Leaving me to curse the empty air.

"Why so vexed, pup?" The Morrigan asked with a raised eyebrow, having sat through that little intervention, silent and still.

"Oh, I don't know." I groused, rubbing my hand through my hair and tousling it in frustration. "Coz I'm no closer to knowing where this other bloody mysterious stone is, and so understand where Knox is going to let all hell loose. All I have is half guesses and the river Thames, which is bloody miles long. No reason to be upset, at all!"

The Shadow fae sighed, reaching for her staff and pushing herself up off the stump. She faced me and shook her head, expression solemn.

"You listen, but do not hear. You ask, but do not understand the answer." She quipped, and I bit back an angry retort, instead just spreading my hands to acknowledge my ignorance.

"Please, do tell what I have missed, oh wise and benevolent granny." I quipped, receiving a sharp thump on my ankle from her staff that I didn't even see coming.

"That you deserved for your lip, pup." She told me, as I hopped to the other foot and tried to clutch my suddenly agonised joint. "*A stone sent by God, that any who touch with their sword should be King*? I suggest you ask your Alpha to search her electronic records for *the London Stone*, for that fits Artur's description almost perfectly. Find that stone, and I believe you will have the location where the mortal Knox plans to conduct his ritual. The mention of the river may assist as well."

"How the hell do you know that?" I couldn't help but ask, seeing a smirk light the face of my Shadow fae relative.

She simply shrugged, a gesture that all too well mirrored my own.

"There are some small delights I allow myself, when I am not walking the battlefields, seeing to the mortally wounded. Or babysitting dense lycan when they cannot think for themselves." The Morrigan started walking off, heading back towards the corpse strewn fields. "Passing amongst mortals, pretending to be one of their ilk, I admit I find a perverse delight in listening to their talk of their history, of their past. Learning how much they get wrong, how little they actually *know*. You should take a walking tour of your London City one day. There are many secrets to be found, right under your nose. If you take the time to look."

With that cryptic and rather alarming insight into her personal life, the Shadow fae left Manisha and I standing there, equally stilled to silence.

Chapter 26

"You sure the Morrigan said the *London Stone*?" Elspeth asked me, cradling a mug of something herbal, possibly rose tea.

We were back in the main boardroom in *Good Deeds*, after I had been ferried through the Veil by Manisha. The Ivory Champion had shown to have less of a sense of humour than the Morrigan, depositing me back safely in my apartment and not in the toilet or the nearby Thames river.

A quick shower to wipe away any lingering charms, and I switched into more appropriate clothing to greet the day. Bear had noted my return by rolling over where he lay sleeping, and snoring a particularly loud rebuke that told me everything of his mood. Leaving him with a full plate of cold sausages I always kept on hand, I was out the door and on my way to the office before Goldspur could show up to talk any more about her tenancy contract.

"Yep, that's exactly what she called it." I savoured the large mug of coffee I had warming my hands, taking a long sip and letting the heat flood down through me. Mortals can keep their tea, I always reckon a properly brewed mug of java could ease all ills and maybe even raise the dead, if the beans were prepared right. "London. Stone. Two words, not easily mistaken for any other ones. Even for me."

"No need for the sarcasm, dear. I was just checking." She told me with a ghost of her usual smile. Ellie had already been on site when I barrelled in the front door, with my good news to impart. Whatever private business she'd had last night, it seemed to have centred her a little, at least so that I wasn't getting over-riding grief and soulful anguish from the witch. More … resigned determination, as if some decision had been made.

Something to discuss with her later, I told myself. Alongside the OPS situation.

I'd forgotten that, as well as setting in place wardings to supposedly protect the office from supernatural intrusions without our permission, Ellie had also installed extra security to prevent eavesdropping by anything that might take an interest or be attracted by the use of their name. The witch had rolled her eyes as I noted the lit candles in the meeting room with a rueful smack to the forehead, their clean blue flame indicating the wardings were in place and we could talk freely. If they flared red, it would mean something was trying to muscle in. If they then went out, we'd know we weren't safe from outside intrusion or anything hearing what we spoke about.

Jessica and Jacob were also in the meeting room, having negotiated for the Furies to take Red Cap and deal with him accordingly. When I had shown up at the office, my Alpha had taken me to one side to give me the wonderful news that Tisiphone had not forgotten our agreement. The Fury had in fact asked after the location of the gnome, but Jessica was wiley enough not to directly lie, just string the immortal incarnation of vengeance along a while longer. But she was onto me and would be expecting me to make good on the deal soon.

Something else to put off till later, I'd also wisely told myself, not believing a word of it.

Elspeth tapped the two words into the search bar and added in *Arthurian Legend* and hit return.

The Forgotten History of the London Stone, an Artifact Linked to Aeneas, King Arthur, and John Dee.

The first hit was definitely promising.

"Yes, this looks like it. The author writes of a mysterious relic, of a sort of stone not found anywhere in the region of England. And, yes, the first image definitely shows a clean break along one side. As if it was part of something larger." Elspeth scanned the web page quickly. "This looks to be your second stone."

"And it's stored where?" I tried to hurry the witch along but quietened under Jessica's cool stare. "Near the Thames maybe?"

"There's a lot of supposition here, stuff about the stone being used by the druids for ritual sacrifice, being part of the original Roman governor's palace when they occupied the city, even linking it to the Greeks and the mythical city of Troy. Typical nonsense stuff." Elspeth shook her head, but then smiled and stabbed a finger at a section on the large screen. "Ah, there you go. *'One of the seemingly newer legends surrounding the London Stone is that this was the stone from which King Arthur pulled out Excalibur - assuming that Excalibur and the Sword in the Stone are one and the same.'* Someone did their homework."

"Location?" I nudged again, this time receiving cold glances from both Alpha and witch. "Hey, I'm loving the history lesson and all, but that kinda seems pertinent."

"You do have a point, Morgan, even if as ever made in a less than elegant manner." Jessica told me, then looked over at our consultant. "Elspeth?"

"I'm looking …" She answered, then flicked the page so that it moved several paragraphs on. "And here you go. *'The London Stone is found towards the southern end of the medieval Candlewick Street - which is known today as Cannon Street - and opposite St. Swithin's Church.'* Bingo."

"Great. So Knox must be renting a room or a building in that location." Jacob spoke up, cracking his knuckles with anticipation. "There can't be too many places he could use opposite the Church, either in London proper, or Lower. I can split the teams, and start searching the area …"

"Hold on." Elspeth had continued reading, always keen to know the full story. "There's more. *Whilst the stone has remained in place throughout the Second World War, and much of the redevelopment of the London district, it has been recently removed and is now due to be on display at the Southbank Centre, on the South side of the Thames. It forms a central part of the Arthurian exhibit that was originally meant to be displayed at The Natural History Museum, before an unfortunate gas leak forced the removal of all items and a change of location …*"

"Oh, you are bloody kidding me." I couldn't help myself. "This has got to be some sort of cosmic joke, or how else do you explain this?"

The Arthurian exhibit at the Natural History Museum, coincidentally, had been a cover that the Mistress of the Sewers – once Lady of the Lake – had meant to use to mask her plans to blow up an old vintage sea mine whilst using Excalibur as a portal key to send the explosion and several thousand pounds of deadly cold iron and silver into the heart of the Ivory Court. To maim and slay those she blamed for leaving her in the Mortal Realm when every other fae involved in the King Arthur debacle skuttled home to hide and pretend it had never happened.

We'd stopped her and her pet shape-changer, as well as my slightly maniacal and now absconded weapons dealer gnome of a contact, but it had been a near thing. And that didn't even cover the fact my ex, Sarah Conner, had been pulled into the mess and almost blown up by the bomb.

But I thought that little event was done with. Case closed, box shut and firmly sealed, stuffed in the bank of the ancient warehouse with the rest of the crazy shit. But here we were, dragged right back into it front and centre.

This. This was why I was almost totally convinced some bastard immortal in the Real had it in for me, and was messing with my life for kicks and giggles. In fact, shits and giggles, to use the phrase correctly.

"Ah understand yer displeasure at events leading us all back tae that particular case." Jessica spoke up, tapping at her keypad and entering in the new data into our file on Knox. "But ah would suggest yer personal frustration is put aside fer a moment, given we now have both the time *and* the place Robert Knox is bound tae for his ritual."

I took a breath, trying to find a sense of calm from the feeling of frustration, panic and just seriously *what the fuck* that this particular revelation caused. Finally, nodding, I took a long swig of my coffee, letting the coffee settle me at least a little.

"So, let us be clear. We have the conjunction, a planetary alignment due at roughly eight forty tomorrow evening, and the second stone's location being the Southbank Centre." Jessica drew these points together at the bottom of all we had put together about Knox and Morgana. "It's clear Morgana seeks tae keep the Courts in a state of turmoil, hence this sudden uprising tae disrupt and turn their attention from her. And here, in the Mortal Realm, Knox has laid out devices tae make the mortal authorities think he will be somewhere he is not. But is that it?"

I looked over all we had added, the notes from our interactions with the man, our struggles and losses … and had to shake my head.

"Nope, that can't be all." I grabbed a pencil from the table and used the blunt end to stab at the keypad in front of me, moving the cursor on the large screen to hover over the devices Knox had planted around London, and the link to his knowledge of and seemingly mastery over the Harrowing. "Knox called on the Harrowing to silence the Nighters already, and again to try and silence Elspeth and me. The threat of true death to immortals? My bet is he's going to use it, a last line of mayhem and destruction this side to ensure no-one is free to challenge him, to stop him. *She,* uh, Morgana has planned this too well, to ignore that sort of tool."

"Ah agree, which is why ah want you tae contact this agent of yers, and convince him of the seriousness of what they face." Jessica told me bluntly, brooking no argument. This was definitely landing in my lap, another small mess to sort out. "If they will nae listen tae advice, then at least we can offer tae help ward against whatever the two have planned tae release as a distraction."

"Uh, won't that leave us a little light, for the actual takedown?" For once it wasn't me being the voice of doubt, but instead Elspeth as she sat back and cradled her mug of tea. "I know the pack has managed admirably against what I would call formidable odds, but if you try to spread yourself to cover both the dummy sites and where we think Knox will actually be, doesn't that increase the risk of being caught unprepared by any tricks he or Morgana might have waiting for us. Remember the Natural History Museum."

"All too bloody well." I growled but then shrugged, ceding the truth. "Thing is, I don't know what choice we really have. If OPS are fixed on the pentagram decoy Knox arranged for them, then they'll need help to deal with whatever trap they'll be walking into. Otherwise, it could be complete carnage."

"I can split the teams but if we're sending help to all six sites, we'll need to call in the other packs." Jacob confirmed, and Jessica nodded her agreement.

"Ah will talk tae the other Alphas and seek their aid." She confirmed, smiling wryly. "Given how we were hired tae find the escapees for these mortals, it will nae be much of a reach tae suggest we support them to ward these sites as well. That ah will handle as an extension clause tae our agreement."

Jessica then looked over at Elspeth.

"We still have nae idea of what ritual Knox seeks tae perform," She prompted, and the witch took her cue, sorting through some papers she had set before her.

"I've studied Knox's journals and the papers we took from his study, as well as the information Morgan and Jacob were able to provide from their brief visit to his laboratory." The witch handed over one piece of paper, where she had enscribed several intricate designs as well as notes on the steps she estimated would need to be followed. "The process he'll most likely attempt, from what I can tell, is a combination of a summoning, to draw Morgana's spirit to the location of the ritual, a binding to then contain said spirit and then finally a bonding to draw her into the vessel he has chosen for her. A three-fold incantation, which I am guessing will require all the stores of stolen life energy he has left to both keep her alive, the vessel in good health and then to seal her into the body permanently."

"Great, a nice easy three step programme. So how do we bugger it up?" I asked, and Elspeth sighed at my – almost expected - trivialisation of what I guessed had to be a very complex thing. But then, I dealt with the plain and simple. Where to hit something, and how hard.

"If we wish to disrupt the ritual and successfully halt their plans, then in my professional opinion, I would suggest either of two options." She answered finally, circling two key points on the paper. "Either we intervene before he starts and remove at least one of the two keystones he is using to tether Morgana with. This should prevent him summoning or tethering the spirit, and his supplies of life energy are not inexhaustible and *should* run out and prevent the ritual's completion."

"Uh huh. That's a lot of *should be's* to be basing our whole play on." I replied, poking holes as ever. "You mentioned two options."

The witch locked eyes with me, an exchange long enough for me to understand what the next words were costing her.

"The second option, in my opinion, has a greater chance of success. If he has already begun the ritual, we have to destroy the vessel he has built for her."

Silence settled around the room, as us three lycans exchanged glances.

"And by vessel, ah am tae understand you mean…?" Jessica queried, and Elspeth nodded, the grim certainty of what she was suggesting writ on her face.

"The body Knox has built from the stolen body parts of mortals, yes." She took a breath, settling herself before continuing. "This thing, it is what we call a *golem*, like the stories of a monster fashioned of clay to house a spirit. Like the guardians the fae use by entombing lesser kin inside models fashioned of metal or stone. The vessel is empty, there is no chance that we would in fact be killing a person. Simply breaking the tool they aim to use to cause untold death and destruction."

"And you're ok with that? Your Goddess, as well? You're kidding, right?" I asked without stopping to think. I immediately saw anger flare in her green eyes as she clenched her fists in her papers so they crumpled.

"Of course not! How could you think …?" She almost spat, and I held up a hand to forestall her anger. She shook her head, taking a calming breath before continuing. "I am not *ok* with any of this. The kidnapping of mortals, the draining of their lives, the dismemberment and cruel medical practices to create a suitable vessel from the unwilling parts of his victims. *None* of this makes me feel ok. But my Goddess and I are aligned. If the situation is so dire then we will do what must be done."

"Morgan misspoke, and ah am sure he is fully apologetic for his unthought accusations." Jessica answered with a tone in her voice that brooked no argument. I simply nodded, taking the chastisement as well deserved.

"As ah see things, we have a lot tae do, and little time tae organise." Our Alpha continued, as Elspeth settled back in her seat and I took a firm grip of my tongue before it dropped me into any more trouble. "Jacob and ah will focus on reaching out tae the other packs, and coordinate support fer the mortal authorities with either their agreement or without. Elspeth, ah would ask you begin preparing anything you can think of, tae help negate what Knox or she might use against us. Especially any way tae disrupt the Harrowing. With nae burning down the building around us this time."

"And me?" I asked as politely as possible. Jessica nodded.

"Time fer you tae reach out tae yer contacts at the mortal authorities. Update them on what we have uncovered, and see if they will change their plans tae include the Southbank centre as potential ground zero." My Alpha saw my immediate doubt and shook her head in acknowledgement. "Ah also fully expect them tae decide otherwise, but we can at least say we warned them. Ah will also seek tae advise *mah* contacts, if they will listen tae me, and seek their aid with what we must accomplish."

Well, that seemed to be about all we had to discuss, so I went to push myself up and leave. Jessica stopped me, raising her hand for one final point.

"Oh and Morgan. See if you can convince them tae give you some better means of contacting them?" She instructed with a slight twist of a smile. "As much as ah can understand the enjoyment they must derive from dragging you back tae the Tower again and again, things are coming tae a head. We may need tae speak tae them quickly, and ah don't think you can run fast enough tae keep playing messenger boy between us and them. Though the exercise *is* good fer you."

"Bloody cheek!" I growled, eliciting a wider smile from her.

Chapter 27

Kay.

Artur's foster brother, also called Cai or Cei, this Knight is attributed with a number of further superhuman abilities, including the ability to go nine days and nine nights without the need to breathe or to sleep, the ability to grow as "tall as the tallest tree in the forest if he pleased" and the ability to radiate supernatural heat from his hands, His sword was also known to cause wounds that could not be healed.

Kay was known to suffer battle rage, ignoring injuries and never tiring whilst in the throes of his madness.

"Look, do we *really* need to do this all over again?" I growled, fighting to control the urge to grab the mortal standing in front of me and toss him on his pompous arse.

The warden of the Tower stared at me with a deadpan look so perfect he *had* to have practised it in the mirror.

It was later that morning, and I'd made my way to the only site I knew where I might find OPS and Agent Cormac Smith. Back to the Tower of London. Of course, since Cormac had not issued me with any means of contacting him directly, that meant running the gauntlet of the Tower guards all over again.

"See? I have a ticket. I know you need for me to have one, so I went and bought one." I waved the bloody thing at the guard, remembering I'd need to add a second to my expenses claim when this was all done and dusted. Knowing my luck, Jessica would classify it as *unnecessary expenditure* and block the refund, just to teach me to find a better way of contacting Agent Smith and his motely bunch. That was my Alpha, always ready to use something as a learning exercise.

"Very good, sir." The guard noted the ticket, his moustache bristling and his back ramrod straight as he faced me. "That allows you full access to all the exhibits around and inside the Tower, including the Crown Jewels … which I must say is my personal favourite sir … as well as the White Tower armoury and the exhibits of the Bloody Tower, Line of Kings and the Medieval Palace. It does *not*, however, grant you access to wander around the grounds looking for this Cormac Smith of yours. Whoever he might be."

"And I told you, he's an agent working for your Queen and government, for the Office of Preternatural Security. I met him here last time, in what I think was an old medical room? Filled with skeletons and stuff in cabinets? Ring any bells?"

"Ah, that would have been the old surgery. We haven't used that since, oh, must be World War Two." The yeoman smiled brightly. "Not on the official tour, mind, so I must ask you *not* to go walkabout and finding such places again, sir."

"As for your Cormac Smith, was it?" He enquired ever so politely. "And this *office of preternatural security*, well that sounds quite important and all, but not something we deal with here, sir. This is Her Majesty Queen Elizabeth's Royal Palace, and as such isn't really the place to use for meet ups with acquaintances, if I might be so bold, sir. There is a coffee shop outside the residence for that sort of thing."

I bit back a growl, trying with some difficulty to remain calm in the face of the guard's stubborn unwillingness to let me through. I *knew* Cormac or Evelyn or someone was watching this play out and probably taking great delight in seeing just how far they could push my buttons before I snapped. The sods were probably running a pool with odds I was stupid enough to get into real trouble before they had to come bail me out.

But this wolf was not biting.

"Fine, no problem. My mistake." I shrugged, looking up and around, trying to sense out any hidden cameras or viewing devices that were monitoring me. "I'll just take a long, slow walk around the place. Maybe pick up something from the gift shop for my friend, for whenever the sod decides to show up. Oh, in the meantime, if you *do* speak to anyone who knows him, please say we think he's completely wrong about where Knox is going to show up, and he's going to look bloody stupid when the shit really starts hitting the fan and people start dying …"

I saw the yeoman stiffen, expression growing serious suddenly behind his bristling moustache.

"Sir, I must say that sounds to be a joke in very poor taste, if that is all it is." He warned, hands shifting infinitesimally as if for a weapon that wasn't there. "If you are not, I must warn you that a threat of harm to *anyone* will be taken most seriously. Now, would you like to repeat that?"

I shrugged, smiling innocently.

"Absolutely. I was just asking for someone to tell *Cormac Smith* of *the Office of Preternatural Security* that …" I began, but cut off as a figure disengaged itself from the nearby office built into the outer wall and walked towards us.

Agent Smith was dressed in his plain grey suit, looking as neutral as ever as he came to stand by the guardsman.

"It's ok, Morris. I'll take it from here." He told the yeoman with gentle but firm surety. The guard didn't even turn, just nodded and gave me one last warning look.

"Right you are, sir." He replied, his dark eyes never leaving me. "I'll be running along then. Have a nice day, sir, but in future please do refrain from such jocularity. *Some* people might get the wrong idea, and then where would you be, eh sir?"

"Good question. Where would I be, Agent Smith?" I asked, but Cormac just shook his head and motioned back the way I had come.

"Shall we walk?" He offered, and I let him take the lead.

We followed the path round the Tower of London, avoiding the wandering gangs of school children being herded as best they could by their teachers, and the smaller but noisier packs of tourists clicking their cameras at everything. Pigeons, yeomen on guard, a section of the castle wall, whatever caught their eye whilst they stumbled into each other's way and ruined most of what they sought to capture.

Cormac led us to one of the free merlins that dotted the Thames wall opposite the castle, facing what was commonly known as Traitors' Gate. That tidal portal used in olden times to ferry enemies of the Crown from any river transportation to their internment within the Tower. It was quite the novel way of foiling most desperate rescue attempts, as most of the time the mortals being brought in had been involved in some plot or other to overthrow the ruling Royal, and mortals as a rule always think some last-ditch effort to free their beloved leader was worth an attempt. The dying for them bit a little less, as they needed to contend with the strong flowing and treacherous Thames river, under the watchful eyes of archers or arbalests stationed safely upon the castle wall and the guards armed to the teeth at the gate itself.

Oh and I have no idea why these little outcrops are named after the famous sorcerer from Arthurian legend. Maybe he liked looking out over rivers, and had a habit of creating these little lookouts for his enjoyment. Or the designer thought they resembled a wizard somehow. It was just one of the many things I felt I *really* didn't need to know.

"I got your message." Cormac leant on the stone, looking out across the water and seemingly paying no attention to me whatsoever. His voice was pitched for my hearing and mine alone, so I played along, leaning on the wall too and watching the river pass by beneath us. "I can only assume you have some relevant details to update me on, given your presence here?"

"If you got the message, then those sods at the Tower know who you are." I groused instead, wanting to make my view of this morning's entertainment clear. "So why did I have to go through the same routine as last time? Hell, if you'd just give me a number to call, we could have saved each other a lot of hassle."

"The yeomen do not, in fact, know any Cormac Smith, or any reference to OPS." Cormac corrected me, a slight smile tugging at his lips. "To them, I am a Doctor Reginald Watts, Royal Physician to Her Majesty but with a side business in working with those society deem mentally … unstable? Morris most likely took you for one of my patients, and any reference to my real name or who I work for will be erased from the Tower security recordings. Most likely it is happening already."

"Great, so the guard think's I'm nuts. How does that help in any way?" I growled, not finding the truth any funnier or easier to swallow.

"It helps because OPS must remain a discreet and clandestine organisation." Cormac told me with the patience of a man explaining something very simple, but very important. "Bandering around our name, the names of those I work with, any reference at all could potentially jeopardise lives and call attention to the work we do. Which defeats the entire purpose of our existence. To keep mortals from ever being exposed to the *truth*."

"Fine, then Mr Clever Dick Agent, give me a way of contacting you so I don't *have* to play silly buggers with the mortals every time." I growled back, knowing his point was valid but the problem was their refusal to work with me directly, give me a means of reaching them when I needed to. "Otherwise I'm going to have to keep doing this *escape from the looney bin* act and keep risking someone recording me with something you can't just erase."

"The matter has already been raised, and my superiors approved having you added to our list of key contacts." Cormac reached into his pocket without looking and slipped out a small, blocky mobile phone which he slid across the wall to me. "Congratulation Morgan Black, you are officially on the OPS's books. Keep this charged, and you have my direct number and that of Agent Jones as well, seeing how she is familiar with your case file."

"Oh gee, thanks. Do I get a code name or something?" I joked but palmed the phone anyway. Great, another mobile phone to try not to break. Given my track record with my work one, this wasn't such a good idea. "Can I call you *Mr Grey* maybe?"

"No, you can't. However if anyone but you uses that phone to call the numbers stored there, or if I receive any calls that I cannot identify but I *can* trace back to associates of yours, the device will be immediately deactivated and we shall have *words*." He calmly told me. "This is for your use, and yours alone. And for official business only. Please don't get inebriated and start drunk-texting either of us for fun."

"Uh, you both are totally safe from that option." I answered him frankly, eliciting a nod and another small smile.

"Now that is dealt with, I believe you had an update for me?" He enquired politely. Everything was just so proper around Cormac. Not the fake *English schoolboy* style mannerism you get with some mortals, from a particular background and upbringing that usually had a strong sense of self entitlement running hand in hand with it, but an actual true sense of decorum and dignity. Not something that could be faked or taught, but that was in the bone. Whatever his story was, Cormac Smith definitely was more than some simple government stooge, and I'd be wise to remember it.

"Yeah, one or two things." I gave him the crib-notes of what we'd put together ourselves from our *not-official* investigation into Knox, despite the agreement for us to leave the matter alone. That and the pertinent details Morgana had let slip in our little chat outside Buckingham Palace.

Finishing up, I explained the steps Jessica was suggesting we take, especially around the site of Knox's ritual and the support of the lycan packs.

"So, way we see it, it's probably a ploy, Knox having those sites dotted around London, just *happening* to form a pentagram and marking the spot with an *x* for you to watch. An easy way to keep you looking in the wrong place, at best letting him do what he likes without anyone gate-crashing the party. At worst, releasing the Harrowing to create a really fucked up diversion for you to handle all on your own. Which is why we reckon you should switch to the place we found, where the London Stone is on display."

Cormac tapped the stone with his fingers, lost in thought, so I just turned and casually watched the mortals passing by along the walkway, wholly absorbed in their day-to-day troubles and concerns.

A man walked past, talking on their mobile, arguing about whether they had remembered to add milk to their grocery order. Two girls stumbled past, linked arm in arm, giggling and whispering about the boys they fancied and which one kissed better. A woman scowled as she talked on the phone and looked out over the river, telling someone she would get the file sent over after her lunchbreak, that it wasn't *that* important for her to go back to the office right there and then.

Normal, boring mortal stuff that to them was still utterly important. Must be nice to have only those sorts of things to worry about.

"I face several issues with the information you came here to deliver." Cormac finally spoke up, still looking out over the Thames. Expression calm, centred.

"Only several?" I joked, shaking my head. "Ok, go on. Point out the plot holes."

"Firstly, there is the small matter your Alpha and pack have continued investigating Robert Knox, when we expressly made it clear he is an OPS matter. To be dealt with by us and us alone." He answered quietly, and I nodded, fully expecting that to be an issue between us. "Leaving that aside, you are basing your argument on information *provided by the very person* who you say is responsible for all the deception that Knox has to date committed. The very individual who would wish the location of the rite he seeks to perform to remain secret. And you think *she* would just accidently, in a fit of pique, reveal this to you? Really?"

I went to reply, feeling I should point out all the other stuff we'd found out. The matter of the Bung brothers being tasked to steal Circe's stone, and the information I'd gotten from Artur. But Cormac tapped the stone with his fingers, showing he was not finished.

"The thing is, Mr Black, I would *like* very much to be able to act as you and your … 'colleagues' do. Find out lone facts, put two and two together, and act upon what your gut tells you is right. I would *so* like to be in that place. But I am not." Cormac sighed, that heartfelt sound that came from the sure knowledge of the twin Gods Policy and Procedure which demanded their followers' unswerving devotion. "We have *rules*, Mr Black, and despite my assertion previously that people in my shoes are granted some degree of flexibility, I also have people I must answer to. And they follow these rules *rigorously*. Rules such as we have to act upon hard evidence, actual findings supported by undiscountable facts that we have thoroughly investigated and proven to be true. Knowing that *everything* we do will be scrutinised for the smallest error."

He shook his head, turning to finally look at me. His expression was apologetic, yet there was a finality to it as well, an unyielding set to his jaw.

"Your *opinions* are based on the word of someone who wishes to distract you. As such, I cannot take this to my superiors and ask them to reassign the teams we have in place, or refocus our efforts. We are not a unit with limitless manpower nor bottomless resources, and they are currently assigned to what we believe are the most obvious locations of Knox's whereabouts. Or will be needed to deal with any *incident* he initiates." Cormac shrugged. "Obviously, we would not turn down the offer of extra manpower, as long as it is understood any units deployed would be under our direct supervision and *would in no way risk exposing citizens to certain truths*. Plainclothes only, I must ask."

Lycan in plainclothes. Only in mortal form, in other words. I knew I couldn't promise that my packmates or any other lycan wouldn't shift if they were faced by the Harrowing or the Harrowed, but I could at least ask them to try to look normal until then. So I nodded, guessing what was next.

"As for the Southbank centre, I can spare no resources to investigate the site, or check the authenticity of this line of enquiry. Into these stones and their possible link to *her*." He continued, fulfilling my expectations line for line. "However, I might as well lift the embargo on you and your team doing anything yourselves, since you've pretty much ignored it anyway. I *would* ask that, if your theory does prove to be true, you use the mobile and let me know so we can arrange Knox's extraction. And that you leave the place in a better state than you did the Natural History Museum."

I honestly thought we'd gotten away with that little debacle, but Cormac shook his head.

"Your Alpha, Jessica Walker may have *discretion-guaranteed* resources she can use to clean up such incidents, but don't for one instant think we are not aware of their operations, or party to the services rendered." He smiled as a thought struck him. "In fact, there have been several instances we provided the expertise she needed without her even realising the fact. We *are* just that good."

"Uh, ok." I shrugged, swallowing the simple fact we were on our own. "So you're giving us licence to investigate, and act on anything we find? As long as I call you if we get Knox in the bag?"

Cormac nodded once, adjusting his grey suit.

"My superiors are more interested that this matter is dealt with and the threat of Knox neutralised, than squabbling over little things like *who did what*. As long as they can deny any involvement and there is no evidence to link them to … well, anything." He admitted, adjusting his cuffs and brushing off miniscule dirt from the material. "That is the madness which my colleagues and I must balance in the daily service of our jobs. To follow strict rules and follow protocol, whilst making sure everything is denied, everything leads elsewhere than to us. And that the truth is *never* known. That *might* help you understand some of the decisions we make."

"Funnily enough, that's kind of how we operate too. Just with less cloak and dagger and more, well, flea powder and belligerent violence." I grinned, unable to resist the urge to joke.

Cormac simply nodded once, showing my attempt had fallen flat as ever with him.

"Some people find me funny." I grumbled, before returning to the matter in hand. "So I guess we're sorted? *Nice to see you, I'll call if we find anything else out* done?"

Cormac nodded, so I took a last breath of the fresh air rolling off the Thames … *mud of so many different flavours, so much history in those decomposing, rotting layers, water so sharp to the taste and yet soft, oil from the boats crisscrossing the surface like maple syrup atop pancakes, fish scales flaking like almonds flakes and bird excrement like crystallised sugar sprinkled on the top* ... and turned to leave.

"Ah, one last thing, Mr Black." The agent stopped me, and I turned to look back at him.

"Yeah? What did I forget?" I quickly wracked my brain for anything I'd forgotten. Something I promised to talk about, to investigate or whatever. "It's not your birthday, right?"

"No." Cormac sighed. Then his next words totally threw me. "It's a matter regarding Detective Inspector Gregory Simon Allen. His death. You were not present when his body was collected, that's right?"

I froze, that memory crystallized in my head.

Of Elspeth curled up on the ground, folded over and around the still, very still body of DI Allen. His blood pooling on the ground from the horrific injury dealt him by Jack the Ripper. Heart pulverised, chest deformed from the savage damage done to him, as the man stood to protect the woman he loved. Defiant in the face of a thing so far beyond him, one frail mortal against a creature centuries old, steeped in evil and hate.

And I'd been unable to stop it from happening. All my Court given powers, my lycan strength, everything that made me better than the mortals counting for nothing in that instant. I hadn't been able to stop him from dying, and I knew that would stick with me for as long as I lived, something that would be there every time I saw my friend, my colleague.

I hadn't saved the man she loved.

"No." I answered truthfully. "Your colleague. Agent Evelyn Jones? She turned up with the *Plan B* squad, too late to do anything but clean up after the event. I told her to get my friends home, to safety, then I had to leave. To go find out what depths of shit we are in. Why?"

Cormac eyed me, those grey neutral eyes of his searching mine, looking for something. And I had no clue what.

"Oh, no reason, really." He replied after a moment, too long to be anything but ominous. "There's just some discrepancies, something I've been informed of that I think needs looking into. But since you weren't there, I'll just have to contact your colleague. Miss Elspeth MacElvy, that's correct? Of 33 Elsworthy Road, Primrose Hill?"

"I think that's her address, yeah." I replied slowly, cogs clunking in my brain as I tried to guess what this was all about. Failing to think up anything that made any sense, I tried the direct approach. "Look, she's had a rough time of things. DI All and her were … well, his death hit her particularly hard. Why don't you tell me what you want to ask, and I'll check with her and call you back?"

Cormac just shook his head.

"No, I think I need to speak to Miss MacElvy myself. Especially if there was some connection between her and the police detective, as you say. It's nothing to worry about, just routine." He smiled brightly, far too chipper for my liking. "I'm sure it's all just a silly misunderstanding, a clerical error. No need to worry yourself."

With that, he gave me a parting nod and walked off in the direction of the main entrance to the Tower, and I guessed our meeting was at an end.

I took a breath, suspicions blossoming like weeds, nothing really making sense but that gnawing feeling of doubt settling in. I thought of the witch's mood, that shift I'd felt from utter sadness, soul-ridden pain and loss, to a resigned determination and weary acceptance. As if a decision had been made, but one that hadn't been easy to settle on.

"What have you done, Ellie?" I asked the air, but my only reply was the shriek of a passing seagull, and the whisper of the wind.

Neither were of any help whatsoever.

Chapter 28

Given Cormac's response to my news, and his sudden interest in our consultant witch, I decided the best course of action was to return to *Good Deeds*, firstly to let Jessica know the way the wind was blowing, but also to check in on Ellie. Explain she'd attracted OPS's attention somehow, without breaking the blood-oath I was bound by.

Oh, and possibly give her a chance to explain, if she wanted to.

Unfortunately, when I got back to the office, I found the witch already gone, headed home to focus on the task assigned her by our Alpha. A good enough excuse, though I couldn't help but doubt it's entire truth.

"Ah did nae see a reason tae deny her request." Jessica told me, sipping her cup of coffee and looking at me with a question in her eyes. "The complexities of Knox's ritual are a mystery ah have tasked her tae unravel, and tae prepare fer whatever surprises he might have in place tae forestall our approach. Neither of which ah think are easily achieved, so if Elspeth asked tae work on them in the confines of her own home, ah could not very well say nae. Why? Is there a reason ah should know of, tae have kept her here?"

I shook my head, knowing I had not a single solid fact to be contradicting my Alpha's decision. Just that doubt, gnawing like Bear on a table leg when he was upset.

"Well then." Jessica obviously considered the matter closed, as she switched her attention to the update I'd brought back from Cormac. "Ah have spoken tae the other Alphas, and they are willing to lend members of their packs tae help ward the locations linked tae Knox. Their obvious concern is whether he plans tae release the Harrowing at these sites, after our previous encounter with that particular weapon."

Encounter. A pleasant enough description for a horrific event that had cost us one entire pack of lycan, and led to the death of another pack Alpha as well as packmates from our own kin, and others. We'd seen lycan we knew and even if we couldn't say liked at least counted as comrades, twisted into monstrous parodies of themselves by some clever machinations of Knox. Perverting the death of immortals to create Harrowed killing machines. Yeah, I could understand the other Alphas thinking twice before facing off against that again.

Hell, the sights I'd seen that night still gave *me* nightmares, and I had been otherwise occupied a lot of the time trying to locate then save the mortal that I loved. Fat lot of good that had done her.

"It is likely Knox will think tae use mortals tae hamper and distract those looking fer him." Jessica continued, aware of my thoughts and sharing at least some of them. "Which is why ah have tasked Jacob and the other packs tae plan enough distractions tae hopefully clear the vicinity of residents, if the mortal authorities dinnae do this themselves. That way, the chance of them having tae face Harrowed in significant numbers should be much reduced."

One thing we lycan had learned early on was that when on a hunt, it was best to plan ahead, identify the most likely location where our target either was laired up already or would head once it realised we were after it. Then clear it of mortals as quickly and efficiently as possible. There were too many stories from way back when, of innocents accidently stumbling across a hunt in progress or a prey about to be captured, and things going sideways fast.

So we got clever. Staked out the neighbourhoods, the overlooks and all the places where mortals might put themselves - and us - at risk of crossing paths at the worst possible moment. The packs became past masters of organising fake events to masque our gatherings or to turn away mortals who might wander into something they shouldn't. What, you thought all the road closures in and around London were for real? Nope, a small but significant number are down to us, using stolen signs and official gear. That and more than one reported gas leak or suspicious package alert could be traced to a pack needing a building cleared and the surroundings off limits, without anyone asking too many questions.

Thankfully, mortals tended to be blasé about mysterious alarms going off or office clearances due to sudden pest infestations that, when checked, turned out to be a hoax or a mistake in the paperwork. We had become experts of targeting those locations where security was minimal, often letting a target of a hunt 'escape' so as to avoid a complicated final stand where anonymity couldn't be assured. We weren't the Men In Black, or the IMF that can pull off amazing stunts with fake masks and the sort of technological wizardry that shouldn't possibly exist. Coz it doesn't. But we do our best, and as long as the headlines in the next day's newspaper *didn't* have our hairy mugs printed all over them, I guessed we were doing it well enough.

The locations Knox has chosen to bury his devices were, one and all, low risk in terms of tight security. The like found in banks, offices in the City of London or the wealthy homes in the more upmarket districts of the city. No, the biggest issue was that all six sites were boarded on every side by mortal homes, which posed a risk of exposure to the mortals, of anything Knox loosed from the devices he'd left behind.

The Southbank centre, however, presented the sort of problems we'd faced with the Natural History Museum. It was too public, with an established security system and operational protocols designed to make sure important people knew what was going on inside at all times. Exactly the sort of place we *didn't* want to have a supernatural event happen, with too many eyes and ears to keep a lid on things.

Jessica had decided to assume removing the Bung brothers from the equation wouldn't stop Knox discovering the location of the second stone, but would hamper him enough to mean he had only one choice. To use the site where it was stored as the ritual's focal point. The Southbank centre was near the Thames, ticking that box for Morgana, and the inside offered enough space for him to work if the bastard figured out a way to get around all the cameras and guards that would normally be obstacles to him. Without simply killing the mortals and destroying the security, which would just bring the authorities down on him all the sooner.

But we faced the same problem. How to get into the centre without alerting all the on-site security as well as whatever Knox had in place to guard him, and deal with the madman in a way that left no evidence we had ever been there.

This was the problem Jessica had turned her skills and talents to solving, and the one I'd disturbed her from completing when I dropped back into the office. Jacob was out, working with the other Alphas to pick who would be helping support OPS, since no matter what happened we'd still need lycan covering the normal, run of the mill craziness we kept from happening in front of mortals day in, day out. Funny how that sort of thing never stops when a world threatening event is about to occur for real. Whilst in stories and movies, the heroes never have to worry about managing the daily grind as well as saving the day. Sucks to be us, at times.

My Alpha was sat at one of the desks on the main floor, normally used by us to log case updates or to file away the closures that meant we'd stop being chased by her Oracle system. Which knew every trick, ploy or excuse we used to try to dodge doing the paperwork. It's hard to argue with something that was an emulation of creatures that could see all possible futures, and peer inside a seeker of the truth's very soul to discern truth from lie without a single mistake over the centuries of their service. It was frustrating, and we probably should have learned by now not to try to fool the bloody thing.

Then again, none of us are perfect.

Jessica had her sleek and very expensive electronic note-pad hooked up to a monitor, and was, from what I could tell over her shoulder, looking over floor plans and security layouts of the Southbank centre.

Not stuff you can normally find online, or even pop to the local planning office to ask for. No, this stuff was from the dark web, that wonderful source of all things not *entirely* legal but generally useful. Mortals filled it with priceless antiques and one-of-a-kind items for sale, or to offer services that if they tried to stick in the local job section would have law enforcement officers calling them up for a brief chat within a very short space of time. That sort of stuff.

But we used it as well, since the immortal residents of the Real often offered items or services useful to us. Like obtaining floorplans to buildings that detailed all the security devices in place, the rota of guards and up to date password details. Helpful information like that.

And yes, I've said before that *normally* denizens of the Real steered clear of technology, due to its habit of exploding in flames or crashing with terminal finality around anything magical in nature. But some creatures were savvy enough to work with the tools they had. Used the supernatural version of oven mitts when handling delicate devices, that sort of thing.

"Anything I can help with?" I offered magnanimously, knowing she'd likely decline. Not that Jessica didn't accept help when it was needed, more that I was not exactly known for my finesse around getting into or out of buildings subtlety. If the Gods had wanted me to be discreet, they wouldn't have made doors so easy to kick in. Or windows to break out through.

"Thank you, Morgan, but ah think we need a better plan than *kick down the front door and run really fast*. Nae offence meant." She answered with a smile before then explaining her current thinking anyway. "Given when the alignment is due, ah expect Knox tae gain access tae the exhibit through fake credentials, so ensuring he is in the building beforehand with all the necessary paraphernalia his ritual needs. Then ah would expect him tae arrange a late-night pass tae *complete necessary changes tae the exhibit* or the like, tae then summon and bind his mistress and make his escape. In his shoes, ah would jinx the security devices but leave the mortal guards tae continue patrolling outside the area of the ritual, tae detain and delay anyone attempting tae stop him. Whilst also ensuring something particularly nasty awaits anyone who gets through them."

She tapped her pad, where she had drawn various routes marked into the building, crossed off one by one.

"The way ah see it, we need tae gain access tae the centre without alerting any mortal guards patrolling the grounds, who might then alert Knox whilst delaying us from reaching him. Then we have tae avoid whatever guardians he has set in place to stop anyone making it past the first line of defence. And finally we need tae find the location where his ritual is tae take place, again without letting Knox know we are close tae him. Three lines of defence tae circumvent with less than forty-eight hours tae plan."

Jessica then smiled brightly.

"But ah *am* guessing a little here. Ah have some ideas and sources that *should* help us handle the mortal guards." She crossed the first problem, moving onto the second and third of our issues to tackle. "Ah also expect Elspeth may be of some aid in learning what sort of aid Knox might be able tae conjure. It is the *other one* who worries me, fer I dinnae know if her current state as a spirit alone helps or hinders us."

She made a mark against problem two, with a question mark beside the letter M circled and underlined.

"As fer the location of the ritual, ah have taken some wisdom from yer recent interactions with Knox, and sought knowledge from those who have had the most exposure tae the mortal." She told me cryptically, smiling again as I tried to work out how the hell I'd been of help here. My interactions with Knox had been haphazard and generally a case of me blundering into him by accident, or him walking in on me. Then something clicked in my head.

"You're asking Molly and Rous for help? Is the Rat God still alive?" I queried, remembering the rulers of Lower London, and their boast that they had used the rats which made up Rous's corporal form to track the mortal, as he went about his nefarious business under their noses. "I thought Knox pretty much vaporised his little furry minions?"

"The God of Rats did indeed suffer badly in yer last meeting with the mortal." Jessica confirmed, and I remembered the shrieks and cries as Knox unleashed the Harrowing on the God, his guards and of course, Talen Orben. The Alpha of the Nighters had not died well, and no matter how much I hated the lycan for kidnapping Sarah, using her to make me betray my Alpha and pack, and using Knox's own experimental serum to turn his own pack into nightmare Harrowed monsters who had killed …

Actually, when I thought about it, the bastard had gotten exactly what he deserved. I was good with that, I realised as I checked my own head.

"Ok. And they're still dealing with us?" I couldn't quite keep the doubt from my voice, knowing Elspeth and I had promised to remove Knox as a threat to the pair, and failed miserably in that singular oath.

"Ah believe Rous's words were along the lines of *'as long as that bloody Redcloak does nae try to help us any more, we're good …'*" Jessica answered with that mocking smile of hers firmly in place, and I sighed, knowing that was another bridge I'd managed to not just burn, but strap with fireworks and set off like a Guy Fawkes' extravaganza. Oh well.

"Ah have faith Rous will be able tae spy out the location of the ritual, as ah expect Knox will need time tae set things in place." She crossed a line through problem number three. "And so, all we can do is wait until ah hear from all mah sources. Thank you, Morgan. That was actually quite helpful tae talk things through with you."

I grinned, shaking my head.

"Just don't make a habit of it, boss. People will start thinking I know what I'm talking about and then think of the mess we'd be in!" We both laughed, before Jessica folded up her note pad and rose from the office seat.

"Ah would suggest rest before tomorrow night, fer you tae be ready fer whatever we face." She told me, laying a hand lightly on my shoulder and looking intently at me with those grey eyes of hers. "But ah know how much you hate tae sit around when things are happening. So instead, ah suggest you spend the rest of the day seeing if you can locate that gnome contact of yers, in case ah am unable tae find a way tae resolve this matter *amicably* with the Furies."

Oh yeah, that small wrinkle. I had to stop forgetting about the shit I was in. Treat it as seriously as it merited. Which, if the Furies decided I'd broken my oath to them and should take Terrigyle's place in their world of horror and torture, was pretty bloody serious.

That said, I *also* needed to find out what the hell was going on with Elspeth, and why OPS wanted to speak with her. That stunk worse that the Bung brothers, and those three trolls were particularly ripe at the best of times.

I nodded to my Alpha as she walked off, checking the nearest clock and finding it was late morning, close to midday. Plenty of time to see about hunting for an errant gnome, before I planned to drop in on the not so wicked witch of Primrose Hill.

And I just had to hope I wouldn't need to use a bucket of water on her before the night was over.

Chapter 29

Bors the Younger.

Sir Bors is always portrayed as one of the Round Table's finest, but his real glory comes on the Grail Quest, where he proves himself worthy enough to witness the Grail's mysteries alongside Galahad and Percival.

Several episodes display his virtuous character; in one, a lady approaches Bors vowing to commit suicide unless he sleeps with her. He refuses to break his vow of celibacy; the lady and her maidens threaten to throw themselves off the castle battlements. As the ladies jump off, they reveal themselves to be demons set on deceiving him by playing to his sense of compassion.

In another, Bors faces a dilemma where he must choose between rescuing his brother Lionel and saving a young girl who has been abducted by a rogue knight. Bors chooses to help the maiden, but prays for his brother's safety. Lionel escapes his tormentors and tries to murder Bors, and Bors does not defend himself, refusing to raise a weapon against his kinsman. Fellow Knight of the Round Table Calogrenant and a religious hermit try to intervene, but Lionel slays them both when they get in the way. Before he can kill his brother, however, God strikes him down with an immobilising column of fire.

At the end of the afternoon, with the sun starting to lower towards the horizon, and colour the sky a blaze of gold and crimson that in another world and life would mean some dragon had set fire to Lake Town, and a bunch of dwarves and a hobbit were sitting pretty in its lair on a whole heap of gold and gems - unaware of the amount of shit about to fall on their heads, I lowered myself onto my sofa with a groan.

Then I soundly, thoroughly and with true feeling, voiced every swear word I knew. Mortal, immortal and even some of the made-up ones I'd heard as well.

Terrigyle Munstrum, one. Morgan Black, zero.

As Jessica had suggested, I'd used the free afternoon to achieve one goal. Find any truce of Teri. I'd started with Camden Town, thinking of starting at the gnome's place of business. To search it for any clues where the slippery bastard might have gone, any little tricks to track him down and pull him back to the Furies by his big bloody ears.

But I'd reached the market and navigated my way through the throng of mortals milling around the outskirts looking at the run-of-the-mill tatt and shiny curiosities designed to attract the eye and open the wallet. Pushed my way through their physical and verbal barrage, like wading through quicksand with someone drumming in my ears, then made my way into the enclosed warren of tunnels fitted with shops one every side like nooks in the cliff walls above the sea. Where sellers of every type of leatherware, alternative gothic and rebellion-fuelled anti-designer clothing brands, ethnic wooden artifice and a host of assorted trinkets and knick-knacks all vied to attract customers and offload their goods.

I'd found the shop that fronted Terrigyle's residence, and made my way past the carved elephant saltshakers and tribal totem poles. Only to find the back room gone. A wall in place of a doorway, where before I knew had been a large room filled with lanterns of every description, assorted paintings stacked one against the other, and one particularly lippy door imp that I had on occasions threatened to burn with a laser lighter to get in to see the gnome.

This time, nothing. Shelves and trade goods blocked my way, and no amount of poking revealed a hidden door or access point. I'd politely enquired as to the room's whereabouts with the staff serving customers but they'd just looked at me as if I was mad, and told me there had never been any extra room. It was just brick wall and concrete at the back of the shop.

I'd forced my way out of the market and circled round back, sneaking in the trades entrance without too much difficulty, but found the same thing there. The entrance we'd used when I brought the gnome back to change clothes and, without my knowledge, pick up the means of his escape, had vanished as well.

The bastard had closed up shop, and then *closed* up the shop fully. Erasing its existence from anyone's memory. And given the sheer bulk of weaponry and gear the gnome had managed to acquire, the fact he'd managed to do so in the hours since he left me in the troll bar with Red Cap and three smelly trolls, well, was pretty extraordinary. And fucking frustrating.

I'd checked in with the bird man, that mortal magician with the gift to speak in the tongue of all things avian, but he hadn't seen or heard anything. I politely requested he get the more sentient birds in and around London to keep an eye out for the gnome, just in case he was still hanging around the area to deal or pick up his post, but I didn't hold out much hope. I then tracked down several other contacts I had who dealt with antique weapons or items of a historical nature, that were in the business same as the gnome. But they too hadn't heard much since his apparent vanishing trick weeks ago, when we'd dropped his furry arse off to the Furies for almost blowing up the Natural History Museum.

The gnome had well and truly scarpered. Probably already back Realside, having stashed all the Accord-breaching weapons that could never travel beyond the Mortal Realm somewhere safe for when he felt it was ok to poke his head back up again.

Oh yeah, the Accords don't just protect the mortals. They may have been originally designed to shield and preserve those souls weaker and at risk from the immortals and creatures of the Real, but there were still things that the mortals had which threatened beings of immeasurable power. Cold iron and silver were prohibited beyond the Veil unless carried by lawful ordained individuals … like us Redcloaks … whilst any enchanted item that had at its core the substance of a creature of the Real was considered red-hot and not to be brought through.

The genie-lamp, for example. Capable of ensnaring magical spirits and binding them to serve the lamp's owner. Anyone found carrying or using that in the Real should expect to be dealt with most harshly, and be taught just how painful a metal spout can be when inserted in sensitive and delicate areas. Especially as metal heats very well.

There were a host of trinkets, magical rings, cloaks, swords and armour that had the blood or body parts of immortal creatures wrought into their makings. Smithed by mortals, to grant the bearers inhuman powers and magical skills. Quite rightly so, these were deemed worse than how mortals perceive serial killers' trophies, and entire clans of the kin who were slain to create the artifact had been known to spend centuries hunting those responsible for its crafting. But also those who used the items in question, making their displeasure known in violent and bloody ways.

The point was, Terrigyle had escaped. Jumped ship, skedaddled and any number of alternative phrases to describe his derriere moving at velocity out of the Mortal Realm and beyond my reach, currently. With time, I'd be able to track the rodent down, but that depended on how mollified the Furies might be by Jessica, and lenient towards cutting me some slack instead of, well, just cutting me.

I'd stopped to grab some lunch from a small café, munching on a less than amazing pastrami on rye and dwelling on the simple fact Danny made the best sandwich. Leastways to my less than refined palate. Then I'd cracked on with my second task for the day, one that I'd set myself.

Find out all I could about Morgana, get to know what sort of enemy we faced. And maybe learn something to give me an edge, if all went predictably and horribly wrong.

Not that I wasn't confident in Jessica's planning skills, or the abilities of Elspeth and my fellow lycans. But this wasn't just some minor river goddess with a beef against her Court, or a hex-crazed college kid hyped up on cursed lore. Or even a university professor stealing the life force of innocent and vulnerable mortals to prolong his own life and build himself a version of his daughter centuries dead.

Nope, this was Morgana. Sister to Madb, a legend amongst legends. And, from how most of the Real characters I knew who were aware of her escape had reacted, a truly terrifying shitstorm about to go off in our faces.

A bit of background reading it was, then.

One of my remaining contacts I hadn't managed to piss off lately was the ever-helpful supplier of all things book related. Edward Keyes, in his little stall under the bridge along the South bank, had supplied me with three solid tomes of ancient design. Much like the books on King Arthur and Excalibur he'd found for me the last time I visited.

Of course, then I'd had a George Knight dagger to trade for the goods. This time I showed up empty handed except for an *'IOU big time'* scrawled on a receipt for a pastrami on rye and coffee to go. Oh, I did include a smiley face, so he knew it was from me.

Keyes hadn't seemed surprised to see me, so I guess words was out that I was on a hunt, but for the first time ever I'd gotten a reaction from the mortal. When I leant in with my pretend purchase and whispered 'Morgana', the man had frozen for a heartbeat, and looked me squarely in the eye. I'd just shrugged and nodded, and I caught the flutter of his heartbeat in his chest, the paling of his skin. All too clear signs of shock.

He'd taken my piece of paper hidden between two paperback romance novels, giving me a stern look as he gathered himself, but thankfully he seemed to know I was good for the favour. Eventually he'd returned with the three tomes, passing them over. And then he'd shocked me a second time, by leaning in as I accepted the books, and whispering two words.

"Good luck."

He'd turned, squaring his shoulders, and simply left the book stall, walking off into the crowds of mortals milling along the Thames. And I had a very strange and poignant feeling that I was never going to see him again.

The bridge where Keyes had aired his wares was just a few minutes' walk from the Southbank centre, so I took the opportunity to pass the massive building as I headed home with my reading material. The place was a solid, multi-tiered presence hunkering down along the south bank of the Thames, of faded yellow stone and glass, set above a small arcade of bookshops and restaurants, and with a plaza out front for those visiting to stand and enjoy the views over the river.

I'd been tempted to head inside, to scope out the place and see if I might 'accidentally' find where the bloody London Stone was being kept. But I'd restrained myself as there was every chance Knox was already on site and might catch a sight of me. Or he'd have his magical defences in place, and me and my big feet would just trigger something.

Instead, I'd simply wandered around the building, noting the main doorways out front, the side entrances and large windows in the upper stories and finally the massive back of the building with its own egress. Market stalls filled this space, offering a variety of foodstuffs to tempt any sort of palate. But alongside these were specialist coffee suppliers, small-time beer producers and for some reason, alternative ice cream sellers offering a new alternative to the substance most mortals found irresistible and more addictive than illegal drugs.

Sarah had been a huge Ben & Jerries fan, and I had come back to the apartment on more than one occasion to find her curled up around a tub, with one spoon and a look in her eye daring me to say that didn't count as dinner. Ah, good times.

Satisfied that I was not going to accidently bump into Knox, knot his arms behind his back and sort things out all on my own, I'd gathered my books and a cheeky tub of mint choc that I hadn't been able to walk past three times without buying, and headed home.

To swear, a lot.

That is how I found myself, spoon in hand and ice cream on the table beside me, settled on my sofa with the three books in front of me, and some serious studying to do. I was well aware that later on that evening, I was due at Elspeth's home with pizza, wine and the bad news she was on OPS's hit-list. To find out what task she needed my particular skill-set to help with, which limited the options as to what sort of trouble she might be in considerably.

But whatever it was, that was for then. For now, I needed to get on with the fact-finding about the immortal we faced.

"The role of knowledge seeker ill suits you, pup." The Morrigan's voice caught my attention as I settled back with the first leather bound tome. I felt her presence fill my living room, a chill not entirely uncomfortable or unwelcome. Looking up, I found her settled on my second sofa like she had always been sat there, her carved staff near to hand, her armour scarred with fresh damage but seemingly intact. The Shadow fae smiled at me with that icy sliver of her lips, as she nodded to the books. "How might I assist your quest, so as to free you for more suitable tasks for your talents? And save you the pain this amount of reading will most likely cause you."

"Dare I ask what things you think I'm good for?" I asked then shook my head. "Actually, don't answer that. I'm not sure I need to know."

"See. Wisdom flourishes speedily, like a flower amongst weeds if nourished and given the right encouragement." The fae smiled wickedly as I sighed.

"I'm just trying to get a handle on the shit we're facing this time. The big bad." I looked around suspiciously, half expecting Morgana to appear like the pantomime villain in a burst of purple smoke. "You know. *Her*?"

The Morrigan cocked her head for a moment, then I saw realisation take root. The fae looked around a moment, then called out.

"Goldspur? I would have words with you."

At her words, the dryad slid free from the apple tree. She was still clad in hand-me-downs from I had to hope Felix, otherwise I had no idea where she could have gotten hold of cut off denim-shorts that hugged her form far too effectively. The t-shirt too was different, a crop top that left far too much mid-drift exposed, but since the white cotton had the message "Hands Off" in prominent letters, I simply assumed Felix was at work here. Her large amber eyes were innocent as she took in the Morrigan and I, hands settling without thought on the hilts of the knives she now always wore.

The Shadow fae noted the dryad's garments with a slight narrowing of her eyes and a disapproving sniff, but forbore to comment.

"Yes, my Lady?" Goldspur enquired, ignoring me. I guess the dryad was probably a little upset with me for not having spoken with her. About that bloody agreement she had left with me. One more thing to take up with Felix when I saw her next.

"We need to speak privately, and not be overheard. Would you please secure this abode?" The Morrigan asked her, a note of politeness in her voice that I wasn't used to hearing except for when she dealt with the High fae of the Courts. Certainly never with me.

"As you wish, my Lady." The dryad stepped back to the apple tree, and set her hands against its trunk. She leant against it for a moment, closing her eyes, and whispering words even I couldn't hear.

A moment later, the apple tree shivered as if touched by a strong wind. A glow, golden like the apples of its name, rippled out along the wood of its trunk and branches, then slid beyond to the walls, floor and ceiling. My skin prickled as I sensed the magic being used, the sense of it very much like the touch of Wyld inside me but also strangely familiar. Like the sense of coming home. Safe and secure.

Goldspur let her hands fall from the trunk and turned back to face the Morrigan.

"It is done, my Lady." She told the fae, giving a small bow. I guessed no one had shown her how to curtsey, or if she could even do something like that in those shorts. I was definitely going to speak with Felix as soon as I got the chance. "Is there anything else I can help you with?"

"No, child. You may return to your watch." The Morrigan told her formally, and the dryad smiled before shooting me one cold, wide eyed look. Then she drifted back into the tree, merging once more with the tree, her amber eyes holding me one last time before fading.

"Uh, I meant to ask." I realised something had been nagging me, and I finally had a way of getting some answers. "About Goldspur."

"Is this *really* the time to be enquiring about the dryad?" The Morrigan asked, cocking one thin eyebrow at me but I shrugged. I could spare a moment to get something sorted in my head, then crack on with the world ending problems we faced. I always was good at prioritising things.

"Goldspur. She's been growing up pretty bloody quick when I thought dryads aged over time. Like they mature with the trees that birth them." I commented, explaining what was bugging me. "Is there … there's nothing wrong with her, right? Or is it just the way the tree was created by magic, in my home?"

The Morrigan shook her head, nodding to me instead.

"You are mistaken in your suspicion, pup." She told me then smiled that wicked smile of hers. "Dryads age in accordance with the health and safety of their ward. Their tree. In this instance, Goldspur is simply responding to the truth that your home and hearth is not the most peaceful place. It has in fact had its threshold breached more than once. As such she has aged to take care of the tree, and also your home, as best she can. So the responsibility for her maturing so rapidly lies solely at your feet."

"Seriously, you're blaming this on me?" I growled but then pushed the fact to one side. It was nothing I could do anything about now, and it had no bearing on my immediate problems. As my immortal grandmother had told me.

"Fine. Back to the matter in hand. It's Morgana I need to know about. Anything that might help us when we face her." I admitted, nudging the books. "I figure we've got enough on Knox to last me a bloody lifetime, but she's the unknown. We're going to go head-to-head with her unless we are bloody lucky, and don't know what to expect. Care to fill in some of the blanks?"

The Morrigan eyed me for a long moment, then settled herself on the sofa.

"I can speak on her, and tell you the sort of creature you will face." She agreed but held out an empty hand. "But I do think it is right and proper for a host to offer a guest a drink if she is expected to speak at length."

"Fine." I grunted, pushing myself up and heading to go hunt out a bottle of wine and some glasses. No matter the time of day, morning or night, creatures of the Real would expect certain basics like a drink and something to eat when visiting someone's hearth and home. No matter what mortal society deemed appropriate, these creatures would continue to request these and not care that it was before midday or long past time for sleep.

A bottle of Merlot, two glasses and some cold meats on a plate later, I set my nourishments down on the coffee table and poured out the wine before settling down. The Morrigan took a long drink from hers, closing her eyes and savouring the flavours before setting it back down and facing me.

"Morgana Na Cruam Crough Se. Sister of our Lady, Madb Na Cruam Crough Si. The younger of the pair, though you would think otherwise from how both like to appear." The Morrigan began, fox face taking on a thoughtful expression as she spoke. "They were closer than hairs on your head in the early days, sisters of battle and blood. They warred together against foes in all Realms, facing any that sought to stand against them. They forged the Court of Shadows into its earliest form, whilst Oberon spent his energies crafting Ivory from law and order. Not for them, the brightness and burning fires of the elemental magics, Madb and Morgana were ever drawn to shadows and ice, the darker and deeper mysteries."

"I *could* tell you many tales of their exploits, their conquests and disasters. Events that shaped them into the beings you know this day. Well, at least as you know Madb." She continued, swirling the alcohol round her glass. "Of the many heroes they vanquished, the many mortal and immortal foes they crushed beneath their heels as Morgana and Madb claimed a Court and destroyed any who challenged them. Until they had proven equal to anything Oberon might summon, that the Wyld Court in the time before your father could raise as champion. In fact, anything from the Mortal and Real Realm."

"But I won't." She set her glass down, looking across at me with eyes that had witnessed the passage of eternity. That had stood amongst the original chaos before order was anything but a distant glimmer of possibility.

And who continued to stand tall and firm. "Instead, you need to know what makes Morgana so dangerous. What she might do, now that she is free. Well, pup, that is the question isn't it?"

I waited, knowing there had to be a punchline, something more than my fae grandmother simply mocking me, teasing me with titbits when Morgana threatened her own Queen.

Thankfully, my patience was rewarded.

"What sealed Morgana's fate, and led to her imprisonment and torture at the hands of her own sister wasn't in fact her actions with Artur." The Morrigan finally continued, as I bit down hard on my impatience. Bear had woken from where he had been slumbering, awakened by the fae's entrance and he obviously sensed my mood. The large troll hound prowled the living room area, circling us, pacing slow heavy steps. Unable to settle, alert for trouble. The Morrigan pointedly ignored him, focused on me and me alone.

"No, what sealed Morgana's fate was her actions centuries before. And this is what I believe you have forgotten, or not considered the import of." She continued, tapping the wooden table in front of her. "This was when a fourth Court still existed, when Ivory, Shadow and Wyld were joined by a sister."

"That of Twilight."

"You may have known of our kin as the Norns, or the Tuatha de Danann. But we knew them as those of Twilight Song." She told me, eyes narrowed and depthless. Pits of dark oblivion. "And they were *savage.*"

"The Twilight fae knew war like it was in their blood, in their very bones. Whilst Oberon, at this time sole ruler of Ivory, fought battles to force order upon the mighty and terrible creatures which existed in our Realm. Whilst Madb took oath to bind Shadow to their cause and force a balance upon all those that existed there. Twilight fought for the sake of war, for the simple desire for death and destruction." The Morrigan smiled coldly, the memories bright and sharp to her. "And Morgana revelled in their nature too. She joined them in their conquests, far from the rigid rules and structures being wrought by her cousins, by her sister. Far enough away that she could pretend that her sister had not moved above her, had not changed since taking the crown of Shadow."

"And then Oberon destroyed Twilight." I could see where this was headed, could read the car crash in the oncoming headlights.

"Oberon. And Madb." The Morrigan confirmed. "The Wyld was still young, too weak to play any part in what took place, where Titania still ruled. But yes, Oberon saw that Twilight would never bend to the new order. Would never accept dominion where he ruled on one side, and his cousin the other. Oh, he also hungered for their power. Let's not pretend his actions were purely for the good of the Realm, to secure a better future for us all. No, he also wanted their might added to his own, so none might challenge him."

"What happened?" I asked, seeing my grandmother shake her head at the needless question. She was going to tell me anyway, so why bother asking?

"Deceit, treachery and all those juicy traits you know and love that lead to a dagger in the back." The Morrigan grinned ghoulishly. "Dagur, Lord of Twilight, was called to meet with Oberon and Madb. To discuss the governing of the Realm, and the subjugation of the mortals. Instead, they trapped him, bound him and drained him of his energies. Making him into the withered thing you faced at Beltane. Then Madb called on her sister, drawing Morgana away whilst Oberon unleashed what he had stolen from Dagur upon his own people, his own Court. Combined with the power of Ivory, joined by the might of Shadow, Oberon waged bloody war on the fourth Court whilst Morgana stood. Imprisoned by her own sister and held from joining the battle."

"Madb sought to save her sister, knowing how closely tied she was to Twilight Song. She had wrested an agreement from her cousin that if Morgana did not raise a hand in the defence of the fourth Court, no action would be taken against her. She would be saved. And so Madb held her with her own will as Ivory and Shadow and Twilight fought."

"Despite the energies stolen from Dagur, Oberon found it was no easy victory." The Morrigan shook head, her braids clacking as the bones wrapped into her hair clattered and banged together. "The sisters, the Norns, they were strong enough to rail against him for a time, even as the rest of their brethren fell. And so, faced with a chance he might fail, Oberon turned from simple conquest to something worse. He used the energies of Dagur to pervert those of Twilight he had captured, turning them into the monsters that now exist within the Veil. He corrupted the very lands of Twilight, turning them into a toxic wasteland that even the sisters could not survive. Faced with their own corrupted brethren turned upon them, their home destroyed, they too eventually faltered. Their strength failed. And Oberon took them, ripping their voices from them so that they might never challenge what he had wrought, never unmake his lasting judgement on their people."

"Fuck." I breathed, as the betrayal of an entire people was laid out before me, explained in so few words.

"Eloquent as ever." The Morrigan smiled coldly. "But yes, indeed. It was truly *fucked*. But that day, Morgana watched comrades fall, watched a people she had counted as allies and friends be ground under Oberon's heel in his desire to force order and law upon the Real. Yet when Madb freed her, she swore binding fealty to her sister, made oaths to obey Oberon as Lord of Ivory. She did not shed even a single tear, and none doubted her sincerity that day."

"Her betrayal of Artur, of Ivory and Oberon's plans to rule the mortals much later … that was just the closing lines of a tale wrought back in the destruction of Twilight Song." The fae concluded, settling back and taking up her glass once more. "Her sister ruled a Court, her cousin ruled over all and Morgana was forced to act as lackey to a halfwit Ivory fae set as a dupe for the mortals to believe in. She had no strength of arms to challenge either of them, no mighty armies to call upon to fight fairly. Instead she used what she knew, seducing Artur with honeyed words and beguiling charm, begetting a monster of her own from the union to have stand as Artur's opposite, his Shadow. Mordred was meant to mock Ivory and Shadow, whilst granting the mortals an opponent to back when it was made clear they had been betrayed. That their divine King was in fact a fraud. Merlin she bent around her finger, sending him Nimue to seduce the mortal mage and lock him away in stone for a thousand years."

"Yet she still failed. She brought the whole thing crashing down around her, but in the end, Morgana found herself in a cell at her sister's mercy. With no power, nothing to call her own."

I sat back, mulling over what my grandmother had told me. It painted a horrific picture, but I wasn't entirely sure it got me any further in knowing how to face Morgana, if we had to. In some ways, she was actually more of a victim here than villain, in how she had been treated by her closest kin. But that just made things messier, more complicated.

The Morrigan obliviously read my confusion, nodding instead of mocking for once.

"Good, you have listened. Think of what I have told you, and draw what you can from the past." She told me, draining her glass and setting it aside. The she rose, facing me. "I must be off, for there are other matters that call to me this night. But three things I will leave with you, to better prepare you for what comes."

"Oh goodie. Here comes the Yoda speech." I quipped but bit my tongue as the Morrigan shot me a withering look.

"Quiet your yap, pup and listen." She told me, raising her hand and counting off three long, slim fingers. "One, you already have the means to track Morgana, gained in her arrogance by scattered salt upon the ground. Take these to your witch, for they will assist you. Two, you will not reach your prize by frontal assault, or by stealthy entrance by the rear. Seek the route that Knox has used himself so many times, that in his arrogance will believe is beyond you. Or *below* you, more like."

"And three?" I prompted, seeing her fingers fold back, giving me the birdie as she smiled coldly at me, showing she knew exactly the mortal meaning of the gesture.

"Three, pup." She replied, as her form began to fragment and fade, the fae leaving as she had arrived. "Morgana has lost twice now. Once when she was at her strongest, and then whilst all believed her true and trustworthy. She will not face you for a battle one on one, nor has the time to beguile and charm you as she did that fool Artur. Expect her to have planned as one weak, without allies and having only had one thing to use. Time, pup. She has had *time* to plan this. Beware that, and you may still survive what comes."

With that, she faded, leaving a faint mocking laugh and an empty wine glass, and me not much the wiser in any way whatsoever.

That's when I checked the clock, and realised time had flown whilst my grandmother spun stories of the end of Twilight, and the fall of Morgana. Leaving me little time to grab the pizzas, and go find out what the hell Elspeth was up to.

It was going to be almost a relief, dealing with her simple problem.

Chapter 30

Accolon.

Renowned as the lover of Morgan Le Fay, and an adversary of Artur's, Accolon was the object of her greatest desire, where she vowed to kill her husband, King Urien, and her brother Artur, for she thought to make Accolon King of Britain either by the devil's help or by magic.

He is known for a foiled plot of Morgan's to slay Artur where she provides him with Excalibur disguised as a normal sword, and entreats him to fight a nameless Knight who she fears. This Knight is Artur, wielding a sword he believes is Excalibur but is instead a feeble weapon that breaks in the combat. With help from his allies, Artur is able to wrestle his own sword free from Accolon and deal him a mortal blow.

Primrose Hill is an oasis of green amongst the sprawling urban London jungle. Like a solitary orchid struggling to break free of the choking chaos threatening to engulf and bury it.

Rising up from amidst narrow streets, railway tracks and the tail ends and dregs coming from Camden way, it somehow managed to retain a sense of nobility and order in so short a supply elsewhere within the mortal capital city.

Walking along the clean streets, littered with chic cafes and urban designer shopfronts, I navigated my way to Elspeth's home juggling two large pizza boxes, a bottle of wine and the determination to put my own problems to bed for an evening, and concentrate on giving my friend whatever help she needed. Hopefully to ease a little of her grief and pain, at least for a few short hours.

After the Morrigan had left me with no real straight answers to my question about Morgana, I'd jotted a few notes down based on the backstory she'd told me, enough to take back to talk with the team about when we met the next morning. I'd felt some satisfaction my little trick with the salt crystals had gotten a confirmation from my grandmother, and I'd brought them along for Ellie to take a look at and see if she could work anything from them.

For clarity's sake, when I'd thrown those crystals at Morgana outside the mortal Royal palace to prove she was just a spirit and not something able to squash me flat, I'd also had the crazy idea that by passing through her spirit, the salt would retain some sense of her. Kind of like imprinting her trace on them, so that someone in the know … like a learned witch I just happened to be bringing pizza to … might be able to fashion a spell to track the spirit with and hopefully help us locate her, and thus Knox. I know Jessica was asking Rous to use his remaining rats, or new ones if he'd had to replace the lost ones, to nose around the confines of the Southbank centre and find where the ritual was taking place, but it was always good to have a backup plan. And the Morrigan had all but confirmed my sneakiness might pay off, so ten points to me.

Anyway, after scribbling out what I thought were pertinent points for the following morning, I'd changed, grabbed the pizzas and wine and left Bear slumbering once more amongst the apple tree roots. I figured I'd be back home later that night to let him out to stretch his legs and scare any still-awake squirrels along the Thames walk, but disturbing him whilst he slept just to force him to go for a walk never ended well for me. So I closed up behind myself, calling for a company cab and mentally apologising to Jessica for the tenuous excuse of a work-related event to use the firm as my chauffeur.

Elsworthy Road sat alongside the rising land which Primrose Hill is famous for, and was a quiet little side street of small townhouses and one solitary small dwelling that would have better suited a country setting rather than the middle of a busy city.

Number 33 had somehow survived being converted into more cost affordable and multi-purpose dwelling. It was a Victorian style affair set back from the street with a gate in the front wall, complete with an actual enclosed garden, paved path and Disney-style wishing well to finish off the oddity.

Easing in through the gate, I walked up the path, checking out the diverse and well cultivated garden Elspeth had managed to grow. No litter to be seen, even the odd empty can of beer or plastic bag that, no matter the upmarket location, always was a sure sign mortals were in residence or used the area for recreation. Instead, I recognised a few of the more well-known plants like holly and foxgloves from sight, and picked out rosemary, mint, basil and thyme from their scent. But there were numerous other boxes and borders brimming with a variety of floral that was far beyond my basic knowledge of herb-lore.

One thing Elspeth seemed to have avoided were flowers based purely on their visual attraction. There was a display of roses, but even I knew someone with a bit of knowledge could do a lot with the petals of that plant. But there was a lack of striking vegetation which mortals grew purely because *they were nice to look at.*

I remembered suffering one of Elspeth's lectures around ignorant gardeners ruining the land they tended purely for the aesthetic pleasure of plants that should never grow in the ground in that location. She despaired when mortals changed the earth type of the place where they lived, increased the temperature and over-watered the soil just to make it a suitable rainforest-type home for something that shouldn't ever have set down roots here in the first place.

Making my way down the path, I stopped under the vintage style porch, a roof set upon four sturdy posts and walled in on the sides to grant a modicum of shelter to anyone walking up to the house. Above me, I noted the dream catcher and forged iron horse-shoe, defenders against most things spiritual and supernatural from breaching her threshold. Alongside these traditional methods of protection, I also noted a small bucket hung almost out of sight, attached to a cord that ran back into the house. High enough to be out of reach, I guessed it was filled with iron filings or salt crystals. The witch's version of medieval murder holes you find in castles, used to shower any invader with something particularly nasty. In this case, something to disrupt whatever unwelcome supernatural visitor came looking for trouble.

There was no security camera to be seen, none of the usual devices that most mortals rely on to keep them safe at home. These would have been useless, given the amount of magic Elspeth probably handled inside her home, short circuiting or catching fire as such things were wont to do. Instead, I caught the glimmer of candles in the windows, the wytch-lights that would act as both alarm for anything approaching and defence against anyone trying to force their way in that way. Many a burglar had regretted trying their luck with a candle-lit window, only to have something unpleasant like their headgear catch fire as soon as they poked it unwisely inside.

A sign hanging from the thick oak door simply noted "The witch is in", which I reckoned most mortals thought was a hang-over from Halloween. Witchfinders had gone out of fashion shortly after the Salem debacle, with so many of them proving to be corrupt and ignorant hunters who had put to death too many innocents either for the pleasure of it, or for money. These days, advertising her true nature was only troublesome for any druids who might show their face, given that nature-loving sect had never truly accepted anyone else tapping their deity's might and still had a habit of settling arguments with sharp sickles curses.

There was a second sign underneath this, which read *"Trespassers will be composted."* I had to chuckle at that one.

Juggling the pizzas and wine, I knocked on the door, hearing movement inside. After a moment, the door opened and Ellie smiled back at me. She was clad in her familiar gypsy-style clothing, but still wore a black wrap around her shoulders which clashed with the other vibrant colours. She'd pulled back the mass of red hair with a band and was wearing some pleasant floral perfume.

"Morgan. You came." She smiled warmly, and for a moment the pain and loss were erased from her expression. I held up my gifts, shrugging. "Thank you!"

"It isn't much, but I even remembered your weird fascination with pineapple on the pizza, so you'd better be hungry. No-one else I know likes the stuff!" I grinned as she motioned for me to follow her.

"Barbarians." She shot back at me over her shoulder. "Mind your step."

Following her in, and nudging the door shut behind me, I stopped and checked my feet, finding a thin line of salt had been run along the edge of the doorway. Just enough to form a barrier, barring anything that wished her harm from passing through.

"You expecting company or just being a little bit more paranoid than usual?" I queried as I stepped over the line carefully, leaving it undisturbed.

Ellie didn't answer, so I figured it was probably just her being cautious. I'd been paranoid at Morgana overhearing any of our conversations, and the witch was doing a lot more than just talking about the immortal. So a little salt spilled was probably just her being careful.

Yeah, right.

The interior of Elspeth's home was homely and cluttered, akin to the rural farmhouses and old vintage pubs you find dotted around the landscape as soon as you left what mortals called *civilisation*. The witch had stripped the ceilings back to the bare beams, and dried herbs were hung from these to fill the air with a delicate scent. She had also knocked through several walls, removing them and leaving only the required support pillars to keep the place standing. This meant the entry hall now opened up into a large style living room, with thick plaid rugs thrown over bare wooden floorboards, and an old-style inglenook fireplace dominating the far-left wall. I tried to remember if I had seen a chimney poking out the side of the outside, but figured I hadn't been looking for one. A large black iron stove squatted in the opening, and the smell of woodsmoke lingered amongst the herbs, telling me the thing was active and well used.

Bookshelves lined the walls, fitted in between windows but taking up the space that other homeowners might use for pictures or mirrors. They were crammed with books of a wide and assorted nature, from the expected herbology and studies of the supernatural, to weather codices charting historic weather patterns across the country, multiple volumes of creatures found in myth and legend, DIY instruction books, cookery series covering starters, mains and desserts from all over the world … the list went on, as I eyeballed the collection.

The books were all well used but dust free, indicating they were owned by someone who wanted them more for their use than for the look of owning an extensive library. Not like those old estate homes where you walk into a room packed with red leather tomes, expensive looking and indicating a serious reader – until you cheekily ran a finger over one of the covers and find they've never been touched. A collector's view of knowledge, for keeping not using.

The witch living here definitely did not subscribe to that.

There was no television taking up space in a convenient corner, no sleek music system to play the various CDs or even records that seemed to be coming back into fashion. There *was* an old-style spinning wheel, the type made famous by a certain princess and her unfortunate allergic reaction to a little prick … of her finger, by a needle. Before anyone thinks anything else. It sat beside a basket filled with balls of wool of different colours, each meticulously bundled and tied to avoid spilling out.

A staircase split the living room, with bare wooden boards leading up to the first floor. Two archways had been formed in the back wall, one that led off to what I could see was a substantial kitchen. A large cast iron range hulked at the back of this, the sort I believe was called an argur or something, with massive doors and large hot plates on top. It looked like she had tiled the floor too, which explained a set of comfy fluffy bunny slippers that sat at the archway since those clay slabs would soak up the cold and be freezing even on the hottest day of the year.

The other arch had a curtain pulled across it, hiding whatever lay beyond. But given the layout, despite this being the first time I'd been inside Ellie's home, I could guess what was on the other side.

Every witch or warlock needed a workroom. A sanctum, a place for them to do stuff without distraction and preferably away from sight so they didn't have to explain the odd scorch marks, paraphernalia and sometimes *things* that hung around such places. In the old days, privacy was needed to stop the locals chancing upon the room and calling for the thumbscrews, or fire and tinder. But these days it was more just to give the practitioner peace of mind and to stop them being interrupted by people knocking at the door wishing to speak about the state of their immortal soul … that or campaign for the upcoming election and their seat on whatever party was in control at the time.

You had to admire the restraints of city living witches and warlocks. If it was me, there would have been a spate of mortals turned into toads and other such creatures for the interruptions they caused. That or I'd have had a whole roomful of voodoo dolls, and a hell of a lot of pins.

I took all this in whilst I eased my boots off and handed over the pizzas and wine for opening, as Elspeth headed into the kitchen for glasses and nominal kitchenware like plates for the food.

"So, what's up. You got some more tests you want to run on me, to see what these tattoos are doing to me?" I prompted, as she clattered around out of sight. "Or do you *actually* have something you want moved, and I'm asking without making a point of you being a weak woman and me a strong lycan or anything, ok? I'm just muscles for hire, you know that."

There was an energy to the air, something that was off-kilter. In anyone else I would have said was nervousness … but Ellie didn't get nerves. She was as solid as the rest of us, used to handling situations with a clear head and a calm centre.

I heard a snort of laughter from the kitchen, then Ellie returned. The pizzas had been left to one side, but she had opened the wine and poured us both a large glass. One thing she hadn't foregone taking advantage of in terms of modern versus classic were the wine glasses. I had the same style, curved and intricately formed so as to help the wine inside breathe. It cuts down on having to open the bottle and leave it for half an hour for it to taste right. The witch knew her alcohol.

"OK, you have my full attention." I grinned as I took the glass, and she nodded before taking a long swig, savouring the strong flavours. "'Fess up."

"Morgan I ... Look, what I'm going to ask you is *completely* outside of anything we've done before. Anything I would think was right or proper for me to ask. Of anyone, let alone someone I call a friend. A close friend." She told me hesitantly, and that nervous energy spiked again. Seriously, if this kept up, things would start flying off the walls before she finished telling me what was up. "It's just ... ah, Goddess, this is difficult ..."

Seeing her so conflicted, so not the self-assured and confident friend I knew and cared a whole lot about, I realised I needed to lighten things up a little. Just for now.

"Hey, I get it. Something difficult you need help with." I told her, grinning to show I wasn't in any way worried over her odd behaviour. "Take a breath, and whilst you work out how to ask, maybe you can do something with these?"

I pulled out the rock salt crystals in their plastic container, and passed them over to her.

"I chucked these at *that fae* when she paid a visit." I explained, only just remembering I had no idea if the house was warded against immortals hearing their names. "Reckoned since they touched the spirit, they might ..."

"Might have taken some of her essence, and be possible to use to locate her." Elspeth gentle shook the container, then popped the lid like a pro and let some of the crystals fall onto her palm. She closed her eyes for a moment, and I felt that brief whisper of magic, a gentle breeze on a summer's day filled with the scents of grass and trees, before she looked back at me with a hint of her old self. "Oh, Morgan. You actually *listened* to me, didn't you? I can definitely bind these in a tracking charm, and work out where *she* is, or will. But even better, if I can use the essence to mimic her, I can maybe even mask us from her sight or any detection Knox might have crafted too. This could be our way to sneak up on them without triggering any alerts! Oh, you clever sod, you!"

I grinned as she shook the salt back into its container, then let her hug me with genuine warmth. I gripped her back, letting her feel my strength and solidity, hoping she could borrow some to settle herself. Then, gently, I stepped back and peered into her face, free hand on her upper arm to try and convey some comfort.

"Now that's sorted, just tell me straight what you need help with." I told her calmly, seeing her flinch then take a long, slow breath.

Finally, she nodded but loosed herself from my grip.

"It's better I show you. Come with me." The witch told me, and I got that sense of finality from her again, decision made and to hell with the consequences. The sort of feeling I was oh so familiar with, but normally going on inside me.

Setting the wine down, I followed Elspeth as she walked across the living room, to the curtain hiding the room beyond. She turned, gripping the fabric, and looked me squarely in the eye.

"Just … Just don't judge me. Please." She asked, and pulled the material back. At the same moment, she grabbed my hand and pulled me forward through the arch before I could react. Stop her. Do anything but take that one step into what lay beyond.

Then I swore. Loudly.

Just couldn't help myself.

Chapter 31

I'd been right. The room beyond was Elspeth's workshop. Used for her craftings, her sanctum where she could practice without interruption.

And, as it turned out, where she got up to total and utter *madness*.

As soon as I stepped through the arch, my senses lit like someone had switched on a light. Or closer to the truth, they'd ripped the hood off my head that I hadn't known I was wearing. Magic sparked to life like sour cherries and fireworks on my senses, thick and powerful enough to make the hairs on my arms stand up like I stood in a static storm.

The room I found myself in was large, far larger than it ought to be so I guessed the witch had cheated, extending the walls into mystical space. A large cauldron sat in one corner, heated by logs and coals underneath and hung upon a black ironwork frame. A long ladle's handle stuck out of this, long enough to have passed for an oar, enabling the wielder to stand at a safe distance whilst stirring whatever was cooking in the pot, and avoiding any splashback or any of the other such dangers when mixing magical ingredients.

Large worktops had been fitted to two of the four walls, and these were piled with books, weird glass paraphernalia and the essential tools of the trade for anyone messing around with the occult and supernatural. Chalks, glass bottles filled with dried herbs and distillery equipment bubbling away merrily. Pestle and mortars, grindstones and enough kitchen implements to tackle any sort of plant. And for those moments when a witch needed to vent her frustration, half a dozen hand stitched dolls, tied with various materials and sat beside a good number of ultra-sharp hair pins.

A large chandelier lit the room, filled with wax candles and keeping a steady light, banishing shadows from the room. Elspeth also had empty jam jars set with candles in niches in the walls, making sure that no matter what, she always had light to work by.

I took all this in with a glance, as my attention was divided between two particular items that sent my panic needle racing to a *what the fuck* moment in record time.

The first was a containment circle, inlaid in the far corner of the room, set directly into the floor to minimise the risk of the lines ever being broken. It sparkled like polished silver, with intricate runes and symbols set within the three-fold circles that comprised its design. And inside this, what I took to be a particularly ugly goblin crouched, eyeing me warily as it poked at the contents of its nose unselfconsciously. Even as I watched, the goblin blurred, shrinking to take the form of a particularly ugly troll, still picking its nose. Then it ballooned, into a towering ogre, still particularly ugly, crouched within the confines of the circle enclosing and imprisoning it.

But this was not what caused me to swear.

The second item filled the centre of the room, having been cleared to encompass its length and breadth. A wooden table, solid oak by the look of it, and set within a second circle of intricate design. Flowers had been lain on the tabletop, circling the figure which lay atop the wooden planks. A candle, burned down to a third of its length, sat at one end, created of vibrant purple wax and chased with silver down its length. This burned warmly and steadily, its flame a strange blue shade.

I looked at the figure lying on the table, arms folded carefully over its chest, clothes carefully cleaned and the posture as of one asleep. At rest. Which warred with the chest wound I knew lay under those hands, caused by a creature of the Wyld, a particularly vicious bastard that also just happened to be my half-brother. Jack the Ripper, released from prison by Morgana and Knox to spread chaos and death, to keep us busy whilst they got on with their ritual.

And this poor mortal had stood against it, thinking to save me and the woman he loved. He'd even managed to land a crippling blow, forcing silver into the fae's body to poison and weaken it, before the thing killed him and then was thrown into the Thames' unbreakable grasp.

Detective Inspector Gregory Allen.

His *very much dead* body, laid out in Elspeth's house. When I was pretty sure it should be in the police morgue, or wherever OPS had arranged it to be delivered whilst I was elsewhere learning of Morgana's escape.

"What. The. Fuck." I slowly enunciated at the witch, as she stood by the archway. On this side of the portal, I could see the shimmer in the air within the arch, a cloaking spell wrought to mask and hide the sanctum from outside view. And to hide what she had stashed away in here from nosy lycan, possibly. "I mean, seriously, Ellie. What the fuck?"

"I totally understand your feelings, Morgan." The witch answered as she stepped away from the arch and moved to stand by DI Allen's body. She gently brushed his face, a lingering touch that spoke volumes. "But if you could enunciate your questions a little better, I will try to answer as best I can."

I took a slow, deep breath, marshalling my thoughts as I switched my attention from the dead body on the table, to the creature bound in the warding circle, and back to Elspeth. Then I nodded to her, working my way through the list of things I wanted to ask.

"OK, let's start with the easy one. How the hell did you get that body here?" I asked, but before Elspeth could begin to answer, my attention snapped back to the creature in the circle as it sat on the ground in the shape of an ugly gnome, and waved at me with one hand. "Hell, is that a shape-changer?"

"Not *a*. *The* shape-changer. Chimera, the Wyld fae released from Shadow's prisons." The witch confirmed as the creature's form shifted once more. This time into a slim and very feminine dryad, much like Goldspur, except for being … yes, still ugly. The creature didn't seem to be able to fix that particular problem. "It's the reason why the staff at Westminster mortuary now have no record of ever receiving a DI Gregory Allen, nor having his body anywhere on the premises."

I eyed the shape-changer, as it grinned and took a deep bow.

"Chimera. The same Chimera we've got packmates out hunting, that's been driving the City police nuts with impersonations of wild animals escaped from London zoo? The one from the Shadow Court's list that *we were hired to hunt and capture?* That shape-changer?" I queried, seeing Elspeth nod at each question. "So what the hell are you doing with it? And why did it steal his body?"

"Because I asked him to." She replied bluntly. "Really, Morgan. Did that really need asking?"

"Uh, sorry. I'm just coming to terms with the fact that you have a *dead body* in your home, and for once it's not my fault." I growled, shaking my head at the sheer weirdness of it all. "Ok, better question maybe. *Why* did you ask a known felon, an escaped prisoner from the Courts and one we're being paid to return to them with a boot up the arse, to steal this body? And how the hell did it manage it?"

"The simpler of the two is the how." She answered, as she faced me across the body of her love. She carefully raised his right arm from his chest, pushing back the material of his clothes to show a simple braided leather band wound around his wrist. "I charmed this when I gave it to him, to act as protection against ill intent against him. Just enough to keep him safe, so I thought. But it means I know wherever he is, like I know where any of the charmed items I have created are at any point. It helps me know the people I care for are safe."

"Given he was wearing the charm when he *died*," She continued, pausing slightly to draw a breath, voicing the damning truth. "I knew where it was they took his body. Westminster mortuary, bound for an autopsy by an uncaring stranger. To lie alone and cold on a slab, surrounded by death."

"After your friends from OPS returned me home, I communed with my Goddess, seeking solace and a way past the pain. She it was that tried to tell me that death must follow life, that all things end. That I should accept this, and remember the joy of what we had, little as it was." Elspeth spoke slowly, her jaw set and her eyes hardening to show just how well she had taken the words of her immortal deity. "But I refused. Why should I lose the man I love, why should his life be worth less than others, when he was a true guardian. A selfless man haunted by tragedy, still trying to save others?"

"I remembered the Chimera was still unchained, that it had so far eluded our attempts to recapture it. It was a simple matter of summoning it to me and binding it to perform one simple act of deception. To the doctors and staff at the morgue, I appeared as an official far above their station, come to provide identification of the body brought in earlier that night. Chimera appeared as my assistant, and when we were taken to where they had him stored, I hexed the cameras and charmed the doctor assisting so that he saw or heard nothing. Then it was just a matter of Chimera creating a copy of Greg's body to be left in his place, and a glamour to change us into morgue staff removing *another* completely different body for transport to the funeral home where grieving relatives were waiting its arrival. No one at the morgue saw or heard anything untoward, and the recording devices will have malfunctioned for a short period."

"Uh, go back to that bit about Chimera making a copy of the body?" I queried, looking at the Wyld fae.

Obediently, the fae furrowed its brow with effort and then stepped carefully to one side. Leaving behind what looked like a mirror image of itself, still in dryad form, standing motionless beside it in the circle. The fae made a *ta da* motion with its hands, and the simulacrum collapsed in on itself, dissolving into a sticky mess on the room's floor before dissipating entirely. "Oh that's just *weird*."

"Not at all." Elspeth countered, gesturing to the fae. "It's an effective defence mechanism, guaranteed to fool any enemy wishing it harm. I knew of it from my studies of the escaped prisoners, and realised how useful it would be for what I wanted. The duplicate will last only as long as Chimera wishes it, so by now the body that the morgue had in storage will have vanished, as will any paperwork or record that he was brought in under that name in the first place. Another hex I left them with, a jinx linked to his name."

"Now that you have *admirably* explained the stunning performance I supplied? As per our agreement, I believe you now must uphold your side of our bargain." Chimera spoke for the first time. Its voice was odd, accents coming and going, not keeping to one but using a meld of all the voices it had probably used in its life. "As we agreed, witch. Release me."

"Oh yes. Morgan, one sec." She told me, walking over to the circle. I probably should have stopped her, asked her to hold on until we'd cleared up this whole mess, but I was still getting my head round finding DI Allen's body here, and the utter insanity of what someone I thought of as rationale and sensible had committed.

Elspeth stopped by the outer circle, facing the fae.

"As bound by your oath to my Goddess and I, sworn upon pain of true death, to serve as I required. I now release you *Chimearam Och Maira*, and bid you return through the Veil." Ellie intoned, raising her hands above her head, and carefully and clearly enunciating every word to avoid mistake or error. "You are bound not to pass back to the Mortal Realm once more for a hundred years, and offer no trouble to any that do not first seek you harm. Begone."

She clapped once, sharply, the sound shivering through the air. Signalling the accord complete, the agreement done.

"Glad to be out of here! Never wanted to come in the first place, if I'm being honest. It smells *horrible*, and Gods, the noise!" Chimera grumbled, before its form started to fray and fragment, disappearing like the Morrigan had until the circle was empty.

I let the moment settle, as Elspeth did a cursory check to make sure the circle was still intact and had not in any way been affected or altered by its recent recipient. Then she turned back to face me, cocking one eyebrow and her expression set into a *next question* expectation.

"Ok, let me just make sure I'm following all this." I swept my hand through the air, taking in everything in the room. "After seeking guidance from your Goddess, who if I'm honest gives *really* shit advice, you decided to go do the complete opposite of what She told you. You summoned and captured Chimera, binding it to perform one task for you in exchange for its release back to the Real with its freedom. Then you broke into a secure mortal medical facility, having tracked DI Allen's body by a charm you gave him … and I'm not going to even comment on that in terms of stalker-instinct … got Chimera to make a goo-copy of him, jinxed all their equipment to remove all trace of him from their records and hexed the staff so they wouldn't remember anything happening. And finally you and Chimera then cloaked yourself in glamour and waltzed back here with a dead body. In some other way than using your cycle, unless you've increased the size of your front basket a shitload. All in, and let me be absolutely clear on this … all this happened in the space of not quite two days. Forty-eight hours. Right?"

Elspeth nodded once, and I shook my head.

"Firstly, I got to say, I'm amazed at just what you've achieved in so short a space of time." I summed up, shaking my head at the sheer scale of her actions. "It'd take me a week or more to get this deep into this level of stupidity. Honestly, you make me look like an amateur!"

I saw Ellie's scowl at my words, but right now I didn't much care if she didn't like what I had to say. *She* had brought *me* into this.

"But ok, it is what it is." I looked her straight in the eye, searching for the truth to what I was going to ask next. "So I guess all I have left is … why, Ellie? Why do all this?"

The witch moved to the workbench behind her, switching aside a tea towel she had used to cover some the apparatus that lay scattered on the worktop. Golden light, warm and alive like a swarm of radioactive bees, flooded the room as she held up two glass flasks. The contents of which was all too familiar to me.

"Because of this, Morgan." She told me, eyes lit by the golden fire, transforming her face for a second so that I didn't recognise the woman standing opposite. "To use this to bring him back to me. To save him."

Chapter 32

Elspeth read my instant reaction as it popped all over my features and held up one hand bearing a flask of stolen life.

"Hear me out, Morgan?" She asked plaintively. "Then you can judge me."

I grunted, thoughts a jumbled mess after seeing the life essence that I remembered she had saved from Knox's sanctum, as we were being attacked by the Harrowing and shortly before I'd gotten us blown out of the house's ground floor window. Ah, good times.

"The thing is," Ellie set the flasks down by the body, and I noted something odd as she moved closer to the table. The blue flame of the candle began to lean in her direction, as if caught in a strong breeze, reaching out as if to touch her. Definitely not a normal flame, then, since the rest of the ones around the room did not move. "Gregory *hasn't moved on.* Yes, his body suffered traumatic injury, and yes, in simple biological terms, he is classed as dead. But his spirit, it's still here. With me. And it wants to remain."

She moved closer to the candle, reaching out to cup the flame gently. Without any coercion or outside force, the flame flickered and waved about her hands, licking over her skin but doing her no harm. Like it was stroking her fingers, her palms. A very loving and intimate gesture.

"This is a *destiny* candle, and it's something every practitioner crafts in their journey of self-awareness and knowledge. Mine was fashioned as I forged the oaths I made to my Goddess, and she to me, and was meant to represent the one event I would face, a challenge that would define who I am. It is different for every one of us. Sometimes it signals a fundamental change the creator must undergo, sometimes danger to the witch or warlock. For me, it was meeting Gregory Allen."

She smiled gently as the flame playfully danced over her skin.

"It would light by itself when the challenge was upon the witch, and would burn until they either conquered that which they faced, or were defeated."

"The candle lit the same day I met him, the one when I met you outside your friends' home. To help try and find Felicity." She continued as I eyed the candle warily. "And I have known that he posed a singular challenge to me, to balance my love for him and desire to share a life with him, whilst being true to myself and my calling. That was the choice I thought I was being given."

"But then he *died*, and I felt the challenge was ended. I came home fully expecting to find the candle unlit, the flame put out. That I had failed." She told me and I could sense the dread and pain she must have felt as she walked in the door, expecting to see a cold, dark candle waiting for her. "But as I walked in, I saw the flame was like this. Blue, not its natural colour, and it *greeted* me. Reached for me as if to welcome me home. It was Gregory's spirit, joined to the candle somehow and it is his will keeping him here. His strength and determination not to pass on."

"That's Gregory?" I asked with more than a dollop of doubt in my voice. There was simply no way that the candle could have heard me since the bloody thing was a *candle*, but the flames still leapt up at my tone, flaring as if reacting. I'd never pissed off a mystical candle before, so just held up my hands and muttered a *sorry* to it. "Uh, ok, calm down! That's Gregory. Fine. He's in your candle. How does that explain this utter level of idiocy you're planning?"

"It's simple, really." Ellie replied, as the flame returned its attention back to her hands. "Jessica had me study Knox's records. His diaries and journals, which have more than enough notes on his research and experiments for me to work out what I need to do. I have Gregory's body, I have his spirit, and I have the energies needed to kickstart things again. All I need to do is convince my Goddess that this is right, that he deserves a second chance. And I will use all my gifts to heal him, and bring him back to me."

"Ellie, listen to me." I kept my voice calm, gentle as possible as I tried to explain my thoughts without causing pain. "You're using *Knox's* work. The mortal whose been stealing energy from other people for over a century, oh and carving them up to make a golem. A body for another spirit. Any of this sound familiar? How is *this* any better than what he's been doing?"

"Morgan, I've thought this through. Argued the same thing myself." She told me, looking me square in the eye so I could see the truth. No attempt to deceive me, or hide anything in fact. "But it *is* different. This is Gregory's spirit, and *his* body. Not some crazed immortal hellbent on revenge, or some broken spirit being housed in a new home to live again. This is Gregory Allen, and all I am attempting is to undo the damage done to him with the skills I have, and some borrowed energy. I can't give the energy back to those Knox stole it from, but I *can* make good use of it, to save another. How is that wrong?"

I bit my tongue as a handful of flippant and glib responses sprang to mind, all too easy to say, to challenge. But the witch deserved better of me, so I stopped myself and tried to think it through.

Fuck, I hate moral quandaries.

"Whilst you think, let me share something with you." Elspeth knew better than to try to force her reasoning on me, knew I'd just head the other way like a mule being pushed by its owner to take a route it didn't fancy. But she did believe in giving me all the facts. "I've told you he was married before. Had a wife and a young daughter. They are both dead, killed by *something* that entered their home whilst he was out patrolling as a younger police officer. This thing left no fingerprints, no DNA, no evidence that it had in fact ever been there … apart from a dead mother and daughter, and a broken mirror with some blood evidence on it that made no sense to the investigators at the time. Both the woman and the child had no marks on them, no visible injuries and no fingerprints, and Gregory said that they were found in a state of extreme anxiety, judging from the expressions frozen on their faces. The neighbours had heard screams and called the police, who broke in to find them dead."

My mind, the logical bit that only rarely got to flex its muscles, took note of what the witch was telling me. The salient details. A broken mirror with weird blood stains. Bodies unmarked and bearing no mortal injuries. Both found looking scared, maybe scared to death.

"Anyone note a weird smell in the home?" I asked, and Elspeth nodded.

"They initially thought it was leaking gas, from the kitchen. There was an attempt to blame a faulty appliance on the deaths." She replied, and I nodded, knowing that would be the default mortal thinking.

"So *something* crawled out of the mirror, killed the woman and child without inflicting visible wounds but in the fight, the mother probably broke the mirror thinking it would save them." I followed the breadcrumbs, stale and mouldy though they were. "The creature then left through the broken mirror, the bloodstains passing with it into the portal and so becoming part of the mirror itself instead of just staining it. Sounds like a boggart or hag, they like to use mirrors to enter homes without breaching thresholds. So what?"

"I thought so too. I checked, and Gregory purchased the mirror at a market a week before, at the time he'd thought it incredibly cheaply priced. Almost as if the owner was trying to get rid of it." Elspeth explained instead. "He thought it had come from a house clearance, since he remembered other household goods for sale there too. A child's cot, some dolls. Some old dresses, possibly wedding clothes."

"Ok, sounds more like a hag now. Vengeful spirit of a child or older woman, comes out of mirrors to kill those it finds before returning to wait for the next victim." I confirmed, then shrugged. "Again, why do I need to know this?"

"Because of how Gregory reacted." Elspeth told me, reaching over to gently touch his pale and cold face. "Most mortals would have been consumed by what happened. Become hunters of all things supernatural, researching the Real and losing themselves in the darkness. Or they would break inside, become alcoholics or substance abusers, trying to forget their own pain and tragedy, the facts that didn't add up."

"But Gregory? He chose the third path." She smiled up at me, a child-like and innocent curve of delight and almost wonder on her lips. "He chose *to protect*. He grieved for the loss of a woman and daughter he loved, but he never let it consume him. He knew there were things in the dark that he did not understand, but he didn't let them break him. Gregory Allen continued to do things as he had done. By mortal law, and logic. It didn't help him in the end, but he tried to live a life that made sense, and to help others with his own strength and nothing more."

"And that is the reason why I love him so much." Elspeth finished, letting me taste the truth in her words. "And why I say no. This is one loss I cannot stomach, one failing I won't stand by and let be. He deserves a second chance, if any of us do."

I could tell there was no arguing with her. Elspeth had made up her mind, was convinced this was the right thing to do not just for her, but for Gregory Allen. If she was being conned, if that *wasn't* him in the candle flame no matter how odd the fact was, then whatever was doing the con was an expert. I couldn't help wonder if this wasn't some trick of Morgana's somehow, some extra little trick to trip us up. But that was just my suspicion trying to find excuses why this shouldn't happen.

"You've got no guarantee this will work." I told her, and she nodded, accepting the point. "Or if it does, that it's a permanent solution. Or what it will cost you."

"I've accepted that my Goddess might refuse me this," She admitted with absolutely honesty. "I've also accepted that this might only give him a little more life. I can't measure what is in these flasks. Is it a lifetime? Half of one? But what I know is it is more than he has right now."

"As for what this will cost me, I think I am better prepared for that." Elspeth tapped her own heart, smiling a sad smile. "She has already told me what I am supposed to do. What I am doing doesn't just go against her express wishes, I risk breaking oath with her. Losing any and all of my gifts, leaving me a simple mortal. But I am prepared for that."

"Uh, ok but *we* still need you in one piece, Ellie," I reminded her, feeling a little selfish but the fact was, she had commitments. "At least until things are done with Knox and *her*. If you lose your talents, you won't be able to brew the witchy potion to help us track you know who, or do that thing you thought up and hide us from her. How's that going to work."

Elspeth nodded, thankfully not taking offence that I was asking her to put us over her own plans. Instead, she took a breath to settle herself, and I got that spike of nervousness again. Like before, when I'd first walked into the house. When she had been hiding something from me …

"Oh gods, Ellie. What haven't you told me?" I groaned, knowing I was going to hate the next surprise. Just coz.

"It's not that bad." She told me, cheeks still colouring slightly though. "I thought of what I am committed to, the promises I've made to the pack. To Jessica. I can't leave you without some help, but even if I do lose my link to my Goddess, I will still have all my knowledge. I'll just need to work with someone who has talent …"

She turned, making a sweeping gesture with one hand. The cloaking she had in place fell away much like the cloak of invisibility from Harry Potter, but this one had completely masked the figure who was hiding underneath it from me. Smell, sound … Everything.

"Uh, hi Morgan." Felix waved a hand at me from where she sat on a stool. "Uh, surprise!"

There you go. Trouble, with Felix making the third. Guess I was wrong about that saying after all.

Oh, and yeah. I swore. Profusely.

Chapter 33

Ector.

Sometimes known as Hector, Antor or Ectorius, this Knight was the adoptive father of Artur after Merlin took him from Uther and Igraine, to learn to be a Knight first and then a King. He is often portrayed as a blustering, buffoon-ness sort of man, but he was known to be stout of heart and willing to lay down his life for his true King.

Much of what the common-folk attributed to Artur's Kingly nature and judgement towards justice and righteousness was taught by Ector.

Shouting ensued.

Mostly by me, a little by Felix. None by Elspeth. Or by Gregory Allen, lying cold on the tabletop.

Eventually I calmed down, as my colleague explained her plans and how Felix fitted into them.

"Felicity has agreed to help me, after I invited her here and explained the situation." She told me, as I shot a look at Felix, sitting on her stool and doing her best *not* to look at the corpse lying in the centre of the room. "I had already decided to introduce her to my Goddess anyway, as I think it will help with Felicity's control of her gifts if she wishes to take oath like I did. Anyway, even if things do not go as planned, her talents and my knowledge will be more than enough to provide what we need to handle Knox and *her*. That I am sure."

"And you're ok with all this?" I asked the younger woman, waving a hand and pointedly drawing her attention to DI Allen. Credit where credit is due, she didn't flinch looking at the corpse, instead looking me in the face afterwards and shrugging.

"I admit I kinda freaked when I first saw what Elspeth had here. But then she told me she needs our help. *My* help. And if I can do some good here, maybe help get Greg back then that's good enough for me." She told me with innocent conviction. "Elspeth and Greg both helped me in different ways when … when Gary killed that man in front of me, They both showed me kindness, and I believe you should pay that sort of thing back. That's all."

"Great. Another karma-happy witch. As if life ain't complicated enough with one of you!" I growled but then shook my head, knowing there was only one decision I could make here. "Fine. Ok, you've planned this out and I can't fault your logic, even if I think you're bat-shit crazy. What did you need me for? And please don't say anything complicated. It's been a rough few days."

Elspeth's smile lit her face, as she walked round the table, coming to stand opposite me and laying a hand on my forearm. That touch transferred some of what she was feeling … happiness that I stood with her, hope that she wasn't wrong and that this might work. And a bucketload of worry, of how her Goddess would react, what it would mean for them both.

I laid a hand gently over her own, leaning in to butt my forehead against hers with a soft touch. She closed her eyes, breathing deeply, then stepped away to stand once more by her love.

"Thank you, Morgan. I cannot tell you what this means to me. To us." The witch told me, then nodded back to the archway. To the room beyond. "All I need for you to do is keep watch. Guard us. When I start the ritual, when I beseech my Goddess to commune with me, the defences around my home will be weakened or even totally negated. I'm not expecting trouble but …"

"These days, none of us do. It just seems to happen anyway." I sighed but couldn't help a small stab of relief that Elspeth didn't need me to arm wrestle her immortal into submission. Or anything like that. I really had been worried for a second. "Fine, I'll just sit my arse on your nice comfy sofa and pick off the pineapple from the pizza until you're done."

"You brought pizza with pineapple? Cool!" Felix piped up, and I put my hands over my eyes, groaning anew.

"Oh gods, there really *are* two of you. What did I do to deserve this?!"

"Oh hush. If you want us to start listing all your faults and mistakes, we'll be here all night. And we have things to do." Elspeth snarked with a smile, and Felix joined her with an easy laugh. Guess I *had* left myself open to that one.

Taking a quick look round the sanctum one last time, I drew a breath and nodded to both women. Then, I ducked out through the archway. Immediately, I lost sight of everything that lay beyond. The curtain swished back across the gap to hide the blurred cloaking Elspeth had in place, and I squared my shoulders.

Guard duty. Fine. After all the crazy shit of the past couple of days, I really could do with just a little rest watching out for any nasties who might come calling.

It was soon apparent that, apart from not having a tv or music system, the witch also didn't have a clock. Checking my phone for the time, I saw we'd eaten into the evening and it was nearing ten already. My stomach rumbled to show its displeasure at having been ignored for so long.

"Might as well make myself comfortable." I told the thin air, and headed into the kitchen to gather up vitals. Bringing back the bottle of wine and the one pizza I had kept uncorrupted by fruit, I settled down onto one comfy sofa and tore free a cold but still delicious slice of jalapeno, double pastrami and extra cheese from the circle. Chasing it with a mouthful of wine, I sat back and let my eyes roam the bookshelves for anything of interest.

Three slices down and a second glass of wine, I hadn't found anything I wanted that much to read. I really didn't feel the need to increase my knowledge of herbs, wildlife or ancient Mayan rituals and lunar prophecies. I know, I'm an uncultured thug at times, ignoring the chance to better myself but that's just me.

I noted the instant the candles in the room's windows suddenly dipped then went out completely. The air grew still around me, silence settling in like someone had turned down the volume on the stereo playing *Life and all its noises*. Everything felt muted. Dampened down.

"Guess they've started." I spoke for the sheer sake of hearing someone speak then set aside my glass. Rising from my seat, I stalked around the room, checking the windows and door, making sure the lines of salt she had prepared were still intact. Not the best defence if anything with any muscle decided it wanted 'in', but the barriers would stop a whole host of middling and weak creatures from chancing their luck.

Power draws power, and Elspeth's ritual was a direct connection to her Goddess. Like ringing the bell on the fire engine to force traffic out of the way. Some things would hear it, and might decide they'd try their luck. See if they could catch a witch unawares, unprotected. Hence my role, to act as dissuader to any chancers. Verbally, physically … whatever it took.

To be fair, it was a role I knew how to play well.

Magic takes time, I was well aware, and quite often that didn't correspond to what passed in the real world. Elspeth and Felix were in a bubble right now, and it might feel like hours had passed instead of minutes, or the other way around. I had no way of knowing how long this might take, so decided the best thing I could do was carry on eating until something showed up.

Midnight came and went according to my phone, but nothing changed inside the house. The un-pineappled pizza was long gone, and the remains of the wine sat in my glass untouched as I casually flipped through *JRR Tolkien's Bestiary – An Illustrated Guide to Middle Earth*. Ok, yeah, I'd gotten that bored, I had been seduced into choosing a book to read.

It wasn't half bad. Hobbits, according to Tolkien, looked more like the gnomes I knew than the Hollywood pretty-boy versions, but he'd been closer to the fae I knew and tolerated with his elves. His dwarves and the dwarrow-folk I knew, were so close that I had to guess he'd been visited by something of the Real to inspire his imagination. They loved pulling that sort of shit. Giving glimpses of their true nature to artists and writers, visionaries or occasionally just the first mortal they met, to mess their heads up and inspire great works of fiction and fantasy. I think it was their vanity, always wanting the mortals to be crafting tales about them in some shape or form.

Anyhow, I was deep in the book, flipping between Balrogs and Ents, when I felt something change in the air. A presence that hadn't been there before. And it wasn't outside the house, but in here, with me. In fact, it felt like it was on the chair opposite me … and I got the distinct feeling I was being looked at. Judged.

So, setting the book gently to one side, I looked up. To find Felix sitting opposite me.

"Finished already? I was expecting fire, smoke. At least some screams …" I queried, looking back at the archway. But it was still closed off by the curtain, and besides I'd thought Elspeth to have announced if she'd succeed or failed fairly volubly. So something wasn't right.

Looking back, I instantly saw my mistake. Whilst the figure was Felix in general appearance, she was giving off a faint aura, like mist rising from her skin. As I watched, I noted a faint emerald tint like a blush to her skin, and even her white dreadlocks began to take on a distinctive tinge. Finally, as the other face me, I saw her eyes shift and change. Orbs of brilliant, vibrant green one moment, then flowing to a dark and rich blue the next. Green to blue, blue to green.

"So. *Not* Felix then." I kept myself loose and at ease, giving no cause to alarm the newcomer. All the while casually reaching for the Wyld inside me, that font of strength to bolster me if things went to shit in a handbasket.

The woman smiled and nodded, but still didn't utter a word. Kinda weird, given how verbose my two friends in the other room were and how hard I found it at times to get a word in edgeways. But ok, if that was how she wanted to play this …

"Look, I'm not sure what you're after here, and as much as I appreciate the company whilst I'm sat out here on my lonesome, I'm going to have to ask you to leave." I politely told the woman, nodding towards the front door. "See, my friend is doing something fairly complicated, and the last thing she needs is anyone gate-crashing the party. If you could kindly use whatever entrance you used to get in here, to exit, I'd appreciate not having to kick you out by your arse. Thing is, I've just eaten, and don't fancy indigestion. That ok?"

The woman smiled and shook her head, laughing quietly. The sound was like the patter of falling rain on leaves, the gurgle of a stream as it bubbled and chuckled along its bed. Definitely not the slightly braying and coarse laughter Felix normally voiced.

"That would present a *small* problem, Morgan Black. Son of Margaret May Black and Herne ne Eachthigheirn, known as the Hunter. Since I am the one your friend wishes to talk to, and is in fact doing so, to ask her favour right now."

One plus one lined up in my head, and I loosed hold of the Wyld as I realised this was neither a fight I wanted or one I could possibly win, no matter the changes in me recently.

"Uh, you're *Terra*? Elspeth's Goddess?" I queried, just to make sure I was getting this right and not making a huge mistake. "I kinda thought you'd be … well … bigger. Since you're the Goddess of the Mortal Realm itself, and all."

The Goddess laughed that tinkling cascade again, smiling at me to show there was no offence taken.

"Size is immaterial, as you well know, lycan." She replied and twitched one finger. Instantly my senses lit with a just fraction of the truth of this immortal, a pressing weight that had nothing to do with her physical form and everything to do with her actual nature. Gravity, falling on my shoulders, making me wince as I felt my bones creak under the pressure. And *power*, so much power it felt like I was standing beside a blast furnace, with it cranked up to its full temperature.

And this was a mere trickle of Terra dialled *down*, lessened to a shadow of her former self so that those who worshipped her could only draw upon a trickle of her essence, not the tsunami of might she once offered. Bloody hell!

"Uh, ok I give. I believe you!" I told her through gritted teeth, and she wiggled that finger again. The air around me cleared and I cracked my neck gratefully, rolling my shoulders to relieve their sudden ache. "Dumb question, but shouldn't you be in there, talking to Elspeth?"

I stabbed my thumb at the arch behind me, but Terra just shook her head, smiling that all-knowing smile. Now I knew where our witch consultant got it from.

"I am there already." The Goddess told me, running a hand down her glowing impression of Felix. "This is just a splinter, an echo of my whole, that I use for a specific purpose or task. In this instance, to speak with you."

"Um, and you chose to look like my mortal friend, why?" I asked, since that point was bugging me. The Mistress, once Lady of the Lake, had taken on the form of Sarah Conner to taunt and tease me. To show me she knew about the mortal I'd been entangled with. "Just asking for a friend."

Terra looked down at her form, holding out a hand and watching as the glow curled up and over it, pulsing with life. Then she simply shrugged, those weird eyes of hers watching me.

"I needed a body, and this is the child my daughter brings me. To take oath with me, and seek help with what has been forced upon her. I thought it fitting." She told me and then leant forward, looking at me directly. "But I did not manifest like this to speak on the child's fate. Instead I wished to speak about what my daughter asks of me."

"Your daughter. You mean Elspeth? Oh yeah, anyone who serves you is a daughter or son, right?" I remembered the brief explanation the witch had given me when I'd once asked how things worked with her and the Goddess of the Mortal Realm. It was one of the reasons why the druids hated anyone swearing such oaths, as they felt they shouldn't have to share the bounties offered by Terra, Gaea, Tellus or whatever title she went by. Nor allow anyone else to enjoy her affection. And since they tended to settle their arguments with very sharp sickles still, no-one had bothered to correct them.

"My children do not *serve* me." Terra corrected me with a small frown. "The oaths they take are to protect, to nurture and to follow the natural course of life. To aid where they can, ease suffering and return this Realm to its once healthy and hale state. But they do not *serve*. They are one with me. As their mother, I instruct them and they obey."

"Uh, ok, they *obey* you. Sorry." I tried to keep the sarcasm from my voice, given I was dealing with a deity of colossal power and majesty who could swat me like a mosquito should she so choose. "You wanted to talk about her resurrecting Gregory Allen. The mortal you sent to challenge her. Right?"

The Goddess looked at me with one raised eyebrow, trying to see if I was accusing her of anything or judging her in any way. But I kept my face as neutral as possible, letting her do the talking right now.

"Yes. The matter of the mortal." Terra mused, settling back and crossing one leg in a very un-Felix like manner. "By rights, his spirit should have passed beyond the Veil to whatever eternity he believed most in. Elspeth should have understood the time she had with him was of most importance, treasured the feelings they shared and the love they let grow between them. And used that to further my influence in this Realm, and in her craft."

"Instead, he has somehow stubbornly refused to pass over, melding with her candle and binding himself to her until it too ends. I would not have thought a mortal capable of such action, especially one with no talent or power." She shook her head, glowing braids clattering together. "And Elspeth refuses to listen to reason, to remember her oaths to me. She seeks to break them, to undo what has been done and bind this mortal to her more tightly with her craft and the life that was stolen from others. In what she proposes, she would make him her guardian, forsaking the companion I gifted her with long ago and instead turning to him for her protection, her safety. I do not understand this."

I sighed, settling on the sofa, realising this wasn't going to be a battle of brawn, any sort of combat where I'd need my muscles and strength. Nope, instead I'd have to use the brains the Gods had given me, to explain something so obvious and yet so complicated to an immortal with the base understanding of mortal nature of a five-year-old.

This was going to be fun. I was glad I'd had the wine to help temper my sarcasm.

"You sent Elspeth her one true love." I started gently, holding up a hand to show I was not pointing fingers or blaming her. Yet. "You could've picked any number of challenges to set her. Find a lost artefact from one of your old temples. Find a way to stop those bloody druids of yours being such pricks and attacking anyone they judge unworthy of you. Hell, solve world peace! Anything like that would have been better than this."

"Why?" Terra asked, and I saw the need in those shifting eyes, those bottomless depths yearning for understanding. I sighed.

"Because love messes up *everything*. Makes you do the craziest thing, risk absolutely everything. Turn your back on pretty much everything you held to before. Just for the chance of it being right, and this being the one." I answered with no small stab of pain, as my thoughts invariably and like a train wreck happening in slow motion, turned to Sarah Conner. "You set her a challenge of overcoming the worst thing that could happen to her, and she's chosen option B."

"To save him, give him another chance. Give them a proper chance."

"I reckon Elspeth could've bowed under the pain and hurt his loss caused, then come to terms with it and moved on. But it's like *this* is the test or challenge or whatever you want to call it. Otherwise *why* was she able to trap Chimera when that bloody fae should have been back freezing its arse off in the Gardens of Ice. *Why* was she able to get hold of stolen life energy, when before we dealt with Knox she'd have had no reason to ever handle the stuff. And *why* it just so happens she's found a suitable pupil who needs your aid. A mortal with nothing to do with magic or witchcraft or the Real until she stumbled into it headlong because of me, and Elspeth. What we do."

"Seriously?" I finished, looking at her. "*Did* you arrange any of that? Coz all that just happening by chance is about as suspicious as marmite flavoured ice-cream. And tastes just as bad, if I'm being honest."

Terra looked at me with those depthless eyes, expression grown calm and statue-like. The glow around her ebbed and pulsed, like the flow of an ocean's tide, as she considered my words.

When she spoke, the immortal managed to throw me a complete curve ball.

"Would *you* let the mortal return from the dead? Would you relent, and turn back what has been done to him?" She asked, and I sucked in a deep breath.

"Uh, that's *way* above my paygrade, your Immortalness." I told her frankly, seriously unprepared for that line of inquiry. "I'm just a poor lycan shmuck with some complicated family matters to deal with. I'm not in the business of the *big* questions."

But Terra shook her head, pinning me with those eyes of hers. I felt her presence around me, not intruding but potent and enfolding me, so that the room seemed to vanish and all that was left was the immortal and I.

"Would you, Morgan Black? Would you let him rise from the dead, whatever that meant for him. For them?" She repeated and I shifted uncomfortably on my seat, seriously wishing we'd ended up fighting instead of this. She nodded at my discomfort. "She need never know your answer. Speak truthfully, and the matter remains between you and I."

Did I want Elspeth to risk her talents, her life for the mortal she had fallen in love with? Did I want Gregory Allen back, when he had been a proverbial pain the backside to me since we first crossed paths? Did I *really* care?

Finally I faced the immortal, weighing up my words carefully.

"Ah, fuck it." I told her, shaking my head and admitting the simple truth. "He and I didn't see eye to eye, and he pissed me off on more than one occasion. But he was … *is* a good man. He cares. And he obviously loves Elspeth, and she him. Even if they get another year together tops, it's worth it. So yeah, I'd let it happen. Just so there's some happy ending out of all this shit."

"But I meant it. This isn't anything I should be deciding. That's for you lot to do. Deal with the big stuff, the life and death questions." I told her bluntly. "Leave me the simple things, like who to hit and how hard. Don't mess with that status quo, or we're all fucked."

Terra smiled at me, her body pulsing with renewed energy.

"You forget your parentage, Morgan Black." She instructed me with no small delight. "Son of Herne, the Lord of the Wyld Court. An immortal. And child of one of my daughters, Margaret May Black. No, you are no mere *lycan schmuck*. You should think on what lies ahead for you. Scions such as you are a matter of mortal fable, facing the direst foes and accomplishing the greatest of deeds. You are born to face the 'big stuff', if only you will admit it."

Great, now I was getting a prophecy from the Goddess of the Mortal Realm. Why couldn't I just be left as a simple finder of lost pets, and eater of free snacks? This wasn't a Disney film, and I most assuredly was not destined to join the gods and goddesses at Olympus, with a snarky sidekick faun and a crazed Pegasus. Let alone a beautiful mortal on my arm.

A thought struck me, as the room started to take shape once more around us.

"Uh, so you're going to let Elspeth raise him, aren't you?" I read the truth in the immortal's expression, the simple nod an answer but the sorrow showing in her depthless eyes so much more telling. "What does that mean for her?"

"Her oaths to me will be broken, child of the Wyld, child of my own." She replied, a single tear coursing down her glowing cheek. "Though I will accept this as her challenge completed, she will be lost to me. And I to her. This I cannot undo, and is the price she must pay."

Crap. So Ellie would get Gregory back, but lose everything that made her a witch in the process. I had no idea what that would feel like, the loss of her magic, her craft. Becoming just another run of the mill mortal. But I guessed it wasn't going to be like ripping of a band-aid, but something much more painful, much more life changing. And I realised I had a very selfish request to make.

"I know you don't owe me anything, but I'm going to beg a favour anyhow." I told the immortal, as she gently wiped the tear from her cheek and touched it to her lips. Capturing her own sorrow. "Is there any way you can, I don't know, *not* make her powerless just yet? We kind of need her as she is to deal with a pretty big problem. One that threatens this Realm, the mortals of this place. As well as us, obviously."

Terra raised one eyebrow, and I shrugged, fully admitting the truth of what I was asking.

"I know I can't ask you not to break up with her. But just hold off for a little bit. Till we're done?" I didn't even bother trying to hide the fact it was a selfish request. "We kinda need her able to function as she does now. All witchery intact, so to speak."

The immortal sighed, shaking her head sadly before answering.

"The oaths she swore will break, there is nothing I can do about that." She told me after a moment's thought. "But there is a way, something I can do. A joining, to allow my daughter and the young mortal to temporarily share the talents one has between them. That way, they would both function as you wish. But they must both agree to this. Besides which, if I am to do as you ask, what will *you* offer me in return?"

Oh joys, bargaining time. I'd almost forgotten that immortals loved their deals, their offers. And I knew enough stories to be certain I had to be really careful what I bargained with, otherwise I'd definitely end up regretting asking.

"So, we're talking *first-born child* kind of deal here? Or *whatever walks over the bridge first?*" I queried, remembering a story of a mortal woman and the Devil, and his attempts to steal her soul. But Terra shook her head, eyes narrowing in thought. "Care to give me some hints as to what's your preference?"

"I am well acquainted with your somewhat ill-fated and tragic attempt to woo one simple mortal female. If I were to await a successful union to produce an heir, there is a good chance this Realm might end before such a thing came to pass." She told me with a snarky smile, as I gritted my teeth. How the hell did everyone know so much about my love life? "No, I ask only one simple thing of you. A task, that I shall name at a time of my choosing, for you to complete for me. One thing, and one thing only."

Pretty much all my instincts were telling me to try and put as many caveats on that request as possible. A time-frame, the sort of things I wouldn't do for anybody, even just asking that she promise the task was actually possible in the first place. Simple stuff like that. But looking in her eyes, I saw that I had no choice here, no wiggle room. I was the one asking a favour, and she was setting the price.

There were times you just had to pay the fiddler, no matter how badly they played.

"Deal." I reached over, and Terra took my hand, clasping it tight. Energy surged and bound our skin, sinking into me with a finality that I knew meant the bargain was struck and I should in no way try to welch out of it. Or suffer the sort of wrath a Realm-encompassing Goddess might deal out. Terra made Oberon and the Furies look like a grimalkin in terms of sheer power.

"Then we are done." She told me and gave me one last smile. "It has been a pleasure speaking with you, Morgan Black. I shall greatly enjoy following your story, wherever it leads."

With that, Terra simply faded away, her glowing form dimming and separating into individual motes of energy which buzzed in the air in front of me like fireflies, before these too vanished. That sense of her, even diminished by such a degree, cleared from the air and I sat back on the sofa, loosing a deep breath.

Time to worry about what I'd just promised to an immortal later, when this mess was dealt with. Now I just had to wait, to see if a Goddess would keep her word and a dead man could walk again.

Chapter 34

The Fisher King.

Also known as the Wounded King or Maimed King, he is the last in a long bloodline of keepers of the Holy Grail. Crippled, all he can do is sit in a small boat and fish outside his own castle, awaiting the day the true Knight destined to find the Grail would come, for they would have the power to heal him.

This was achieved by Percival, who was able to heal the wound inflicted on the Fisher King for wooing a woman not meant for him. It was lore that the Grail itself would choose the partner of every keeper, and inflict such terrible punishment if any should go against its wishes.

Terra didn't keep me waiting long, thankfully.

Maybe a half hour after I'd finished talking to the Goddess of the Mortal Realm, the curtain swished aside from the archway, and Felix stepped back into the living room. I'd decided the best thing I could do was stretch out on the sofa, legs hanging off the ends, and just stare up at the ceiling until something happened. Given I'd just been chatting to a goddess and been told a few things about myself I needed to digest.

"Lazing on the job?" Felix snarked softly, as she stepped carefully over to the nearest empty chair and collapsed into it. "Gods, that was *intense*. I feel, shit, I don't know what I feel!"

"Congrats, you've just met your first goddess. It doesn't get any easier, I promise." I told her but laboured up from my stretched-out position to crouch down beside her. "You doing ok, kid?"

"Ask me in a week, when I've slept like the dead." She told me but nodded once to show she was good. "Oh, shit, that was in poor taste wasn't it?!"

I shook my head. Somethings reassuringly never changed.

"I take it things went to plan then?" I asked gently, but before Felix could answer, I turned at the touch of Elspeth's presence as she entered the room.

Tears stained her cheeks, and she had a frailty about her that I had never seen before. But she wore a smile like the rising sun, and I could almost feel the heat of her happiness, a counter to the sadness welling inside her.

She stepped across the room and I rose, enfolding her in a big, gentle hug. Just holding her for a long moment as she leant into me, soaking up my strength.

Finally I pushed away enough to look her in the eye, setting my hands on her shoulders to steady her.

"So it worked? He's...?" I didn't finish the question, not knowing the exact word to use for what must have taken place in the sanctum.

"Asleep, but yes. He's back, and it's really him. Healed of his wounds." Elspeth told me, tears coursing down her face, eyes brimming with them. "Morgan ... *she* told me what you did. What you bargained for. I can't ... you didn't need to. I was willing to pay the price."

"Ssh." I gently shut her up, shaking my head. "That's not for now, and nothing I regret so let's not do the telling off bit just yet, ok? For now, I'm hoping your Goddess kept her end of the bargain, is all."

Elspeth nodded, and freeing one hand, gently lifted it palm upward. Energy coursed over her skin, a pale shadow of what she had once summoned but still there, still alive in her. The biggest difference was the scent of the energy. Where before it had been clean, alive like the touch of the forest and grass. Now, it was tinged with a purple hue I had last seen Felix conjure against Baba Yaga, and carried just a faint taint of the Veil.

Definitely sharing whatever it was Felix was tapping into, but this wasn't Duracell.

"It'll take some getting used to, and it's only temporary." Elspeth told me, nodding over to where Felix had slumped into the chair, eyes closed and was now snoring in a very unladylike manner. "Normally this is something witches do to empower one of their coven, to perform a single task that would be beyond them. The bond between Felicity and I, well, it was wrought by the Goddess, so is a little different. But I don't expect it to last more than a few days. Then, well, I guess we'll see."

The witch looked back at me and I saw a sudden thought cross her mind. She reached into a pocket in her multi coloured skirt, then tossed me something small that she palmed from there.

"Before I forget. Catch!"

I almost fumbled it, feeling my fingers clench around something cold, plastic. I looked down at what she had thrown me, and had to resist the urge to flinch when I saw it was the inhaler from the Blooding. Marked with tiny script and housing a corrupted part of the Harrowing.

"Are you trying to give me a bloody heart attack?!" I growled, easing my grip so that I didn't accidently crush the container and loose all manner of hell in a small, confined space.

"Oh stop being such a baby. It's safe as long as you don't break it. Or push the button on top." She told me with a familiar smile. Then she placed a hand over mine, covering the cursed item. "I want you to have it, Morgan. I won't lie. After what happened to Gregory, I gave thought to hunting Knox myself, and letting that thing loose on him. I … I don't think I should be trusted with it."

"And trigger happy me is a more suitable candidate, *how* exactly?" I shook my head, the thing making my skin crawl where it lay on my palm.

"I'm like Boromir, when Frodo has the One Ring. Not the right guy for the job."

"Tsh, I always thought he got judged too harshly. He meant well." She replied glibly, then smile at me. "*I* trust your judgement and that's enough for me. I worked out what Knox did, how the thing works. It's a simple binding ritual with one unbreakable instruction upon release. It forces the shard of the Harrowing contained not to kill but to bind. To create a Harrowed, no matter the creature it first contacts. In some ways, he has managed to *change* the weapon of the gods, make it both less and more powerful than the actual Harrowing itself. For that, I have to admire the man, no matter how I feel about him otherwise."

"Just don't start liking him *too* much." I growled, slipping the small container into a pocket gingerly. I wasn't all that happy to have been given it and had no idea what the hell I'd do with it, but better I kept it than Elspeth went off all gung-ho and tried to take Knox on alone. Especially now that, well, she wasn't herself. "We still have to stop him, no matter the fact he kind of helped bring DI All... ah, Greg back."

Elspeth nodded, her expression set, that jawline of her's firm.

"Don't you worry. I still blame him for Gregory getting killed in the first place, and for the trail of death and destruction he has left in his wake. Innocents have suffered at the man's hands, and for that, Robert Knox must face judgement." She told me bluntly, and I squeezed her shoulders before nodding off to the sanctum.

"So. What next?"

Elspeth looked over her shoulder, her expression softening, before turning back to answer me.

"For now, I think it's time you went home and got some rest. We have a lot to do tomorrow, if we're to succeed in stopping Knox. I'll let Felicity sleep here for a bit, then wake her and we'll work on the salt crystals together. Gregory will most likely sleep for hours yet, and won't be ready to do much until he's eaten and … well, I still have to explain things to him." She admitted, cheeks colouring slightly.

"Yeah, like how come he's alive, what you had to do. What this whole thing is about." I prompted, and she nodded. "Oh and the small issue of him not being an active policeman anymore."

"There's that, and the small detail that part of the ritual, the breaking of my oath to my Goddess, transferred what she had bound to me to him." She admitted, and I tried not to laugh. "So I no longer have a guardian to summon to my aid, a familiar. Instead, I have Gregory … and he's got some nice new tattoos and a sense of me he never had before. It'll take some explaining."

"Oh, good luck with that." I chuckled, trying to image the stolid, sensible police detective coming to terms with his resurrection and new job role. "If OPS get in touch, I'll do my best 'ignorant grunt' impression. But you are going to have to work out what this means for him. People saw him dead, and the fact you jinxed the mortuary records doesn't mean others don't know what happened. He can't just walk out onto the street and back into his life."

"I know. But we'll figure it out." She replied with firm determination. "Now, thank you for coming, Morgan and, well for everything. But I'd like to be there when he wakes up again, so if you don't mind?"

"I'm going, I'm going!" I grinned and gave her a last, hearty hug. Hell if she hadn't thrown me the biggest curve ball yet, planted me in one hell of an awkward situation, but it had ended well. Something good had come out of this mess.

I could live with that.

"You going to be safe?" I nodded to the unlit candle wards, and Elspeth struck her head with her palm gently. "I'd hate for something to come calling and mess up tonight's fun and games after everything we've been through!"

"Thanks for reminding me!" She replied and clicked her fingers. On the sofa, Felix's snoring broke for a moment, disturbed from her sleep by Elspeth's use of their now joined craft, but slipped back into the slumber the next moment.

The candles sprang to life again, as that sense of protection settled back down inside the house. A warm, safe feeling.

"Oh, and I left you the pizza with pineapples." I admitted as I opened the door and stepped outside. "There's a lot I'll do for you, but eating that thing? That's just plain wrong!"

The door closed on her response, and I let myself enjoy a good, hearty laugh as I walked off into the night.

Chapter 35

If I'd known the hell that was going to break loose the next day, I'd have stayed in bed.

Honest to gods.

I'd heeded Ellie's instruction, and headed home to crash out and get what sleep I could before we gate-crashed Knox's party and seriously messed things up for him and Morgana. Or got messed up by them, which was equally possible.

Bear had greeted me with much headbutting and slobbery licks to anything he could reach, so I'd veered from my intended plan of slumber and took him out for a long walk along the Thames. By this time it was gone one in the morning, time stealing away from me dealing with a goddess with a capital *God*, having a comrade in arms resurrected from their horrific death, oh and having the substance of my being and who I was put to question.

I'd stood looking out over the river, listening to the gentle rush of the water from the strong current, listening to the whisper of wind in the trees behind me whilst Bear waited patiently on the concrete beside me. I didn't *feel* different, not after learning who my parents were, where I came from. Fine, I had the touch of Shadow, Ivory and Wyld bonded inside me now, nothing that any lycan to my knowledge or Jessica's had ever had. But that didn't make me the son of a god. A demi-god, as Terra had intimated. The hell, no. It just gave me a really weird family list for Christmas cards and birthdays, and some pretty messed up obligation that I still didn't fully comprehend.

Me, a quasi-immortal? Don't make me laugh.

With my troll hound finally bored of scaring sleepy squirrels and imaginary enemies amongst the shadows of the Thames path, the pair of us had returned to the apartment and had a rustle-up snack of whatever I could find in the fridge, washed down with the remains of an open bottle of wine. Goldspur had peered from the tree, and I'd given her a nod, not in the mood to talk about contracts or her dress sense or any of the foolishness Felix had filled her head with. But admittedly, it was nice to see her, and I realised I'd started to include her in my sense of home. Troll hound, apple tree and now dryad guardian. I was definitely starting my own collection.

At least it wasn't cats.

Food done with, plates cleaned and dog settled back to sleep amongst the tree roots, I'd dived into a hot shower to wash away any lingering enchantments from anything I'd come into contact with at Elspeth's home, then with a towel wrapped around me to provide decency, I'd crashed.

Hours later, I surfaced from a deep sleep and dreams filled with glowing figures telling me I was a wizard, a demigod, a power and then changing to Hagrid from Harry Potter, offering me cake. I washed, again, then changed into suitable attire and then went through the rituals I'd grown used to performing before any major hunt.

Pack any and all armour, weapons and ancillaries I might need to face off against a host of nasties. Check. Lay out enough clean bandages and wipes to deal with anything I came home with. Check. Make sure I had enough films and series to watch on Netflix to watch whilst I healed. Check. Make sure there was wine and food within reach for whenever I got in. Check. Top up Bear's bowls so he didn't get hungry and go hunting for munchies. And check.

Bear wouldn't be coming with me on this hunt. Not because I didn't trust he'd keep me safe from harm, from whatever Knox or Morgana might throw at us. It was just I had no idea how I'd explain him if we ran into any mortals, or keep him from being recorded on camera. He'd stay in the apartment, safe, until either we succeeded or … well, otherwise.

With all my preparations done, I took the troll hound out to stretch his legs and relieve himself, then returned back upstairs.

To find Goldspur waiting for me.

"Uh, hi." I greeted her as Bear huffed a welcome, pacing over to her side and leaning over for her to scratch his head. A rumbling grumble rolled from his chest, and he panted with a lolling tongue as he leant into the dryad's strokes. "Look, I'm heading out…"

"You go to war, Morgan Black. I shall guard our home, and our friend." She cut me off, one hand settling on the hilt of a knife. Her glowing amber eyes held mine for a long moment, then she smiled. "Fight well. We shall see you when you return."

With that vote of innocent confidence, the dryad patted Bear's head then slipped back into her tree. My trollhound snorted, padding forward and settling down amongst the tree roots. He eyed me with those mournful eyes of his, but I knew it the was the right thing to leave him behind this time.

"Keep her company. I won't be long." I promised him, then nodded towards the kitchen. "You've got enough chow and water to keep you happy for a while. *Don't* eat the tv remote."

The troll hound's response was to close his eyes and give me a deep, rumbling sigh.

I took one last look around the apartment, memorising things. Just to hold onto, a little charm to help me focus when the shit got Real, and I needed to remember what I was fighting for. What I needed to get back to. Then I shouldered my bag and headed down.

I called up a taxi, and was walking in the front door of the office am hour later.

As I stepped inside *Good Deeds*, it was apparent Jessica had called in the cavalry. In fact the whole darn army. I immediately sensed the presence of the other Alphas, as well as a large number of the other lycan packmates. I took the stairs quickly, reaching the first floor to find everyone gathered and in the middle of what I guessed was a debrief.

"Morgan, ah am glad tae see you." Jessica spoke up, as I felt everyone's eyes fall on me. "If you would care tae join us, we were just covering off the assignments fer this evening's ... *entertainment*, shall we call it?"

I grinned, setting my roll-bag down on a desk, and sitting down beside it. Emma nodded to me as I collected a mug of steaming coffee from a tray that had been left nearby, and sipped the deliciously strong liquid. I shot a look over the large whiteboards that had been erected with all the details we'd collected as I took another swig.

"We have agreed tae provide support tae the mortals, securing these six positions around London." Jessica told the gathered packs. "Yer Alphas have divided you in tae groups, the first tae continue tae manage the hunts whilst the second help secure these sites. We suspect Robert Knox intends tae release the Harrowing there, or tae try in some way tae cause enough chaos tae keep the mortals occupied. Yer priority is tae handle anything the mortals are nae equipped fer, whilst they get as many innocents tae safety as possible."

Chuckles echoed round the room, with more than one half muttered comment voiced along the lines of *what are mortals equipped to handle?* But the gathered Alphas; Josh and Bree Saunders, Jarthi Patel, and Sean and Patrick Boseman, simply glanced around their packs and silenced them without a single word.

"Now that you have had yer little jokes," Jessica continued when everyone was silenced. "Remember what came tae pass at the last Blooding. What happened tae the Nighters. Tae Sal Orben. That is what Knox would unleash on the mortals, to spread panic and fear whilst he is about his true business. That we cannae allow."

Jessica turned away from the first board. The next one showed the Southbank centre, photos taken from all angles alongside building schematics and a list of guards, routines and security camera placements. Each entrance had been methodically crossed through, with notes against them such as *too exposed, blind spots* and *killing ground perfect for ambush.*

"This is where we believe Knox aims tae complete his ritual. The Southbank building has reasonable security, and Robert Knox has left this in place, tae warn him of any attempt to access the centre." She tapped the various entrances, each one crossed through. "After some checking, ah believe he is masquerading as a Professor James Mews, an expert in Arthurian artefacts from Bristol. The real Professor is most likely dead, his identify stolen. Added tae the mortals, there is a high possibility Knox will have Real security warding him as well. Morgan here negated Red Cap, so we dinnae have tae worry about that particular creature, but Chimera is still at large, as well as Black Shuck. Nae forgetting the last remaining members of the Twilight Court. Creatures you may know of as the Norns, Nordic fae from legend."

Our Alpha tapped a third white board, this one taped with printouts and articles. Research she or Elspeth had done on the old Nordic legends, specifically the Norns.

"We know little about these fae, except fer the simple fact the Lord of Ivory wishes them forgotten. Erased from memory." She told the gathering with a grim smile. "And since Shadow has helped him with this endeavour, I nae think they should be underestimated fer their ability tae – speaking politely – fuck with us. And that is nae covering anything the one who's pulling Knox's strings might be able tae conjure."

"All in all, we are agreed. A small strike team will attempt tae disrupt Knox and his ritual before he completes it. As all entrances have proven tae be useless, ah have reached an accord with the rulers of London Lower." Jessica picked up a red marker and drew a circle underneath the building on the plan. "They have agreed tae allow a number of us through the Lows, and use a portal up into the Southbank centre which circumvents the mortal security. This gets us inside and hopefully with a chance tae surprise Knox and *her*."

"Uh, one small thing?" I raised a hand, and Jessica nodded for me to speak.

"What is it, Morgan?" She asked, and I took a swig of coffee before answering.

"Um, that bit about the Lows. I kinda thought I'd screwed up any chance of us going back there anytime this side of, well, whenever." I admitted, remembering Rous's words just before he went in and got most of his rats fed to the Harrowing. "What did you have to offer them?"

"You are nae wrong." She replied with a wry smile. "Rous and Molly decried their feelings about that last meeting with Knox most vocally tae me, especially in relation tae you. But they are first and foremost the rulers of London Lower. They have asked, and after talking tae the other Alphas, *we* have agreed tae grant them immunity from judgement and hunts fer the next hundred years if they allow us tae travel through the Lows and tae use one of their personal portals where we wish tae go. Enough time fer this matter tae be settled, and fer them to restore order where Knox has caused so much damage."

"Oh great. Another deal." I commented dryly but then shrugged. "One hundred years? Surprised Molly and Rous didn't bargain for more, given that's like a good night sleep to them. Cheers for clarifying."

"Mah pleasure." She told me sincerely, then looked back around the other lycan. "So, as ah was saying. A small number of us will travel through the Lows, tae the portal Rous and Molly have prepared fer us. We will go early, and aim tae steal at least one of the two stones Knox is using tae focus his ritual. If we can remove even one from the location, ah have been assured this will disrupt things enough tae thoroughly ruin his plans."

"And if you can't get the stones out?" It wasn't me asking this time, instead one of the lycan from the other packs. But I knew the answer, even as Jessica nodded.

"A fair question. If we are delayed in reaching Knox and his summons, then our only other choice is tae destroy the vessel. The body he has fashioned fer the spirit he is conjuring. Ah will nae ask any other tae do this thing, which is why ah am leading the team entering the Southbank centre."

A weighted silence greeted Jessica's statement, everyone in the room knowing what 'destroying the vessel' meant. Give us any of the nasties from the Real, any of the nightmares that crawled, swam, flew or slithered into the

Mortal Realm and we were fine with stopping them. Terminally. But this thing? It was blameless, a combination of body parts stolen from unwilling mortals. Hell, was the thing even *alive*? Was there a mind in there, or was it just the blank slate Elspeth had said it must be. Could we be sure?

As I've said, I hate the moral ones, the questions that niggle at your *right and wrong* line that we all have, the one we never cross. That make you second guess any decision. But we didn't have much choice here.

"You said a small number. How many is 'small'?" Emma asked this time, filling the uncomfortable silence. "It took most of the pack to deal with the Mistress and her shape-changer, so are you thinking this is any less dangerous?"

Jessica went to answer, but was interrupted by footsteps on the stairs and a familiar scent entering the office. I turned in surprise, since I'd figured Elspeth and Felix would be occupied for most of the day brewing up both the tracker and the cloaking ritual the witch had suggested she could make. But it seemed whilst I'd slept, they'd simply cracked on with the work in hand.

Intermingled with the familiar natural scent of Elspeth, and Felix's sharper fragrance from some bottle combined with a lingering trace of the Veil, I immediately identified a distinct third smell … something like the air after a lightning strike, or the fading dregs of spent fireworks. Gone was the soulful weariness, the weight that seemed to drag this mortal down, replaced instead with a sort of latent readiness, like a guard dog awaiting the command to attack.

I eyed Gregory Allen as he followed the two women up the stairs, looking entirely out of place in a t-shirt emblazoned with '*Burnham on Sea Folkfest 1990*', faded jeans and a pair of worn-in trainers. He had a coat thrown over his shoulders, but left open at the front given the late summer weather. The tattoos on his face, curling script over his forehead and running down over his left eye and cheek, stood out against his pale skin like a brand. Which I guessed they were.

"Seven, I think." Elspeth replied to Emma's question as she nodded first to Jessica, then to me. "That's about the limit the charm will cover, if we want to remain undetected on our approach. I'm assuming four lycan, including Morgan here and the three of us. That should allow us to handle anything we encounter but remain small enough to avoid most conventional means of detection."

"Seven? And only four pack?" Emma replied with more than a trace of disbelief. "Against Morg … *her*? Or just Robert Knox with the Harrowing, most likely the Chimera and these other Twilight fae they broke out of prison. You are kidding, right?"

"You can take Chimera out of the equation. He's been dealt with, and won't be a problem for us, or anyone this side of the Veil in fact." Elspeth replied firmly, brooking no argument. "And no, I'm not kidding. Jessica, might we have a word in private?"

"Ah believe we need *several* words, Elspeth." Our Alpha replied, her eyes on Felix and Gregory. "Mostly about involving mortals in our business, and the line we agreed tae draw fer you and your outside involvements."

The lycan Alpha looked around the room, nodding to the other of her kin.

"Whilst my colleague and ah talk this matter over, ah believe you have enough tae be getting on with. Find yer teams then ah suggest you head tae yer locations and familiarise yerselves with the locale." She instructed the room, as she nodded to the meeting room's door. "Remember, the mortal authorities are tae handle the residents. You need tae settle in, and instead worry about anything from our side of things. Unless of course the mortals look tae need a hand."

Chuckles rolled around the room again, as lycan from all the packs eased themselves up and started heading over to their Alphas, or in our pack's case, Jacob to find out who'd drawn the short straws.

I was about to head over to the coffee machine and top up my brew, when I felt Jessica's attention settle on me.

"Morgan, ah would appreciate you joining us." She told me in that *it's an invitation but one you can't turn down* sort of manner she had.

"Uh, ok. Sure." I set my mug down and rolled my shoulders, feeling the tension ratchet up a notch. Time to go play piggy in the middle, between the big bad wolf and the wicked witch.

I got *all* the fun!

Chapter 36

Gingalain.

This Knight bore the title The Fair Unknown, and is the son of Gawain and a fairy. He had many adventures whilst sojourning through the wilds to join Artur's court, saving many a maiden from an unwanted marriage and defeating enchantresses along the way.

Finally, he takes part in a tournament organised by Artur, and in doing so wins the hand of the Queen of Wales. The title he bore is taken from the many romances written about him at the time, as he was known to be the saviour of ladies' virtues and most uncommonly handsome – from his fairy lineage.

"Ah would like an explanation. Several, in fact." Jessica spoke quietly, her hushed tone that in an animal would have come as a warning growl. "Fer the mortals' presence here, fer what ah am sensing about Detective Inspector Gregory Allen and fer the simple fact, the man was *dead*. Yet here he stands, in mah place of work. Please explain."

Our Alpha had waited until the four of us had filed into the meeting room, closing the door firmly behind us and then letting everyone take a seat before speaking. Felix was nervous, over-tired but at the same time buzzing with energy I guessed was a left over from whatever crafting she and Elspeth had been up to whilst I slept. She sat halfway between her new witch-sister and me, obviously not sure who was going to shield her the most from my Alpha's obvious displeasure.

For her part, Elspeth was, at least on the surface, her usual calm and collected self as she settled into a chair almost opposite Jessica. She was dressed for work, foregoing her colour gypsy colours for the muted greys and blacks I had last seen her wearing when we broke into Greenwich University. Remembering how that had gone for us, I *really* hoped this wasn't an omen, at least for me. Gregory Allen, expression settled in a slight frown and with his jawline firmly set, stood at her side with one hand resting on the chair's headrest. Not quite touching her, but it was a matter of breaths between them was all.

The witch faced the lycan Alpha for a long moment, eyes locked as they both read what they could from the other. Finally, Elspeth nodded and sat forward, setting her hands on the meeting room table.

"First things first." She reached into a pocket and pulled out one of the warded candles, the ones she used to protect against intrusion and anything overhearing our conversation. "Felicity, dear, if you would be so kind?"

I had a sudden memory of Felix and Danny talking in my apartment, of what had happened to the café and to their home when she had been upset, not in fully control of herself. Kinda like now with the amount of energy she was putting out, but I had to hope Elspeth knew what she was doing, and resisted the urge to dive under the table.

Felix looked at the witch, who nodded once, then closed her eyes and held a hand over the candle. For a moment nothing happened, then purple-grey flame erupted around her hand in a blazing inferno. She quickly dipped her flaming fingers against the candle wick, then quickly shook her hand to douse the blaze.

The witch smiled at her encouragingly, then shot me a quick look with one cocked eyebrow, obviously catching my less than subtle flinch. Then she pushed the candle into the centre of the table as the blanketing effect filled the room, shrouding us from any interference or anyone listening in.

"Now that we are secure … this is how it is. Using what I learned from Robert Knox's journals and through the intercession of my Goddess, I brought Gregory Allen back from the dead. We are now bound, he and I, and that oath is what you sense has changed about him." She spoke calmly, in no way trying to appeal to Jessica like she had to me, simply giving her the facts. "By doing this, I have severed my oaths to my Goddess, and am no longer her daughter, or one of my coven. But thanks to … *a friend*, my Goddess reconsidered fully stripping me of the craft for my actions. Instead she offered a temporary binding between Felicity and I, so I might still be of aid. We share the font Felicity has access to, and I will guide her in her use of it as well as tap into it myself."

"So, Felicity is here because without her, I couldn't have crafted the charm to hide us. Nor this." She continued, reaching into her clothing and pulling free a small glass vial. Inside, the salt crystals I had given her glowed with a faint violet light, floating in the container without any seeming means of support. "Morgan was kind enough to supply these salt crystals that had been in contact with Morgana's essence. With them imbued, we can use them to track her and hopefully locate her exact position once we are within the Southbank centre."

"And as for me," Gregory spoke up. His voice had gained a raspy quality, so I guessed coming back from death hadn't been a complete joyride for him, and there was a weight to it that he hadn't had before. The anger though, that was still there. "I'm here to look after Els. She's explained things to me. Stuff I don't quite believe, or understand. But I know I almost lost her once, and I'm not risking that again. Where she goes, I go."

"Besides," He smiled crookedly, shrugging his shoulders and reaching up to touch the intricate runic tattoos that now marked his forehead and left side of his face. "I'm officially dead, and the Metropolitan Police force isn't in the habit of accepting detectives back once they're deceased. Let alone with this stuff on my face and body. I'm at what you might call a loose end."

I wisely kept silent, not wanting to put my size ten foot anywhere near the storm that was brewing between my Alpha and my witch-friend. Possibly also because Elspeth hadn't specifically named me as the one who'd bartered with her Goddess for the bond, and I didn't think that needed doing anytime soon. I'd promised to stop making rash decisions, to think of the pack more and me less. Yet here I was again.

Jessica let loose a pensive sigh, settling back in her chair and steepling her fingers as she thought through the mess that had landed in her lap. Elspeth's actions, whilst not breaching the Accords per se, skirted a number of moral and very real arguments about the rights of the dead, and what could and couldn't be done without their prior consent.

She'd also risked falling into exactly the same trap as Robert Knox, believing she was working to bring back someone she loved but instead playing *find me a new body* with any number of nasty fuckers from the Real. And then there was Felix, pulled into our business when all she'd really done was be in the wrong place at the wrong time, and be oblivious to the intense and twisted emotions of a fellow student.

As I've said, you couldn't pay me to be an Alpha. Far too many difficult choices to make.

Finally, she nodded, squaring her shoulders and looking around the small gathering.

"Ah cannot say ah am happy with how this has played out." She admitted, and I had a sudden and sharp insight into how this might be affecting her.

Jessica had lost David four years ago, hunting the Real and tracking a particularly nasty immortal, a *kikimora* from Slavic mythology. Normally the creature would steal into mortals' homes and either strangle anyone it found sleeping with their long shadow-spun hair or enter into the sleeper's mind and bind itself to them like a parasite, draining them of life whilst targeting those it's host encountered to feed off next. But this one was sly, deciding it needed a steady source of sustenance without the risk to its life. So it had begun stealing children from London foster homes. It had been easy, given how such places had little or no threshold to stop it, and the fact no one questioned an orderly or staff member acting strangely. The pack had picked up its scent after it strangled several attendants as they slept at work, and three children could not be accounted for afterwards.

Mark and Jessica had tracked the *kickamora* to the Real, deep in the heart of the Verdance. This was when Herne still hunted any lycan venturing into the Wyld's domain, so the Alphas had taken lead, choosing to hunt the creature themselves. It should have been a simple snatch and grab to drag it back for judgement, but the bonded pair had found the creature with over twenty mortal children still alive, still feeding its hunger whilst suffering non-stop nightmares. On its own turf, the beast had been horrendously strong, and Mark had made the call to keep it occupied whilst his packmate freed the captives and got them to safety.

Jessica had done so, returning with Jacob and a half dozen of the pack to save him, not caring of the risk of the Wyld Hunt. But she was too late. The *kikimora* had overpowered Mark and was feeding off him, bound to him and gripping his spirit tight in its talons. In a moment of sanity, he had made Jessica promise to kill him as he trapped it into its own nightmare, keeping it from fleeing and so ending its life with his own. We had no witch then, no knowledge of how to free Mark but keep the bastard imprisoned, and so our Alpha reluctantly obeyed the lycan she loved.

Mark Walker never returned from the Real, and on that day she lost a partner and love of centuries.

And now she was faced with the fact Elspeth too had lost her love, from even so short a time. Yet the witch had broken her oaths and brought him back to life, whilst Jessica had kept her oath and killed the man she had spent so many long years forging a life with.

"The fact of the matter is, this is nae the time for us tae be divided." She continued calmly. "Fer now, ah will cede tae your terms. Morgan, Jacob and Emma shall accompany mahself and you three in tae London Lower, whilst those of the pack not engaged elsewhere shall be stationed close by in case we need them."

"However." Jessica laid her hands flat on the table, and looked directly over at Elspeth, expression set and grey eyes flat. "Once this matter is attended tae, ah believe we need tae look at the contractual agreement between us and consider what yer actions mean in terms of *Good Deeds*."

"I thought we'd get to that." The witch replied, reaching into a pocket again but this time pulling out an envelope. This she placed in front of her, laying her hands on its flat surface. "As such, I have prepared a final statement of any work I believe should be billed to *Good Deeds*, and a notification of termination of my consultancy with yourselves. I have also included several contacts who I think might be interested in working with yourselves in a similar manner as I have done, with references to their skills and history."

Crap, she was leaving? I looked between Elspeth and Jessica, seeing no reaction from my Alpha except a slow nod of understanding. I opened my mouth, thinking of all the reasons this *shouldn't* happen, but the witch held up a hand, forestalling me.

"Morgan, it's what needs to happen." She told me with a sad smile. "The bond between Felicity and I will not last long, and once that is gone, I'll just be another mortal with some interesting hobbies. I need to use that time to help her and guide her so she doesn't come to harm or harm others. And, well, Gregory and I need some time. To work out what life has in store for us, and what I did really means for him. That's not something I can do if I'm still chasing down miscreants or researching hunts for you all. I'm sorry."

"Nae need tae apologise." Jessica replied as I sat back, shutting my mouth. "Up until today, ah cannae think of a time you have not proven tae be an asset tae our endeavours. You will be missed."

She turned to look at me, those grey eyes catching and holding me.

"Ah believe it's time you reached out tae your contact at the mortal authorities, tae let them know of our plans and the support they should expect shortly tae arrive." She instructed me. "Ah would hate fer there tae be any trouble between the packs and the mortals, as ah fear there will be enough confusion and problems later without our adding tae it."

I shrugged, safe in the knowledge that now I wouldn't have to slog all the way over to the Tower of London and face off against the Wardens there just to give an update to Cormac and OPS. They'd just have to find their entertainment elsewhere, the sods.

"Ah believe we are done then, unless there is anything else you think we need tae cover off?" She offered up, but Elspeth and I both shook our heads. "Good. Ah will go speak tae Jacob and Emma. Ah suggest we leave the office no later than half past five this afternoon, as we need tae reach

London Lower in good time. Time acting differently once we're there, remember."

Felix shot me a look as I pushed myself out of my chair, but I mimed making a phone call and she rolled her eyes. I guessed she probably wanted to check in with me, maybe see how I was treating Goldspur, but I really had to check in with Cormac and see what other fun we weren't aware of, to cause us more headaches.

There was always something.

Leaving the meeting room, I found most of the packs had already cleared out, having checked in with their Alphas and been given their assignments. Those of ours not out with them were loitering near the coffee pots, with Jacob and Emma instead standing by the whiteboards, discussing strategies. I skirted them, leaving Jessica to give them the good news, and made for the front door and fresh air.

I found an empty park bench overlooking the park, far enough away from the traffic to mute its roar and off the main thoroughfare so as not to attract any mortals wanting to feed the pigeons or squirrels. Stretching out my legs, I pulled out the OPS phone and dialled the first of the two numbers stored in its memory.

It rang twice, then connected.

"Morgan Black, what a surprise. How can I help?" Cormac's voice managed to convey dry sarcasm and a total lack of patience in so few words. It had to be something he practiced, to deliver it so easily.

"Uh, Cormac. Lovely to speak to you. How's the wife? The kids? The dog or cat or goldfish?" I queried jovially, trying to imagine his expression at the banality of my questions. "I'm good, thanks too."

"I will obviously sleep much better for knowing that, and everyone is well, especially the goldfish." He replied without even a hint of gritted teeth or patience being tried. "I *am* rather busy, trying to organise six strike teams in separate locations and the logistics of removing non-combatants from the areas without alerting the media or alarming them significantly, so if you would mind being as brief as possible? I would so appreciate it."

"Fine. Spoil all my fun." I quipped back, then quickly gave him an update on what the Alphas had agreed and were already putting in place. "So, just so you don't go shooting any suspicious looking characters or try to arrest anyone lurking in the general vicinity, they'll be on hand to help if things do go to shit."

"Their help will be appreciated, as long as they stick to the stipulations I mentioned last time." The OPS agent replied with far less gratitude than I thought was due. "There were three things I wanted to discuss with you, so it's handy you called."

"You're welcome." I belaboured the word, but he simply ignored my implied hint. "Go on then, shoot."

"Tempting, but not yet." He snarked, and I shook my head. "Firstly, I was wondering if you had managed to catch your colleague, Elspeth MacElvy? We do so need to speak to her."

"Uh, no sorry." I deadpanned my answer, only now remembering I was supposed to be warning her of OPS's attention. Now that I knew what she had been up to, I was willing to bet it had something to do with a missing Detective Inspector, and a not so subtly hexed London mortuary. "Haven't seen her."

"Hmm, most odd." Cormac replied dryly. "I sent a car round this morning to see if we could catch her before she left for work, but it somehow encountered engine trouble two streets from her home. And my colleagues reported a sudden squall of torrential rain which forced them to seek shelter when they made their way on foot. Most odd, as it seemed localised to a few streets, including hers, and those alone."

"Got to love London weather. It's got a mind of its own." I joked, whilst wondering whether that had been Elspeth and Felix playing silly buggers with the OPS guards, or possibly Terra stepping in to protect them despite the broken vows. You never knew with gods and goddesses. "If I see her, I'll be sure to tell her to grab an umbrella."

"You do that. Hmm." Cormac obviously didn't believe a word I said, but we were both playing the game so I was happy to keep bullshitting as long as it kept Ellie out of one of those grey dreary interrogation rooms below the Tower. Or someplace worse. "Secondly, ah yes, Bran had a message for you. I wrote it down here… ah yes, here it is. *Tell the boyo not to trust the rat. Nasty things, full of fleas and disease. Don't trust 'em.* Yes, that was it. Apart from more intimations of doom and gloom approaching rapidly, but I think you already know that."

The rat? Don't trust it? I wracked my brain for anything that dire warning could link to, but the only immediate thing that popped into my head was Rous, the Rat God. But Jessica had struck the deal with it and Molly, so what was one of its rat's going to do to cause me trouble?

"Great, very helpful. As ever." I told him, locking that little nugget away to check later. "You said three things?"

"Oh yes, the third point I wanted to raise was based on our earlier conversation." Cormac drawled dryly. "The fact you and your boss are so sure we are wrong about, that our *mutual friend* will be in residence at the Southbank centre. Remember?"

"I can hardly forget." I answered truthfully, seeing how that was all we were focused on right now. "What about it. You lot giving up on your suspicious six points of the pentagram theory?"

"Not quite." He replied. "The thing is, I think we have discussed this already but there are *seven* points on a pentagram. The six cardinal points, or energy lines, which all, when connected form a junction. A seventh point."

"Yeah, where you think he's going to show up and do his voodoo. You're wrong but what about it?" I was convinced we were right, that the whole buried artefacts were a blind or distraction, at worse a trap for anyone tracking Knox to them.

"Oh I just wondered if you'd checked a map of London, and worked out where the lines all bisect?" He asked, and a sudden nagging feeling of *oh shit, what now?* ran cold shivers down my spine.

"We didn't expend too much effort coz it's obviously a play by Knox. I think we had a map up with the points drawn out, and they intersect roughly in the Thames. So either he's rented a bloody big boat or learned to walk on water. Oh and managed to work out how to stop running water short circuiting his ritual." I growled down the phone. "Either way, it's obviously either a trap where we die a horrible death or a way to keep us twiddling our collective thumbs whilst he does his thing *at the Southbank centre*. But go on. You're going to tell me what we missed, right?"

"Of course. We *did* agree to share relevant information, did we not?" He told me with that slight cutting tone to his voice. "The six lines actually converge on a location on the south bank of the Thames, not on the river itself. Further down from the Tower of London, and Tower Bridge. A little place called …"

"Bermondsey Wall E." I growled out the address, certainty like a stone in my stomach. "The six points all point to my fucking home, don't they?"

"To be fair, I didn't make the connection." Cormac admitted ruefully. "It was Agent Jones, given how she was AIC for our little altercation there previously. But yes, whilst we cannot pinpoint an actual location, the lines either intersect there or very close by. An odd fact, unless you take into account Knox's obvious animosity towards you. I *did* warn you."

"Thanks. Warning duly bloody noted." I snapped and ended the call.

Ok, Morgan, think. I told myself. Just think for a second and don't go charging off and make a bloody fool of yourself.

We were *sure* the Southbank centre was where Knox aimed to summon Morgana. The stones were key, Artur had no reason to lie about his liaison with her and the stupid shit he'd promised whilst they were making out. Morgana had even mentioned the broken promises herself. And we were fairly positive the locations dotted around London were there simply to distract OPS, keep them focused elsewhere whilst he broke the Accords and then did a runner.

But it was my *home*. Could I take the risk?

And if I did believe something was due to happen, what could I do? I could go grab Bear, bundle up anything irreplaceable. But what about Goldspur? What about her father, the apple tree the Morrigan had grown there to remind me of my roots? They couldn't run. The dryad would in fact fight to the death to remain by her father's side.

Could I leave them to face whatever Knox was planning? Could I desert my Alpha and leave them to face the bastard and Morgana themselves?

Neither really bore thinking about, let alone choosing the lesser or greater good shit here.

Instead, I did what anyone in my furry shoes would do.

I asked for help.

"Morrigan, I bloody need you and please don't make me do the three-times summoning shit!" I growled, causing a passing jogger to shoot me a troubled look and start running that bit faster.

"So please get your bony arse over here, so we can speak?"

Chapter 37

"We really do need to do something about that tongue of yours, pup." The Morrigan's voice snarked at me from the bench. I turned, finding the fae sat upon the empty seat beside me, clad in dark robes hiding her armour, carven warstaff set against the seat's arm. "Before someone removes it for your impertinence, perchance."

"You can send me to finishing school when this is all over." I growled, twisting to face her. "Been keeping busy, I trust, granny?"

She shot me a dark look, black eyes glimmering pools without a single shred of humanity to them. Well, they wouldn't have, would they?

"War reaves our home, pup." The fae told me as she settled her hands in her lap, gazing out over the rolling green of the park, the mortals lazing around sunning themselves or laughing in small groups, running along the beaten tracks or chatting to friends on their phones. A picture of calm and serenity. "Traitors within Ivory and Shadow, even the Wyld, spring up like weeds to tear and trip at us, seeking to choke the Courts and leave the Realm open for *her* to return as conqueror. Oberon is not yet recovered enough to take to the field, so Titania stands as Lady of her Court, defending with all her might. But when you cannot trust even the swords at your back, how long do you think she will stand?"

"Hey, we're trying to get this mess sorted mortal-side as soon as we can," I reminded her. "If we can stop *her* from getting her mitts on a new body, this is all over. Right?"

The Morrigan's silence was enough to quell my hope, and I shook my head.

"Let me guess. It's like the evil baddy in book one who the hero gallantry confronts and overcomes to win the day. But you just know the bastard isn't dead or gone, but will be back by book three to really ruin the day. This the same thing?"

"I know not of books." My grandmother told me sharply, her eyes switching to fix me for a moment before she turned back to gaze at the mortals playing like lambs whilst the wolves tied their napkins and sharpened their knives. "But *she* is like nothing you have faced before, pup. I told you, do not think to win this day by trial of combat, or strength of arm. There will always be another trick she has to play."

"Yeah, and I think I know the one she's throwing at me specifically." I outlined what Cormac had told me, the key locations around London and the unsubtle fact they centred on my home. "I can't help but think I'm meant to go rushing off to save Bear, Goldspur, my bloody home and let everyone down. But I can't just forget them either."

The Shadow fae made a tsking noise, shaking her head in obvious despair.

"You are still so *mortal*. So tied to things, when in truth everything ends." She told me, her tones sharp like jagged ice crashing together. "Your home will crumble and fall, your dog will age and die. The river on which you live will rise up and engulf this city. The mortals you know will wither and fall away. Until you accept this, anyone can use your weakness against you, and they will."

"Maybe so, but right now, I count those things as strengths. Things that keep me centred, stop me from losing the plot and saying a big *fuck you* when stuff from my past, from the Real, keeps becoming *my problem*." I shot back, angry at her words but also feeling the pain of knowing she spoke at least a little of the truth. "I didn't call on you to have you point out where I'm going wrong."

"Pity, for that would be an easy thing to achieve and might bring me a modicum of pleasure this day." The Morrigan smiled that wicked smile of hers, then waved her hand for me to continue. "Let's be about the business in hand then. Why did you call on me?"

"Not to help take down *her*." I answered, seeing her eyebrow quirk in surprise. "I already got the inside track on what sort of help I should expect from the Courts, by dear pappy."

"He spoke you to?" The fae queried, with an expression that on anyone else would have earned the description *a trifle vexed*. "That is unexpected."

"Tell me about it. In fact, don't. I can guess." I answered quickly before we went off down another tangent, another shortcut to my failings. "No, what I want to ask for help with is, well, protect my home. Guard those living there. Just for tonight, whilst we're dealing with *her*. I don't know what's going to happen but I can't be there. So would you, grandmother, help me?"

The Morrigan eyed me for a long moment, those dark eyes of hers reflecting no thought, no emotion that I could read. In her lap, she tapped one finger against her other hand as she thought.

"You know what you ask?" She finally spoke, voice cold as the devil's freezer. "If I am to guard your home, keep those you care for safe from harm, then you cannot limit me. I must be able to act as I see fit. Do whatever I think is right, no matter the cost in life. If a mortal seeks entry, I will be free to do whatever I wish to them. With them. I shall break no Accord, as you will have given me freedom to do as I will."

I could have thrown a whole load of stipulations at her. Asked the Morrigan not to harm anyone, just deter them. Use only necessary force, and definitely stick to the mortal rules. But I had no idea what Knox was planning, and I reckoned whatever it was, he wouldn't be playing with gloves on.

"I, Morgan Black, ask you Morrigan Na Crob Derg to guard my hearth and home this night against any and all who come against you. Keep those I care for safe, no matter what, and you shall not be bound by mortal or Real law whilst guarding against attack." I asked in hushed tones, since I was already getting enough odd looks from passers-by to make me think the fae was hidden from their sight. "Will you accept?"

"I accept." She replied instantly, that smile curving like a knife. "Focus your efforts on Knox and *her*, and worry not about your home and those that reside there. They will be safe, and waiting for you to return."

I knew I was probably going to live to regret what I'd just asked, but the key point was I'd *live*. My home would be safe, hell I'd call up Danny and get him over there. Bear would be ok, Goldspur too. I'd handle the fallout later.

"Thanks." I told the fae, but she just shook her head, dark eyes narrowed.

"Learn to focus on the task in hand, and survive the day. Then you can settle accounts with me properly, pup." She told me, letting me know this wasn't some simple favour, just something she'd let slide. No matter that we were family, there would be a debt owed. Oh joys.

The next moment she was gone, leaving only a chill in the summer's fresh air, a touch of ice where only warmth had been before. And a single crow feather on the bench beside me. A touching reference to how I'd first gotten to know the Shadow fae, back when I just some simple kitten finder. Simpler times.

I needed a little more time outside in the fresh air, feeling the sun on my face and letting its warmth soak into me. Just a little longer, before I headed back to let Jessica know OPS were ok with our deal, without revealing any more details and triggering the bloody charm I still had bound to my blood.

Before we went down to the Lows, and into the darkness.

Chapter 38

Nimue.

Also known as the Lady of the Lake, Nynyve, and Viviane. She was instrumental in providing Arthur with the sword Excalibur, eliminating Merlin, raising Lancelot after the death of his father, and helping to take the dying Arthur to Avalon.

There is much discussion on whether there was but one Lady, or a Sisterhood that aided Artur and his Knights throughout his reign. And even her role is at times questioned – 'though Nynyve is sometimes friendly to Arthur and his knights, she is equally liable to act in her own interest. She can be also selfish, ruthless, desiring, and capricious. She has been identified as a deceptive and anti-patriarchal equally as often as she has been cast as a benevolent aid to Arthur's court, or even the literary descendant of protective goddesses'.

Things went to absolute hell just in time to thoroughly ruin everyone's day.

The clock was just closing on five, and our small company had gathered in the office. I'd finally dragged myself back inside to update my Alpha and dig out whatever kit I thought I'd need. Thanks to my new Ivory brand, I could leave a lot of the bulkier armour behind and feel less conspicuous walking around London looking like an extra from some 90s sci-fi horror movie.

Felix had grabbed me as soon as I was back in the office, and we'd had a quick catch up. I'd called Danny and told him to head over to mine, but to stay downstairs and ignore any weird noises or stuff happening upstairs, and that seemed to help put his daughter's mind at ease. For my part, I'd argued and cajoled and eventually gotten Felix's agreement to stay back and not get involved in any of the fighting unless she absolutely had to. I remembered how she had handled Baba Yaga, but that had been luck more than training, and there was a real chance she could get seriously hurt this time.

Thankfully Felix saw reason and agreed to let us take the brunt of anything came against us. And to follow Elspeth's lead. She was smart enough to know she was well and truly in over her head right now, and that for once we seemed to know more that she did. So she'd listen, and probably only give me grief later if we messed up and things got complicated.

Emma and Jacob had not liked the stipulation of only four lycan going in, but the fact Jessica was in with us helped allay some of their concerns. Having an Alpha along for the ride meant we had the big guns to play with, even if she'd dock us for any accidental damage we caused and had no way of hiding from her.

It happened. Sometimes a wall just got in the way.

Clad in our not *quite body-armour but close enough* gear, carrying a bag of tools and weapons carefully packed so as not to make too much noise, the three other lycans finished checking each other over and eyed my slightly more casual outfit dubiously.

I just grinned, giving them a twirl.

"Ah hope yer faith in this Court armour does nae let you down." Jessica told me, as she shifted one of the armour plates on her thigh to a more comfortable position. The three members of my pack looked like they were attending a paintballing event where they expected to take serious damage, leaving aside helmets as they'd only get in the way if they Changed.

I looked down, patting my less bulkier cargo pants, t-shirt and under-armour that was so much more comfortable to wear when the weather was this muggy. Summer in the city was never really that pleasant to run around in heavy armour, so my gift from Ivory was an unexpected boon I might actually need to thank Titania and Manisha for. If things ever settled down for us to have that sort of conversation.

"You can soak up whatever they throw at us, and I'll be the one to do the dodging and bouncing around if it makes you feel better." I replied, doing a quick check of my pockets. All the vials and flasks of useful items were where I'd stored them, including that ticking timebomb Elspeth had given me.

The inhaler holding the altered Harrowing.

I'd kept it on me for the simple fact I wasn't comfortable leaving the thing lying around, and didn't have anywhere I'd call secure enough to leave so dangerous an item. So, I'd left it in my pocket, just in case. Hell, I had no idea when I'd need the thing.

Elspeth was still in her dark gear, only adding a few items from the office to her belt of many pockets. Including the wand I remembered her having at Greenwich, but thankfully never needing to use its stored magic.

Wands, staffs, the equipment you see wizards and witches use in films or read about in books didn't mention how troublesome the bloody things were. Each had a certain amount of stored magic inside them, dependent on how they were made, from what materials and other factors. That energy leaked out over time and needed to be topped up to keep the things useful. Unfortunately, there was no way of knowing how much magic the things would take, and had a nasty habit of exploding when the owner imbued too much into the thing. That or they went off and released all their might when accidently triggered. Think rubbing the genie's lamp to make it shine, not meaning to release its prisoner, or a broomstick that started flying when someone unknowingly picked it up to clean the floor with.

Beside her, Felix was clad in her usual coloured melange of fashions that was a statement all to herself. Her white hair was bound back, and she didn't carry any weapons but then I'd seen her call Veil-fire to her hands to light a candle, and I reckoned anyone who thought her the weak and an easy target would get a short but very surprising shock.

And finally there was ex DI Gregory Allen. Still in clothes Elspeth had scrounged for him, still with that aura that set our lycan senses on edge. Not what he seemed, like he was slightly out of focus and causing us to squint to see him properly. He'd asked, possibly thinking back to his encounter with Baba Yaga and Jack the Ripper, and I'd dug out another cold-iron and silver shortsword he now carried in a bag slung over one shoulder.

I'd give him that one. He obviously learned from past experiences even if he wasn't entirely convinced they were real.

Like dying.

"So, there's seven of us." I commented dryly, nodding around the team. "Do we just go with the names of the dwarves from Snow White, or is anyone else here a Marvel fan and can quote the sides from Civil War?"

Jessica gave me a steady look but I just shrugged, grinning.

"Hey, we're heading into battle. Might as well do it laughing." I argued, seeing Jacob shake his head whilst Elspeth sighed a long-suffering sigh.

That's when my phone started buzzing, as did Jessica's. And Jacob and Emma's too.

"Uh, that's weird." I noted with little need, grabbing out the phone to find it was the OPS one. "This does not bode well."

"*Snow White's Seven Dwarves. We do mining, thieving, the occasional banditry* …" I started, but stopped as Agent Evelyn Jones's voice overrode me.

"Morgan Black, shut up and just listen." She instructed sharply. "The six sites were as you suggested. A trap, not anywhere Knox meant to ever be. The devices are somehow leaching the life from anyone close to them, and the area of effect is growing steadily. We've already lost a dozen agents who were caught when they activated. I don't believe any of your kind are hurt. But if we don't stop the devices, the radius of effect will soon breach our initial estimations and hit inhabited areas."

"Fuck. He's siphoning more life energy!" I growled. "Can't you just, I don't know, bomb the bloody things?"

"We're OPS, not the army or royal air force, you idiot." She reprimanded me sharply. "But we'll handle it. Besides this, something has happened on the Underground. We're getting reports of some sort of incident, possibly a terrorist attack. Gas or something, causing the tube trains to fail along the Circle Line. There's at least a dozen trains stuck in tunnels, with commuters on them all."

My blood ran cold, that shiver running up and down my spine like a marathon sprinter on speed. Some sort of gas, electrics failing. In a confined space. Maybe nothing, maybe …

"He's let the Harrowing out." I told the room as well as Agent Jones. "Those carriages will be filled with the Harrowed, and as soon as they work out how to break open the doors they'll be out and after anyone in the Underground. You've got to clear the tube stations and lock the gates. Contain them, then we'll handle them."

"Again, we are already on it." She replied, as Jessica nodded to me, speaking quietly into her phone. I guessed at least one of the other Alphas, giving us the good news. Emma and Jacob were talking together, directing our pack on staying out of the energy drain's effect until OPS worked out how to stop the bloody things. Or we'd have to start doing things old school. Like dropping buildings on the bloody things.

And that still left however many Harrowed Know had created in the tube tunnels. Fuck!

"Oh and Cormac told me to tell you, something's going on at your home. Some sort of conflagration maybe, the reports are sketchy at the moment." Evelyn wrapped up the call. "I don't have the details but I think something was set to go off at the centre of the pentagram. It's damaged an area around your apartment block but I think it's still standing. I'll let you know as soon as I hear anything more."

The call cut off, and I slowly slipped the phone back into my pocket, a cocktail of feelings and thoughts warring inside my head to be the one in control.

"That fucking bastard!" I snarled, as my packmates finished up their calls. "I know the guy's nuts but this? It's psychotic!"

"I cannae argue with you there," Jessica replied as she snapped her phone closed. "Ah have advised the other Alphas that unless the mortal authorities can destroy the devices before any more lives are lost, that they should act as they see fit tae stop them working. Whatever the cost."

"What's going on?" Felix asked, her face paling at my sudden rage. "You said something about the Underground?"

"The guy we're after. The guy who taught Gary Weatherby to do what he did to you?" I told her, knowing Felix needed all the facts if she was joining us. "He's released something really nasty on the Circle Line, just in time to catch people leaving work or heading out on the town. Innocent people, and they'll either have the life ripped from them or be left as vicious killing machines. We call them the Harrowed, and they're like the worst kind of killer zombie you can imagine, then triple it. Just to cause more distraction."

"Shit! Can't we, like, switch them back? Isn't there a cure?" She asked, looking back at Elspeth who shook her head, expression grave. "They can't be …"

"They were dead the moment the Harrowing touched them. There is no cure, and the only thing that can be done is to kill the things they've turned into." The witch told her, not pulling any punches. "They'll feed off the living, be drawn to life if only to devour and destroy it. The mortal police, security services, they won't be enough to stop this. Maybe Morgan's friends will be able to, but they'll need help. Lycan help, let alone anything from the other side."

"We're on our own." I answered that question, not wanting us to waste any time appealing for aid. "The Courts have got their hands full, another little distraction designed to keep them occupied whilst this shit goes down. It's down to us to fix this, or we could lose London, maybe worse."

"He's playing Chase The Lady. A street game." Jacob spoke up, having finished giving instructions to our packmates. "Knox is trying to take our attention off him, the Queen, and keep us looking elsewhere until he's ready to be revealed. We just need to find him, and let the others deal with all the fires he's set to keep us distracted."

"All well and good, but the bastard *set fire* to my home." I growled, catching a look from Jessica, the question obvious. "It's ok. I … I kinda guessed he'd be trying something, so I asked for some help. The sort we can't get anywhere else, to just keep things safe whilst we get this done. The place should be ok."

My Alpha gave me a long look before she stepped amongst us, instantly attracting all our attention.

"This changes nae a thing." She told us, looking each one of us in the eyes. "Knox is the key tae stopping this madness. We must trust our kin and the mortal forces already in play tae cope with what this man has let loose, and remain focused on our target. Stopping the ritual, stopping *her* from being reborn. Nothing else matters. Agreed?"

One by one we all nodded.

"Good. Then let's get tae the Lows, and see about ending Robert Knox's madness once and fer all." She growled grimly, heading off to the front door. "Fer I'm beyond bored of this mortal causing anyone any more pain or suffering."

"This ends fer him tonight."

Chapter 39

Back down the Lows. A place which after my last brush with the immortals in charge, I reckoned I'd steer clear off for a good few years. Maybe a decade or two, until they forgot who I was.

I should know by now, life doesn't like me keeping those sort of promises. Even to myself.

Word that something was up, a situation affecting the mortals of the city, seemed already to be out as we left the office and headed towards our nearest route down. The Peter Pan statue that Elspeth and I had used before. When I'd been out in the park only a few hours ago, it had been packed with people chilling in the sun, eating picnics and laughing out loud, playing loud music and generally filling the green space with noise. Typical mortals.

Now, the park was eerily empty. The seven of us moved into the grounds without coming across a single jogger, sun-bather or group of frolicking teenagers in the late afternoon sun. Normally you couldn't swing a cat without hitting a mortal, but now, the only people I saw were those hurrying off in the distance, urgently speaking into their personal phones or huddled around small radios or tablets playing the news. Police sirens echoed on every side, joined with the more laconic wail of ambulances, the emergency services out and about.

Poor bastards, I thought, hoping to the gods OPS intervened in time to stop any of the emergency services heading down into the tunnels and confronting the Harrowed. It'd be a blood bath, but only the start of the horror in store for the dwellers of London Upper if the beasts got free.

Reaching the statue, Jessica took the lead. Where before a Sister of the Arch had been waiting for us, this time the space around Pan was empty.

Instead, our Alpha simply stepped up to the statue, leaning against the cold metal and whispered a phrase too low under her breath for me to catch.

Pan shivered, waking to life as whatever she uttered was accepted. Again, he looked over the small gathering of those seeking passage below, his metal orbs alighting on me and I could swear a mocking smile bending his child-lips even though he was cast iron. He gave a sharp toot on his pipes, and the entrance to the Lows ground open with the sort of creaking groan that makes most people reach for the WD40 or at a pinch any oil to wet the hinges.

It seemed we were expected, given how when the small company exited the staircase and stepped into the entrance lobby, it was to find a contingent of hobgoblin guards waiting for us. That and the two rulers of London Lower.

Molly, clad in wraps of transparent gauze which hugged her earth mother curves and left little to the imagination, smiled invitingly as we entered the small circular hallway. Beside her, Rous gave a small chittering hiss, the sound echoed from a multitude of rodent throats. The Rat God was diminished from when I had last seen him, barely half his size and made up of a motley disparity of rodents of shapes and colours. I guessed even though London was a breeding ground for grey rats, only a small percentage made it down to the Lows and escaped the cookpots and traps of the locals. The rest were whatever Rous had summoned from further afield.

"Welcome, Jessica of the Walker Pack." Molly greeted us, looking around the small company. Her eyes rested on me for a long moment, then passed on but I'd felt the judgement in her gaze. The unspoken accusation. No matter the fact Jessica had brokered a deal with the rulers of London Lower, they hadn't forgotten or forgiven me.

Something twitched in the back of my head, something someone had said. A message. But too much had happened, the news of the Harrowing and my apartment block being attacked. It'd have to wait, to pop up probably at the worst possible moment. That's how these things normally happened for me.

"Thank you again, Lady Molly, Lord Rous, fer allowing us tae pass through yer domain and make use of yer portal tae London Upper." Jessica gave them both deep, formal bows and we all hastily copied the gesture. "As we agreed, the Lows will be immune from hunts fer the next one hundred years, and we shall only venture below upon yer direct invitation. Those were the terms we agreed, ah am correct?"

"That is so." Molly commented, before nodding in my direction. "Though *that one* is not welcome full stop. Too much suffering follows his shadow, and too much pain can be placed directly at his feet. The Lows will never forget."

I went to speak, at least to apologise or explain how it wasn't *exactly* my fault Rous had stormed in on Knox, gung-ho and sure in his own safety when surrounded by guards, only to be fed to the Harrowing. But Jessica shook her head once and I bit my lip instead.

"Ah understand. He is necessary fer what we seek to achieve tonight, but otherwise he will nae venture this way again." She agreed with the earth mother, and I simply shrugged my acceptance when both shot me a look.

"Good, then. We will guide you through the Lows to the place you must enter through." Rous chittered, speaking up now that the terms had been agreed and I'd been soundly put in my place. "Once there, one of my kin will guide you through the portal and take you where you wish to go. Then you are on your own."

That little niggling doubt jumped up and down, begging for attention but I shoved it to one side, telling myself I'd work out whatever I had forgotten later. It can't have been anything important.

We passed swiftly through the tunnels and by-ways of London Lower, surrounded by the guards and following Rous and Molly as they walked on ahead. I figured we were being taken the long way round, avoiding all the inhabited and well-used locations of the Lows since we did not set foot in the market even once. Instead, we took tunnel after tunnel, branching out and delving ever deeper into the shadow and darkness.

Steps led down to lower levels paved with old flagstones and intricate patterned tiles, with pillars of stone crafted from the very bedrock to reach up like petrified trees to the roof above. I recognised some of the designs as Roman in nature, from pictures I'd seen online and also displays I'd attended with Sarah in an attempt to appear more cultured than I really was. You do those sort of things when you think you're in love, and want to be the sort of person the other thinks you are, even if they're missing key facts about you.

Like me being a lycan, not mortal. Small stuff like that.

Finally, after what felt like hours, we stopped in a small antechamber, a junction of several tunnels that led off into the shadows. Steps reached from the stone-clad floor up to a stone arch set in the earth wall, detailed with vines and leaves, as if the portal had been filled in long ago but its structure kept from being buried. As a reminder of what lay beyond, maybe or just because it was actually a portal to elsewhere. I could feel the latent magic of the doorway, so different to the doorway Knox had used to ward his private sanctum before. That had required a special sequence to unlock and reveal its true nature, done so by Elspeth in one of her particularly clever moments.

This one, however, did not hide its nature. It was obviously a way through. Just hopefully to the place we wanted to go to, and not some random location halfway across London. Opening in someone's bathroom or toilet, if my luck ran true.

"This is the place." Molly told us as the guards filed in behind us. "Rous will send one of his servants with you, but other than that, from now on you are on your own. And bound by your agreement to us. Do not think to renege on it, unless you wish to suffer dire consequence."

"Aren't you going to ask us to swear to deal with Knox once and for all, or promise we won't let him know you helped us?" I asked, remembering how insistent the pair had been when Elspeth and I attended their Court, to ask their permission to hunt the mortal. They had practically demanded we promise such a thing before they offered us any help, whereas now …

Molly looked at me, the weight of her immortal nature settling on me like gravity.

"Would it matter if we did? You have proven unable to keep your word, lycan, so why should we be foolish enough to trust you to keep it again?" She enquired and I had to agree, she had a point. "No, you go to face Knox. If you succeed, we have a hundred years to rebuild what we have lost. If not, then, well, we shall see."

With that, the earth mother strode off towards the nearest exit. Rous remained standing before us a moment longer, then his body gave a violent shake and one rat dropped from the mass and landed on the stone floor.

"Feris here will be your guide." Rous told Jessica, pointedly ignoring me. "He has been instructed to take you through the portal shortly, when the time is right. Once through, he will then take you to where you need to be, if you wish to stop Knox."

I eyed the rat standing alone on the stone dubiously. Even a non-expert on rodents like me could see this rat was not in its prime. One foreleg was a stump, the claw gone, and its fur was motley and patched, violent pink skin showing through pebbled with lumps. This rodent was definitely not well.

With that, the Rat God slithered off to join his mistress, the hobs glaring at us a moment longer before falling in behind their Lord and Lady. In moments, the gathering were lost from sight, the heavy tramp of the guards' feet slowly fading away as they speedily put distance between us and them.

"So, anyone feel like they *really* wanted to get as far away from us as possible?" I quipped, staring off into the darkness, back the way they had gone. "Or is it just me?"

"Just you, I reckon." Emma told me, as she set her bag of weapons down and opened it. She began strapping on a small arsenal of silvered cold iron, now that we were beyond mortal view and no-one was going to start asking inconvenient questions like *are you intending to do some violence with all that cutlery, Miss?* "By the way, what did you do to piss them off so much?"

"I reckon Rous blames me for getting most of his rats nuked by Knox the last time we were down here." I admitted, looking to where the sickly Feris stood silent and still. Almost a statue. "A bit unfair, really, since I *did* try to stop him charging in. Jacob, you can back me up, right?"

"Hnh." My packmate grunted, reverting to his mono-syllabic responses. I guess he'd used up most of his monthly allocation of words, giving me grief over my behaviour.

Seeing how it didn't look like Feris was in any rush to get us through the portal, we all got on with the job Emma had started. Getting kitted up and ready for trouble. I strapped on my replacement shortswords and a few knives for good measure, loosening them in their sheaths so I didn't have that awkward moment if any of them got stuck.

Jessica had brought her favourite sabre, taken from a Russian horse guard she had fought centuries ago on another continent, but had braced it with an old English sword-breaker. This was a blade of cold iron, sharp enough to deal considerable damage, but the slots that ran up and down its length were meant to catch and snag an enemy's weapon, effectively disarming them with a twist of the wrist. I'd practiced with her on a few occasions, and had my arse handed to me as she effortlessly sent anything I used flying across the gym floor as she wielded the tool like a martial arts professional.

Jacob, true to his calling as pack tank, had brought a small arsenal of weapons that would have outfitted a modest medieval army. He slid twin swords over his shoulders, and strapped machetes to his thighs, with a bandolier of knives slung across his chest. To this, he added a spike-headed mace and a long-handled truncheon studded with cold steel and silver, for anything that was resistant to sharp edges.

Looking at the four of us, I realised the small oddity. None of us, in fact no lycan I knew, ever used a range weapon. We didn't carry guns as they would usually fail against creatures of magic, but crossbows, bows, slings, javelins, hell there were a host of weapons Terrigylle had shown me on many an occasion that were great to deal damage to our foes from a distance, and remove any risk to ourselves.

But instead, we always got up and personal with the creatures or Accord breakers we faced. I think it was something to do with it always being a hunt for us, which we looked at differently than mortals. They did it for sport, hiding and shooting their prey from places of safety then crowing about the achievement afterwards as if it took any real skill to kill something when it didn't know the danger. Instead, we wanted our prey to know what they faced, to see that knowledge in their eyes as we tracked them down. The guilt for their crimes or actions, the certainty that they hadn't gotten away with whatever it was they'd done.

Still, I reckoned our stubborn pride and the need to go toe to toe with our prey came at a cost. Just ask Mark Walker.

"Uh, you think you're going to need all that stuff?" Felix asked, looking at Jacob's armoury with a slightly horrified expression.

Jacob shrugged, adjusting one machete so that it sat flatter against his thigh.

"What my packmate of many words means," I spoke up, smiling across at her. "Is that in these kind of situations, it's often better to bring everything and use nothing, than risk showing up unprepared and at a serious disadvantage."

"Like *don't bring a knife to a gunfight* kind of thing?" She asked, and I nodded.

"Yeah. Though more like *don't bring a stick to a bazooka fight,* but close enough. But speaking of which, just remember you promised to hang back and let us take things head on. No heroics, ok?" I reminded her, seeing her shake her head at the suggestion.

"Looking at all that stuff, oh don't worry. I'm happy to hide behind you and let you take the hits!" She replied, grinning impishly.

"Good, coz Danny will *kill* me if you scrape your knee or dirty your dress, Princess." I snarked back, to which Felix stuck her tongue out as a suitable reply.

I shot a look over at Elspeth and Greg … it felt weird not thinking of him as DI Gregory Allen. Hell, it still felt weird thinking of him upright and mobile. But I saw the man had slipped the loaned sword free of its carry-all and, with the witch's help, was strapping it on.

He slid the weapon free and made a few circles with blade. Nothing fancy, not like a kid smacking weeds with a stick as they imagined smiting their enemies. Instead, Greg seemed to be feeling the weight and balance of it, adjusting his swing automatically to snap the weapon back from one thrust to another slashing strike. He wouldn't be winning any swashbuckling awards, but death seemed to have gifted him a few more talents than he had had before. Worth noting, I told myself.

With preparations done, and no sign of the rat making any movement apart from the occasional blink of its rheumy eyes, we all settled down to wait. Felix sat down on the floor with me, and I dug in a pocket, handing across an energy bar. The sort with nuts, honey and all things crunchy rather than the gooey sort that felt like you were eating wet cardboard.

"Eat up." I told her, as she looked at what I was offering. "You'll be surprised how much energy you'll burn when we get to the fighting. If you do any of it, that is. Nothing worse than a grumbling stomach whilst you're trying to appear badass, fighting off a bunch of nasties."

"Is it always like this?" She asked, around a mouthful of nuts. I looked around, taking in our surroundings.

"What, dark, dismal and a little wet underfoot?" I asked, eliciting a grunt from her. "Yeah, sadly it is."

"God, no. Idiot." Felix told me. "The waiting around, with nothing to do. Is this normal?"

"Normal? Hah." I snorted, earning a raised eyebrow from Jessica as she turned from talking to my packmates. I shook my head to show there was no problem. "You're sat in a place beneath London that should not exist, surrounded by witches, werewolves and moth-eaten rats. Oh, and you know a man who came back from the dead but no-one is calling him the Messiah. And we're heading off to go fight a certified lunatic whose been alive for centuries, and a creature from Arthurian legend that should only be a bedtime story, one of the scarier ones. Normal? That word really doesn't apply to what we do here."

"But the waiting? Yeah, that's about right." I added, as I read the reassurance she needed in her open and honest face. "Most of what we do involves hunting down leads, checking facts, investigating details to lead us to the thing we need to find. That can be incredibly tedious and boring. But then, when we do find our quarry, there's a few minutes of frenetic activity before we're back to the boring part of dragging their usually unconscious body off and cleaning up after ourselves."

"Enjoy these moments of calm. When it gets crazy, they help keep you grounded." I wrapped up, giving her a shoulder nudge.

It could have been minutes later, maybe longer, when the rat finally did something other than sit on the floor and moult. With no sign that I saw to alert it, Feris suddenly shook itself, shedding more fur onto the cold stone underfoot then scampered over to the gate embedded in the wall.

"Ah see it." Jessica spoke up even as I went to alert everyone. "Ah think it's time, people."

Everyone pushed themselves up and stepped forward, giving the rat plenty of room but making sure we could reach the gate quickly when it opened. I positioned Felix behind me, drawing one of my swords but not Changing yet, in case anything popped through when the portal opened to greet us accordingly. On a whim, I reached for the Shadow mark inside me, feeling ice gather and spread out from my tattooed hand. In a moment, my sword glittered with hoarfrost, steaming with extreme cold.

"Very pretty." Emma remarked dryly, eyeing my frozen blade. "Remind me to invite you to my next house party. I'll save a ton on bagged ice."

"The duties of a Knight Errant are never done." I grinned back at her, rolling my shoulders and readying for the fight ahead. "Add *popsicle supplier* to my *kitten finder* credentials on my cv, would you?"

She flipped me the bird, and I bowed to the witty rejoinder.

"Enough." Jessica spoke quietly and without force, but we both nodded and focused back on the matter in hand.

Feris reared up on its hindlegs and with a certain amount of arthritic jerkiness, clawed at the mud which filled the archway. For a moment nothing happened, then where the creature had scratched the surface, longer lines began to spread out like a spiderweb of cracks. Bright white light began to shine through these, spearing out as lumps of mud and other unidentifiable matter started to crumble and fall to the stone floor. I felt the wakening magic like a caress over my skin, and cracked my neck, bracing myself for whatever came next.

The next instant, the remaining mud vanished in an explosion of bright white light. We all shielded our eyes, squinting against the glow until it slowly faded to a more bearable level. The arch was now filled with rippling liquid, glowing with a pulsing hue as circles spread out across its surface like miniature waves on the ocean.

Feris twisted its spine to stare at us, having somehow managed to evade the falling clods of dirt. It gave a rasping hiss that I had to assume was rat for *come on*, then darted into the portal. It left an after image of itself in the glowing surface, which slowly faded as the ripples spread.

"Jacob, Emma, if you would?" Jessica instructed, and the two packmates nodded. Squaring their shoulders, weapons ready, they stepped up to the portal. Emma motioned for Jacob to take lead, she covering his back as he stepped through. Then she vanished as well.

A moment passed, then Emma's head ducked back through the rippling surface.

"All good. Comes out in a storage closet by the looks of things." She told us. "Big enough for us all, and that rat's acting impatient-like. Reckon we should head on through."

"I'll take the tail." I volunteered, seeing Jessica nod in agreement. Made sense one of us hanging back to make sure nothing from this side tried to follow over, for whatever reason. We didn't need any more surprises.

Elspeth and Greg went ahead, and my Alpha stepped up with Felix. The young witch to be ... wannabe-witch ... witchling ... whatever she was, shot me a slightly worried look but I grinned and motioned for her to head on through. If Jessica was with her, she was safe as anything.

Finally it was my turn, as I was left standing in the antechamber alone. Somewhere far above us, people were dying, my packmates most likely fighting Harrowed and gods knew what was going on at my home. I just had to trust the Morrigan wouldn't leave me too much of a mess to clean up whilst protecting my hearth. But if Bear and Danny, and Goldspur to be fair, were all safe ... I'd weather that shitstorm happily.

Time to go kick some mortal ass, and hopefully ruin an immortal's well-planned and incredibly complicated comeback tour. Or possibly walk into a horrendous and devious trap, and find out just how stupid we'd all been.

With that pleasant thought, I stepped through the portal.

Chapter 40

The Questing Beast.

This strange creature was much sought by the Knights of Artur, after it appeared to the King in a dream. Merlin explained the origins of the beast as born of a human woman, a princess who lusted after her own brother. She slept with a devil who had promised to make the boy love her, but the devil manipulated her into accusing her brother of rape. Their father had the brother torn apart by dogs as punishment. Before he died, however, he prophesied that his sister would give birth to an abomination that would make the same sounds as the pack of dogs that were about to kill him.

The beast was renowned for making the sound of yelping or barking of thirty or more hounds. It is often described as having the head and neck of a snake, the body of a leopard, the haunches of a lion, and the feet of a hart.

It wasn't a trap. Just a broom closet, if the number of mops, buckets and cleaning bottles cluttered around the place was any indicator.

As I stepped into the Southbank centre, I felt the portal snap shut behind me. A one-way trip, ensuring we didn't head back into London Lower and cause Molly or Rous any more headaches. Ahead of me, I could see Jacob and Emma at the doors, easing them open to check outside. Jessica stood with Elspeth and her two companions, the witch having taken out the vial of glowing salt crystals and was holding it at eye level.

"Morgan. Ah was just asking Elspeth if she was sure the charm is working tae cloak us?" Jessica greeted me as I stepped away from the blank wall where a moment before had been a glowing portal to the Lows.

"And I was just replying that, to the best of my knowledge, everything is working just fine." The witch replied, shaking the vial a little and staring at the crystals. They were glowing a brilliant violet hue, and had floated to the top of the container. She turned the glass in her hand but the crystals remained pointing upwards. "Of course, I can't wholly test the charm until we bump into one of Robert Knox's guards. Then we'll see."

"Handy, that." I grumped, but knew it wasn't really the witch's fault. Charms to obscure and hide you from people's attention required, by dint of how they worked, the people to be present so you knew if the crafting was working or not. Otherwise you might as well just throw a blanket over your head and tell the world *you can't see me.*

"Doesn't the fact we haven't heard alarms going ape-shit or the pounding feet of an angry horde running to attack us kinda mean all's ok?" Felix spoke up, her voice a little hesitant but with a note of defiance definitely there. I guessed she was a little sensitive given how she'd helped craft the charm, and didn't have the experience of ignoring doubting lycans like Elspeth had.

"Fer now, let's assume things are working as expected." Jessica answered, keeping her expression neutral. It took a special kind of patience to handle Felix's sarcasm, and not remind her that she was practically a tag-along on this mission. I know I was tempted to make a sarky reply about things always looking ok just before they went to shit, but I took my Alpha's lead and held my tongue.

Jessica pulled out her slim electronic pad from one pocket, the display lighting up under her fingerprints. I'd once commented on her reliance on something so advanced and technical, when we were around magic all the time that would short circuit the thing eventually. Jessica had duly revealed she had invested some resources with a dwarrow of her acquaintance, and the clever little bastard had crafted her a shielding for the device to sit in that grounded it from latent energies. Effectively attaching a lightning rod to the tool, and ensuring it would survive all but a direct strike from anything supernatural.

Thankfully the cost had been high enough to convince her *not* to enforce all her pack used such a device to keep our contracts up to date. Otherwise it would be another thing for me to lug about, and probably break given my history with work phones.

After a quick search of her history, Jessica motioned for everyone but Jacob to gather round. He stayed on the door, keeping watch.

"Ah downloaded the schedule of events before we set off, and verified a few details with mah contacts." She told us, showing the floorplan of the Southbank centre laid out in full on her screen. All six floors of the building.

"Everything indicates the Arthurian exhibit is located within the roof pavilions. At the top of the building."

"Of course it is." I groaned quietly. "Villains never think about giving the bloody heroes a break and organising their diabolical plans on the ground floor, to save our bloody legs."

"They are *so* inconsiderate." Jessica smiled at my lament before continuing. "We are here, on the ground floor at the rear of the building. Away from the main thoroughfare and stairwells. Public lifts tae levels one tae five are set on either side of the building, with the security office located alongside the auditorium on level three. Cameras cover every floor, set tae view all four internal aspects as well as the exteriors of the centre. A team of ten security guards patrol on the hour every hour, with two always remaining in their office whilst the other eight walk the floors and report in via handsets. Finally, the office has a direct line tae the police and also tae a private security firm engaged solely tae respond tae threats to any person or possession whilst on the premises."

"Oh goodie. Just a walk in the park then. What's the bad news?" I growled, and Elspeth rolled her eyes at me with good natured exasperation at my constant need to make jokes.

"The *good* news, Morgan, is three-fold." Jessica tapped the screen, zeroing in on the sixth floor. "Mah sources indicate that due tae certain last minute stipulations enforced by the organisers of the exhibit, all security cameras on the top floor are turned off. Instead a private security feed was installed, with the centre assured all liability is waived in case of any sort of incident."

"Oh that's gotta be Knox pulling his usual bullshit. Meaning no cameras to worry about up there?" I queried, and my Alpha nodded.

"Ah believe you are right. Second, the top floor is restricted tae 'members' only', accessible only by a single elevator from the ground floor, avoiding the other levels. And that route was also named in the *camera exception* stipulation, with even the on-site security banned from its use tonight." She tapped the one shaft leading all the way from the ground level to the top, marking it in red. "Ah reckon if Knox thinks tae expect trouble, he will see this as a perfect way tae channel his enemies in tae one place, and deal with them at his leisure. Which, of course, we won't do."

"Instead, it would seem the owners of this building became *very* concerned with the state of its exterior recently, and have engaged a company tae clean and repair the bottom five levels. Discreetly, of course, so as not tae ruin any advertising fer the event already in place." She smiled, tapping the east side of the building, where a set of steps led down to an alley between the main building and its twin, the Queen Elizabeth Hall. "Ah arranged fer mah contacts at this company tae leave scaffolding and mechanical lifts in place tae access up tae floor five, through the side entrance here. And ah just happen tae have the security codes to get us through the gates."

"Once we gain level five, there is a staff stairway we can take tae the top floor. Again, there is a code tae use, which ah have." She smiled, the extent of her network of contacts obvious from what the Alpha had organised in so little time. "Ah very much doubt Knox will have thought tae ward any route used solely by mortals tae bring sustenance tae guests, given his low opinion of the young women and men he has kidnapped over the years to use tae repair him and build himself a body too."

It all sounded so simple, a sleight of hand like something out of an *Oceans* movie. If we'd planned a little more, we could've probably chosen a soundtrack to go with our snatch and grab. Something peppy, given we had a young witch-to-be along for the ride.

Of course, in my experience, it was when things looked so simple and easy that it invariably went wrong.

"What about the third thing?" Felix asked, as she poked around the closet, inquisitive as ever. "You said three-fold."

"Ah did indeed." Jessica nodded at the young mortal. "We dinnae know what allies Knox yet has, what guards still exist tae ward their efforts. So ah arranged fer a little distraction, a demonstration against the Arthurian event after posting on the relevant sites fer such things. *Selling out our country's history, encouraging elitism and bigotry against the common man. Just another rich-list fascist appropriation of our country's soul.* The fact this sham is selling its tickets fer upwards of five hundred pounds per person just tae pass the door, let alone the upper tier priced tickets fer sustenance as well, helped me encourage certain groups with the need tae voice outrage fer it not being open to all, no matter their social standing. Ah expect a sizeable mob of mortals tae rally outside the building, and unfortunately several security guards were taken ill suddenly tonight. Ah foresee the first-line of defence being much weakened, with the guards focused on keeping the protestors at bay. Knox will nae doubt be aware of what is happening, and will most likely send what guards he has tae keep an eye on the fracas, giving us a chance tae sneak past them."

"You know you're risking mortals mixing with whatever nasties Knox has up his sleeve?" I queried, knowing it was one of our cardinal rules *not* to use the inhabitants of this realm as bait or cannon-fodder, no matter the temptation at times. Yeah, I know we shouldn't even think it, but you try to keep a good thought in your head when you have places to be, and the person holding up the queue ahead of you is chatting about their day, or the funny thing that happened to them last week *that they just have to share*. It happens.

"Only a risk if we delay, and dinnae put an end tae things here quickly." She replied and I shrugged, it being her call.

Checking my watch, I saw Rous and Molly had dropped us back into the Mortal Realm at just gone half seven in the evening, with just shy of an hour before the sun had set and the alignment would be visible. Dusk, that point between light and darkness, such an important time for spellwork and craftings.

"The mob should be gathering as we speak, so all we need do is wait here until we hear the discord start, then make our way out the side entrance and tae the upper level. From there, ah expect us to breach the fifth floor, the stairwell, and land on Knox well before twenty to nine, with time in hand." Jessica finished up, setting the pad back into her pocket and looking around us. "Any questions?"

I raised a hand, since one thought had been troubling me. It was completely immaterial to our problems at hand, but it was nagging like a hangnail.

"Yes, Morgan?" Jessica enquired lightly, but with just enough of a tone to tell me not to waste what time we had.

"It's about the tickets." I saw her expression grow a little stonier, so rushed on. "I thought this whole Arthurian exhibit was a sham created by the Mistress to get a load of mortals in one place, to be blown to kingdom come when she nuked the Ivory Court. But then we went and arrested her ass, ruining the whole plan. So how come the exhibit's still going, and where the hell is the money going? Five hundred a ticket, baseline? That's a shitload of cash for a fake event that was never meant to happen?"

"Whilst I dinnae think this is anything we need worry about *right now*," She told me with a mild reprimand, but then continued. "Ah would hypothesize the actual event is nae a fake, but something the Mistress learned of and took advantage of fer her plan at the time. So the organisers, whomever they are, would still be keen tae show off their exhibits. The fact they have the London Stone is nothing less than a massive coincidence, otherwise Knox would nae have needed tae seek help from the trolls tae steal the thing if he in fact already possessed it. Ah would imagine he simply has had tae alter his plans, pretend tae be a dead man and fake the pertinent details to allow him tae be left alone tae perform the rite tae summon *her* all last minute. Or we would have nae found it so easy to infiltrate a place he properly controls."

"As fer the money?" She eyed me, then shrugged. "Ah just reckon that is a sad sign of the mortals' greed, and their innate desire tae derive wealth from something that should be free tae all. History is a thing unbound, not owned."

"Any other *more pertinent* question then?" She asked again, but this time no-one spoke. "Nae? Then we await the mob."

Chapter 41

Thankfully, mortals can be depended on to organise a mob fairly quickly as the need arises. Probably from all the practice they'd had throughout the centuries, dealing with vampires, mad scientists and yes, even the odd blood-hungry lycan destined to be someone's fur mittens and wrap.

The sound of angry chanting filtered through to us as we waited in the utility room, accompanied fairly speedily by the sound of running feet and the crackle of hand-radios delivering the bad news to the guards on the ground. The noise was far enough away to make me think Jessica had also planned for the staged protest to occur at the main entrance, near the Thames and far enough from us to cause no problems. Also, if magic *did* start getting chucked around, having a fast-flowing river to neutralise the worst effects was no bad thing either.

Jessica nodded to Jacob, who had remained near the door with Feris the moth-balled rat. He creaked the door open, scanning around but quickly shut it as Elspeth suddenly fluttered her hand in the air, eyes closed.

"Something. Yes, definitely a sending of some sort." She spoke up, sensing whatever it was that was passing near. "I don't recognise the crafting but it's powerful. A watchdog of some kind, to keep an eye out on what's happening."

We waited for a long moment, before she opened her eyes and nodded to Jacob.

"It's gone now. Moved on, to probably check on the noise."

Jacob quickly ducked his head out of the door, looking around then turning back to us.

"All clear." He informed the company, and Jessica motioned for him and Emma to head out.

"Let's be quick, people." She commanded, as we left the room with Feris scampering ahead of us. "Rous said our furry guide would lead us tae where we need tae be, but fer now, let's get to the fifth floor. Morgan, if you would?"

Grimacing but nodding at the polite order, I lengthened my stride and reached down, scooping up the rat and imprisoning it carefully in one hand. It gave a muffled screech of protest, struggling in my hand, and I swore I could feel its ribs poking through its moth-eaten skin.

"I don't like this either furball, but accept the free taxi service and don't bite me!" I warned the little beast, as we quickly made our way towards the glass doors leading to outside. Through them, I could see scaffolding and security fences, a gate firmly locked and fitted with a punch-pad to stop idiot mortals from risking broken limbs whilst clambering where they should not.

As we neared the way out, Elspeth made a quick gesture and high up in the ceiling, the black globe of a surveillance camera made a cracking noise and spat a short rain violet sparks as her hex fried its inner workings. Jacob opened the nearest door, ushering us through one by one, with Jessica taking the lead now.

"Oh for fucks sake." I growled, as we hit the fresh air. Jacob shot me a questioning look, and I held up my hand holding our furry guide. "The bastard just pissed all over me."

My packmate snorted a laugh, and I shook my head, resisting the urge to toss the probably rabid and flea infested little shit as far as I could.

Jessica punched the code into the keypad beside the door as we huddled close by, trying to look as inconspicuous as possible to any passers-by. The lock made a satisfying clunk and the door swung open, Jessica ushering us inside quickly and pulling it shut behind her.

"Elspeth, if you would take the lead with Jacob, ah would like us tae avoid any wards or traps Knox might have prepared fer us." She told the witch, ever suspicious from a lifetime of dealing with tricky bastards. "We cannae take too long out here in case we are spotted, but we do nae want tae stumble into anything blind either."

The witch nodded, and started up the switchback stairway that the workmen had kindly provided, the sort of winding steps made up of scaffolding and rough planks that threatened splinters at any unwise grip or stubbed toes not clad in solid workboots. Jacob moved to her side, a solid shadow warding her from any potential harm but Greg was only a step behind, seeming drawn along in her wake.

I motioned for Jessica to join Felix next, and I took the tail again, doing one last check to make sure nothing was following us. I tried to sense any malignant intent, anything beyond the bubble and rush of the mortals all around us. The noise from the protest had risen as they faced the guards hiding behind their locked doors and hastily erected barriers, chants about *save our culture* and *robbing from the poor to give to the rich!* filling the air as the gathered mortals worked themselves into a fever pitch. It was reassuring not to hear screams, meaning no guard from Knox had decided to intervene.

Level after level we traversed, as the sun dipped lower towards the horizon and a chill slowly replaced the warmth of the summer's day. Snatching a moment to glance through the criss-crossed scaffolding bars, I enjoyed the chance to see London from on high, above the pall that hung over the ground that was part pollution, part mortal funk that blighted my heightened senses. Above, looking down, it was easy to see the beauty of the city. The pride that men and women had taken in the buildings they erected, the patchwork of green spaces and river walks breaking the monotony of stone and concrete, glass and metal.

It was a beauty of hard work and pride taken in each and every building raised, ever foundation set. Mortals get a lot wrong, but in this one thing, they can excel. They build for permanence, and make a lasting mark on wherever they call home.

Elspeth stopped at every new level, casting out her senses and questing for both traps and guardians waiting for us. It was possible Knox hadn't been fooled by Jessica's plans, and had rigged the platforms to break underfoot or explode in flames. Anything to stop enemies from approaching this way. But at each point, the witch shook her head and carried on upward, with Jacob stalking close behind.

We reached the top of the stairs without incident, and Jessica stepped up to join Elspeth and Jacob as they stopped by the floor to ceiling windows that comprised the fifth level's walls. Our Alpha seemed to be hunting for something as she ran her fingers over the first window frame, then the second. Finally, after three fruitless searches, something went click under her touch and the fourth window slowly swung inward.

"Ah arranged fer one of the windows tae be unlocked, with the excuse the glass had been damaged and needs replacing." She explained as we stepped inside again. "Elspeth, if you would?"

The lycan Alpha nodded toward the hall into which she'd stepped, where another black globe lurked on the ceiling. The witch twitched her hand and more sparks rained down. I was looking for it now, and saw Felix react as the power was channelled through her, her fingers curling and twisting as she mimicked the other's gesture. I pitied Danny's electricity bill or cost for replacement fittings if his daughter learned how to hex things as easily as Ellie did. Whilst she was still living at home, and the pair still argued over trivial matters. Danny had told me his daughter tended to simply storm off in a huff whenever they argued.

Now, the storming part might have a whole new meaning.

With the camera hexed, we moved quickly along the empty corridor. The central shaft of the building from the third to the fifth floor had been hollowed out and formed one massive auditorium where musical events were held, famous orchestras from around the world enchanting their audience for an hour or two, or speakers came to deliver both comic entertainment or serious diatribe to whomever was paying to listen. It was there as well, two floors down, where the security office was located. Where those guards not trying to hold off an angry mob of protestors were probably weighing up the threat level, deciding whether to call for help or just let the people outside shout and expend their energy without escalating to possible violence.

Hopefully they were distracted enough not to notice the odd camera frixting out, as any alert they raised would probably trigger Knox's personal guards as well.

Jessica led now, stalking along the floor with purpose, only stopping twice more to let Elspeth destroy more surveillance equipment. We ducked down a side corridor, moving away from where visitors would congregate, and instead started passing signs indicating *Staff Only* and *Not For Visitors* in bold red letters. Subtle enough messaging for mortals, who usually needed at least three visual warnings before realising where they were headed was against the rules or not allowed.

Feris had quietened in my hand as we moved up the side of the building, but after we entered the fifth floor he started squirming again, emitting those muffled squeaks that were probably rat equivalents of swear words. Finally, I stooped to the floor and let him free, wiping my hand on my trousers and trying not to think too much of the slight dampness that clung there.

The rat reared up and hissed at me, red eyes glaring myopically at me but I just shrugged and nodded toward where my Alpha had stopped, watching as I released our guide.

"Hey, I just provide the transport. You got a problem, take it up with the travel company." I told the creature and nodded towards my Alpha, as it scampered off through the carpet.

"Something up?" She asked quietly as the little thing bounded over the floor, scampering past her.

"No clue. It started getting all antsy as soon as we got back inside." I told her, shrugging. "Rous said it would act as guide to us this side, so am guessing it's picked up something?"

We watched as the rat headed down the corridor in front of us, then stopped at a small intersection.

"The stairs tae the sixth floor are on the left." Jessica commented, watching the rat as it jerked its head back and forth, as if searching. "All we need do is use the access code on the staff door, and Knox should be none the wiser of our approach."

"Then why is the rat going right?" Elspeth asked as Feris, true to her observation, scarpered in the other direction. It stopped just down the hall, rearing up by a door and scratching at its lacquered surface.

"Could be *she's* not upstairs yet? Maybe waiting until the ritual is done. Like resting or something?" I conjectured, as we all looked at the furiously scrabbling rat. "Maybe in some old sarcophagus or magical trunk. The sort from the movies you know you should never open, but some idiot always does?"

Elspeth rolled her eyes at my childish attempts at an explanation but she had no better suggestion to offer. Jessica pulled out her electronic pad to check the floor plans once more, then slipped it back into a pocket, turning back to face us.

"Ah am of a mind tae see what Rous's guide may have found." She told us, nodding towards a clock on the wall. "We have time, and if it is indeed some sort of periapt or vessel tae contain her until the ritual, we may be able tae stop things even quicker than ah planned."

She started forward, quickly followed by Jacob and Elspeth. Emma stepped up beside Felix, whilst I tried to ignore a niggly thought that was bouncing up and down at the back of my skull, vying for attention.

"Besides, ah have nae reason not to trust Rous at his word." She added, as she reached the door.

At that point, Felix shot me a slightly worried look, and whispered.

"Morgan, I ... I can hear those voices again…"

Trust. The Rat.

That warning in my head finally decided to make sense, and I had a moment's clear recollection. Of Agent Cormac Smith speaking to me, passing on a warning.

… *"Secondly, ah yes, Bran had a message for you. I wrote it down here… ah yes, here it is. Tell the boyo not to trust the rat. Nasty things, full of fleas and disease. Don't trust 'em."* …

I went to shout, sensing danger where there had been nothing before.

But Jessica had already reached for the door handle, and eased the portal open.

Chapter 42

Tom Thumb.

Also known as Bawd Tom, this character is no bigger than his father's thumb. He is known to have been swallowed by many creatures, to have tangled and overcome giants and was a favourite at court with Artur. He joins in the hunts with the Knights on his own steed, a mouse, and has many adventures where his diminutive size enables him to escape certain doom.

In later years, Tom was also linked to a supernatural creature used by maids and nannies to frighten young children into good behaviour.

The room beyond looked to be some sort of storage room, this time free of cleaning products. Instead, there was a clutter of wooden crates and large jars, containers with straw stuffing spilling from their insides and rolled swathes of heavy materials that looked to be old tapestries carefully stored.

I'd seen the like hanging in the Mistress's lair, displaying scenes from days of yore ... a term which normally meant armoured clad idiots riding full tilt at each other with long pointy-ended poles, or winsome maidens atop towers looking down as their brave knight beat some defenceless creature hard enough to shift it from zoology to mythology.

Jessica was already in the room, following Feris as the rat scampered through the open door. Jacob and Elspeth had fanned out on either side of our Alpha, the lycan braced for trouble whilst the witch had her eyes closed, one hand raised and glowing faintly with violet light.

"There's definitely something." She spoke, slowly turning as she scanned the room's interior. "Old, very old. Oddly familiar somehow."

"Uh, Jessica?" I called as I slid inside the room after Emma and Felix, eyes hunting for the obvious trap. "We might want to get the hell out of here. *Real quick.*"

Our Alpha looked back at me, eyebrow raised as she let one hand stray to the hilt of her sword.

"What's the problem?" She asked, as Jacob took a step back to her side, flanking her and Elspeth opened her eyes, shooting me a worried look.

"Our mutual friend, the one who hired us to clean up the escaped prisoners?" I was as ever mindful of the charm still bound to me, preventing me from naming any details about my source of all things governmental and spooky. "He gave me a warning, *not to trust the rat*. Slipped my mind until just now."

"That's a pretty fucking big slip," Jacob growled as he slid a machete free with a steely hiss. "They tell you *why* we shouldn't trust the little shit?"

I shook my head, as I nudged Felix.

"Nope, but Felix here is starting to hear voices in her head, and that seems to be linked to her powers. Which come from the Veil." I saw her nod in agreement, eyes wide. "So it can't be anything good."

It isn't.

The voice rasped from nowhere and everywhere, lilting with odd and fractured tones. But amongst them, for the weirdest reason, I thought whoever speaking sounded a little Nordic. Behind us, the door slammed shut, as the air in the room lit with that unmistakable crackle of magic, and the now familiar stench of the Veil.

It suddenly looked like Knox *hadn't* been as distracted and ambivalent to the other route we might take as Jessica had thought. Or we just hadn't been as clever as we thought we had. Circle back to my worry about things seeming too easy.

I was set to guard against intruders, and those who would stop our plans. The voice continued, and I tried to focus on its source. Beside me, Felix was turning unconsciously, head cocked as I guessed those voices in her head started to get louder. *We have lost so much, and this is our only chance to right the wrong done us. So here you will stay till the deed is done.*

Violet fire flared around both Elspeth and Felix, as either one or both witches channelled the power they shared to ward off any attack. Jacob growled, machete glinting in the fluorescent light as he bowled forward in a rush, hoping to catch the unseen guard as it spoke. Emma warded Jessica, the pair with drawn blades, whilst Greg had moved to his love's side, sword drawn and held low.

No, I don't think so.

The voice spoke once more, then a single pure and brilliant note split the air.

Then everything …

Stopped.

It was like the air around me congealed, pressing in from every direction. I was suddenly blind, sight lost in a haze of gloom that was not quite shadow, not quite light. Something in between. I couldn't breathe but after a moment's panic I realised I didn't in fact need to. Whatever it was, it gripped me tight and held me, unyielding as I strained to break free. Twitch a finger. Do anything apart from stand there like a complete fucking idiot.

Noise filtered through the murk, distant and muffled like I was underwater in a fishtank trying to listen to people talking in the other room. And I actually know what that sounds like after having my head shoved into one as a spirited attempted to drown me by the friends of a ghast I was tracking, whilst they argued with the mean bastard to get it to run instead of fighting me. Ah, fun times.

I struggled, trying to reach for the Shadow mark, the touch of the Wyld, hell even Ivory's gift just to help me break free of whatever had hold of me. But it was like fighting fog, nothing to connect with, nothing I could strike or slip free from. Just constant pressure all around, locking me in place.

The muffled voice or voices continued, too indistinct for me to understand any words or work out even how close or far away whoever was talking was. Whether I was about to get a knife somewhere particularly painful, held defenceless and blind, mute and almost deaf. My brain, given no other option, focused on the few words our attacker had spoken, the strange accent that I swear was Scandinavian or Norwegian or something. Viking maybe?

Sent to stop those who would stop our plans was fairly self-explanatory, but the fact the guard knew of whatever plans there were upgraded it from simple muscle to a partner to the crime. *We have lost so much, and this is our only chance to right the wrong done us* was slightly trickier, but it helped when I realised I'd heard a voice similar to its.

More rasping, broken and definitely way less sane, but the odd lilt was there.

Just like the fae I'd fought in the Beltane tournament. And whom I'd found out later had been the once Lord of the Twilight Court. Before Oberon sucked all the power out of him like a mosquito on a series blood drive, and used it to break his entire race and home into a virtual horror-scape.

A Twilight fae, then. One of the few who had been freed along with the convicts from Ivory and Shadow. I tried to rack my grey cells for the names of them on the list we'd prised from Oberon's reluctant grasp ... *Höðr, Vár, Urðr, Verðandi and Skuld* if I was getting that right. The last three being the Norns, the sisters who had their voices ripped out by gentle-Obie-ben to stop them using their craft. The voice had sounded masculine, so I discounted those three straight off.

That left *Höðr* and *Vár,* and to be fair, I knew so little about them I wasn't even sure I was pronouncing their names right in my head. Hodur? Vair? Either of them was a contender, and had sung some sort of hex against us. No matter that as lycans the bloody thing should have bounced off like rubber bullets used against a tank, or the fact Ellie had been channelling power when it happened. We *should* have been untouched.

I began to get a small inkling of why Oberon had thought them so dangerous, as to nuke the entire Court into oblivion.

More voices, or a voice, and I thought it was closer this time. If I could just ... what, overbalance and fall on the bastard, I could squash it. Him. Whatever, if the Twilight fae was anything like its King, it would be in pretty bad shape from its long imprisonment. I might even be able to stab it as I fell. Except I'd forgotten to draw my sword before we were attacked. Too distracted realising I'd been a complete idiot and let us walk blindly into a trap.

The voice sounded again, and then I think it choked off. Stuttered or definitely faltered in some way. Silence settled in, that imprisoning grip like a vice, unbeatable.

Next thing I know, I felt something grab me and shake me roughly. The fog started to break from my eyes and ears, shredding so that noise and light rushed back in with a confusing chaotic burst of static.

A sharp, hard pain cracked my cheek, even as my ears finally unblocked.

"For fucks sake, Morgan! Wake up!" I realised it was Greg shaking me, and it had been he who had slapped me just now. I grabbed his wrists, shaking my head to chase away the lingering fuzz.

"I'm awake! Fucks sake, Greg, stop it!" I growled, pushing him back and forcing his hands down. "Why'd you have to bloody *slap* me?"

"Uh, coz you were standing there like a complete prick, not responding to me shouting in your face and shaking you?" He answered glibly, and I bit back a growl. He was right, he'd just been trying to break whatever hold the hex had over me. But I bet the bastard hadn't touched Ellie.

"Next time, go get me a cup of coffee and a pastrami bagel. That'll do the trick a lot quicker." I told him, but the ex-police detective just shrugged, turning away.

I shook my head again, trying to clear the remaining fug from the hex. It seemed everyone else had been affected and were still in the throws of whatever had been used to hold us, given how stiff legged and statue-like their postures were. Ellie had been frozen with a hand outstretched as if to ward off a blow, whilst Felix had been in the process of ducking out of the way. Jacob had been running forward, machete swinging, whilst Emma and Jessica were a step behind, bared blades lashing out on either side at the unseen attacker.

Speaking of which. I looked around, my eyes finally alighting on the extra body in the room that hadn't been there a few moments before.

Emaciated like the fae from the Tourney, clad in rags of once finery, bearing what looked like broken manacles at its wrists and ankles with the chains removed. It had long uncut hair, silvered and tangled, but I could see rough charms marked with runes bound into the shaggy lengths. Tattoos marked its grey skin, that once again reminded me of runic script I'd seen used by the Nordic mortals except these were harsher, more savage somehow.

The biggest difference of course between this fae and the prisoner in the Tourney was the shortsword sticking out of the thing's chest. Buried to the hilt, spitting the thing through and having hit so hard that its breastbone had been dented inward.

That was definitely new, as I'd had to freeze the fucker I'd fought, then accidently exploded it after a mis-use of my Shadow gift. This one had been killed with a single blow. But by who?

I knelt, in my periphery vision seeing Greg gently start to rouse Elspeth, as expected in a much less rough manner that he had done with me. Leaning over the body, I confirmed my suspicion, finding the sword in the fae's chest the very one we'd leant our newly resurrected mortal in *Good Deeds*. The scabbard at his waist was empty so I had to assume he'd been the one to kill the creature. With a single blow.

That wasn't worrying at all.

Leaving that aside, I pushed myself up and went over to start waking my packmates from the hex. It only took a few moments, the charm obviously only lasting as long as the fae remained alive and keeping it powered. I remembered the sound, the single note I heard just before the air closed in all around me, and guessed that had been the fae.

It's voice. Oberon had destroyed the Norn's voices to stop them from using their gifts, and Felix was hearing voices in her head after gaining her Veil-linked gifts. I had a sudden and horrid certainty she was somehow linked to the Twilight fae, somehow tapping *their* power. And we were using a charm to hide us from being discovered based on those gifts of hers. Which possibly came from them. No, that wasn't a mess waiting to happen *at all*.

"What the hell was that?" Jacob growled, lowering his machete as he shook himself, shedding the last of the freezing hex. I'd dodged his reflexive slash as he'd awoken, that blade of his carving the air and almost doing me a mischief as he tried to fight an enemy now dead.

I nodded to the corpse on the floor.

"Say hi to one of the sods Oberon was keeping in his private prison, before they were broken out." I told the group as they moved in closer to look at our attacker. "I dealt with one of them at Beltane, and the bastard nearly dumped the Veil in our lap, as well as a particularly nasty tentacled horror that put me off calamari for a while, I can tell you."

"Ah remember you telling us." Jessica commented as she knelt by the body, easing the hair away from the creature's face, studying it. "Ah also remember you saying the creature was strong. That it took all three champions tae defeat it. Not this one, then."

"Nope. Reckon Greg's the hero of the hour." I nodded over to the once policeman, as he gave support to Elspeth. The hex seemed to have affected her the most, leaving the witch unsteady on her feet and leaning on him for support. "Care to give us the gory details?"

Greg shrugged, expression neutral.

"Nothing much to say. We all walked in, then that note went off. Like a whistle or something. You all froze like you were stuck to the floor, and I felt *something* try to do the same to me. But it just kind of fell away." He wrinkled his forehead, the whole experience of suffering a hex new and strange to him. No wonder he wasn't any better at explaining what had happened. "I figured as soon as the creature appeared I should play along, pretend to be frozen like you. It was walking around you all, talking to itself. Sounded imbalanced, or at least not all there in the head. Then it stopped by Elspeth and went to touch her, and I had a feeling that was a very bad thing to let happen. So I stabbed it. Only needed to do it once. It just looked surprised then fell over. After that I just started waking you lot up."

"Remind me to teach you the art of the storyteller sometime." I joked as I reached down and very carefully, eased the sword out of the fae's body. Black blood, rather than the normal silver, coated the blade but I wiped most of it off on the thing's ragged clothing before handing it over. "Note to self, you only need to stick the pointy end into your opponent a little bit to stop them. Shoving it all the way through risks trapping the weapon in your opponent and leaving you defenceless against the next opponent. Plus its always icky having to pull it free afterwards, what with all the blood and gore."

"Gee, thanks, sensei." Greg quipped and I shot him a hard look. Back from the dead he might be, with unnatural strength and the ability to throw off hexes, but he was still new to all this and was in *no* position to throw me lip when I was trying to help. He accepted the sword, flicking off the last of the black blood and sliding it into its sheath in one fluid motion and without looking.

The man was definitely learning, as I'd seen untrained idiots try that move before and lose a thumb.

"Anyone seen that fucking rat?" Felix snarled, shivering slightly from the aftereffects of the hex. I cast about, but the room was a maze of boxes and clutter, perfect to hide something so small as the rodent. I tried to smell for it, but again there was a host of scents to follow in the air let alone the masking stench of the Veil so recently channelled. No matter how old and smelly the rat had been, it was hidden from even a lycan's senses just this moment.

"Bastard is probably long gone," I growled, looking over at Jessica. "I think it's fair to say Rous sold us out, as I can't imagine his little minion decided to lead us astray all on its lonesome."

"As much as it pains me, ah cannot fault your logic, Morgan." She replied, a hard scowl furrowing her normally untroubled expression. "Ah had thought ah bargained with the rulers of the Lows fairly, but it would seem their grudge against us, and you in particular, has blighted their judgement. It will be something ah shall address when we next speak."

"Can I be a fly on the wall for *that* conversation?" I quipped but she shook her head.

"That is fer later. We have an appointment tae keep, that this one was keen tae make sure we were late fer." She looked down on the dead fae for a moment, then turned away. "How long were we imprisoned?"

There was no clock in the room, so I dragged out my phone and checked the display.

8.23.

"Shit, we've only got seventeen minutes before the alignment." I growled, realising we'd been held longer than twenty minutes despite Greg's explanation. I guess the fae had taken longer to get to Elspeth than it had at first sounded. Maybe. "We need to hustle."

"Agreed. Knox may know his guard is slain, so there is nae point us delaying further." Jessica turned on her heel, stalking out of the room and back the way we'd come. Jacob and Emma let Greg and Elspeth go ahead, Felix following quickly behind before they went through the door.

I cast one last look at the dead fae, slain long after his kin had lost their lives, fallen so far from his own ruined Court and realm. The poison from the silver and cold iron was already working its way through his corpse, organic matter flaking away into dust so that soon there would be nothing left of the creature except its rags and a few scattered shreds of ruin. In one way, it was a true tragedy that this was where his story ended.

On the other hand, the idiot had brought it on himself by messing with us. So for that, the fucker deserved what he got.

With that thought, I pulled the door shut behind me, and followed my pack and friends.

Chapter 43

We took the staff staircase up to the sixth floor, Jessica using the code to get us through the final checkpoint. No wards had been set to guard the way, so we had to assume Knox had relied fully on the Twilight fae to deal with anything that got all the way to the fifth floor without expending any more energy on protection.

His mistake.

We fanned out on the final floor, Emma and Jacob taking either side with weapons held ready in their hands as Elspeth held up the vial of glowing crystals. They hovered within the glass jar, batting against the thin wall in one direction only, pointing us to the left. The Weston Roof Pavilion according to the floor plans.

Using hand signals only now, Jessica sent us forward, lycan stalking silently over the thick carpet. The staff area where drinks and food were brought up was wide enough to allow the two pack enforcers to stand shoulder to shoulder, blocking anything we might face from coming at those of our company not built for combat. Jessica and I brought up the rear whilst Greg stuck close to the centre and Elspeth's side.

We moved quickly, knowing time was trickling away, our goal ahead. If we could surprise Knox, get at least one of the Arthurian stones away from his ritual then we'd short circuit the whole thing. If need be, we could probably throw one of the sodding things out of the glass window and into the Thames from here, thoroughly ruining his plans. If not, well there was always plan B.

Jacob listened at the door leading to the next room, the Pavilion, and nodded back our way, holding up one finger to his lips. Then he made a circle with his hand and pointed back down where we had come from. So only one person talking, but he could sense others like the bastard from below, just he wasn't sure how many. I recalled the prison list, and held up four fingers since that was the number of Twilight fae I knew were free and hadn't already been dealt with. The Norn sisters plus one more.

Jessica motioned for us to go on the count of three, with Emma and Jacob to divide left and right as she stepped up to take centre. Elspeth looked like she was going to argue as the Alpha brushed past her, but Greg drew her to one side and let the lycan through. The witch threw him an irritated look, but he just nodded to Felix, reminding her the pair were linked. Any danger she drew, she's most likely pull the younger mortal in with her. At that, Elspeth's expression softened and she reached up to cup Greg's face in an intimate gesture by way of apology.

Jessica looked around the six of us, and we all nodded. I drew my swords, settling their familiar weight in my hands.

Her fingers came up, counting down.

Three.

Two.

One.

And in we went.

Chapter 44

Tristan.

A Knight to stand toe to toe with Lancelot, the pair fighting to a stand-still after a prophecy from Merlin, engaging in the greatest duel in living history. He is linked with Isolde, loving her from a young age, but his uncle, King Mark, proves jealous and seeks the maiden's hand himself to spite the younger Knight.

Through trial and danger, Tristan wins through to prove his love to Isolde and the pair of them seek a life together – yet King Mark is unable to leave them be, and ends their love by mortally wounding Tristan whilst he is distracted.

The Pavilion was a wide, long room, with floor to ceiling windows on three sides and glass overhead to give the impression of being open to the air. It normally would have had long tables and chairs laid out, or at least places for mortals to stand and sip their drinks whilst listening to whatever speaker had been hired that evening, or to look at whatever expensive display had been arranged for their entertainment.

This evening, the décor was decidedly different.

The fading rays of sunlight speared in through the glass windows, unobstructed by any furniture. Tall candelabras of dark iron stood at the corners of the room and at intervals along the centre in a specific pattern to form a circle and cross bisecting the floor space. A large mat had been set under these, covering the carpet. Woven into the material so as to be unbreakable, was one large complicated summoning circle of silvered thread, complete with intricate runes surrounding its rim. Four other smaller circles had been set around the main one, these no more than a couple of feet wide.

Sat within the largest circle and directly beneath the open sky where someone had removed panels from the ceiling to let in the fresh air, were two large hewn stones. Massive in size, they must have weighed six or seven hundred pounds in weight at the very least, and together they formed a rough anvil shape of overlarge proportions, bisected by a break near the sharp point. Age had weathered their surfaces, pitting them with rain and frost, weathering them from harsh winds, but it was still possible to see carven into their sides were numerous faces, staring out with blank cold eyes. Mouths silent yet agape, either in song or lamentation.

And atop this lay a still, motionless figure.

Clad in a simple shift of white cotton, the sort of thing you'd expect to see in a period drama or play, worn by a young lady of reasonable means. The figure wore no slippers or shoes, and her skin that could be seen was pale, almost marble. Blonde hair had been combed carefully to fall down from her head and cover the stone underneath, tresses be-ribboned glowing in the fading sunlight with the only life and warmth about the figure. Her features were composed, her eyes closed, and her lips were just as pale and bloodless as the rest of her. No breath stirred her chest, no movement of eye to show that she simply slept.

This was Knox's *golem*, his vessel for Morgana.

The man himself had his back to us as we entered the room, with the stones between us and him, bent down and adjusting something on the floor. He was clad in an old coat of dark material, stiff collared and cut to fall mid-thigh. Again, of a design that had gone out of regular fashion hundreds of years ago. He was humming to himself, a broken rhyme in his native Scot's tongue that rose and fell in pitch as he worked.

Apart from the stitched-together corpse on the stones and Knox, the room seemed empty. No other guards to be seen, no Twilight fae or Real cronies to challenge us. The air however stank of magic, the reek of the Veil intertwining the crackle of lightning and pervading thunder. Elspeth closed her eyes for a moment, reaching out with her senses, and held up a hand as we entered, obviously sensing *something* but so unsure of what that she shook her head, unable to define what we faced.

Jessica nodded, accepting we were going in blind, and pointed her sword to the stones and body. Either was our objective, removing them from the circle and the ritual would end Knox's madness. Time was running out, as the light from outside dimmed further, and evening darkened the sky overhead. Soon the planets would be visible, pinpricks of brightness in the velvet embrace of space, aligned in a way not seen for hundreds of years.

Granting a grief-stricken mortal this chance to break the Accords and do something utterly monstrous.

Not on our watch.

The carpet helped, muffling our footsteps as we approached. But Knox must have set some wards in place, an alert for any surprises, since we haven't even got within five feet of the summoning circle when it erupted into violet-grey flames, blazing with power.

Spinning, his eye locked on us as his face crumpled with anger and frustration. The burn marks I'd caused him when I set fire to the remains of his daughter were still hidden under tight fitting gloves, but his single eye narrowed with rage as he caught sight of me amongst the group.

"I told you! Leave us alone!" He raged, leaping with more energy than a mortal several centuries old should have, and entered the circle. The fires melted away from him, most likely keyed to his nature so as not to burn him. For the rest of us they offered a very painful warding. I remembered the fires in Gary Weatherby's boathouse, and didn't fancy tangling with whatever the one who had taught him could pull off. "Just leave us alone!"

"We cannae do that." Jessica told him sternly, as we halted our approach. "What you seek tae do is wrong. It is not yer daughter you are summoning, but a spirit of ancient cunning and dark desire, hellbent on revenge and destruction. You have been *used*, Robert Knox, though you nae will accept it. So we must stop you, else more lives will be lost, more pain done in the name of yer insanity and guilt."

"No!" He bellowed, shaking his head from behind the circle of roaring flames. "It is my Emily Rose, my sweet Emie. She calls to me, and I *will* not let her die this time. Not again! Help me!"

Wind assaulted us at his summons, battering us back from the circle as we struggled to remain upright. The flames surrounding Knox and his Frankenstein vessel roared up, and the air blurred like oil on water as some sort of fog seemed to rise from nowhere to writhe and knit the air before us.

"Something's in there!" Elspeth shouted over the roaring gale, as we prepared for whatever had come at his call. "He won't be able to unleash the

Harrowing on us whilst he's in that circle and it's active, so we need to keep him there!"

"And yet somehow get the bloody stones out of there too?" I growled, as I circled to ward her and Felix. Greg had moved to stand before her as well, sword drawn and still discoloured with the fae's blood along it's tip. "Anyone see a small flaw in that plan?"

Before Jessica could tell me to quit whining, the fog blurred and lashed forward. A spear blade darted out, shivering through the air with a whining cry, slashing first at Emma and then Jessica. Both lycan hammered the strikes aside with their own weapons, as Jacob charged forward but the spear reversed with inhuman skill, its end fitted with *another* spearhead which almost spitted him as he hurled himself aside from the counterstrike.

The spear blurred, slamming blows to the left and right, as a figure slowly coalesced amongst the fog. Tall, slim like the immortal we'd faced downstairs but this one was clad in ornate leather and burnished bronze armour. Its face was free of helm, braided white-blonde hair adorned with curved white feathers knit amongst the locks. A tattoo, blood red in colour, marked the ridge side of the face, covering one eye, cheek and forehead. This branched like a tree or trident, so that her one eye peered from behind this, bisected by the prongs.

"Slayer of my kin!" The fae hissed as she brought the twin-headed spear round in a tight arc. "Know that you face Vàr now, the Keeper of Vows. You may have slain my brother, Höðr, but pass me you shall not!"

The fae levelled her spearpoint at Greg, expression tightening in a vicious scowl.

"You! You bear his blood on your blade. Your death shall be truly excruciating."

Greg shrugged, raising his sword.

"You're a bit late to the party, ma'am." He quipped with far too much jollity for a mortal still struggling with the unreality of his situation. "I died once already, had my heart pulverised. Try to top that."

"Oh, for fucks sake, enough with the quips!" Emma snarled, shaking her head as the familiar crackling and disconcerting noises filled the air. She

Changed, her blonde shaggy mane whipping in the wind as she snarled through a mouthful of vicious teeth. "One of them is bad enough. Did we have to get another?"

"Emma, Jacob, with me." Jessica commanded, as the three lycan squared off with the Twilight fae. Jacob rolled his shoulders and Changed as well, his darker fur spiking out and great jaws parting with a snarl of anticipation. "Morgan, you and the others. *Get the bloody stones!*"

"You. Shall. Not. Pass!" The fae replied, slamming her spear down so that one point struck through the carpet. The fog behind her thickened, reforming into three … five … six replicas of her who now stood shoulder to shoulder. All armed with long spears, forming a wall across the room.

"New plan! Kick this thing's arse!" I snarled as a blade shivered through the air to try to carve me in two. The images of the fae reacted as if they were alive and of their own mind, not mirroring the original's movements but instead attacking of their own volition. Which was a pain as they tried to pair off against each one of us, meaning Felix and Elspeth were suddenly under threat.

"Oh no you don't!" I snarled as one fae tried to push past me and attack the younger of the two. I hammered its spear back even as I saw a second weapon striking low to gut me. Instead, I summoned the Ivory mark, feeling armour thicken around me in a heartbeat. Grinning, even knowing they wouldn't see my expression, I knocked the spear aside with a casual flick of my backhand.

Their eyes, dark orbs pulsing with violet energy, widened as they saw me switch up to my Ivory Errant persona, both snarling with renewed fury.

"Spawn of Ivory! Betrayer! Kin-slayer!" They both cried, shrieking with one voice that made the glass around us vibrate in its casing. "Die!"

"Rather not!" I snarled back, barrelling forward and hacking at them with my swords. And then I realised my mistake, as not one or even both of the fae, but all seven leapt at me, spears lashing like serpents to strike me.

I desperately parried two strikes, rolling under a third. Searing pain hammered into my leg as one spear found a way past the armour and drew blood. But that left three spear points set to turn me into the dumbest kebab ever.

Thankfully I wasn't alone. Jessica turned aside one blow with her sabre, the sword licking out with delicate skill learned from hundreds of years of practice. Jacob was less refined, barrelling into the blows and bashing them away with his machete, with Emma a step behind to harry the fae as they staggered off balance.

"Way to piss them off, dumb ass!" Jacob snarled at me as I hopped back, feeling the pain of my wound start to numb and fade as it knit together. Just as long as the bastard Twilight fae didn't use any wolfsbane, I was ok.

"Got their attention, didn't I?" I griped, testing my leg and finding it ok to put weight on. "Now how about we finish this?"

"Back off!" It was Felix, calling out behind us as the fae circled amongst the mist, fading from sight and obviously planning to strike from the protective veil. "I got this!"

I clocked a look from Jessica, and shrugged. The young witch had agreed to stay out of the fighting, but the enemy wasn't exactly playing fair and Felix was still stood safely behind us. What was there to lose?

We backed up a step, warding the witch and witchling. Elspeth had her hand on Felix's shoulder, leaning in close and giving her instructions, to which she nodded and raised her hands.

Violet grey fire erupted around her fingers, writhing in a frenzy of destructive power. Felix gave an odd-sounding cry, modulating her voice to strike a single note that quivered in the air but then gained strength.

From within the churning mists, something reacted. Something flinched, as if shocked.

"How is this? You are not one of us!" Vàr cried out from where she and her mirror images hid. "You, child! Stop!"

"No one calls me child." Felix snarled, breaking the tune for a moment and thrust out her hands.

Power hammered out, lashing the churning fog and lighting it with flashes of thunder and explosive flame. Vàr gave a high pitched scream, the six other forms convulsing in the grip of the attack as the fire jumped from one to the next. Each mirror image exploded in a burst of sparks and fury, until one figure remained. The Twilight fae writhed in the grip of Felix's attack but then seemed to gather herself, setting her spear to the floor and leaning into the power hammering at her.

"You will not stop me, child!" The fae yelled, as her own power thickened around her, attempting to push Felix back and shred her onslaught. I winced, guessing what was coming, what happened when you didn't listen to a young woman like my friend.

"I told you, don't call me *child*!" She screamed and the fire around her hands roared out like dragon flame. The mist was shattered, shredded in an instant, and Vàr was picked up and bound in the inferno. The fae bucked and writhed, her spear falling from her hands to clatter on the carpet as she screamed out her own fury.

In the next breath, Felix threw all the remaining flames around her hands forward like she was shoving against something heavy. Vàr gave a final cry, then her body was shoved out through the glass window in a splintering crash of broken panes, arcing out over the Thames in a trail of fire and fury. Like a comet, she roared over the turbulent waters before dropping into their dark depths, lost from sight.

For a moment, the roar of the flames surrounding the summoning circle was the only sound in the room. That and the rush of air in through the broken window. We all turned to look at Felix, as she slowly lowered her hand.

"What?" She asked to our slightly bemused faces. "I *told* her not to call me a child. It pisses me right off, ok?"

Jacob looked across at me, eyebrow cocked as his jaws worked to frame the question.

"You *sure* she's just a mortal?" He growled quietly. "No chance one of her ancestors mixed things up with, oh, I don't know, one of the Furies?"

"Had bloody har." Felix snipped back at him, eyes narrowed. "Don't make me light a fire under your furry ass. Aren't we on a deadline or something?"

"Fury. Definitely." I whispered to him, then nodded. "Ellie, think you're up?"

We approached the summoning circle again, Elspeth leading Felix this time as the other hung a step back, obviously aware just how dangerous things were right now. The witch stopped just short of the fire, studying the construction of the barrier we faced. Inside the flames, Knox stood by the stones and the body he had built from harvested mortal parts, eyeing her warily.

"This is a piece of work, and then some." The witch commented as she knelt down to study the markings. "He's used four different types of seals, all from different cultures and history. There's the main one, I think, which are in Hebrew, with gothic German and Nordic runes added to bolster and increase the strength of the working. And then this other one, it has to be fae of some description but I don't recognise the language so I assume from these Twilight ones you mentioned Morgan. I've never seen anyone combine this many rituals into one, let alone use it for a warding."

"You'll never break through!" Knox mocked, as he stood by the corpse on the stones. "Go home, just leave us in peace!"

"Can you undo what he's done?" Jessica asked, coming to stand beside the witch. "Is he right?"

"It's not that simple." Elspeth replied, pushing herself up from her inspection. "This circle? He's channelling life energy into it, from all those sources I guess he had stored around London, maybe even further afield. You normally only need a little bit of magic to seal the circle, then it is self-sustaining. What's he's rigged here? It's like he's strapped a ton of C4 to a crate of dynamite and then doused the whole thing in petrol and planted it atop a factory full of fireworks. If I try to unpick it and get it wrong, it could blow up this entire building, vaporising everything in its blast radius. Us included."

"So, uh, don't get it wrong?" I helpfully suggested, receiving a withering look from her. "Oh and Jacob, no defusing this bomb, ok?"

Jacob snorted as he bent to pick up the Twilight fae's fallen spear.

"Worked didn't it? Museum's still standing?" He snarled his response, referencing his inventive way of disarming the deep sea mine Terrigyle had supplied the Mistress with, to enact her revenge on the Ivory Court. Reaching in and ripping out the clockwork mechanism *had* worked, but I'd felt like I needed a new pair of boxers for a little while afterwards.

Weighing the carved spear in one hand, the lycan enforcer then stepped over and held out the weapon to, of all people, Felix.

"Here. It's yours." He told her, distracting her from watching Elspeth as she peered at the summoning circle again.

"Uh, why?" She asked, eyeing the long length of intricately decorated haft and the wicked twin spearheads dubiously. Felix barely topped five foot eight, whilst the warrioress she had set fire to and shot out the window like a cannonball had been closer to seven. And the spear had been crafted with her in mind.

"Weapon of the vanquished, winner takes all, yada yada." I spoke up before Jacob could explain. "You kicked her butt, so you get her belongings. It's an old rule but still valid. Plus, it *is* a pretty neat weapon."

Seeing me nod encouragingly, she gingerly accepted the spear from Jacob. Finding that it weighed little, she set one spearhead to the floor, leaning on it like a staff.

"What do you think?" She asked me, and I shot her a grin.

"In about twenty years' time when you've grown into it, you'll be bad-ass." I told her, receiving another well-earned poked-out tongue.

"Children. I am *trying* not to blow us all up here." Elspeth spoke over her shoulder, somehow managing to shoot us a withering look even though she was facing in the opposite direction. "Now, there is something I can try …"

Even as she spoke, the fires running around the circle suddenly guttered, dying down to run as glittering rings of script and lines around the warding, then finally even these winked out. The roar of the flames was hushed, silence settling in as the six of us looked at Elspeth.

Within the circle, Knox stood frozen, stock-still beside the body on the stones. His lone eye was fixed on us, the discoloured glass hiding his other dark under the ever-encroaching shade of dusk.

I did a quick pat-down, checking to make sure everything was in place, then slapped the witch on the shoulder as I grinned.

"Thanks for not blowing us up!" I told her happily but stopped as she turned slowly to face me. Her expression was grave, her eyes wide.

"That … that wasn't me." She told us, voice suddenly fearful. "I didn't even …"

And within the circle, the corpse suddenly sat up.

Chapter 45

"Oh shit." I voiced my eloquence in that moment.

The corpse, for that was what it had been up until a moment ago, swung its legs down and laid its hands in its lap. That wealth of golden hair fell over its face for a moment, before it was brushed back with a simple gesture as the young girl looked across at us.

"My Emmie." Knox crooned, his hand settling on her shoulder, expression losing any trace of fear, anything but loving adoration and the simple relief that his wish had come to pass.

"Nae so. Knox. That is Morgana." Jessica answered, there being no reason not to say her name now.

The girl shook her head, stepping down from the stones gently, wobbling slightly like a colt trying to stand for the first time. Her face was round, young and untouched by any sign of fear or anger, her eyes wide and a deep, mortal brown.

"I fear you have me mistaken. I am Emily Rose Knox, and this is my father, Robert Knox." She told us with simple innocence, a small smile touching her lips as she entwined her fingers with her father's as they rested on her shoulder. "I must say I am confused as to your presence here, and your outlandish attire, but I know not who this other you name is …"

"Oh, just cut it out." The lycan Alpha over-rode her, setting her sabre's point down so that it rested against the carpet. Behind, Emma let herself Change back into her mortal form, whilst the rest of us eyed the child warily. "If yer foolish enough tae think we rely upon only our eyes tae tell us the truth, then yer long imprisonment has truly made you senile."

Knox bristled, anger breaking the unnatural calm suffusing his face but the child shook her head and patted his hand, settling him back once more to silence. Instead, she faced Jessica, expression confused.

"Your manners are most aggressive towards me, but I have done you no wrong. What ill do you think I have done you, to warrant such?" She enquired, looking across from one to the next of us. "What have I done to any of you, to bear me such anger? Pray tell me, so I might set things right and make amends. So I and my father may leave in peace this most odd place."

I'll give her this, the child had me wondering. Was it *actually* possible, after everything that Knox had done, that I'd uncovered and been dragged through … that he'd actually managed to resurrect his dead daughter's spirit instead of Morgana? Could an immortal fae have fucked up *that* badly?

But Jessica was unconvinced.

"Take one more step forward. One step closer tae any of those that stand with me and ah shall test whether yer *father's* skills keep yer head attached tae those shoulders after a well-placed blow." She told the child, grip tightening on the sabre's grip so that the leather creaked. "If you want tae know yer first mistake, you've been speaking modern day English for the past few moments. A language the child's spirit would nae know tae speak when so recently returned tae life."

The moment held, the child looking up at Jessica, my Alpha standing stock still, almost like an old samurai warrior with sword drawn and facing its enemy. Before the music suddenly turns dramatic and then there is blood and screams, and lopped off limbs falling all around.

Then the child's eyes slowly bled warmth, from chestnut hazel brown to deepest darkest shade. Bottomless pits, much like those I faced every time I visited the Court of Shadow. Faint black veins traced across the untouched and smooth skin of the child's face, and her lips bled colour until they had the blue blush of oxygen deprivation.

She smiled, a wicked and evil thing on one so young and innocent-looking, and performed a little twirl in mockery.

"Fine. Ruin my fun." Morgana spoke, then pushed back her golden hair to look at us with those black as shade eyes of hers. "Was that my only mistake? For the record since I have you all here."

It was her voice, from the prison cell, dripping with inhuman tones and an acidic lash that no mortal could ever utter. There was mockery in every word, the tell of a creature that thought itself so far above you that it found the fact you were even speaking to it almost beyond belief. The arrogance of the immortal, tempered and sharpened from the long centuries of no-one setting them straight.

I realised I was almost growling, the hair on the back of my neck standing up in place of hackles, as I felt her utter contempt for us. I could feel my hands tightening on my sword hilts, my muscles burning with the desire to lash out, wipe that smug smile from her face.

And then her eyes fell on me. Just for a moment, before she switched back to my Alpha, but it was enough. In those dark orbs, I read the fact she knew *exactly* how I was feeling, what I was thinking, and it mattered not a whit to her. Not a single flicker of worry … in fact, the bloody creature seemed to enjoy knowing my fury at her.

Knowing that, I strangled the rage from Shadow, Ivory and Wyld melded inside me, breathing slowly in and out to calm myself. I wasn't going to be baited, not by her.

"Ah *did* say yer first mistake." Jessica reminded Morgana, standing cool and calm. At ease as she faced the reborn immortal. "Yer should have reacted far worse seeing mah packmates transformed, as any poor mortal might instead of ignoring a woman or man with a wolf's head. Just saying."

Then she nodded to Knox.

"And finally, yer *father*. You've hexed him or something, but the last two times Morgan here tangled with him, he released the Harrowing with nae a moment's thought. Let alone the fact he's proven tae use *hexen-wolfen* belts tae transform like those idiot students he messed with." Jessica smiled her toothy smile, as Morgana looked over at the mortal beside her. "If you *were* simply his child reborn, ah would have expected tae have faced either him transformed in tae something suited tae protecting you, or that other abomination the moment we showed. Nae matter our witch here saying anything tae the contrary. Instead he's standing there like some besotted fool, probably not even fully aware of what we say here."

Morgana cocked her head, a truly creepy gesture that had so much of the child about it. Then she smiled crookedly, shrugging her shoulders.

"You can't blame a girl for wanting some fun to pass the time. It's been so *boring* waiting for you all to arrive." She sighed, raising one hand to her brow as feeling wearied, before focusing back on us with that shark smile. As comprehension dawned amongst us. "Oh my dears, I am sorry but you were *never* going to get here in time to stop Robert Knox completing the ritual. I just told your little packmate that 'fact' about the alignment to give my pet the time to finish the ritual and bind me to my new body. I've been lying here waiting on your arrival for *hours.*"

I ground my teeth as Cormac Smith's doubts came back to bite me in the ass. Hard. I'd trusted what Morgana told me to be the truth, when instead she'd just used me. Fed me the right information to allow her to know exactly when we'd show.

Gods, I was an idiot.

I felt the rage of Wyld surge inside me, fighting to break free. I bit down hard, tasting blood, trying to control the urge to step forward and attempt to do damage to that smug smiling immortal. *Attempt*, as I was well aware of just who we faced.

"So why bring us here. What is this?" Jessica asked, nodding to the trappings, the ritual laid out to convince us we'd had a chance to stop this thing being reborn. "Why the farce?"

Morgana settled back onto the stone anvil on which she had been summoned, wearing that smug smile as she watched us. The heroes sent to confound the villain, standing like idiots when they found out they'd been duped.

"Why? Oh it's simple really. I wanted you all gathered before me to see that *you lost*." She replied, voice dripping acid as I'd heard before, when she delivered her message to Madb in the cell. "Despite all your attempts to block my puppet, frustrate my minions and generally spoil plans that I have laid carefully for longer than you have drawn breath, *I won*. I have no desire to fight you. I have far better uses for my time now that I have a body once more. But I did want you to know this, so you can move on. Leave me be, and do the pitiful things that you feel are important. They are no consequence to me now."

"You. You want justice?" She asked, looking across at Jacob. "I see the pain you struggle to bury inside you, the loss of one you loved so raw. I see the truth that you blame me and my puppet for this. Well then, I am feeling magnanimous and so … I give you justice."

Morgana turned to Knox, the mortal obeying some unspoken command and kneeling down beside her so they were almost face to face. Before any of us could act, could say anything, stop her or whatever, Morgana cupped the other's face. She stared into his eyes, pulling him close.

"My Emie." Knox crooned but Morgana shook her head.

"No, not so. I think it is passed time you saw the truth." The fae told him, and power flared around her fingers. "Robert Knox, behold what you have wrought."

Knox writhed in the grip of whatever she was doing to him, spasming for a moment before calming. But then his lone eye grew wide, expression changing from its happy slackness to true and utter horror.

"What… what are you?!" He cried, trying to jerk free from her grasp. "You aren't my Emily! What… oh god, what are you?"

Knox then stared in horror down at himself, ripping off his jacket in a frenzy as Morgana held him close. His head jerked as he looked down at the discoloured skin of his arms, the faint marks where scars had formed from his surgeries. The different pigments of his own flesh. Stolen from others.

"Oh god!" He howled, a sound wretched and agonised. "The children! What I did to … what I took … Oh god, their cries are in my head, their screams! I can *feel* them in me!"

"You took their lives, their energy. Even their flesh." Morgana told him, her voice turning harsh and unforgiving. "You cut them apart, ignoring their pleas to stop, to set them free. You destroyed hundreds of lives, mortal, and drained the lives of many, many more. You are an abomination, a blight upon your fellow man."

"You made me!" He screamed, hands reaching up to wrench at the grasp she had him in, struggling to break free. "*You* were in my head, whispering to me. Telling me things. You made me do it all!"

"I? I did nothing but answer your wishes." She replied grimly. "Did you not beg me to aid you, to show you what you needed to do. No matter the cost? Am I to blame, when it was your hands that cut their flesh, your hands that held them down and did *unspeakable* things to them? Children, young women, men cut off before their prime. You reaped a heavy harvest, mortal, to salve your own guilt."

"No! It was you!" He screamed, and I caught sight of the now familiar grey fog rising from his skin, boiling from his eye. Knox was unleashing the horror he held inside, something even Morgana was wise to be wary of. "You are to blame for everything! God above, hear my prayer and help me kill this vile thing!"

"Oh no. I'm sorry but *I'm* the only God here, and I wish otherwise." Morgana told him primly, and did something, another surge of power. The touch of the Harrowing suddenly cut off, its fire dimming as Knox writhed under the lash of her touch. "As you have stolen from others, shall I now take from you. You asked God to be rid of this vile thing? I grant your desire, Robert Knox."

Morgana leant in close, and her mouth opened as if she was going to take a bite from him. But her jaw extended, dropping lower than any mortal could do without dislocation and severe pain. From that maw, a single tone sounded, grim and final as the tolling of death's bell.

Energy burst from Knox like gas escaping a burst balloon, golden fire burning from both his healthy eye and the one hidden, from his skin and under his clothes. It writhed in the air between them, surging out of the mortal and down into the mouth of Morgana as she swallowed all the life energy he had stolen over the centuries.

Elspeth gave a sickened cry, unable to watch the grotesque scene playing out before us, and Greg at some unspoken sign from her stepped forward as if to try to stop it. But Morgana gave a negligent wave of her free hand and golden fire burst around the circle, forcing him back.

Knox writhed, his body thinning and aging as the life was drained from him in a torrent. He managed to twist his head, that one eye falling on us beyond the circle, and he groaned.

"... *Oh god ... H...heell..p ... me!*" He hissed as the skin on his face decayed and peeled away, the flesh underneath blackening and rotting. "*God ...fooorrr...ggive ... mee...*"

Flesh and muscle withered and decayed like some B movie horror special effect, as Felix made retching noises behind me. Knox finally stopped writhing, as his internal organs collapsed and Morgana was left cradling a wretched skull and withered skeleton beneath. This she tossed out of the circle, to land in a crumpled heap at Jacob's feet.

So ended Robert Knox, once eminent physician, member of OPS and later a thoroughly twisted and corrupt mortal who had murdered countless victims and stolen the life from even more to fuel his guilt and desire to right a wrong done in his own mortal lifetime.

He still didn't deserve to die like that.

"There you are. Justice is done." The fae commented with a shark-toothed smile. "The mortal who inflicted so much suffering is dealt with. Your *case* can be closed, and off you trott to salvage whatever good you can from the damage he has done. I believe there are Harrowed still to be dealt with, as well his victims laid to rest. Lies to tell their families, to appease their sorrow. Mortal stupidity like that. So run along."

"Ah think nae." Jessica told her, expression hard from watching the fate of Knox.

"Nae? No? Didn't you hear me?" Morgana asked, wiping her hands on her white dress and leaving smears of Knox's remains down the material. "You *lost*. You cannot remove the stones or take down the mortal puppet I used to bring me over, to stop a ritual that has already been done. Your plan is in ruins, dear one."

She laughed sharply, the sound cutting over the sound of the wind coming in through the broken window.

"Oh yes, I knew what you planned. I was there, as you laid things out so eloquently before your rush to reach to me." She grinned and gestured with one hand. From the shadows of the room, a small figure slunk to breach the fiery summoning circle and come to rest by her feet. Moth-eaten, fur sticky and rank, the rat peered at us with its mad red eyes.

"You are acquainted with my construct, I believe? I crafted it to keep an eye on those silly rulers of London Lower." Morgana admitted, reaching down to stroke the creature. "With Rous so badly diminished, it was easy to slip it in amongst the other rodents that petty creature uses to make himself whole. Then I simply whispered in his head, binding him to me. You thought you had made a deal with him for safe passage, to have a guide to lead you to me."

The fae laughed cruelly.

"Instead you accepted my creature without even verifying it's nature, and spoke in its presence without thought."

My skin crawled as I remembered carrying the bastard up the floors of the building, how it had pissed on me before leading us into the trap. I hadn't felt a thing wrong whilst holding it, not even a whisper to think it was anything other than an old and manky rat with incontinent issues.

"So you see, I knew your plan and what you intended. The mortal has been punished, and the ritual you sought to stop is complete. I am here, bound to this body as if it were the one I was formed with." Morgana ran her hands down the young girl's body, tracing it's gentle curves before raising up her hands like a supplicant. "So there is nothing more for you to do here. Simply ... leave."

"There is one action ah believe ah can still take. One ah voiced with my colleagues and friends, tae stop you." Jessica replied calmly, as she raised her sword from the carpet. "Elspeth, have ah given you enough time tae decipher the circle? Ah grow weary of yapping with this deviant."

"More than enough time." The witch replied grimly, as purple grey fire erupted around her hands, and outlined Felix was well.

"Then let's get this done." My Alpha commanded, grinning wolfishly.

"Oh *really*." Morgana shook her head sadly, then gestured with her slim young hands. "So be it."

Raw power hammered down into the room, a raw torrent of might that hit us like a tsunami. Violet fire, reeking of the Veil and so fierce it burned the air around us, exploded about Elspeth and Felix, hurling them back across the room as they screamed under the fiery onslaught.

Greg threw himself forward, sword seeking to spit Morgana, but she waved one hand and deepest shadow leapt at him. It wrapped all about him, encasing him in inky shade, freezing him to the floor like some obsidian statue. Mouth open in a snarl, sword arcing out to break the summoning circle and hew at the immortal.

Tentacles, much like the monstrous appendages which assaulted the Champions in the Beltane Tournament, burst from rents in mid-air. These lashed out at those of us still standing. Jessica ducked and rolled from the first questing limb, but it suddenly split, branching into leaner spiked whips that now ended in gaping fanged maws. Emma and Jacob hewed at their own attackers, but Jessica disappeared under a mass of biting, snapping fury as the tentacles bowled over her.

Howls erupted from under the boiling mass as our Alpha Changed, flesh and gore shredding the air around her as she surged upright, bits of tentacle and gouts of purple gore splashing all around. No mere calamari was going to stop a lycan Alpha. Eyes fixed on Morgana, jaws set in a thunderous snarl, she paced toward the summoning circle, sabre carving anything that came at her to ruin.

Yet Morgana faced her, unperturbed. Calm.

Like a hydra, the stumps that Jessica had hewed through sprouted multiple heads, gnashing teeth and vicious spikes filling the space around the Alpha. Hidden amongst these, whiplike spears darted in as she hewed at the fresh onslaught. Her snarls turned pained as these pierced her through, binding her as she snapped and chewed at those she could reach. But the tentacles writhed and boiled over her, sending her sabre crashing to the floor as she was lost from sight under the onslaught.

Blood, scarlet and thick, soon spilled out to mix with the purple gore staining the carpet.

Massive coils writhed from the rents in the air, burying Emma in the next breath and forcing Jacob back as his wolfshead ripped at unnatural flesh and machete spattered purple blood all over the carpet until he too vanished from sight.

I faced Morgana alone, seeing my packmates and Alpha negated in a heartbeat, my friends set ablaze and lost from sight. Calling on Shadow and Ivory, I encased myself in the mystical plate armour and sheathed my swords in steaming cold.

The reborn fae eyed me calmly as she walked slowly and gracefully out of the summoning circle, growing more confident in her new body with every breath. She stepped around the heaps of writhing tentacles burying my packmates and stopped by Greg's frozen form. Behind her the flames flickered and died, the circle once more quiet.

"I can taste the stolen life in this one." She told me with a hungry smile. The fae ran a hand over his darkness clad form, tracing along his outstretched arm with one finger. She licked her lips, and eyed me with those hungry, depthless eyes. "And you, I know you. Morgan Black. Knight Errant of Shadow and Ivory. Child of the Wyld. Son of Herne and Margaret May Black. Oh, I have heard the whispers about you."

I circled her, knocking aside questing tentacles and their fanged mouths, but the creatures … things … whatever guided them seemed less inclined to attack me for some reason. Only if I drew too close to where I knew Jessica lay, where Emma and Jacob were, did they snap and lash at me.

"Shouldn't believe everything you hear. Like I heard you were the smart one compared to your sister." I replied glibly as I held my swords low, ready. I was facing an immortal on par with Oberon and Madb. More powerful than the Morrigan, and she could hand me my kidneys any day of the week. But I wasn't done yet. "Besides. Your sister does the little girl thing way creepier and scarier than you. The blond pigtails just *really* don't have the same effect."

I stepped over the summoning circle's perimeter, keeping my opponent in front of me as I mentally prepare myself for the insanity I was planning. It was a massive gamble, probably one of the stupidest things I'd thought of ever doing. But what choice did I have? Really?

Morgana eyed me, then reached up and caressed her long hair, the locks bound in ribbon. Smiling like the end of the world, she swept her hand back over her head, and as it passed her hair went from golden to alternating ebony and silver, entwined. It braided together like snakes mating, falling into dreadlocks bound with small skulls and blood red gemstones, as the dark veins on her face pulsed with renewed vigour.

Yup, that was a helluva lot more scary to look at now.

"Tell me why you think I am not clever, when I have outwitted you at every step. Blocked your every attempt to thwart me." She commented dryly, taking a step away from Greg's still form and settling in one of the smaller circles drawn on the floor, opposite me. "And oh, how I will punish your foolishness for thinking me any less fearsome than my sister. You may not scare me, none of you do. But I can be your worst nightmare, *pup*."

She hissed that last word, the sound low and malevolent. But I just shrugged, and allowed myself a hard smile.

"Well for starter, how dumb are you? You break out your *sister's* prison, with all the Real to hide in, but instead you breach a bunch of the Accords and mortal rules by coming *here*. The Mortal Realm. Arse-end of magic-ville." I mocked her, then grinned more widely. "And yeah, I don't scare you. None of us do. But I know who does. The creatures who make Oberon wet his big boy pants at the mere thought of them showing up. Of them coming for him. And I just happen to have one of them on speed dial."

I knew I was going to regret this, but it was time to toss the dice.

"Oh, and my worst nightmare? Finding pineapple on my pepperoni pizza, and you don't even come close, *babe*." I glibly shot at her before drawing a breath. Past time for any regrets.

"Tisiphone, I call on you!" I shouted over the wind, over the muffled sounds of my packmates fighting to break free, over the muted screams of Elspeth and Felix.

"Time to come collect!"

Chapter 46

The air split with ragged howls, the screams of the damned filling the Pavilion. Tisiphone stepped through the rent she had carved in reality, her cloven hooves sinking into the carpet beside me. Her tattooed skin smoked in the cool air of approaching night, and her hidden eyes burned holes into me as she stood within the circle.

I looked across at Morgana, grinning like a madman as I pointed a thumb at the Fury.

"*Her* I know you are shit-scared of."

And Morgana …

Smiled.

"**MORGAN BLACK, I SEE YOU.**" The Fury thundered, towering over me. "**BUT ONE I DO NOT SEE, NOR SENSE, IS THE GNOME TERRIGYLE MUNSTRUM. EXPLAIN.**"

"Tisiphone I see you." I told the Fury, edging a step away from her, out of the summoning circle. Morgana's smile had unnerved the hell out of me, and I was trying to work out just what the fuck I was missing. "Teri's not here. But *she* is. Morgana, the escaped fae. The reason for all the mess in the Mortal Realm right now, for what's fucking up the Real too. She's all yours."

"**THAT MATTERS TO ME NOT.**" The Fury replied and my stomach dropped about fifty feet straight through the floor. "**THOUGH I SENSE OATH BREAKERS NEARBY …**"

"What do you mean you don't care!" I snarled, gesturing around us and to London beyond the windows. "Can't you see what she is doing to my packmates? To *mortals*? She's summoned things from the Veil to attack them! She's breaking the fucking Accords! Mortals are *dying* out there, coz of her!"

"YOU ARE MISTAKEN. YOUR KIN ASSAULT NOTHING." Tisiphone looked around the room, taking in the tentacles, the burning fury, the chaos all around us.

And Morgana gestured with one hand, smiling that devil's smile of hers.

The tentacles vanished. The fire wrapping Elspeth and Felix shivered and was no more. Greg stood, still as a statue but untouched by any darkness.

It had all been a fucking glamour.

I hadn't even felt it, and lycan were normally proof against hexes, charms and beguilement. Let alone the fact we had our witch along with us, to see through anything the fae should have been able to throw at us. But she'd done it anyway, as I saw my Alpha grappling with thin air, Emma unconscious on the floor, her wolf's head lolling to one side. Jacob was stabbing nothing with his machete, teeth gnashing and ripping as if chewing through something binding him. But they were all untouched. Unharmed.

And I remembered the Morrigan's warning, as ever too late.

She will not face you for a battle one on one, nor has the time to beguile and charm you as she did with that fool Artur. Expect her to have planned as one weak, without allies and having only had one thing to use. Time, pup. She has had time to plan this. Beware that, and you may still survive what comes.

I should have guessed, seeing my Alpha taken down so quickly when to my knowledge Jessica could level a building if she so wanted, and wouldn't break a sweat swatting some freaky-ass tentacles from the Veil. But it had been so *real*.

"Fuck it!" I snarled, as Morgana laughed at my frustration. "Fine, she tricked us. Me. But she's still broken the Accords. Loosed the Harrowing on mortals, had a bunch of them killed to make her a new body. Drained *thousands* of their life to break her free of prison! How the hell are you ignoring all that?!"

"BECAUSE SHE DID NONE OF THESE THINGS." The Fury answered, pointing a finger to the gory remains of Robert Knox. "I SENSE THE TRUTH

OF WHAT YOU SAY, BUT YOU ARE MISTAKEN AS TO WHO WAS THE PERPETRATOR. THE MORTAL YOU KNEW AS ROBERT KNOX, HE DID THESE THINGS. I CAN SENSE THE TRUTH OF IT, SEE THINGS CLEARLY FOR WHAT THEY ARE."

"But she made him do them! She beguiled him, making him think she was his dead daughter!" I almost grabbed the Fury and shook her, so pissed off was I feeling. "How does that make her blameless?"

"WE PUNISH THOSE WHO BREACH THE ACCORDS, WHO BREAK THEIR OATHS. THAT IS WHAT WE ARE, ALL THAT WE MAY OR MAY NOT DO." The Fury replied, looking at me from behind that blank helmet. "EVERYTHING MUST HAVE THEIR LIMITS OTHERWISE ALL WOULD NEED TO BE JUDGED, ALL WOULD BE DEEMED FITTING FOR PUNISHMENT."

I found her answer singularly unhelpful, made worse as Morgana decided to chip in.

"I told you, Morgan Black. *I have done nothing wrong.*" She laughed, those dark eyes of hers shining with evil delight. "You have summoned a Fury here to punish me, but I have broken no oath, no law. If others have done so at anything I may or may not have *said*, that is not my fault. Nor my burden to bear. Your arbitrator of justice will look elsewhere for her prey."

I felt Tisiphone's hidden eyes fall back on me, hot as the fires of hell.

"MORGAN BLACK, YOU SWORE AN OATH TO RETURN THE PRISONER TERRIGYLE MUNSTRUM TO ME WHEN THE TASK YOU UNDERTOOK WAS FULFILLED." She told me, voice like the crunching of metal. "YOU HAVE NOT KEPT THAT PROMISE. YOUR OATH IS BROKEN."

Oh shit.

"Hey, I just hit a little snag is all. Dealing with this bloody lunatic!" I told her with all the conviction I could manage. "Are you *really* going to let her off the hook, believe her flimsy as fuck excuse? Deal with her shit, and I'll find the little bastard and hand him right back to you!"

"I HAVE HEARD COUNTLESS SOULS OFFER THE SAME." Tisiphone told me bluntly and I took another step back, starting to think this had been a really bad idea. "YOU WOULD THINK THEY WOULD STOP TRYING IT ON..."

"Morgan, what's going on?" Elspeth's voice caught me, and I looked over to find her upright, held there by Felix. It seemed the pair of them had fared better than my lycan kin, since Jessica, Jacob and Emma were still caught up in the throes of the glamour Morgana had used on us all.

At her voice, Tisiphone's head snapped round and the tattoos on her body boiled with fervour.

"YET YOURS IS NOT THE WORST OATH BROKEN HERE!" She uttered, raising one clawed hand. "I SMELL SHATTERED PROMISES BETWEEN MOTHER AND DAUGHTER, KIN OF SPIRIT AND BOUND BY WORDS OF SERVICE AND FIDELITY. I SENSE THE PAIN OF A GODDESS REJECTED, A MORTAL DEFYING HER SWORN DUTY."

An unseen force grabbed Elspeth, snatching her from Felix's grasp and dragging her forward even as Greg started to rouse from his stupor. The witch's guardian shook his head, sword lowering his sword as consciousness slowly returned. Too slowly, far too slowly.

"DAUGHTER OF TERRA, I TASTE THE BROKEN FRAGMENTS OF THE OATH YOU YET BEAR INSIDE." Tisiphone thundered, as the air seemed to boil around her. "IT'S RUIN CALLS TO ME, DEMANDING PUNISHMENT. YOUR GODDESS'S PAIN MUST BE ANSWERED."

Elspeth's eyes opened wide as she was dragged towards the Fury, frantically trying to resist. To summon the craft she shared with Felix to defend herself. Grey violet fire burst around the scarlet monstrosity, but Tisiphone simply shrugged off the attack, untouched, as she continued to reel the witch in to her waiting grasp.

Fuck! I hadn't even stopped to think of the witch and what she had done. What she had been forced to do to raise Greg from the dead. Terra had told me the price Elspeth would pay, had made it clear the bonds between them were broken by her actions. And now I'd summoned the one creature whose very existence relied on it punishing those who broke faith, who betrayed those they had sworn service to.

Fuck, fuck, fuckity fuck!

There was nothing I knew that worked on a Fury, no trick I had or skill I'd been given that would stand up against the immortal's innate power. But Ellie was my friend, and I'd be buggered if I let some tattooed, blood-skinned behemoth with a penchant for torture drag her off to eternal punishment without making her fight tooth and claw for her prize.

I threw myself forward, summoning Shadow to freeze the Fury where she stood. Wyld strength to aid my strikes as my swords carved the space between us. Ivory to ward off her answering blows that would probably leave me a broken mess on the floor still.

But I was too late.

Morgana got there first.

Chapter 47

There was a sound, like a background hum. I'd mistaken it for air conditioning or machinery. Just the sort of the thing you always hear in larger buildings of a certain age, when providing a cooling working environment meant more than investing in the latest Dyson product. But this suddenly cut out, as if someone had flicked a switch. Silence rushed into the Pavilion, and with it, a change that altered *everything*.

Where before, the four smaller circles around the main summoning ward had stood empty except the one where Morgana casually stood, now all had occupants.

Three tall, willow-thin and rag-clad fae now stood proud within the silvered circles. Their hair was long, falling unbound below their waists, and knotted with fetish charms and silver trinkets. The women's faces were gaunt to the point of skeletal, ash-grey skin stretched tight over their sharp cheekbones and high foreheads. Tattoos similar to those I'd seen on the other two fae we'd recently tangled with marked the three, intricate in design but still with that Nordic runic look to them.

The Norns. *Urðr, Verðandi and Skuld*. And I could see their bared throats with oddly discoloured skin and faint pale scars marking where Knox had performed his surgery. To restore their voices.

The one thing that had made Oberon so afraid, he'd buried them for centuries in the darkness. Voiceless and broken.

The Norns now raised their heads, focusing on Tisiphone as she stood in the central circle. They opened their mouths, eyes slitted with concentration, and power lashed out as they *sang*. A harsh and overwhelming chorus that hammered from all three sides against the Fury. She screamed, her rage so great that her skin burned with a hellish hue and her tattoos boiled and thickened to almost cover any and all her flesh.

Elspeth's advance halted, the witch stumbling and falling to her knees as the Fury snarled, her scythes springing to her clawed hands as she turned to face this new threat.

The power solidified, forming blackened chains that clamped down on the Fury's wrists, ankles and neck. Muscles bunching and flexing with inhuman strength, she shattered the one bearing her left arm down, but the next instant another chain appeared, refastening and forcing it down again. Chain after chain appeared, latching onto Tisiphone and binding her as she raged and screamed so hard the glass in the room fractured and shattered, the frames warping and groaning with the effort of remaining in place.

As the Norns sang their song of containment, Morgana stepped from the circle she was in, walking across the carpet floor until she stopped near to where Felix had dropped the spear of Vàr. She leant down and picked up the finely crafted weapon, before looking across at me and giving me a hungry, satisfied smile.

And a final nod of thanks.

Then, with speed born of her inhuman nature, Morgana leapt into the summoning circle. Spear held high, hair fanning out around her as she cried out loudly.

"By this act, I claim the Court of Twilight as mine own!" Her voice boomed out, overscoring Tisiphone's bellowing cries and the song of the Norns. "I restore what was taken, right the wrong done. Be done, and mine by right of conquest and desire!"

And down came the spear, as the Norns tightened their chains and forced the Fury to bow under the weight of the restraints. The spearhead flashed with arcane fury as it hammered down into the immortal's exposed back, down through her body as Tisiphone's angry snarls turned to cries of utter agony. The sharp-edged spear burst from her lower body, slammed into the floor underfoot, spitting her as Morgana loosed hold and stepped back.

Energy burst from the Fury, an onslaught of power that howled as it arched upwards like a shaft of burning brightness. It pierced the gloom closing in on us, rising higher and higher to paint the sky. Under the flaring brightness of four sparks of brilliance shimmering in the heavens. Four planets, aligned in a sight not seen for over four hundred years.

Dusk. I felt everything crumbling around me as I remembered another name for this time of day, a step between sunlight and night's shadow. Twilight. Their time, with a footstep in both darkness and light, yet of neither.

"Finally!" Morgana crowed, as the energy pulsed and flared, burning upwards from the Fury. Tisiphone had quieted now, slumped upon the spear that pierced her through, blind head bowed and tattoos fading. "You know, I *really* thought you were going to make me kill one of your companions before you summoned her. You really are a stubborn one, lycan."

The fae turned to look at me, and I started, seeing her dark hair now adorned with a circlet of glittering silver entwined with shining ebony. A crown, bearing a single rune carved into a stone that sat atop her brow.

"This. You planned all this." Elspeth was recovering, gathering herself from almost suffering an unimaginable fate at the hands of the Fury. Beside her, Greg seemed to have gained most of his mind back, sword drifting between Morgana and the prisoner in the summoning circle, unsure where the threat to his love was. Felix looked on with terrified eyes, glancing across to me to find some hope, some sense that all was ok.

Which it definitely was not, in any shape or form.

"This was never just about you escaping from prison." The witch continued, drawing a breath and facing the immortal. "This was about the Twilight Court. What was done to them. All this. For them?"

"They were my sworn brothers and sisters of battle." Morgana replied coldly as she eyed the energy pouring from the Fury, her smile turning hard at the memories evoked. "My cousin of Ivory has never known the meaning of the word *enough*, and his jealousy of the power of Twilight was only equalled by his fear that they might do exactly as he did. Seize control, decide *they* were right to rule the Courts. So he struck first, a betrayal made so much worse because my *sister* stood with him. She bound me, held me in check whilst Dagur innocently accepted Oberon's offer to meet, to talk of the future. To plan."

"Instead he was stripped of his strength and made to watch as his people were butchered, his home broken and corrupted. Those few who remained strong enough to resist either changed into horrors beyond comprehension or thrown in prison with him."

"So yes, you could say I felt *aggrieved* that whilst my cousin in Ivory, and my sister in Shadow may speak of justice, they are in fact the worst offenders ever. They both should suffer the wrath of the Furies, but he was crafty enough to avoid such a fate. He bargained with them, to remain free so long as the Courts maintained order and justice in our Realm." She shook her head, eyes falling to Tisiphone. The drain of energy was undiminished but its effect on the Fury was starting to show. The Fury's skin was cracking and flaking away, her great frame starting to shrink as her very essence was drained from her. "So I decided to wait. To plan. To right the wrong done to them all. To restore even a portion of their home, and those of their people that still live."

"Yeah, not *quite* so altruistic though," I replied, nodding to the crown sitting atop her head. "With Dagur dead, I'm thinking you saw a chance to have your own Court, your own throne. Not the one promised by Artur, but something you won by your own hand. One step above your sister, am I right?"

Morgana reached up to caress the runic stone, and smiled sharply.

"And why not? You did me a great favour, ridding the throne of its foolish occupant when I would have had to do the same thing myself to achieve my goal. Instead, I shall restore Twilight to its glory, and neither Oberon or Madb will have the might or knowledge to stop me. None of you will."

Her eyes then narrowed in thought, that smile like a predator's. Just before it sank its teeth into its prey.

"But as Queen, I shall need courtiers. Those to advise me, those to act in my stead when I am otherwise engaged." She took a step closer to where we stood, and I raised my sword to ward off any attack, not really having much hope I could do much against her now.

She ignored my gesture, only shooting me a disdainful look before moving on to face Elspeth.

"You. You know the Mortal Realm and its rules, its peoples. I have been long gone from here and I would seek one to offer me advice and counsel." She told the witch, who stared at her with a mixture of fear and confusion. "If you would join me, you might do your fellow mortals some measure of favour, tempering my inclination towards them."

Behind her, Tisiphone gave a rasping groan, as the energy began to flicker and pulse, the raging torrent diminishing as her body broke apart and slumped down onto the floor within the circle. The Norn's song swiftly changed, the tone easing and becoming less strident, and I felt the energies respond to the different flow. This felt more alive, less an attack and more … like anticipation?

The beginning of something?

"You are fucking kidding aren't you?" I snarled, off-balance and wholly unsure how we could make this right. We'd come up here to stop Knox, interrupt his ritual and prevent Morgana being reborn. Now he was dead … horribly so … Morgana was standing before us in a brand-new body, and she was going to be Queen of Twilight? And she wanted Elspeth to work for her? I mean, what the actual fuck?

"I am little surprised your simple mind struggles with what I desire to achieve here." Morgana shot back, her dark eyes alight with cruel mirth as she switched her attention momentarily to me. "I would offer you a role as my Court jester, or possibly boot cleaner, but you are tainted too much by Ivory and Shadow. Let alone your disreputable Wyld nature. But to spell things out in terms you will understand. I am refashioning Twilight. Here and now. The energies Knox stole from his fellow the mortals, those he drew from his victims as the sun set today? These combined with the eternal essence of this Fury shall remake a small portion of what was lost. Twilight, founded here in the Mortal Realm. And I shall rule over it, alongside my Court, where Oberon cannot reach without breaching the Accords. Nor my sister. They will be powerless to challenge me, their will and desires for naught as I take my rightful throne."

"Lady, you're insane." I answered bluntly, stepping in front of Elspeth and Greg. "This is the *Mortal* Realm. Not some kiddies sandpit for you to build your own little castle and play princess, just coz daddy didn't buy you a fucking pony when you were a child. Just fuck off back to the Real, and leave everyone here in peace."

"What your tongue, pup, or I shall remove it and use it to slap you to death." She answered with a snarl. Behind her, the remains of Tisiphone had crumpled to ruin, leaving the spear standing upright as energies still sang up its length. The air around it vibrated, changing somehow so that to my senses, it felt *heavier*. Like it was gaining mass.

"The fact is, witch," She continued, turning away from me as I was dismissed. "The Furies now know of you and your broken oaths to your Goddess. This one is not destroyed, I have merely stolen her energies for my use this night. When she is reformed, they will hunt you down. Seek to punish you for your actions. No matter the reason behind them, the fact it was done for the love of another. You *will* be made to suffer."

"And besides. I can taste the stolen energy you used to raise this mortal of yours. Those are mine, taken by my puppet for my use alone. I am owed for what you used, given what I attempt here. I can simply take them back ..."

Morgana made a clawing gesture, and Greg gave a muffled cry and collapsed, clutching at his chest and writhing in agony as the tattoos on his skin boiled like they were seeking to rip free. I snarled a curse as Elspeth cradled him, whispering words as she drew on Felix's shared power, trying to keep him alive.

The fae made a cutting gesture, and Greg's convulsions quieted, his breath rasping harshly but slowly steadying.

"Or you can join me. Become my advisor and keep your mortal at your side." Morgana told Elspeth, that smile of hers so cruel, so confident. "I care not for one small life if you would swear to serve me. These creatures, these *friends* cannot keep you or your loved one safe from the Furies. But I can."

"You can't do this. It's a breach of the Accords. You'll have everyone rise up to put you down!" I spat back at her, but it was not Morgana who replied.

"Nae, Morgan. It's nae so." Jessica rasped, as she slowly struggled to her feet. Jacob and Emma were slowly recovering their senses as well, the big lycan kneeling by his second and checking her over as she slowly roused from unconsciousness.

"You're shitting me?" I spat, not caring this was my Alpha. But she seemed to understand my current mood as she just shook her head, expression set.

"The Accords say nae a thing about resurrecting a fae Court within the Mortal Realm, nae even in the Real. For no-one thought it was anything ever needing tae be discussed." She replied, as she slowly walked towards us. "Twilight was long destroyed, Oberon and Madb agreed tae keep this matter quiet, and none of the mortals' business. So technically, the bitch is correct in her thinking. Pardon mah language, Elspeth."

The witch just smiled sadly, the pair sharing a moment.

Morgana dipped her head, smiling sharklike at the name calling but offering no rebuttal. She instead locked her eyes with Elspeth, and held out one hand.

"Join me. I will even open a Way for these others to leave before Twilight is reborn. They will be safe." She offered, dark eyes glittering. "Well, at least for now."

Giving up on trying to glare the fae down, I turned my back on her and faced Ellie. She was back on her feet, supporting Greg who seemed to be regaining his strength after almost having his jump-start back to life reversed. His expression was grim as he realised he was being used to force the woman he loved to make a terrible decision but I could sense his helplessness as well. Nothing he could do would change her mind … if he took himself out of the equation, Elspeth would still be at risk, still hunted by the Furies.

"You can't do this." I told her, seeing the anguish in her eyes, the pain. The realisation of what choice she faced. "I'm sorry, Ellie. It's my fault for calling the Fury. I didn't think …"

"Oh hush, Morgan." She told me, shaking her head once. "Stop trying to be the noble hero, it really isn't your thing. I made my choice long before now, and I knew there would be a price to be paid. I can't lose him. Not now."

Looking up over my shoulder, she faced Morgana.

"You promise to get them clear of here? No tricks, no fae glamour or shit pulled to make them suffer for any reason. Get them safe back to their office. You promise?" Elspeth demanded, face pale but eyes fierce.

Morgana shrugged but nodded.

"It matters not if they survive this night. The pup at least, I know, will cause trouble for me later but nothing I cannot handle." She dismissed me with a single glance. "So yes, I promise to offer them a Way to safety, if you swear to join me now."

The witch squared her shoulders, pulling away from Greg and motioning for him to go stand in the circle with Morgana. He looked ready to refuse, but she leant in and whispered in his ear. Whatever she said, it had the intended effect. His shoulders slumped and he slid his sword back into its sheath and with slow, heavy steps, left her side and moved to stand as far as he could from the fae whilst within the ward.

"Open the Way then. I want to see them safe before I swear." The witch told Morgana, her tone brooking no argument even though she was in no position to demand anything. The fae cocked her head, that smile of hers sharp as a blade, as she considered for a moment before finally nodding.

"We shall speak of your attitude, and changes to be made when this matter is dealt with." She promised, and Elspeth fought hard not to flinch at the barely concealed threat.

Morgana looked across at the Norns, some sort of unspoken communication passing between them. Whilst two of the Twilight fae continued to sing their strange song, as the air in the Summoning circle writhed and shimmered with strange shapes and colours and the stink of the Veil threaded the conjured phantoms, the third turned and faced us.

Her voice modulated, the song shifting to a quick and sharp string of notes, Power was threaded through every element, channelled in a controlled stream to strike the far wall by the door where we had first entered the Pavilion. The surface of the wall shimmered like oil on water, then collapsed inward as if there was nothing behind it. The well expanded until it covered the entire room's end. And the tangle of colours finally coalesced like a picture coming into focus so that we were looking in on the *Good Deed's* office floor. Red flames flaring in the fountains, the familiar wards reacting to the intrusion.

"There. A gate to their nice little rabbit hole where they can scurry to, to hide." Morgana told Elspeth coldly, and flicked a finger at us. "Now get them gone so we can be about *my* business."

Elspeth looked across at me, blocked from Morgana's view and mouthed one word. *Wait.* Then she turned to face Jessica.

"Please, just get yourselves and Felicity out of here. This is something I have to do." She told my Alpha, who eyed her for a long moment before finally nodded.

The lycan slowly and carefully sheathed her sabre, motioning for Emma to help Felix, the young woman still shivering from the effects of everything that had just happened. The mental assault from Morgana making her think she was burning alive was enough to short-circuit any mortal's headspace, let alone all the other shit she had witnessed tonight.

"This is nae over." Jessica told Morgana, who gave a shrug of indifference, accepting the truth.

"And when I am settled with my Court, wolf, I'll be happy for you to come calling. Then we can *discuss* matters at our leisure." The fae told her with dripping sarcasm. "But now, get you gone if you don't want to waste the chance your friend has bartered for you."

I could sense the struggle Jessica was having, feel the emotions running through her. The desire to fight, to save one of her own even though she wasn't technically pack. Warring with the logic this wasn't a fight we could win, and there was a young woman we could get to safety.

She shot me a quick look, and I shook my head once, acknowledging we were done here.

"Say yer goodbyes quickly, Morgan." She told me, then motioned for Jacob and Emma to wait whilst she took lead through the Way. "Ah shall be waiting on the other side."

Jessica stepped through first, wary of any trap or trick. Ripples spread across the image as she passed through, and finally settled as she appeared within the office on the other side. Jacob's phone pinged, and he checked the text before nodding once. Then he and Emma gently carried Felix into the Way.

A moment later, my phone pinged. Sheathing one sword, I pulled it out to check I had one new message.

We're safe. Whatever you're thinking, making it count.

Jessica as ever on the case, making sure this hadn't been some weird trap of Morgana's. Not trusting the immortal to keep her word without twisting it somehow. Fae were tricky bastards at the best of times, and this was far from that.

Also knowing me too well, realising I wasn't done.

Elspeth then turned to me, and I pushed the phone back into my pocket.

"Come here, you bloody idiot." I told her quietly and enfolded her in a tight hug, careful not to spike her with my remaining sword. "Just stay safe, ok? Until we … *I* can fix this. We're not leaving you with her, you know that."

The witch hugged me back, then leant in to whisper in my ear. At the same time, I felt her hand brush my thigh pocket. The one opposite where I kept my phone.

'The Harrowing. Revenge on Knox.'

With that she pushed away, stepping quickly over to stand with Greg. He set one hand on her shoulder, either to give her some of his strength or just reassure himself they were together still.

Leaving me standing there, as her words blazed like wildfire in my head.

Chapter 48

Brunor.

Known as Brunor le Noir, and The Badly Cut Coat, this Knight travelled to Artur's court wearing the bloodied and damaged armour of his father, also Sir Brunor. Slain by two villainous Knights, Briadan and Ferrant. Through many perils, the younger Brunor eventually meets and defeats the pair despite being wounded from a previous challenge.

He is known to have wed The Ill-Speaking Maiden, a woman who journeys with him on his quests and constantly belittles his efforts. As a true Knight, he never once rebukes her – and it takes words from Lancelot himself to force the lady to admit she was instead seeking to test his strength and resolve for finding his father's killers.

Despite having avenged his father, Brunor refuses to change out of his old armour, wearing it as a badge of honour until his own death in battle.

The Harrowing. Revenge on Knox.

"Best you leave as well, pup." Morgana told me dryly, as she motioned for the third Norn to return to the crafting of a new Twilight with her sisters. "The gate will not last much longer, and you *really* do not want to be stuck here with me when it closes. That I promise you."

The Harrowing. Revenge on Knox.

The five words tumbled round my head as I desperately tried to work out what Elspeth had been trying to tell me. A way out of this, a last *last* throw of the dice, when the previous gamble I'd taken had so royally fucked us all.

The Harrowing. Knox had it, but Morgana had shut him down before he could call on it when he finally saw what he'd done. Who he'd summoned. She'd consumed all his energy, and most likely destroyed his link to that entity. I had no connection to the weapon, and didn't know the first thing about how to summon it. Elspeth had read his notes, *she* knew, but unless I'd missed the hand-over meeting somehow, the witch never mentioned she had learned its secrets. So why that?

"Pup, I will not warn you again." Morgana hissed, the air throbbing with violent intent. "Leave us whilst you still can. Do your friend a favour, and spare her the sight of your death, which I will make *most* painful."

Revenge on Knox. He was dead, the bastard. I had wished ill on him many times, had wanted him shut down and, ok, yes, felt the desire to smash his skull in after what had almost happened to Sarah. But he had died a gruesome death, the life literally sucked out of him after Morgana had ripped off the veil from his eyes and let him see just how badly he had messed up. The damage he had done to so many. He had died in utter torment. Was that revenge enough for his actions?

But Elspeth had specifically said, *revenge on* him. And suddenly I remembered a conversation, the witch admitting something to me as we stood in her house. Just after she had raised her love from the dead.

… After what happened to Gregory, I gave thought to hunting Knox myself, and letting that thing loose on him. I … I don't think I should be trusted with it …

It. The Harrowing. Knox's little gift to the Nighters. To Talen Orben and his packmate Sal. A corrupted version of the killer of immortals, meant not to just drain life from the first thing it interacted with, but to corrupt and warp them into something truly horrific. One of the Harrowed. Knox had prepared small containers to house the abomination, bound with hexes and rituals, and the lycan had used them in a failed coup against the rest of the packs at the Blooding.

That had ended badly for everyone that night.

And Elspeth had rescued one of the containers from the scene. Then given it to me for safekeeping when she admitted she wanted to hunt Knox down and use it on him.

Did she mean…?

Would that even work?

I looked up, catching Morgana's glare loaded with vicious intent, but I ignored her after a moment. Instead I met Elspeth's eyes, the question naked in my own.

She nodded carefully, once.

The witch then turned, capturing the fae's attention as she slowly knelt on the carpet, head bowed. A supplicant before her ruler to be.

"I, Elspeth Viviane Elmerra MacElvy do swear to serve and honour you, Morgana, Queen of Twilight. That I will bear true and faithful allegiance to you, and you alone …"

Her words cut through the roiling maelstrom of the burgeoning Twilight realm, the energy storm muting for a second as I heard my friend start to bind herself to the mad Queen. Giving me the distraction I needed.

Ok-ay. This was officially going to be *the* stupidest thing I had ever tried, in a long line of stupid and crazy. Thankfully Ellie had waited till the rest of the pack and Felix got clear, guessing I wouldn't risk their lives doing something this idiotic with them still in the blast zone. Just my own, showing how well my friend and colleague knew me.

I needed Morgana off-guard, convinced I was desperate and not thinking rationally. She already thought me stupid and slow, so it wasn't going to be hard to push her expectations even lower. To let her face me, instead of granting the pleasure to one of her minions who could probably wipe the floor with me and ruin the one chance I had of stopping her.

"Hey! There's something I just don't get." I shouted out loud as I focused on the wannabe Queen of Twilight, settling myself on my feet. Drawing a slow, calming breath and loosening my muscles for what I planned to do next.

"Many things I would say you, of all creatures, would not get. A hint to 'leave this place and live' being the most obvious right now." Morgana replied archly, then smiled cruelly. "But if you insist on wasting your life with idle chatter, pray do tell what bothers you so."

"Thanks, Moggie." I grinned that insolent smile of mine, guaranteed to put anyone's back up. "Oh, you don't mind me calling you Moggie, do you? See, I like to nickname all you crazy-powerful immortal fuckwits. *Obie*, *Tits* … ah, I still don't have one for your sister apart from *scary-as-fuck*. But you, well, you remind me of a little black cat, yowling and spitting. So … Moggie it is. Or Mogs."

"I am going to take great pleasure in eliciting each scream of agony from you." Morgana answered with her own smile, but I saw the black fire rippling in her eyes, the anger stoked and flickering to life.

"Yeah, good luck with that, Mogs." I shrugged, before continuing. "As I was saying, there's something bugging me. You *couldn't* have known I'd call up one of the Furies. Fine, you set all this up. Giving us the wrong time, sticking Rous with a dummy rat to spy on us, hiding Twilight fae around the place to slow us down. All this effort with Knox and the Harrowing, draining the life from mortals to feed your pet project. But you needed something like a Fury to jumpstart the whole thing. So how the fuck did you know I would call her here, just when you needed her?"

Morgana shook her head, braids clattering as she sighed in disappointment.

"You think in such small terms, pup." She answered, gesturing around her. To the singing Norns, the remains of Tisiphone. The burgeoning *other* that was growing under the Twilight fae's ministrations. Their new home. "All this has been planned across the span of *centuries*. Whilst my sister tortured and tormented the body in which she thought I was still imprisoned, I have wandered far and wide. Between the Realms. Touched the lives of mortals and immortals alike in my search for revenge. For a way to remake what was unmade."

Morgana pointed a finger at me, then gestured to the gate behind me. Which I guessed was starting to fail, given the lack of magic keeping it open.

"Long have I known of your kind, of the *noble* task you pups undertake. To uphold the Accords. Keep the stupid and ignorant mortals safe from harm. And to *whom* you report." She explained with spiteful smugness. "You have captured my tools without knowing I saw what they saw. Knew what they knew. And so you were revealed to me, when you slew the Mistress's pet shape-changer and handed her over to the Furies for judgement. When your little gnome friend, so invaluable to you, was returned to you in your pathetic efforts to track Robert Knox. I *knew*."

I couldn't help but want to kick myself, despite all the precautions we'd taken to keep her spirit from listening in and learning our plans. I'd been the one to practically invite her in on anything we said or did, as long as anyone she'd been working worth was on the scene. Even those I had no clue were linked to her in the first place.

"Terrigyle." I sighed ruefully, shaking my own head. "The poor bastard didn't even know he was serving you, and you still used him like a fucking puppet. Even after he'd been tortured by the Furies for his stupidity."

"Where do you think he obtained a trinket to escape his judgement, *just* when he needed it?" She mocked, and I growled despite myself. "All for just a little information, a little knowledge of what you had promised. To a Fury. Then it was simply a matter of making sure your debt remained owed, and that you felt in such a state of hopelessness that you would call on her. Thinking she would see me as the bigger prize. The juicer steak to bite. Your idiocy is a match only for your naivety, but I should not complain. Both have served me well."

"Naive and stupid. Yeah, I've been called that and worse. But the fact is, you aren't taking my friends. And I'll be fucked if I let you conjure Disney-land slap bang in the middle of my backyard." I growled, adding all my anger and frustration to the sound. I hefted my sword, loosening my shoulders.

Morgana laughed, the sound like shattering glass, and shook her head once more.

"I would call you fool, but we have established you are not fit even for that role." She spread her hands, taking two steps to leave her outside the summoning ward. Unprotected if it was brought to life. The Norns continued singing, as Elspeth leant back against Greg, eyes fixed on me. "Still, let us be done with this. I might yet find a use for you ... as a lesson to any who might come later, to see what happens when a jumped-up *kitten finder* thinks himself an equal to his betters. As if you *ever* could be a threat to one such as I."

Morgana beckoned to me, eyes flaring with angry fire and insolence.

"Come, Sir Pup. Show me what a Knight Errant of Ivory and Shadow, born of the Wyld, can do."

I hurled myself forward, summoning all my gifts as I focused everything on reaching Morgana.

Ivory armour clad me, as I Changed from one breath to the next. Muscles sang with the strength of Wyld, making me feel invincible, unstoppable. My sword was a feather in my hand, catching the light as it carved the air, aimed to strike at that evil smile. Frost coated the weapon, steaming with frigid wrath as I drew on everything I had for this one last gamble. My free hand scrabbled at my thigh, then came up as a fist to hammer at her head if she blocked my sword strike.

Barbed whips of Shadow lashed at me, striking at my armour and tearing through it like it was paper. Fire, real this time, howled around me, drawing the breath from my lungs and scorching my skin as I powered across the floor. Thunder hammered down on me, forks of lightning that speared through the space between Morgana and I, a flash-fire of agony jumping from muscle to muscle like a hundred taser-strikes. Spearing up my spine and exploding in my skull so that my eyesight blackened and dimmed, my brain pounding like it was set to implode.

Agony wracked me, the breaking of bone, the tearing of flesh. An assault of fury no mortal thing could endure, and no immortal thing could withstand for long. Morgana unleashed the merest fraction of her might at me, and I bled and howled, uncaring who heard my cries as the pain wrenched my jaws apart and dragged primeval sounds from my very core.

Ten feet … five feet … three feet …

I hurled everything I had into those last remaining steps, as I felt my skin break and burn, my blood spill upon the carpet underfoot in bucketloads. Something hammered into me, either real or conjured, and I felt my armour shatter and ribs break in an orchestra of agony. My sword was shaking in my grip, relentless forces grinding down on it as I sought to slam it home in Morgana's flesh … silver and cold iron battling the forces assaulting me …

Battled and lost.

Metal broke, shivering with a ruined cry as the blade shattered into minute fragments and were blasted away as Morgana stood untouched. The merest stub of the weapon remained in my grip, and I snarled with bestial fury as I sought to carve her open with the jagged remains.

One foot …

I loomed over her, a bloodied, broken mess of lycan, Knight and kitten-finder. Morgana gazed up at me with pure contempt, untouched as I staggered the last distance between us and thrust the broken weapon at her. Hurled my fist at her head, in simple defiance.

I felt my wrist break as she lashed out, inhumanly fast, slapping the weapon away before it dared draw close to her. The fae's smile was all encompassing, all devouring as she faced me and watched my fist fall slowly, so slowly towards her.

And she laughed, raising her face to meet its strike.

I felt my fingers break as I hammered at her cheek, bones popping and grinding against her crafted flesh. I howled, feeling things pulverise and shatter, forcing open the ruins of my fist to drag my palm down her face in a final inglorious slap.

"Is that it?" She drawled, and with a casual backhand, sent me tumbling back across the floor towards the slowly decaying gate. "Is that everything my cousin, my *sister* ... even that halfwit Herne, could manage to have stand against me in their stead? Are you all?!"

Pain assaulted me as I drew a shuddering breath, broken ribs grating harshly and the many wounds bleeding profusely. My head pounded, my eyesight swam and I swallowed hard to force the blood that was filling my mouth to clear it for a moment.

And I laughed.

A harsh, guttural sound, ripped from something torn deep inside me. A part of me that howled with anguish at all the pain, the loss we'd suffered, the reality that we'd failed. All falling from my wolf jaws as I spat blood and gasped through the pain. But still able to find a moment's joy as my broken hand flopped on the floor beside me.

Fragments of plastic, enscribed with runes, falling from it.

"What? Why do you laugh?" Morgana scowled as she casually reached up to trace the damage I'd done to her face, the bits of what I'd had in my hand embedded in her flesh. "This? You think this was worth you dying for? I shall heal this in a ... moment ... ahhh ..."

Her voice stuttered, a faint tone of worry stealing in where before had only been cruel arrogance. I panted and gasped through the pain, forcing down the frantic cries of my body to just lay still, let it heal and then do something stupid, and instead pushed myself up. Finding my feet, I wavered as consciousness fought against the agony, and finally won.

"What ... What is this?" Morgana hissed, as grey smoke billowed from her wounds. Alive, unstoppable. And very, very hungry. "What have you done, lycan?"

I slowly raised my hand, revealing the shattered remains of an inhaler, the faint runic script almost lost from sight. The container that had housed Robert Knox's hybrid Harrowing. Now mostly and firmly embedded in Morgana's flesh.

"Robert ... Knox sends his ... hnh ... regards ... and wishes you to ... hnh ... rot in hell." I snarled as I watched the Harrowing boil and pulse with vigour, driving in through the gashes and slashes, burrowing into her skin and flesh. Warping and writhing as it began to re-write her genes. "I guess ... I should say ... hnh ... happy birthday, *bitch*."

"*NO!*" Morgana screamed, hands clawing at her face. Purple-grey fire erupted, an inferno seeking to scour the Harrowing from her flesh but the smoke simply writhed and dug deeper, covering her cheek and forehead and one eye now. Grey flesh, tattooed with the markings of Twilight, now boiled and shifted, blackening and tightening like the Harrowed I'd seen at the Blooding. "This will not be! I shall not be undone!"

Power flared in the Pavilion, an inferno of might and rage summoned by the fae to scour the hateful thing from her flesh. And a sliver lashed out, enfolding me and gripping me with surprising gentleness. I didn't even try to fight, all my energies focused on keeping the darkness at bay, at staying conscious.

I was picked up and carried back across the carpet floor. Into the decaying gate. Realising this was my last chance, I threw out my undamaged arm, my one good hand reaching out to grab for my friend.

And failed.

My last sight was of Elspeth standing with Greg, as the energy in the summoning circle exploded outwards, spilling colours and images across the whole room and out through the windows in a tide of creation. My friend's eyes locked on me, her skin already stained with black veins from the oath she had sworn, binding her to Morgana. Her hand was held out, reaching for mine.

Behind her, the fae Queen raged as she fought the death of immortals now bound to her body. The corruption sank deep, her flesh already changing to something foul, something born of horror and pain. A fitting punishment for Morgana to suffer, branded by the mortal she had used so badly, who she had ended in such an inhuman manner. Only to suffer at the hands of *his* corrupted offspring of a weapon to kill such as the fae, when she had pretended all this time to be the daughter he sought forgiveness from.

As my vision dimmed, a thought struck me. The magic throwing me into the Way. It had not come from Morgana, but neither had I felt Elspeth's familiar touch. Whomever had cast me from the room was strange, unknown to me. But who else was there still upright to have thrown me to safety?

As the question burned in my head, I sank into darkness.

Chapter 49

There are many more characters and players in the legends of Artur Pendragon, each with their own tragedies and triumphs. Some may seem the oddest ever, whilst others more like the man or woman you face in the mirror each morning.

It is for you to decide what your own story will be, and what will be retold in pages like this in future times.

It was later the next day. In fact, evening was drawing in and I stood on my balcony, glass of wine in hand and a plate of fine black pudding sausages sat beside me. Bear was snoring loudly at my feet, and I leant carefully on the railing, looking westwards.

My cracked ribs were healing leisurely, reminding me of my foolishness with the occasional stab of pain. My left hand, the one I'd punched Morgana and unleashed the corrupt Harrowing on her with, was pretty much functioning as it should though the bruises were a livid counterpart to the Ivory brand. And I still ached from head to foot from the wounds I'd taken across my entire body, like someone had taken a cheese grater to me and scrubbed *really* hard.

I'd woken in *Good Deeds*, a bloodied and broken mess on the office floor. Jessica and my pack had watched from the other side of the gate, unable to pass back through to offer any aid, seeing my insane charge against Morgana. Then the revelation that I'd unleashed the Harrowing on the fae before I was hurled back through the gate and it collapsed, cutting us off from whatever happened at the Southbank centre.

My Alpha, assisted by Jacob and Emma, had bound my worst wounds and strapped the bits of me that were broken too badly to let flop around on their own. Felix had been in no state to help, suffering some sort of feedback from her connection to Elspeth and the oaths she had sworn to Morgana. Leaving the young woman unconscious on the nearest sofa and not responding to any attempts to wake her.

When my packmates were sure I wasn't going to expire just there and then on them, Jessica had gotten on with the job of finding out what the hell had happened whilst we were trying to stop Knox and Morgana, and also what the state of play was where we'd just come from.

Neither had yielded answers easy to swallow.

The six devices Knox had set to replace the lost life energy which I guessed Elspeth and I had wasted whilst setting fire to his sanctum and tackling the Harrowing, had managed to claim the lives of over a hundred mortals despite best efforts by OPS and our packs to keep the areas clear. Mortals just can't be told to leave their homes, stay away and not be stupid enough to sneak back in to find out if the big secret was aliens, evidence of supernatural life or just a good news story they could sell to the papers for a tidy sum and appear on the front page the next morning. Over a hundred dead mortals, drained of their lives.

Cormac had lost a dozen of his team to the life draining hex as well, agents trying to help mortals get clear of the thing's influence. Thankfully, our packs had managed to escape unscathed, being able to move faster than anything mortal and resist the hex longer with their lycan nature.

That hadn't helped as much down in the tunnels of the Underground, facing over seventy Harrowed created when Knox released his corrupted version on the circle tube-trains. They'd managed to lock down the routes out, keeping the mortals from witnessing the monsters that had once been brothers, sisters, fathers or mothers. But down in the narrowed confined spaces, with Harrowed erupting from every side, another seven packmates had died. Bree Anders had been lost as well. Torn apart by a mob of the beasts as he held them back from an unguarded gate which would have let the things loose in Aldgate. A disaster he could not countenance.

This left the Bosemans as the only pack Alphas not struck down by the madness of Knox and Morgana. We had lost Mark Walker years ago, but in the space of a few weeks, four pack leaders had been butchered or corrupted, lost to their packs.

The toll was already too high, but it had not stopped there.

Agent Evelyn Jones was one of the agents lost to Knox's trapped devices, I found out later. She had come across a small family barricaded in their squat-home, immigrants afraid that the warnings were a trick by the British law enforcement agencies and they'd be deported as soon as they stepped outside. Both parents and five children, all whom she'd rescued from the life-draining hex before she herself succumbed.

The news from the Southbank centre, in fact that entire section of London, had been at the same time difficult to obtain and yet easy to at least grasp from the simplest method of checking the news-feeds, and following the obvious chaos and confusion spreading like wildfire.

From the south end of Blackfriars Bridge, across the Waterloo and Westminster arches over the Thames and ending at Lambeth Bridge, a wall of roiling grey nothingness had risen shortly after I had tumbled through the Way and back into my office. A chunk of South London, encompassing Lambeth, Elephant and Castle, Waterloo and Newington seemed to have completely vanished behind this veil. Nothing could enter the mists, and helicopters flying overhead had found themselves beset by strange weather patterns as they neared the area and forced to veer away or risk crashing.

A small enough area of London as a whole, but within those districts, at least thirty thousand mortals lived and worked there. Thirty thousand souls suddenly cut off from the rest of the world, instead exposed to whatever twisted reality Morgana had crafted as a home for the remaining Twilight fae.

OPS had responded with surprising speed for an agency of the government. All access points were blocked off, air traffic re-routed and a cover story released about a suspected leak of chemicals in the vicinity that meant none could enter or leave safely. This was then linked to the story about issues on the Circle line, with possible terrorism blamed.

Stay safe, obey the rules and listen for updates, had been the message pumped out over news channels, radio stations, signs and from word of mouth by the hundreds of uniformed policemen and women and volunteers deployed to deter worried relatives and friends, angry business owners and more than a few tourists looking to experience something different in the city.

Mortals being mortals, they tend to be drawn to acts of stupidity and insanity if it meant they could say they'd achieved something singular and special. Even if that was a shortening of their lives to absolute zero, and was only noted on their tombstone.

Cormac had been in touch, verifying that the disruption in South London was definitely Morgana's fault, that Knox had been dealt with but unfortunately was in no condition to be handed back to them, and that he had been partly right not to trust the word of Morgana. Generously, he left off pointing the finger directly at us for allowing the shit to royally hit the fan, but I figured that was because I'd stuck him on speaker-phone when he called and he couldn't have missed the various growls and snarls from the pack as soon as it looked like he was raising the subject of blame.

Once we'd checked in with all our pack, Jessica had deployed as many of them as she could spare to support keeping the Twilight-bound section of London ringfenced and off limits. She'd drafted a short but very to the point communication to Rous and Molly, explaining how the Rat God's actions voided any and all agreements we'd put in place with them and that they should expect to hear from her and the other Alphas soon on the matter of the immortal selling us out so easily.

We'd only had silence back from the rulers of London Lows, but they were generally never quick to respond to enquiries from the Red Cloaks, let alone when we'd found out that at least one of them had been serving Morgana and had sold us out without even trying to warn us.

Rous was probably in the darkest, deepest pit he could find, hoping no-one found him.

With my wounds bound and having given my full debrief to Jessica - and suffered a harsh dressing down for my last attempt to take on Morgana alone despite having the Harrowing to use - I'd grabbed a lift back to the apartment. Mostly because I was in no condition to help anyone, but also to check in on what the hell had happened there and to make sure everyone was ok.

Felix had finally wakened by then, with only shredded memories of what had gone on the evening before. Apart from that and as she put it *the sort of hangover headache I think I'd deserve after a truly god-awful bender,* she seemed to have no lasting damage from what Morgana had done to her, what she'd felt through her link to Elspeth.

That link was silent now, not broken but Felix said it felt numb, cut off somehow. She'd joined me in my ride home, eager to see her Dad but I also reckoned she needed some time to herself, to make sense of everything that had happened after we'd filled in the gaps.

Before we'd left, Jessica had taken me aside one last time. I'd expected more of the earbashing for my failed attempt at stopping Morgana, but instead she surprised me. As always.

"Ah see you think tae carry the blame fer our failure tae stop Knox and Morgana." She had told me, giving me a look that brooked no bullshit or argument. "Ah know I cannae convince you tae stop blaming yerself, but think on this if you will. Morgana could nae have known *everything* she claimed. She is nae omnipotent, and despite having centuries tae plan fer her escape, she also left things tae chance and simply takes credit fer getting lucky when things could easily have turned out differently. She is *arrogant*, Morgan, as yer fae contact did try tae warn us. We may have lost this round, but this is nae over, and now we know her better. We know her weakness, and ah fer one will be looking tae make use of that fact. So cut yerself some slack, if you can."

With those words of advice meant to soothe my stung pride and general *I fucked up* mess of a head, she let us leave.

It turned out Knox had definitely been looking for a little payback from my setting fire to his daughter's remains and the hurt done him when he grabbed them to keep them safe. He'd suffered from fire, so had wanted me to do so too.

The backlash of energy he had directed from the pentagram he'd arranged around London had unleashed a tsunami of chaos on the Thames path near my home. A whole chunk of the walkway and river wall had been blasted to a glassy ruin, the wall bending inward by thirty feet or so like something had crashed headlong into the bank and melted its way inward until it stalled.

All the trees in a hundred or so foot stretch had burned down to barest stubs sticking from the concrete underfoot. This too had been shattered and melted, creating a strange marbling effect that looked like someone had taken a massive blowtorch to the ground. Possibly God, or Godzilla. One of the two.

My apartment block stood almost at the edge of the destruction, with maybe twenty feet of solid ground between the melted wall and my home. Enough to mean the foundations were safe, the building not at risk of subsidence and easily explained away without anyone but me knowing the Morrigan must have held back the destruction herself. Otherwise I reckoned my home would have been a smoking pile of rubble and ash, and I didn't want to think of what would've happened to those inside.

Danny had greeted us as we came in through the door, grabbing hold of Felix and holding her tight as she let loose pent-up sobs. I gripped his shoulder with my good hand then left the pair to it, staggering up the stairs to my home floor with the occasional growl and curse … to find Bear waiting for me. The trollhound did his various best to floor me, crashing into me and subjecting me to a thorough inspection and tongue licking until I wrestled him away and indicated I was in no condition to handle his *I missed you* act until I'd healed some.

Goldspur had also put in a brief appearance, blurring out of her tree and grabbing me into a tight embrace without any word. No explanation. But the dryad had seemed genuinely pleased to see me, so I bit my lips against the pain and hugged her tightly back before I begged off to go deenchant myself under a hot shower and then salve my wounds and address my immediate needs.

Those being wine and sausages.

The Morrigan was gone by the time I arrived, leaving only a rolled-up parchment on my coffee table. I knew I could leave it, but I'd learned it was wise to read anything she left lying around or specifically for me since there was usually something she wished me to know … and I'd only suffer if I left off learning whatever it was.

Grandson. I trust this finds you with all limbs attached and generally in one piece.

Your hearth is safe, the wrath of this mortal averted though I believe I may have blown all your and your tenants' electrical systems from the complaints I have heard since. Your friends are safe, but know that they felt your suffering, your pain. The bonds you have forged speak of your true nature, for no mere lycan could create so strong connections. It is almost … Courtly.

The winds tell me of the ills that have befallen this Realm, and of what new challenges we face. I must inform our Queen, but will return before long to collect what is owed me.

Good luck with the angry mortals. You can always feed them to your hound.

I'd read that second paragraph several times, trying to make sense of just exactly what the Shadow fae was trying to tell me, but eventually giving up and heading to find a hot shower.

Only to remember the power was out, and settling for a freezing cold one.

Now I stood, looking back towards where I knew the Southbank centre lay, at the centre of the strangeness now engulfing that portion of London. Even in the dimming light, I could just about pinpoint the roiling grey mist as it rose above all the buildings, the cranes and other clutter that made up the London skyline. In the distance, I caught sight of a blinking light moving haphazardly through the night sky, seeing it suddenly veer off and dip back the way it had come. Another news or police helicopter, maybe even military, finding out that flying too close to the walls was bad news for everyone onboard.

Bear suddenly rose from where he had lain snoring, ears perking up and eyes alert as he ponderously shifted his bulk from a prone position to something approaching on guard. Ready for trouble.

"What is it, bub?" I asked quietly, but even my frazzled senses sparked as *something* intruded. Familiar, a sense of vastness dampened down to a trickle, of majesty in a very humble and down to earth way. Which, given the being this had to be, made perfect sense.

"Hey, Terra. What's up?" I turned slowly, finding I was no longer alone on my balcony.

The goddess had retained her mask of Felix, probably as a nod to me and how we had last interacted or possibly just the fact she liked appearing as her maybe soon-to-be next follower. I hadn't pushed my friend on whether she had sworn any oaths but guessed that now, without Elspeth to guide her, Felix would need all the help she could get in managing her powers. And having a goddess on tap, to support and encourage her growth of all things witchy-woo, wasn't such a bad thing.

Just as long as she didn't go do anything stupid and get a Fury on her case. Who knew?

"Greetings, Morgan Black." The immortal replied, nodding her head in acknowledgement. She still glowed with power, her skin faintly smoking and her eyes unmistakable as anything mortal. But Bear gave her the once over anyway, the trollhound pulling the trick all dogs know from birth. Have a cold wet nose, stick it in as uncomfortable a place as possible to see how the newcomer reacts.

Terra simply smiled and scratched the mutt in exactly the right spot to earn her a rumbling purr deep within his chest, and his hindleg making a concerted effort to thump a hole through the planking underfoot.

"I'm pretty sure even my piss-poor and severely depleted wards should stop immortals I haven't *strictly* invited from dropping in for a casual ear scratch session with my dog." I politely commented, knowing with everything that had gone on, I *really* needed to have them redone. And properly this time. "So I'll ask again. How can I help?"

Terra looked at me with those blue-green orbs of hers, cocking her head for an instant before leaving Bear's side and walking towards me. I felt no threat from her, and besides I wasn't in any condition to throw down with anything right there and then. So I let her draw close, and tried not to back up when she reached across and laid a hand on my chest.

Over my heart.

Energy, warm and fuzzy, washed through me. Sluicing a measure of the pain from my wounds down the proverbial toilet. My broken wrist dulled to a comfortable ache, my ribs calmed from their jagged cries of pain and my skin quit feeling like someone had taken a belt sander to me and removed several layers.

"You swore an oath to me, Morgan Black, and I have come to collect." She told me as I drew a deep breath, mentally jumping up and down with joy when it didn't feel like I was grinding my innards together with the movement.

"I remember." I gestured down at myself, still wrapped in bandages and braced. "Look, I'm not in a real good shape for much right, but if you come back in a week or so …"

The immortal simply shook her head, keeping her hand over my heart.

"I am not seeking a deadline. Simply that you do as I ask." Terra told me, those strange eyes of hers flashing. "You swore oath, and you will keep it. And now, I ask you."

"Find the one who is lost. Find. My. *Daughter*."

Those words hung in the air as the goddess slowly melted away. Leaving me alone with my wine, sausages and trollhound. Who was eyeing the plate of food with far too much interest for my liking.

"Great! I'm home not even twenty-four hours and I'm already back on another bloody case." I groused to the mutt, as I tossed him one sausage and scooped up another to bite. "I think I need a better *out of office* message."

Looking back out over the water, I caught sight of movement in the grey veil so far away, and yet literally on my doorstep. As I watched, I thought I caught sight of coiled scales glinting in the fading light, of batlike wings arching out to catch the air. And of a head built like some fanged monstrosity from the ocean's depths, the sort of thing that turns up occasionally in a fisherman's nets to make him pack up shop and go stay on dryland for a while. And probably take up drinking hard spirits to forget.

Or it could have been my imagination, and just the mist moving in interesting patterns.

Yeah, right.

"If Morgana's brought fucking dragons back, I'm gonna be *seriously* pissed." I told Bear, who chuffed his agreement on principle before darting forward and snatching the plate and its remaining bounty of sausages. This clasped firmly in his lips, he bounded inside. To devour his stolen goods, then turn those big puppy eyes on me to avoid any recrimination.

Leaving him to his prize for a moment, I focused on that grey wall, of what lay beyond. A new Court, returned from its ruins, and a mad, possibly corrupted fae Queen who had good reason to want me dead many times over now.

"Just bloody well stay safe." I told the empty air as I thought of a wealth of long red hair, bright green eyes full of laughter and a mischievous smile. A friend, a colleague and someone I'd failed badly. Who needed my help, And whose goddess, it seemed, hadn't given up on her no matter the pain she'd caused. No matter the oaths broken. "Coz I'm coming for you both, and no bloody way am I leaving you behind again."

And being *truthful*, what was a Knight Errant for, if not to go save the damsel in distress? To drag her and her loved one back by the scruffs of their necks, whilst convincing any and all parties to leave them the fuck alone? Dragons notwithstanding.

I'd just wait till my bones stopped crunching, and I'd finished my wine.

Then, Gods help anyone who tries to stand in my way.

Coz I am lycan. Hear me bloody roar.

Morgan's story, and that of the Pack, continues in Book 6 –

Old Dog, New Tricks

Coming soon.

About the Author

Born the fourth son of the sprawling Cameron Clan, JP Cameron was introduced to the wonder of words and story-telling with the magical tale of The Hobbit, as one of the first books he remembers.

Taking The Lord of the Rings to primary school as his book for class set his feet firmly on a path, an endless road and a love of the fantastical, strange and magical.

Through school, work and into adult life (what little of that he knows), JP continues to expand his library and scope of writing, exploring other genres and inventing strange new worlds. But his love of fantasy remains at the core of his writing. Living with his wife and their hairy behemoth disguised as a Chow Chow in the green rolling hills of West Sussex, he is often found gazing happily at bookshelves groaning with volumes by Sir Terry Pratchett, Terry Goodkind, Terry Brooks and many, many more authors not called Terry.

Otherwise you may meet him up and down the UK coastline, celebrating a rich and happy history of piracy in fine company.

His published works to date include Tales of the Blade, and The Spire set, and now his debut into dark fantasy – The Lycan Files.

Find him at @bandycoot_74 for tweets and questions.

Printed in Great Britain
by Amazon